A thick smell of iron coated my throat and I retched. Blood was in

the air, mixed with rage in the violent gusts, and fear burst into my

heart. I could swear I heard my name swirling in the blasts, the sounds

of an unknown or dead language, and pressed my hands over my ears

to stop it. I fell back, wiping the assault from my face and searched

Mom's stone, eyes wide with panic.

BOHERMORE
The Pirate Queen: Book One

CITY OWL PRESS
www.cityowlpress.com

Cover Design by Olivia at MiblArt. Map Design by Jake Peterson. All stock photos licensed appropriately.

Edited by Amanda Roberts.

For information on subsidiary rights, please contact the publisher at info@cityowlpress.com.

Print Edition ISBN: 978-1-944728-14-4

Digital Edition ISBN: 978-1-944728-21-2

Printed in the United States of America

BOHERMORE

Jennifer Rose McMahon

CITY OWL
PRESS

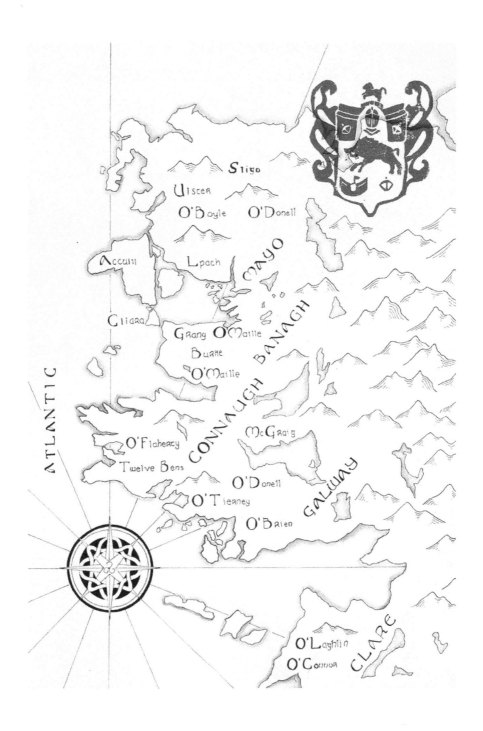

For Patrick Joseph O'Malley

My Joey

grá mo chroí

I feel the wind coming.

I know it's going to kill me this time.

It's been trying for so long.

Chapter One
The Hunt

Clawing up the steep hill, slipping on loose gravel, I cursed the new rip in my favorite jeans as I vanished into the town cemetery. Every inch of the place was familiar, from the oldest tombstone to the freshest newcomer. It used to be a playground to me for as long as I could remember; hide and seek grew into manhunt, sniffing fresh-laid flowers in the sun turned into stargazing in the black night sky. But it was different now.

My feet dragged through the old section of the graveyard, passing the centuries-old stones of early Massachusetts settlers. The thin slate hand-carved headstones, some cracked or fallen, leaned toward me, straining to be noticed.

I slipped past the World War II monument, avoiding eye contact with the weathered bust-sculpture of some famous general. His eyes supposedly possessed your soul if you looked directly into them. It always gave me that unsettling feeling like I was being watched, so I moved with purpose, flinching at every little sound. I kept focus, past the cannons and into the new section of thick granite stones, shiny on the front, rough on the back, all the same.

The straight rows were packed tight with cold efficiency, draining the warmth of the old section from my core and replacing it with the chill of mass-produced memorials. I shimmied through to the far edge, avoiding stepping directly on any plots, especially ones with fresh-cut sod because, well, the possessed thing again. You're just not supposed to.

Grateful to be somewhat on the outskirts of the grid, I found my mother's grassy patch by the young maple that shaded it.

"Hi, Mom," I whispered as I dropped to my knees in front of her, looking around to be sure I was alone—wondering if every time I looked up, whatever it was that was out there hid, with stealth timing. "I'm gonna hang out with you for a little while. I think I need your help." I paused and tried not to feel dumb.

I plucked the dead leaves from the pot of pansies my grandparents had left and gently pulled a tuft of grass away from the base of her stone to be sure my senior picture was still buried there.

"It's like something's wrong with me," I mumbled. The comment seeped out of my mouth like the sick bile that was churning in my stomach. "Like something's following me…or someone. I don't know."

I flashed back to the smell of wind and rain, the echo of words spoken just out of my hearing. I'd been having the feeling more and more lately—not quite the disturbing visions I had before Mom's death six years ago, but subtle reminders of them.

"Mom, it's my awake dream. The scary wind, the screams, everything. It's coming back. I can feel it. And now that you're gone, I think I'm next."

My heart palpitated in my chest. Hearing my harrowing words made it all the more real. My grandparents and the doctors—they'd all claimed Mom's death was caused by a "heart condition." But I knew better. I knew the truth. It was behind their hushed whispers, behind their tears, behind the hands brushing me away from grown-up talk. My awake dream killed my mother. She was always in the visions, being pulled away from me into the mist. And now…now, it was my turn.

"Am I going crazy?" My exhale expelled resignation and even submission as my hands pulled across my face and into my hair. "I just need to know everything's okay. Like there's not really anything wrong. Can't you just give me a sign?"

A falling leaf, a swooping bird, a rainbow? Anything.

My anxiety twitched in my eye. It lurked in my sweaty palms and my racing heart. I really hated that out-of-control feeling, and it was poisoning every day for me now.

All I needed was reassurance. For my mother to say yes, this was all just my imagination, a ghost story. Maybe my mind had taken my stress and my longing for her and spun it into a remembered nightmare, bad movie-type: *Deadly Wind With a Vengeance*. But now, facing my high school graduation, it was time for me to get a grip.

I sat in the grass tracing the engraved letters and shamrocks in her headstone, waiting for answers that never seemed to come. Finally, I curled up, leaned in against her stone, and rested.

The clink of metal on granite disturbed me—or did it wake me?—and I sat up on my knees, frowning. If I wasn't alone anymore, I'd be out of there so fast.

I peeked over Mom's headstone. The wind had whipped up without warning, flinging mist and twigs at me like shrapnel, making me squint and shield my face. My hair twisted wildly and my jacket flapped against my body, raising alarm in every nerve. I gripped the top of Mom's stone, straining to see past the wind, trying to figure out who was out there.

A thick smell of iron coated my throat and I retched. Blood was in the air, mixed with rage in the violent gusts, and fear burst into my heart. I could swear I heard my name swirling in the blasts, the sounds of an unknown or dead language, and pressed my hands over my ears to stop it. I fell back, wiping the assault from my face and searched Mom's stone, eyes wide with panic.

Desperate for a response, I stared into her monument as if looking into her safe, nurturing face. I blinked for better clarity, leaning in to it, when somewhere deep in my mind, her voice exploded as she commanded me—

"Run!"

My legs sprinted before I was even standing. I had never run faster in my entire life. Every obstacle was against me—rigid headstones, flying petals, loose sod.

I flew out of the cemetery without looking back, my hair trailing behind me, arms pounding me forward. My lungs burned, not only from the effort of sucking extra oxygen, but actually my chest was burning, on my skin, like fire. Something had hurt me. Something unseen.

My pace slowed only when I was within a safe distance from home. Evil self-consciousness washed over me as I considered how crazy I must have looked—early morning May, running for my life, out of a cemetery. Aw, jeez. What an idiot. I prayed the neighbors weren't looking.

What was I running from anyway? Guilt again? Probably. The truth behind my mother's death? I always wondered if I had something to do with it, if I was responsible somehow…I mean, of course I was. Maybe I just wasn't strong enough to help or, more likely, too afraid.

Closing myself off from the rest of the world had always been my best defense from facing it. Worked like a charm, I thought. No one to question me, nobody to need me, no chance of letting anyone else down. I preferred it that way.

But if these crazy visions were coming back, forget it. I couldn't face them. Not again. Especially alone. Without Mom.

No way.

Not a chance.

***

"Maeve Grace…." My grandmother's sing-songy voice called to me from the porch. "Time fer dinner. Fetch some extra tomatoes on yer way up, dear."

Lost in her backyard in my own roaming thoughts again, feeling safer since my earlier "episode" at the cemetery, her voice snapped me back to my present job: filling the wooden salad bowl for dinner. My drawn-out sigh was louder than necessary.

The house would be full of Irish visitors in no time, gathering with my grandfather to watch Ireland play Italy in the World Cup. Michael O'Brien might come with his uncle, Paddy. Blush burned my cheeks just thinking about him and I threw myself back into the vegetable patch.

Searching for more tomatoes seemed way better than a loud soccer match laced with Irish swearing, and definitely better than making an idiot of myself in front of my life-long crush, which was what I managed to do any time Michael was near. I poked around behind the St. Brendan statue, moving the dense greenery in search of anything worthy.

"Are yeh comin', loov?" Gram's voice sounded like a distant echo from the porch high above.

In a knee-jerk response to her call, I tripped on some zucchini vines and landed at the base of the St. Brendan statue in the middle of the garden, my face nearly hitting it.

"Jesus!" The accusation rang clear in my voice. I blamed him for a lot more than nearly breaking my face on one of his anointed ones.

A handmade shelter enclosed the three-foot whitewashed statue of Brendan on three sides. From the back, I couldn't see the religious icon but knew its every feature by heart: peaceful, bearded face, robe-like clothing, cross in one hand, gesturing to the open expanses with the other. Always mocking me.

He was Brendan the Navigator. A courageous mariner, in search of paradise or the Garden of Eden. My grandmother's bedtime stories retold *St. Brendan's Voyage*, his epic travel to the promised land, a million times, engraving his fearless curiosity onto my soul.

White paint peeled down in delicate rolls from the outer back wall of Brendan's enclosure, moving my eyes toward its stony base. And there, in the statue's foundation, was a hidden metal door the size of the long side of a shoebox, with countless coats of paint, rusty hinges, and a small, aged padlock.

My eyes widened. How could a little door be here all this time and I never noticed? I cupped my palm around the lock to inspect its tiny designs: Irish artwork, Celtic-type swirls and knots pulled me in, whispering their secrets too quietly for me to hear.

I closed in for a better look, pressing the overgrowth out of my way, drawn to the mystery that only a secret door in an Irish garden could create. A faint burning returned to the skin on my chest, reminding me of my strange injury from the cemetery, heightening my senses.

The pressure of a comforting hand rested on my shoulder, nudging me closer. I turned to ask Gram what it could be and gasped for air when I saw no one there. My eyes darted back and forth, finding only green around me. I snapped back to the secret door without blinking, ignoring the sting of my drying eyes. Strange sounds filled my mind, lonely, haunting sounds of tin whistles lost on the wind, maybe coming from inside the statue.

I reached for the lock again and rubbed the Celtic carvings with my thumb. The metal door was sealed by the paint of countless years. I pushed my fingernails into the top line of the seal, moving along the length, trying to break through—

"*There yeh are!*" My grandmother's voice pierced through my soul.

I flew back from the statue and landed in the zucchinis. "Jeez, Gram!"

"Didn't mean ta startle yeh, dear. Go on, now. What's keepin' ya?"

Gram positioned herself between the statue and me, blocking my view of the secret door. I pushed left and then right, trying to get another glimpse of it, desperate to confirm it wasn't my imagination. But somehow, Gram was able to block it no matter how I squirmed.

"Gram, behind you, in the St. Brendan statue…." I started, dying to show it to her. "What *is* that?" I tilted my head for a better look, reaching around with my curious fingers.

"Oh, nothing." Gram swatted with her dishtowel, stopping my hand from further exploration. I pulled back, feeling like a small child caught with her hand in the cookie jar. "Another one of yer grandfather's projects, 'tis all, his handiwork, sure. Prob'ly keeps some old tools in there or whatnot."

My chin pulled in as I scowled at her. Did she think I was dumb? Her efforts at distracting me from the secret door were useless. I was going to find out what was in there. My eyes were drawn back to it. What *could* be in there?

"Come on now. Stop yer dilly-dallying and daydreamin'. Time to come in. Scooch." She swatted at me again with her dishtowel. God. That was really annoying.

Could she actually be *hiding* something from me?

Walking up the rolling lawn toward the porch stairs, I looked back at the statue. Its head was tipped a little—maybe it always had been— but now it was more obvious. It knew something. I had discovered its secret and now its gentle face was encouraging me to do something about it. Daring me even. The hairs on the back of my neck stood up as we held eye contact.

"Come along now, loov," Gram said.

Climbing the high stairs, I was paralyzed with the need for answers. Real answers. Not just the ones you're given as a child, hollow and flat, that let the adults avoid or move on, but real, concrete answers…about Mom, about my grandparents, about Ireland. Lots more about Ireland. Why was it always shrouded with mystery and secrets in my family? No one ever wanted to talk about it, but it was who we were. It didn't make sense, all the silence.

**

"Are you ever going to *really* tell me why you and Joey left Ireland?" I'd asked a million times before but was never satisfied with the simple or unfinished answer, like I was always "too young" to be told.

Gram's pace slowed on the stairs and she turned to look at me. Her eyes were usually soft and bright, but today, hidden behind her veil of gray strands, they looked steely and guarded.

"Nothin' ta tell, Maeve. You're always lookin' for some grand story."

Did she think I was still ten? I waited for more, not budging.

"There was nothing left fer me at home. Twelve siblings, tiny cottage, no jobs. I had ta go and, sure, I met yer grandfather around that time and he was in a great hurry t' get to America."

Same story as every time. I was sick of all the pleasantries. *Just be honest for once and tell me what really happened. Say what you mean.*

She played with her necklace, the one she loyally wore everyday no matter the outfit, and rolled the heavy, vintage charm around in her fingers. The Celtic swirls and mythical beasts danced on it.

"Ah, there's nothin' left there fer me now," she said, clearing her throat to dispel the tightness in her voice.

"What about Joey?" His name rolled off my lips the way 'Grampy' or 'Pop Pop' would for any other grandchild.

"Never." The word came out of her like a shot, smacking me upside the head, and she was quick to soften her reply. "I mean, yer grandfather won't go back now either, dear. Been hiding for too long.

He's too old. 'Tis a shame, really."

"Hiding?" My head cocked to one side.

"Hmm?" Gram reached for her necklace and looked away.

"You said, 'He's been hiding'. From what?" My tight gaze bored into her back.

"I'm just sayin' he's lost touch with home, is all." She stuck her head in the fridge, looking for nothing.

My grandfather used terms like "fled" and "escaped" when he talked about his journey to America at eighteen. He would tell stories, after a bit of whiskey, of struggles for land and wealth, for country and clan. I had faded memories of his fairy tales and legends—battles among clashing chieftains, castles, and ships.

Visitors began to arrive for the soccer match and a symphony of brogues livened up the living room. "Uncle" Paddy, one of Joey's closest friends, filled the space with welcomes, his booming voice bringing a smile to my face. Then I heard Michael. My heart stopped. He was greeting Joey, talking stats about the match and cheering some sports chant, making my grandfather laugh.

I pictured his fitted Irish soccer jacket, the lucky one he wore for every game, and his friendly smile. I'd had a crush on him since kindergarten. Butterflies tickled my stomach, but I snapped back to Gram, looking for a distracting kitchen job so I wouldn't have to go out there.

Gram readied her cast-iron skillet for the steaks. The smell of boiling spuds and the hot, garlic-laced pan filled every inch of the kitchen. As I leaned in against the fridge, my shoulder flinched off its surface as if I'd been tazed.

"Wait. When did you tape my acceptance letter to the fridge?"

I specifically remembered burying it at the bottom of the papers on my desk. But now, the Boston College letterhead was staring out at me, waiting for a reply. Or, worse, a commitment.

Thoughts of my looming college plans made me feel like I was going to puke. My grandmother had been so brave in her journey to America, and here I was, squeamish at the thought of going away to the college down the road.

"I haven't made a final decision, you know." My insecurities flooded to the surface. It was obvious to everyone I would be attending BC. Both my parents were alums.

"Nonsense, dear! Yeh're headed off to university, for pity's sake, not the war. Ya just have the nervous jitters." She looked at me sideways. "Sure, when I was yer age, I was on a ship to the States, eighteen years old, with only a dream in me pocket."

Uncle Paddy wandered into the kitchen and Gram was quick to move her attention to him.

"How're me girls?" he asked as he hugged us, planting a kiss on Gram's head. I looked past him to see if Michael was on his heels, but no sign of him. My breath steadied itself.

"Ach, lassie." He looked at me. "You've grown. Not a kid anymore; sure, those big green eyes of yours would hold any lad hostage. Git out there and say hello to Michael. You'll bewitch 'im completely." His smile was wide and his eyes twinkled. "It's that Norwegian beauty. Ya got that from yer da'."

Noting the look of disappointment in my curled lip and crunched nose, Paddy turned to Gram, looking for more Jameson whiskey.

"Though you're Irish in every way, young lass." He patted my shoulder with his heavy hand, trying to take back his earlier suggestion that I could be Norwegian in any way.

Too late. I'd already heard the message—I wasn't Irish enough.

"Sure, ya should send her off to the Ol' Country, Kate. It'd be good fer her. Stop with the shelterin'. You've kept her hidden long enough," he said over his shoulder as he moved back toward the match with his whiskey and more glasses. He gave a final shout: "Time she found out who she really is. Where she came from. No?"

Gram eyeballed him with a look that could kill. Her eyes spelled each letter of *shut your mouth, you drunken fool.*

Paddy turned to me like a reprimanded puppy and said, "Forgive me, lass, for me big mouth. Yer special though. Destined for greatness. They just don't want ya to know it yet," followed by a wink. He turned back toward the living room and shouted, "Hey Michael, Maeve's in the kitchen waitin' ya."

Gram went after him with her dish rag, like chasing a fox out of a hen house. He ran for the hills.

My knees turned to liquid as I prayed Michael wouldn't listen to him. I froze, wondering.

Paddy's words made me burst with a million more questions for Gram and I turned to her, wide-eyed, ready for information. But she was closed off tight with her back to me, humming an Irish ballad, a little too loud. The kind that always made me cry.

Paddy's comment played over in my mind—how I didn't look Irish. I already knew that but it hit me like a bus anyway. My family looked Irish: strong hands, broad shoulders, twinkling eyes. But I looked more like my dad, and what's ironic about that is he left us when I was a baby. I didn't even know him.

What I did know was that I didn't fit in here. Surrounded by the Irish all my life and still I was different and awkward.

It was weird because when Mom died I didn't fit in at school anymore either. I had just turned thirteen when it happened, so I guess you could say it stole part of my childhood, like I grew up that day. My friends and the other kids around me noticed too. They were still worried about how many likes they got on social media, who they were going to semi with, and if they had the latest phone app. It was all white noise to me. I didn't fit from that point on. I didn't even want to.

And now, I wasn't even fitting in with my own kind. Always hiding in the garden, the kitchen, the cemetery. I was more comfortable alone.

"Hey, Maeve."

I turned like I'd been electrocuted. Michael's smile melted me into muteness.

"Heard you were headed to BC. Go Eagles." The artificial lack of enthusiasm in his tone made me chuckle. He leaned against the door jamb, looking at me with a familiar fondness.

"Um, yeah, well, I don't know yet." I looked at Gram, annoyed about the acceptance letter and now about her telling people. "I guess." I looked down at my phone on the table and pressed the button, hoping some message would appear and whisk me away.

Silence.

"Had you pegged more for a UMass Amherst girl, no? The Zoo?"

He laughed, knowing that was the furthest thing from the truth. He didn't seem to care though.

Stuck, as usual, I was blank without any form of witty comeback. The more I tried to come up with one, the more I froze.

"Yeah, BC. That's the one for me." I did not just make a rhyme! Is it possible to die by choking yourself? I envisioned reaching for my own neck.

Michael grinned, probably to be polite. "Well, keep in touch. I'll be workin' with Paddy as his apprentice. Stoneworking, you know. You'll have to keep me up on the college stuff."

"Yeah, okay." I smiled and reached for my phone again. What was wrong with me? He went back to the living room. I blew it. Again!

I dropped my face into my hands trying to erase the previous moment. I snuck a peek through my fingers at Gram and then pulled my face up.

"I should go. To Ireland."

It was like an epiphany. Paddy was right. And he had said something about me finding out where I came from and who I was, like he knew part of the story that was always kept from me. And Gram seemed fixed to keep it that way.

Gram's lined face awakened as she considered my interest in going to Ireland. Then her eyes squinted, closing the topic, and she paused for a second. Her spatula hovered over the pan and she opened her mouth as if she was going to say something. But then she stopped.

Gram was scared.

***

Once the house settled after the match, I found myself in the kitchen again with Gram as I reluctantly helped with the cleanup. I preferred the torture of cleaning my own room. At least I could sweep everything under the bed in there.

"Gram, seriously. What would you think of me going to Ireland?" I pressed her to re-engage as I sat down with my cup of tea, drying the "special occasion" silverware.

Then a sudden sense of urgency flowed through my veins, a chill that hit my marrow. I dropped the serving spoon from my hand onto the table with a loud clang.

Gram blurred out into streaks of color blending into the kitchen. I froze with my eyes bulging and my heart racing.

The wind was coming.

Terror filled me in an instant, reminding me of its occupation of my soul.

I grabbed the wooden legs of my kitchen chair and held on for dear life. Wind, screams, fear—it was coming but I wasn't prepared. I wasn't strong enough. My mother wasn't here this time to help me and—

The wind surrounded me before I had time to draw in a full breath of air. I squeezed my eyes shut and pressed my lips together to block the violent assault. The gusts burst into my ears and up my nose, filling every space in my skull, whirling around in my head, searching for the source of my being.

The urge to look for my mother held more power than my good judgment. I snuck one eye open, hoping for a glimpse of her beautiful face. Maybe she was still trapped there, in the wind, but all around me a vast emptiness swirled with mist and angry gusts.

Wetness clung to my skin as I stumbled forward into the void, shivering through the darkness and confusion. Alarm rose, widening my eyes as thoughts of death swirled around me. My heart pounded with such force I thought it would burst out of my chest. Gram's words of Mom's "heart condition" echoed in my thoughts. My shoulders rounded in as pain surged out of each spastic beat.

I raised my head to gasp for air as a rolling grassy slope appeared. It was like an Irish countryside, so familiar that a wave of relief blanketed my erratic heart. But only for a split second.

A massive rock flew up in front of me then, like a wall, nearly smashing me. I slapped my hands on it, annoyed as it blocked my view and my movement, and maybe a chance to see my mother.

Cold mist and salty spray pelted my face again in harsh slaps as I pushed through the blasts and the thick scent of marine life.

A bone-chilling sensation shuddered up my spine, warning me I wasn't alone and definitely not welcome. My eyes darted around, trapped in my rigid body, searching for my age-old stalker.

I fought the primal urge to run, risking my safety for a possible second of contact with my mother, when from deep within my subconscious a sound began to rise unlike anything I had ever heard or had even known existed in this world. It was a heavy, guttural moan, one of loss and sorrow, and my hair stood on end.

As I squinted into the fog, following the direction of the sound, a form began taking shape and a face came together in the gray haze. It snarled and came at me out of the mist.

My instincts took over. I turned in an instant and ran for my life blindly through the fog. I tore across the green expanse and stumbled on the uneven ground. I didn't have a chance.

Too terrified to look back, I flew through the mist and rain, leaving swirling trails off my elbows and back. The horrifying sound rang louder in my ears as I lost ground. The figure, though I didn't know what or who it was, thundered just steps behind me.

A frozen chill ran through my heart—whatever that thing was had caught up to me. With a newfound burst of energy driven by pure terror, I hit high gear only to be brought to an abrupt halt.

On a shore, I had hit water's edge. Splashing through the shallows, my pace was slowed to molasses, just like a freakish nightmare when you can't run and your voice is lost. With no other option, I turned, hands raised, to face my attacker. A glint of bright light blinded me for a split second and—

SMASH!

My body dropped back down into my chair as my muscles released their death grip on my bones. I drew in a life-saving breath to fill my starving lungs and clutched at my chest to relieve the intense burning on my skin.

I recognized my surroundings: Gram's kitchen. No one chasing me, no massive rock, no wind pounding me. I was safely sitting in my chair at the kitchen table, my cup of tea still steaming in front of me.

Gram stood by the sink, frozen, eyes wide with panic. Fragments of the broken plate she must have just dropped were strewn around the floor.

"I'm okay, Gram," I lied, trying to convince myself as much as her. "I'm okay. It was just a dream."

Yeah, a dream that was stalking me, luring me, maybe even trying to kill me. The nagging burn on my chest raised my inner alarm toward hysterical.

Gram blinked and then shifted her eyes to look directly into mine. Her expression loosened as she glided toward me, reaching for me with outstretched arms, as if she'd almost lost me. She smothered me in her hold.

"T'anks be t' God you're all right."

"I'm so sorry, Gram. I'm okay now." I tried to hide my panic and confusion from her. "This is just a weird thing that used to happen to me sometimes…when I was little."

My awake dream had truly come back to haunt me, and right in front of Gram. Those were the two worst things that could ever have happened. Losing my mind was one thing, but for Gram to have any notion of it was quite another. She would only isolate me from life more now. She already controlled me too much as it was.

I blinked and squished my eyes to release the imposing images. I sniffled to clear the salty mist from my nostrils, surprised by the smell of the sea and damp earth still left there.

"It just hasn't happened in a while, since before Mom…." I paused, smoothing my hair that was still strewn across my face. My dream's connection to Mom and her death was undeniable now, at least in my mind. "But I'm okay. Really."

Her mouth still hung open and her eyes were brimming with tears, proving she needed a better explanation.

"Mom used to help me when this happened, when I was little. She would hold me and talk to me until I came back. We used to call it my 'awake dream.'" I hoped to normalize it as she listened without breathing.

With an uneasy sense of foreboding, I added, "I think it's coming back."

I peeked up from under my lashes, watching for her response.

Gram's face dropped as her eyes searched mine for a different explanation. Judging by her lost stare and the anguish on her face, you'd think I had told her I was dying.

Chapter Two

Taking Flight

...and I was.

Gram knew it too.

The pale, drawn look on her face left no doubt in my mind. I was in trouble.

The gnawing in my gut hollowed me out, making me heave. I'd never imagined my own death before. I'd feared it, constantly, but never actually pictured it...until now.

Pursued.

Stalked.

Hunted.

My heart skipped out of rhythm, making me gasp. I clung to my chair, hovering in limbo, until my pulse came back to its steady pace. My hand pressed to the middle of my chest to confirm my heart was still beating. Was this how it started for Mom? Her "heart condition?"

The wind took her from me. I had no idea how, but its responsibility was clear. Had she had the same warning as me? Would she have been able to escape it? Could I?

Maybe there was a way I could have some control over this crazy curse. Find out what it wanted. Maybe put an end to it.

I pushed against the table, grinding the legs of my chair across the floor, and jumped up.

"I need air." I left Gram in a blur behind me and ran for the backyard.

I jumped from the last few porch stairs into the grass and sailed down toward the garden. St. Brendan held the same look in his eye and welcomed me back, head still tilted, this time in curiosity.

On my knees, I inched closer to the statue, looking deeply into its face. Instead of feeling its familiar nagging judgment of my fear and insecurity, I felt understood.

"What should I do?" I asked in a whisper. "I know you know." I goaded it with a stare-down, feeling a strong spine for once.

Images from the visions returned in a flood, showing the green rolling fields, the mist, but then I could hear the sounds too. Ancient tin whistles, tribal and Celtic. Sounds I'd heard before from Joey's old radio when he'd had too much Jameson, feeling nostalgic for home. The sounds were in my awake dream, though they were masked by the whirling chaos and my distracting terror. My vision pulled me away to Ireland, every time. I was sure of it.

"It's in Ireland, right?" I asked Brendan. "The answer to all this mess. *Right?*" My voice grew louder and more persistent as I realized I *was* right.

Behind Brendan, on the back wall of his enclosure was a prayer. I'd seen it my entire life but never actually read it, until now.

THE PRAYER OF ST BRENDAN
Shall I abandon, O king of mysteries
The soft comforts of home?
Shall I turn my back on my native land
And turn my face toward the sea?

My eyes darted back to his, as if he had spoken. And I listened. I heard. For the first time in a very long time.

There was something in Ireland, luring me there. It couldn't be denied any longer. Had it killed my mother? Was it trying to kill me? All I knew was that it had to be stopped.

But I was on my own now. More than ever.

***

"I want to go to Ireland," I said. "I know it sounds crazy and impulsive…." My hand rose up to stop Joey from saying no too quickly. The idea of going to Ireland had hit me like a brick after my awake dream in the kitchen the night before and nothing else mattered anymore.

With Gram nowhere to be found, this was my chance to get Joey on my side. "And I know it's not what you had in mind for me, but, seriously, it's what I really want to do right now." My wide eyes begged him.

Maybe Mom could have escaped. I needed to escape. I needed to change my direction, fast. My life depended on it. If I could find out the cause of the dreams, end them or find out what they wanted, then maybe it would all stop. Maybe I would be safe.

If only I had been able to do this for Mom, before it was too late. I hated myself for not being able to protect her.

Joey's jaw fell and he stared blankly, shocked by my announcement. His expression went long and limp. Was he traveling back to Ireland in his mind, thinking about what it used to mean to him? He looked…lost.

Worried for him, I tilted my head and took a closer look. Standing over six feet tall and two hundred fifty pounds, Joey was strong and intimidating. Family stories described him as a scrapper, a street fighter, who never lost a match. His temper was something to fear—but in that moment, his eyes became misty and red and he struggled finding words to say.

I waited, like a verdict was about to be read, my fingers grabbing the fabric of my pants.

One last push. "I want to find where you and Gram came from, learn more about Ireland and who I am."

Joey stumbled back and collapsed in his chair with his head down. I jumped to him, regretting every word, for causing him distress. My backpedaling was already forming in my mind. I'd go to BC. I'd go through the motions. Anything to keep him happy.

He raised his eyes off the floor, causing my heart to skip triple beats just as the doorbell rang.

"Joseph!" Paddy's voice filled the house as he let himself in. "Joseph, me boy. I've come for the bloody mower."

"Jazus, Paddy. 'Tis around back. You know the way."

Joey's assertive efforts at redirecting him failed. He was upon us in an instant.

"What have we here?" His arms went for miles as he embraced us both before we'd fully stood. "I miss somethin'?" He looked back and forth at us, sensing the intensity of our moment.

"She's goin' back to the Ol' Country, Paddy." Joey looked at me, lips in a thin line, mind made up.

I clapped my hands together and jumped as tears filled my eyes. "Thank you!" I flung my arms around him.

I loved my grandfather. I thought of all the times we played cards and how he would pass me slices of apple off the end of his tobacco-tarred jack knife. But I was determined to learn more about my family history and find a connection to my awake dreams. My last vision had been steeped in Irish images, sounds, and smells. I could only hope the answers I needed were hidden somewhere there.

I didn't want to raise any alarm with my grandparents by disclosing the true nature of my trip—to understand Mom's death and also, potentially, avoid my own. They were too old. Judging from Gram's terror after my earlier awake dream, they might not have let me go if they realized that I was really planning on finding the source of my visions.

"Well, Joseph," Paddy interjected, "I'll be needin' ta get Michael over here straight away to catch this lassie before some other bloke finds her." His elbow jabbed at me as my heart jumped into my throat.

"Ah, 'tis too late now for poor Michael. Sure, she's already on her way now, can'tcha see." Joey stood proud, with his shoulders squared.

Could I really be going to Ireland? For real? I could go tomorrow—pack my bags, get on a plane, and find the answers I've been searching for. After all these years, I was finally getting my chance to actually figure things out.

***

"Have yeh a proper rain jacket and wellies?"

"Has yer passport arrived yet?"

Gram's endless questions poked me in the eyes, raising my already spiking anxiety. Joey watched our pressure-cooker dance play out over the time it took to get organized and he planned his moments strategically, staying out of Gram's way and catching my ear whenever he could.

He motioned for me to sit in my chair, next to his, in the living room. He looked back toward the kitchen to be sure Gram was nowhere around.

In a hushed tone he said, "I think me brother Eddie may still be in Claremorris. He was sixteen when I left. Big fella. Learning the way of the farm. Find him. Tell him about me and he'll know who ya are then. He'll have stories for yeh, I'm sure, grand stories even." His eyes widened. "Don't let 'em go to yer head. The rest of them, well, I can't be certain. Some kind of crazy carry-on when I left...I just don't know."

His rambling proved *he* wasn't even sure about what he was saying.

Gram flew out of the kitchen with her internal sonar detector flashing like a strobe.

"Ach, sure, don't listen to yer grandfather." She swatted at his arm with her dishtowel. "Don't be scarin' her now." Gram looked to me and added, "Mind you, his family stories are just one big exaggeration."

Gram eyeballed Joey to shut him up.

Her overreaction to his stories halted our conversation—and it was odd because my grandfather hadn't really disclosed anything alarming to merit her response. Or had he?

***

As ambitious freshmen battled for parking in Boston for the big move-in day to their respective college dormitories, I sat on my bed and stuffed my backpack, clicked the buckles on my suitcase, and drew the cords of my cinch sack, preparing for my transatlantic journey.

Could this really be happening?

"Take care of yerself, me Maeve." Joey cleared his throat as he spoke and swallowed hard. Fighting tears, he said, "Find the O'Malleys in County Mayo and ye will find...."

He coughed and cleared his throat again with his closed fist at his mouth. He reached into his pocket and pulled out a folded paper.

"Use this map to find the O'Malleys in Claremorris. It will lead you to everything you're looking fer. And maybe you'll find some answers. Bring 'em back to me, will ya? Promise me."

The simple map, drawn on a page ripped from a notebook, sat folded in my hand, small, but it held so much. Its weight made my hand drop slightly. A chill quaked my shoulders, making me shudder. I hoped I wouldn't let him down.

"Maeve…." I turned toward the echoing voice behind me.

The emptiness of the room crushed in on me as my eyes bulged out of my head, searching for the unseen source.

I shot my gaze back to Joey, though he remained unaware.

Movement at the window made me flinch. A black bird perched on the narrow sill. It stepped to the side, exposing its regal red shoulder. A red-winged black bird. My mind filled up with thoughts of Mom. That was her favorite bird.

I ran into Joey, hugging him with all my might. Half for the sorrow of missing Mom, half for saying goodbye. His chest heaved against my head as he took quick, shallow breaths.

"God bless, me Maeve. I'll miss ya, dear." His voice cracked, barely audible, then he released me to lumber into the backyard and vanish into his shed.

I stood in the same place he left me. Self-doubt crept in to dampen my spirit, adding at least twenty pounds to my self-burden. What was I doing? My grandparents needed me. This was my home. I was happy here…and safe.

But *was* I happy here? *Was* I safe?

No.

I wondered, though, if I had what it took to actually do this. I was pretty much a coward up until now, like the shell of a real person. I couldn't realistically expect that to change any time soon.

I straightened, took a deep breath and grabbed the handle of my suitcase. Time to find out.

***

"I'm not sure this is such a good idea." Gram's reluctance seeped out of each syllable as she took the exit for Logan Airport.

"Gram, it's fine. We have it all planned out. I've got a place to stay and everything. No worries." *Don't fail me now, Gram.* But regret shined out from deep within her guarded eyes—regret about my trip before I had even taken it.

"It's too uncertain. Anything could happen. It's too dangerous." Her voice trembled with worry. She started to veer out of her lane from distraction.

"Gram, it'll be no different than here," I protested. "I'm signed up for those courses you wanted me to take. It'll be fine." I rubbed the back of my neck, frustrated about agreeing to take a couple of college classes while I was there. It was Gram's one demand so I wouldn't lose focus on my education, blah blah blah.

She frowned at me after hearing my flippant tone, but after a second she steered back into the correct lane.

I looked at my documents as Gram parked the car in terminal E and opened my newly assigned passport. *Maeve Grace O'Malley* was printed next to what looked like my mug shot. The blank pages begged for their first stamp.

"Check-in. Aer Lingus." A man in a green uniform ushered me into the corral ropes in the terminal. Gram followed.

But before we could reach the check-in desk, Gram stood up tall, straightened her jacket and said, "No. Ya should be comin' home with me." She looked back, but people were already queuing behind us. Her eyes darted around. She held the charm on her necklace and rubbed it between her fingers, then she took my elbow and began to turn me around, ready to push through the people in line. "It's fer your own good."

I planted my feet to my spot, pretending I didn't notice the pulsing, burning on my chest. The exact same painful sensation I felt after running out of the cemetery back home.

"Gram, no." I left no room for negotiation. "I need to do this. This is about who I am. You *need* to let me go. I know you're worried. But I'll be okay. I promise."

I rubbed my chest to soothe the rising burn, but my breathing became shallow as my blood pressure dropped, making me dizzy. My heartbeats had slowed to a pace where I heard their dull lollops in my ears, fading out all the other sounds.

"Next." The Aer Lingus attendant called for me.

Gram had wilted, like a frail, thirsty flower, unable to build a solid comeback to my defiance.

I dragged my bags onto the scale and handed my passport and ticket to the woman as my heart rate finally normalized.

"But what if something happens t'ya?" Gram wiped a tear from her cheek fast, as if it could go unnoticed.

If I turned back now, I would be a prisoner to my awake dreams, waiting for judgment day, never knowing what truly happened to my mother. I would lose my mind, literally. I had to face it now. Find any answers that might be hiding in Ireland because I surely wouldn't find any answers here, sheltered like a wallflower in Boston.

I was going.

"I love you, Gram." I hugged her, but winced as the burn on my chest hit a new level of agony. I pushed my face into her shoulder to hide my pain, biting my lip.

"I love you, me Maeve Grace." Her voice broke as she struggled to regain her composure, unaware of my condition. Then she said, in a low, foreboding tone I hadn't heard out of her before, "Goodbye, m'loov."

Actually, I had never heard more harrowing words in my entire life, and they knocked the focus off my burn. I didn't know what it was in her goodbye, her choked voice or the finality of her tone, but it sounded like she was saying goodbye to me today, and forever.

My grandmother knew something. She was afraid.

But *now* was not the time to push her about it. I was one step away from the gate. So I just nodded, gave her one last pat on the shoulder, and stepped into the beginning of my journey.

Chapter Three

Turf War

Waiting for Aer Lingus flight E132, I held my foam coffee cup as if it were the outstretched hand of someone trying to save me from a fall. The burning on my chest had faded but left me with an uneasy chill in my heart. As I moved in for my sacred first sip, I looked up, only to be met by a girl's direct gaze, right in my face.

"Oh my God! Where did you get that?" She plopped her designer bags down, lifted her Chanel sunglasses, and eyeballed my coffee like she was going to steal it from me.

"Um, right over there…at that stand." I pointed with a weak wrist toward the kiosk with a larger-than-life coffee banner above it. "I'll watch your stuff if you want to…." I said to her back as she was already barreling toward the coffee cart.

Minutes later, she dropped herself down in the seat across from me. She pushed her blunt-cut, perfectly straightened hair behind her ear, crossed her loafered feet at the ankles, and took a moment to worship the warm cup in her hands. She was smitten, inhaling the scent with a look of true love on her face.

"I've been waiting all day for this." She used a low, throaty voice as she smiled dreamily into the cup. Her perfect manicure managed to make even the foam cup appear dignified.

"Me too, actually. All my life even." I exaggerated the simplicity of my existence, speaking into my cup, referencing more than the coffee.

She burst out with a thunderous laugh, shocking for such a

proper-looking girl, and it made me laugh too. Her stiff, straight posture released as she slumped in her chair.

"I'm Michelle, by the way. I'm studying abroad in Ireland for the year." She'd clearly just burned her lip on the hot coffee but was going in for another attempt anyway. "I've been dying to get away from Tufts. Okay, and my family." She rolled her eyes. "Too stuffy. This is my chance to go to the school of *my* choice. Far away. Finally." The words blew out of her in one long exhale.

I tried to size her up, though the signals were crossing left and right. It seemed like she was on a personal journey too, different but the same: dropping her preordained trust fund identity and trading it, rebelliously, for her newfound freedom. I huffed to myself, wishing my trip could be more like that.

We sipped our coffees as a guy shuffled past us with a larger-than-life carry-on, bumping Michelle, hard, nearly spilling her cup.

No apology. A total jerk.

She turned to me, eyes bugging out of her head. "Oh my God. He's gorgeous! Did you see him?" She leaned out of her seat for one more look. "I hope he's sitting next to me on the plane. Maybe he's Irish." She lifted her eyebrows and pouted her lips.

I had to admit that, though she seemed a bit flighty or like a bull in a china shop, I wasn't sure which, I already loved her carefree spirit and honesty. She had no filters at all, like she wasn't afraid of anything.

"Last call, boarding flight E132 to Shannon."

The crackling announcement jolted us to reality. How had we missed the previous boarding calls? We darted urgent looks at each other, grabbed our things and raced to the gate. At least fifty apologies and excuse-mes parted the crowd for us as we bounded through.

Out of breath and giddy, we flew down the gangway toward a green plane with a shamrock on its tail. We stepped through the open door and made our way down the narrow aisle of the airbus. Michelle stopped early and I continued on, deeper into the tight rows.

When I finally found my seat, I slumped into it with a disappointed sigh. We were miles away from each other. I looked at the guy next to me, out of the corner of my eye. His suit, wedding ring, and laptop separated us like a stone wall.

I watched Michelle hunt down a flight attendant and after a brief exchange the stewardess made her way down to me.

She looked at the businessman and said, "Are you interested in an upgraded seat, sir? We have an open spot in first class."

He was gone in a flash. Michelle came bouncing down the aisle and threw her bag into the overhead bin.

"I'd much rather sit here with you than those stiffs in first class. My mom's such a snob. She thinks it's *safer* up there for me." She made air quotes around the word "safer" while rolling her eyes at the wasted expense. Or at her mother.

Another flight attendant checked our buckles and gave us extra blankets. "More college students, yeah?" Michelle nodded at her. "The flight's full of 'em. NUIG must have arranged for all of ye to arrive at the same time." She pushed crappy headphones into our seat pockets and moved up the isle to the next row of passengers.

"Are you going to NUIG too?" Michelle's eyes begged.

"Nah. I'm actually supposed to be at BC right now, but I'm kind of ditching the full-time college thing for the moment." I sounded like such a fail.

Michelle's face fell.

"I'm taking two courses, though, at the National University of Ireland in Galway. My grandmother insisted." My mouth pursed to one side, still unsure if that was a good idea.

"That's NUIG! You idiot!" She burst out laughing. "Awesome!"

She pushed her fashion magazines into the netting on the seat in front of her. "I wonder if there are any cute college guys on board. We could get a head start." She propped herself up to survey the cabin. "I swear. I'm going to hook up with whoever I want in Ireland. No one will ever know! Ha!" Her sinister smile went from ear to ear. "I hope you're not tied down with a boyfriend. Tell me you're single. Pleeeease."

I side-smirked at her. "Yeah. I'm single all right."

"Thank God." She nestled down into her seat as if the problems of the world had been resolved. "I have a super-full schedule, five classes. Sucks. I have to get enough credits so I can graduate next year." Her fist moved to her mouth as she contemplated her words, probably second-guessing if they were her own or her mother's.

"Hey, did you register for that philosophy class? The one they force on every exchange student?" She held her breath for my reply.

"I don't know. I think I'm in Irish history stuff." I dug in my cinch sack for my travel binder. My course registration was in there somewhere. I didn't pay too much attention to what the classes were when Gram and I were enrolling. I only cared that they were back to back on the same days—to keep it simple, and basically get them over with.

Michelle's eyes widened as I pulled the registration out. She grabbed it from my hands.

"Hell, yeah! Same class!" She pointed to the first one. "I knew it! She beamed as she repositioned herself in the small seat and lifted the plastic-wrapped blanket between two fingers, examining it. She flashed me a cheesy smile and added, "And you totally have to help me with my mission to find myself a gorgeous Irish lad." She laughed at her plan but shot me a look like she totally meant it.

"I…I'm not so sure I'd be…."

"No." Her finger shot up to silence me. "You're helping me."

***

Six hours to Ireland flew by. Though we left Boston in the early evening, it was now early morning the next day in Shannon.

"Passports." The customs official sounded like a robot as he reached for my documentation. Michelle passed hers to the official at the adjacent desk. I dug into my cinch sack and rifled around but my passport wasn't where I left it. I pulled the bag open so I could see inside.

"Leave no bags unattended." The overplayed announcement boomed in my ears. "Keep all belongings in your sight and report any unusual characters or events."

My blood pressure plummeted and I nearly crapped myself. Where the hell was my passport? Did it fall out in the plane? *Think, Maeve, think.* It was impossible, my mind already went into panic mode and I couldn't think clearly enough to retrace my footsteps.

I looked back toward the official in his formal white shirt with badges and nametags and credentials all over it, my face blazing. Behind him, beyond the check point, more officials lingered, one with a dog standing at attention. With a lost gaze I turned to him and he was there holding my passport, tapping it on the counter, with an overly judgmental look in his eye to match his smirk. My water bottle and nuts were still right next to it, where I left them all.

"Oh. Right." I scrunched my shoulders up to my ears and gave a toothy grin. "Thank goodness."

"Where're yeh from?" he asked as he flipped through my passport, looking for a blank page, realizing then they were all blank.

"Massachusetts," Michelle and I said in unison. Then rolled our eyes at each other, in unison.

"Ah, two girls from Boston. What's the nature of yer trip?" The customs official looked at me for an explanation.

I was caught off guard, still coming down from my "lost passport" heart attack and had no idea how to answer the question—which had actually grown into a full-blown interrogation in my mind. Crazy dreams, family secrets, ditching Boston College, lost, confused, deranged? It all sounded bad.

The two officers held stern glares, waiting for a response. With each passing millisecond I worried they were becoming suspicious and preparing for full-on terrorist protocol, which pressed my panic button even further. I looked to Michelle like a deer in headlights, begging her to answer for me.

She looked directly at the customs officers and said dryly, "Personal enrichment."

The guard stamped my passport and leaned in, arms crossed on the counter. I looked up at him like a convicted criminal, wondering what my next offense might be.

He said, "Oh, and happy birthday, Maeve O'Malley."

What? Oh, right.

"Th-Thank you!" A huge smile lit up my face. Today *was* my birthday.

Walking toward baggage claim, I grabbed Michelle and said, "Jeez, I had no idea what to say to those guys. I totally froze."

"Not like it was a hard question, Maeve. *Nature of your trip?*" She teased me. "You gotta toughen up a bit. And besides, all you had to do was bat those fabulous lashes at them and you'd own them!"

She gathered my hair at the back, twirled it into itself and tossed it around my shoulder to the front. "And one more thing." She tilted her head at me. "Happy birthday." She snorted a laugh and took my arm, leading me straight into our Irish futures.

***

My bus ejected me on iconic Eyre Square, the center of Galway City, alone. I nearly pulled Michelle's arm off when she got out on the outskirts of town for her housing, but now, I was on my own. I watched the water splashing in the big fountain with huge sails rising out of the spray. The mesmerizing motion and sound held me to my spot, making it even harder to take my first step.

For a minute, I thought I was in an old movie or a throw-back episode of some kind. Everything was so nostalgic and historical, from the ancient architecture to the cobblestone roads. My eyes moved along the rows of attached buildings built right at the edge of the streets, mostly pubs judging from the Guinness signs hanging over their doors. The word "quaint" came to mind, more than once, but grand at the same time.

Like an obvious tourist, I opened my city map and oriented myself, using Eyre Square as my landmark. Bohermore wasn't far. I turned, placing the fountain at my back and found my direction.

Overloaded with bags, I took my first step from the curb, looking left for a clear break in traffic. Before my foot even hit the road, a car horn blasted me, sending my soul right out of my body, leaving the shell of a crepe-paper human in its wake.

They were driving on the other side of the road! Burned into my memory was the long black and white license plate. My first true warning I wasn't in Boston anymore.

"*Céad míle fáilte*, a hundred thousand welcomes, Miss O'Malley." Mr. Flaherty, my landlord, greeted me by the fantastic bright blue door of 122 Bohermore. The brass knocker in the center added to its appeal. He removed his cap and smoothed his thinning, wispy gray hair as his eyes smiled at me. My flat was directly above his paint shop.

"All th' way from Boston, yeah? Brilliant." He spoke quickly with a thick brogue. "Yer grandparents are from the west, I hear. Nicest part of Ireland, sure." He took my heavy case as he pushed open the blue door. "Bein' an O'Malley in the west is quite a thing now. Yer lot go way back, ya know." His tone took on a hint of pride.

My ears perked up at the sound of my family name as I followed Mr. Flaherty through the blue door and into a long outdoor corridor space. It would have been a narrow alley between two buildings if not for the door we had just come through.

"Do you know much about the O'Malleys?" I pried, moving behind him like an eager puppy.

We reached the end of the alleyway and I could see around back of the building. The yard was filled with building rubble and trash. It was a total waste site. My heart sank. "Yer entry is 'ere." Mr. Flaherty opened the white door on the right. "Go on, have a look-see. I've got yer bags."

I moved up the stairs to the second floor, holding my breath waiting to see what my apartment—no, my *flat*—looked like. The shiny black and white alternating tiles of the kitchen floor struck me first. The bold statement set the personality of the newly renovated space and invited me in. I looked back at Mr. Flaherty with a huge smile of relief and approval.

"Do you think I'll find any O'Malleys around here?"

I looked out the back window over the kitchen sink. Green hills rolled in the distance, but tightly packed housing estates filled the close-up view.

Mr. Flaherty hesitated again, but had no way of avoiding the question a second time. His silence was deafening and I turned to him. I caught a look in his eye that unnerved me, like he had seen a ghost…but he stared right at *me*.

"Ach, sure," he mumbled and snapped back to the moment. "The O'Malleys are in Mayo. That's where you'll need be goin'." He checked his pants pockets for something that likely didn't exist and said, "Now, that should be everythin'. Gimme a holler now, Miss O'Malley, if I can help ya at'all."

And he was gone before I could draw my next breath.

***

Michelle's voice crackled and popped over my antiquated landline in my flat as she instructed me to meet her in town in exactly two hours. Her giddy voice assured me nineteen was The Big One, "true adult," and she intended to celebrate pub-style. A sour twang shot through me as I realized I was saying goodbye to eighteen. It would be a memorable age. The age when I woke up and started breathing again.

Clothes flew in every direction as I dug through my bags for a decent outfit. I chucked my unresponsive cell phone out of the way and eyeballed it like a traitor. It would be unfair to judge it too harshly for its incompetent international service issues, yet a growl escaped through my teeth. Somehow it found its way back into my hand anyway, like a missing body part.

I ran to the tiny grocer a few doors down for some quick supplies, cell phone attached like a bad habit. Maybe I'd find a SIM card or whatever technological upgrade it needed. A stack of turf briquettes sat by the door, like a necessary last-minute item for all shoppers. I lifted a bundle to test the weight.

"'Tis the sod cut from the ancient bogs in Connemara, dried and turned into briquettes. Used for fuel, for the fire." The clerk gave a half smile at my obvious greenness. "Go on." He nudged his chin at me, lifting one eyebrow.

I keeled to one side as I grabbed the heavy stack—the smell of burning turf had tickled my nose all the way up Bohermore.

As I checked out, he added, "You'll be needin' ta get a new one of them." He tapped on my old phone with smug certainty. "Tesco's have got them pay-as-you-go phones." I shot him a sideways glance and grabbed my phone, pretending to protect it from his negative judgment.

The turf bundle got heavier with each step as I grumbled toward my blue door. Maybe it was the insult to my phone, but likely the extra ten-pound load. I readjusted every few feet, rubbing the deep red lines out of my hand each time.

In the midst of my inconvenience, my eyes were drawn up Bohermore toward a sea of crosses gazing at me. A small church, surrounded by a cemetery of Celtic crosses, nestled itself into the landscape. Each ornate cross was decorated with a ring around its intersection and stood with pride for Gaelic Ireland.

They tilted their curious expressions at me with a hint of recognition. An unnerving chill ran through me as I looked around to see if anyone else was noticing this. A light pulsating on my chest warned me that my old burn was awakening.

Bags dangling, I grabbed my heap of briquettes and picked up my pace, wasting no time slamming the blue door behind me with a thud. The burning sensation eased and as I rubbed it, I was pretty sure it never really existed.

Feeling stupid, I began arranging the briquettes in my fireplace, one at a time like a teepee. They tipped and fell flat as I fumbled with their positioning, now ruing my reluctant participation in Girl Scouts. As I leaned in to check the flue, an uneasy sickness turned my stomach, like I was going to throw up. The sensation came in the exact moment that I felt—

The wind was coming.

I braced myself on the hearth, holding onto the edges, preparing for the terror and abuse of the winds. Ice ran through my veins, confirming the wind had found me again. But I had changed my direction, fled across the ocean in search of answers, and still it continued to attack me.

My eyes squeezed shut and I covered my mouth to control my sickness as the wind continued to blast me. Holding my breath, I opened my eyes one at a time. The whipping wind filled my vision with swirling salty mist.

I searched through the drizzle and swirling fog, looking for my mother. She was trapped in the wind and I had to find her.

I stumbled forward and reached out blindly. My hands struck damp stone: cold, solid rock—a high stone wall. I shuddered as chills shot through me, straight to the bone. Could it be the same stone wall I'd seen when I had my vision in Gram's kitchen?

"Mom?" I whispered. "Mom? Are you there?"

I missed her. Just calling out to her split me in two.

A desperation rose in me, years of yearning, with the thought of seeing her again. It grew like a swarm as each painful, empty day I had existed without her came back to me in a flood. Flattened by its weight, I tried to push the ache off like every other day, but in this unnatural place it was even harder than normal.

Weakened from the crush of missing her, I leaned against the wall, pressing my cheek to it for support. Then, through the thick mist, I saw it—the ominous figure racing toward me.

I sprinted away on a bolt of adrenaline, keeping the wall on my right as I searched for a place to hide. The wall continued without end, like a sick nightmare, offering no shelter, no end to turn around. I was exposed. Like a defeated victim, I looked back toward my attacker in surrender.

The dark gray mist held no shape at first, and I caught my breath in the borrowed moment. Then my mind exploded with the war cry of a banshee. A mangled screech, like crushing metal and scratched chalkboards mixed with pure death, rose into one ringing, terrifying sound.

I flattened my back against the wall, trying to become part of it, to disappear into the mist before I was caught. My eyes darted upward, searching for safety and, through the dark fog that surrounded me, I could see an expanse of white sky drawing me upward. Was it "the light?" Was I supposed to head toward the light?

I blinked at its calm sanctuary, unable to resist its lure, and my muscles began to relax. My eyebrows rose up in slow motion as I focused on it—no, not on the light. On my ceiling. It was the ceiling of my flat, on Bohermore.

My hands, still on the stone wall, or so I thought, gripped the stonework of my fireplace. The stone wall vanished. The return from my awake dream went from slow-mo to face punch as the sound of my own voice hit me with its freakish, high-pitched scream.

"Who are you? What do you want!"

My voice echoed in the empty flat.

Then that troubling feeling seeped through me, the one you get in a horror movie when the slasher is creeping up and the ominous music is mounting. I wasn't alone. Someone was near, just out of my view, watching me, stalking me.

My blood pressure plummeted, making me light-headed, causing the room to swirl. The jolting return of my heart's steady beat brought me back, shocking me like a defibrillator, and I wondered how long it had actually been stopped.

My head reeled back as my life force surged through my veins and in a violent jerk I proceeded to vomit all over my new turf briquettes.

Chapter Four
Twice as Nice

Rain sprinkled my face, annoying me as I kept a steady pace down Bohermore toward the city center. The drizzle wasn't quite wet, but almost sticky, coating my face with a soft film of moisture. I was already ten minutes late for Michelle, and the rain slowed me even more.

My mind raced, but it wasn't near as fast as my heart as I passed the shops and pubs without really seeing them. Scenes of my awake dream were on replay and I searched the reels for clues.

Should I tell Michelle? Would she think I was nuts? She turned out to be the best friend—okay, only friend—I had in this new country, and telling her could be a mistake. I didn't want to lose her already.

There she was, standing by the statue of some famous poet on Eyre Square with a huge smile on her face. My mind made itself up on the spot.

"So, I have these weird dreams…." I spilled it, feeling like a head case as I listened to myself explain the inexplicable. Michelle listened, motionless, as I talked about Mom and the awake dream where she fought to stay with me but got ripped away—by the wind. And then she was gone for real.

"So the visions are back, big time now. They're filled with Irish details, like green hills, stone walls and tin whistles. That's why I came here. Crazy, right?"

Speechless, Michelle studied my face like we were strangers. She took a long, slow breath and reached for my hand. "Maeve, I'm so sorry about your mom. I had no idea."

"It's okay. I didn't mean to bring that up. I'm fine. I just wanted you to know about my weird visions. That's all." I took my hand back, pretending to brush an itch off my forehead.

"Yeah, okay. But wow." Her head tilted as she tried to understand.

Ahhhh! That's not what I wanted! I didn't want to talk about my mom. Ever. My knees started bouncing as I fought to escape Michelle's sorry-for-you gaze.

"Come on." I grabbed her elbow. "Let's find that pub you told me about. The one with the cool band."

It didn't take long for Michelle's solemn pace to pick up to one I could tolerate. We passed a young man and woman playing a guitar and singing Irish ballads. The guitar case was laid out in front of them, filling with coins from passersby.

Michelle stopped out of nowhere and her eyes widened as she stared at me. "Okay, wait. So, you're awake...but you're dreaming?" Her eyebrows shot up, waiting for an answer. Insecurity twisted my guts as I nodded.

"So, these head trips, they must mean something, right? They're a message or a sign." Michelle's eyes became saucers. "I'll be your dream interpreter. I'm really good at this kind of thing. I got an A in Psych 101."

"Well, they're actually, kinda...terrifying, to be honest." My frown had no effect on her. "I'm getting a little freaked out about it now. Like I could be hurt, badly, or worse. Like something's after me, or someone."

"Maeve!" she squealed. "Are you kidding me? I knew it the second I met you...you're *enchanted*!"

Okay, now she'd gone off the deep end.

"An old soul returned to Ireland, following your dreams, literally." Her eyes bugged out beyond belief. Then her voice went quiet and the tone took on a lower, steady hum as she looked straight into my eyes. "You have to figure out what this is...what it's all about." She leaned in to me without blinking. "Seriously."

Her eyes flicked back and forth as she studied me, trying to make sense of what she saw—reading me like a book. I smooshed my face into a colorful boutique window, faking interest in whatever was on display. Mesmerized by the kaleidoscope of Celtic designs in the window, I knew it was time to start searching for answers.

But where?

***

"I can't believe they can squeeze so many people in here!" Michelle yelled at me from our tight spot inside Lynch's Pub. The flyers had led us here with the promise of a great band.

My mind still wandered around the millions of places I could start searching for answers to my potentially deadly visions. A pub was not the place to begin, I was sure of that, and my racing thoughts distracted me.

"Let's try to find space closer to the band!" Michelle screamed into my ear, leaving a high-pitched ringing. I pressed a finger into my ear to bring it back to normal functioning.

"This is good!" Michelle motioned to a short bench against the wall. "I bet these are all the college kids here."

"Yeah. Cool." My voice sounded hoarse already and not as convincing as I wanted. The music was too loud for me but didn't seem to be bothering anyone else.

"So this is Mojo…." Michelle was already checking out the band at the back of the pub. "They're supposed to be awesome."

The band was set up behind the ancient stone arch that spanned the entire width of the pub.

"What the heck's a mojo anyway?" she said in their direction. Her lip pulled up on one side, scrunching her nose.

"I have no idea," I blasted back. "But I think we're about to find out."

The music filled the pub again with the burst of a guitar solo and I thought my eardrums would do the same. I couldn't help bouncing in my seat though. The music was actually whisking me away.

Squished against the wall by the crowd, we strained for a better look at the band. Four guys from what we could see. A big, burly man with a long beard on bass, another guy with a black leather biker jacket and graying handlebar mustache on drums. The other two were mostly blocked by a bunch of girls vying for their attention.

The crowd shifted for a split second, exposing the final two—two young guitar players. Michelle pinched my leg so hard I let out a yelp. I leaned to see the one who was hidden mostly by the huge amp but the other, the lead vocalist, drew all the attention with his sparkling blue eyes flashing at all the girls.

"He's gorgeous!" Michelle gushed, grabbing my knee. It was love at first sight for her. "Oh my God! I'm staying here all night!"

"Totally." I faked my enthusiasm. My relentless visions that now tracked me down in Ireland made it tough to get too excited about a couple maybe-cute guitarists.

I took another look at them. Okay, hot. A couple of definitely hot guitar players.

Michelle's huge puppy eyes begged me for more. Fine, I could do this. I looked back at the band for inspiration.

"I like that guy over there behind the amp." I pointed with just the tip of my finger toward the guitar player who remained almost out of sight, letting the frontman take all the attention and credit. "He seems mysterious or shy or something."

She didn't hear a word I said. She was already totally gone. I'm pretty sure I even saw some drool.

I glanced back to the hidden boy in the shadow of the amp. His tall frame was more of a silhouette with strong shoulders that rolled in. He scratched his scruffy stubble, seemingly unaware of his public position on stage.

I flinched with a sharp gasp when, suddenly, he looked directly at me, as if I had called his name. His eyes held mine in a lock, staring right into me. Before I could stop them, my eyes darted in another direction for safety. My cheeks burned from the obvious insecure response. His deep blue eyes shocked me as they stood out against his pale skin. Almost like he was caught doing something wrong. I used every ounce of strength to not look back.

After last call, we poured out of the pub with the flow of the crowd, leaving behind a swarm of girls hoping for a chance to chat with the guitar players. I stole a last glance at the mysterious one. He moved silently about the stage, putting away his instrument and shutting down the sound amplifiers, oblivious to the attention from his fans.

***

Back at my flat, the clock read 12:00 exactly as dance music blared through Michelle's phone, sounding like it was lost in a tin can.

"It's midnight. Let's do something dumb," Michelle huffed as she pulled the two cozy chairs by my fireplace together, facing them toward one another.

Holding a wooden spoon in one hand and a box of elbow macaroni in the other, I pursed my lips and scrunched my eyebrows as I frowned at her, wondering what the idea might be and half-hoping it didn't involve my awake dreams.

"I was thinking we could just make some mac 'n' cheese," I said lamely, holding up the box.

"I learned this from an old book my hippie aunt had in her apartment in Cali," Michelle said, ignoring my suggestion as she struggled with positioning the chairs perfectly. "It's a way of finding out who you were in a past life. We have to try it!" She dimmed the lights.

Gesturing for me to sit in one of the chairs, she said, "Don't you just love that Hollywood kid on TV, the medium who crosses over and speaks to people on the other side?"

I tipped my head. "I love that guy." More than a million times I'd imagined meeting a clairvoyant. Maybe someone who could contact Mom, see if she's okay.

Michelle sat in the chair across from me, pulling her seat close to mine so our knees were touching. Somehow she had lit the briquettes in the fireplace, like an accomplished Girl Scout, vest covered in badges, and the flames threw shadows and dancing light around the room.

"Okay," she started, "so, we keep staring at each other, but through squinted eyes. Let your eyes kind of lose focus and blur out and just staaaare at me while I staaaaare at you."

A giggle slipped out of my mouth and she eyeballed me like an angry teacher. I nodded my head and bit my bottom lip, concentrating on doing it right.

Cozying into our chairs, we shook out any excess energy from our arms and started the game. Leaning in toward each other, we started to stare. I gazed at Michelle with her serious face and squinting eyes and I focused, hard, trying to see her past life and then…burst out laughing. Spit flew.

She fought hard, trying not to laugh back but finally, laughter blasted out of her. A massive snort vibrated the room as she drew her breath back in. My legs crossed like a clamp as I curled over, sure I was going to pee myself.

"No, really, Maeve," she said, all serious, wiping her tears. "Come on, we have to do this. Let's try again. More focus this time."

"Okay, I'll be good. I promise."

We squinted in the flickering glow of the fire and gazed at each other again. The shadows on Michelle's face made it look long and drawn and her eyes were larger than normal. Her hair looked like she had a fancy, old-fashioned bonnet on with banana curls coming out of the bottom.

"You're a pilgrim…or a settler of some sort." I tried harder. "Wait! A well-to-do pioneer. Maybe…wait, an 1800s New York City woman. I can't decide!" We fell over laughing again but then I sat up straight with heightened intrigue. Maybe this stupid thing worked?

"I want to know what I am," I blurted. "Be serious! Let's do it again so I get my turn!" I was dying to hear what Michelle saw in me.

She readied herself, sat up in perfect posture, and squinted at me. Under her intense scrutiny I forced myself to stay relaxed and natural, which of course had the opposite effect. My left eye started twitching.

"Your hair is wild and unruly," she said. "It looks like there's fabric tied in it, randomly, to hold bits in place." She went on. "You look like you're wearing ruffly, lacy stuff around your neck…like a queen. Queen Elizabeth! No! Wait. Not Queen Elizabeth. You look more lawless and rebellious than her. I know! You're a pirate!" She pulled back in surprise at her discovery. "That's it." Her laugh snorted through her nose and resonated through the room. "A pirate!"

We stared at each other, taking in our new identities with nodding satisfaction. But as we sat up, ready to get our snack, a loud clang came from the fireplace, the sound of metal hitting off stone. We jumped and reached for each other as our eyes darted around the room.

"What the hell was that?" Michelle whispered as she moved closer to the fireplace.

"No, stay away from there." I grabbed her sleeve.

"Why?" She pulled away, squinting her eyes. "What was that?"

"Wait. Please. You don't know what it could be." Fear coursed through me, freezing me to my spot, forcing me to accept that I recognized the sound. And it was bad.

"Is it your dream?" Michelle looked at me, eyes bright and ready for intrigue. She moved closer to the fireplace as I remembered the familiar clash of steel and stone. I'd heard it in the cemetery back home, mixed with the fury of the wind.

"Maybe."

We held each other's gaze, as if for safety, and then turned to the fire. Our arm hairs bristled as we considered how to move. I blinked into the flickering flames, hypnotized, and in the millisecond-darkness of blinking, a face appeared. Like looking into a mirror, I gazed into the face of a woman, hair wild with fabric tied into it. Just like Michelle had described to me in the game. When my eyes popped open, she was gone.

Michelle looked at me sideways, without moving her head away from the fire, and as our eyes met, a loud, crackling sound of frenzied sizzling came from behind us. We reached for each other and jumped toward the sound in practical hysteria, holding on for dear life.

Slapped back to reality, we dove toward the stove to save our pot of pasta from boiling over and splattering everywhere.

Looking like complete idiots, we collapsed in a fit of nervous giggles as we attempted to rescue what was left of our hard-earned midnight snack—but not without an insecure peek over our shoulders now and then.

***

It was the first day of class. And I was a mess. Literally. I might as well have had bits of rag tied in my hair like Michelle saw the other night.

It hadn't been raining when I left my flat. I even saw blue sky.

And then, *splash!* The sky dropped buckets on me and the wet soaked through every layer. By the time I got to campus, drowned-rat-style, the sun was out again.

I stood in the quad, squeezing excess water from my hair. The gothic, medieval quadrangle of NUIG looked just like the website and brochures. Covered with collegiate ivy, it had two spire-topped towers rising from the far corners with a large clock tower in the center. It set the perfect stage for an old-world campus.

I raced to Smokey Joe's, the college coffee shop, to meet Michelle. I sloshed my bag down and checked my feet to see if pools were forming where I stood.

"Where the heck's all my stuff?" Michelle rifled through her backpack, arranging and rearranging everything. "It sucks we don't have more classes together." She spoke into the depths of her school bag, searching for a pen or something.

She looked up for the first time and pulled back with an unfiltered grimace. "What the hell happened to you?" Her perfect hair proved she'd somehow dodged the rain dump.

I smoothed my hair and wiped moisture from my eyebrows. "What?" My eyebrows shot up in defense along with my right shoulder.

She stared and then blinked. "Nothing." And went back to rummaging.

"Figures. My first day of class and I'm gross," I mumbled to myself, Michelle having validated the obvious. I pulled my new phone from my pocket to wipe it dry.

"What the heck is that?" Michelle's face twisted as she stared in disgust.

"Shut up! It's my new pay-as-you-go phone. My other one won't...." and I burst out laughing, from her spoiled-girl reaction and from the crappy disposable phone sitting in my hand. It was only ten euro. But at least I could text now. I hoped.

We wandered the halls, glancing at glass cases filled with old sports photos and artifacts, until we found our philosophy classroom.

The professor ignored us, prepped and ready to go, hiding behind his long wisps of thinning blond hair parted with precision down the middle. One of Michelle's eyebrows lifted as she looked from him to me, probably double checking to see if we were on a movie set with this perfectly cast middle-aged professor character. I bent to see if he had pads sown onto his jacket elbows.

We pushed straight for the back, holding hostage any giggles that threatened to escape as we watched the other students file in, ignoring the professor right back. And actually, ignoring us too.

Just as the big hand struck the hour, our teacher stood, introduced himself, and began a monotone overview of the syllabus. The drone reminded me of the steady hum of a fan, or one of those white-noise makers that smother other sounds. An hour later, I snapped to from moving chairs and flying backpacks.

Michelle's jaw had gone slack and her cheeks hung like meat. One look at her and my giggles blasted through my nose.

"No. Hell, no. We'll never survive this," I whispered.

Please, I prayed, let my next class be better.

Fortunately, we had time for coffee at Smokey Joe's before my Celtic History class and I was able to feel my face again. Unfortunately, I had time to visit the bathroom...which had a mirror...which proved my hair did not agree with rain and the Irish humidity. I was a total freak with spaz hair! Not to mention that my underwear was still wet and stuck to my butt cheeks, making them itch. Bad first day, so far.

Waiting in the hallway for my next class, two tough-looking Irish girls, "fine strapping lassies" as my grandfather would say, stared me down. My self-consciousness rose up without hesitation and poisoned me, making me fidget. If the door to the classroom wasn't locked, I would have hidden under a desk.

Glaring at me like professional boxers, they sauntered over. I could practically hear their intimidating fight song trailing behind them. I held my breath.

"You're new, right?" the husky one asked. Her rugby shirt said it all. She could break me.

"You a Yank?" the smaller one asked, more to the point, looking me up and down with her mouth pursed to the side.

How'd they know that? I looked at myself. Right. No heavy rain jacket. No big boots. Clearly caught in an earlier "shower" without proper gear, all-around unprepared. It was obvious. Not to mention my fading tan and highlights from the summer sun back home.

"Yeah, I'm from Boston."

"Sorry, Tish here's the bold one. I'm Fiona, the normal one." The rugby player twisted her fist into Tish's arm and said, "Ah, Tish, just slaggin' ya'."

Fiona turned back to me and said, "So, have ya met teacher yet?" She winked and moved her eyebrows up and down.

"Um, no, not yet." I looked sideways at her and then over at Tish, wondering what the big joke was.

Fiona nodded at her friend and together they started, quietly and then louder, a sort of sports chant: "Ooh ahh, Paul McGratt. *Ooh ahh*, Paul McGratt!"

It was catchy and they repeated it a few times and made it even funnier by bouncing to the beat and poking their fingers into the air. It was clearly a song or rhythm that had been sung before, many times.

I cracked a nervous half smile and was about to question their quirky performance when he walked around the corner.

I knew it was him.

Paul McGratt.

Ooh ahh, Paul McGratt!

He was gorgeous.

Like he'd just come off the soccer field, he was full of energy and life. His eyes were bright and inquisitive as he surveyed our group. I drew a line up his squared jaw, avoiding the pull of the late summer sky in his gaze.

I couldn't keep myself from staring. His hand moved through his wavy, chestnut brown hair and snapped my awareness back to my own appearance. Oh my God. My hair came in a close second to Frankenstein's bride. I looked at the ground for refuge. Maybe he wouldn't notice me today.

He fumbled at the door, looking for his keys. His sports jacket and fresh white oxford were nothing like my last professor and I was sure I could smell fresh air off him. There was no way he could be a PhD. He was too young, twenty-two or twenty-three maybe. He must be a teaching assistant or something.

"Well, pretty clear I'm new at this. No hidin' it now," he said to us, still hitting his pockets for the keys. He flashed a weak smile, swoon-worthy, and then stopped, hearing a jingle in his breast pocket.

Fiona and Tish were staring at me with smug smirks, enjoying every moment of my reaction to him. I couldn't resist turning back to him for another peek.

Just as he was finding the right key, he dropped them. "Ach," he groaned.

The keys were right by my feet and without thinking, I bent over for them. We nearly bumped heads as his hand got to them before mine. Our fingers brushed and he jumped like I was electric, yanking the keys upward.

Without enough time to dodge his hand, I pulled back but the keys brushed my hair and had no chance in the world of clearing the tangled frizz. They got stuck.

"Ow!" I bent toward his tugging hand as his cheeks blazed in blotchy red. "Owowowow...." My voice followed his efforts at freeing the keys from my rat's nest.

"Sorry. Sorry." He continued to shake and tug as the beet-colored patchwork moved down to his neck.

Fiona and Tish burst out laughing without any attempt at subtlety, and now full-blown passing out was my only option for escape.

"Wait. Wait. I got it." His hand rose up, stopping me from moving and making matters worse. He picked at my hair, freeing his keys as I stood staring at the ceiling, the wall, anywhere but at him or Fiona and Tish.

"Sorry 'bout that. I didn't mean ta...." His deep-set, bright blue eyes smothered his words and put me into a mute trance. "You okay?"

Fiona was snickering in the corner of my eye.

Digging deep to find my voice, I said, "No problem, really."

I ran my fingers through my hair by instinct, to smooth the 'snared key' site, which made matters worse as they got stuck too. It was no use.

In defeat, I pursed my lips to the side and lifted my shoulders up toward my ears, accepting the fact that my first impression was that of an idiot. With that resignation, I was then able to look him in the eye.

He held my gaze and lingered there, like he recognized me. I pulled my eyes back to the safety of the floor as my cheeks began to blush.

But by the end of class, I had fallen full victim to his enthusiasm for Celtic history, his brogue that rose up at the end of every sentence, and his chiseled jaw and dreamy eyes.

At least I'd have one good class in Ireland.

***

I fell right into the routine of having two courses on Tuesdays and Thursdays, with the rest of the week free for exploring. NUIG was great for researching my visions, and I spent my free time poring over ancient maps, Irish history books, and historical photos. I looked for anything familiar or something that might spark a memory. My head was full, but still no clues.

Sleep, back at my flat, was my only chance for calm.

"*Méabh….*"

A whisper brought me from the peaceful bliss of sleep to subtle awareness.

"*Méabh….*"

My eyes shot open. The sound was in my room, not my dream. My heart pounded in my ears before I had a chance to talk myself out of the irrational thought. I was frozen in fear, my eyes darting around the room.

Rays of sun streamed in through the window and the sheer curtains danced in the light morning breeze. I drew in a deep breath and let it flow out of my pursed lips in pure relief for my safe surroundings. But as I pushed myself up on my elbows, I heard it again. This time it filled my entire room with its echoes.

"*Méabh.*"

It was my name. I could hear it plainly, but in another language of some sort. It was calling to me.

I jumped out of bed and moved to the window. The curtains were billowing now in the breeze and I raced to close the sash, to stop the eerie sound from entering my room again. I fought past the flapping curtains and squinted my eyes into the wind to reach for the pane. I drew back in an instant, standing like a statue, staring at the locked window that hadn't been opened in days.

"*Méabh.*" The sound surrounded me again and reverberated through my bones.

I turned on my heels and bolted out of my room, flew down the stairs, and smashed out the door of my flat. Bent over in the alley, hands on my knees, I panted for gulps of air. My hands covered my face as I paced, talking to myself, coming up with reasonable explanations while shivers quaked out of my body.

How could I go back up there? There was no way.

I was barefoot, in an old T-shirt and underwear, and I had few options.

***

"I ran outside in my underwear this morning." I looked at Michelle with a sheepish grin as we walked toward Lynch's Pub. Street lights flickered to a gentle glow as early evening darkness settled in.

"Ooookaaaay...." She raised her eyebrows in judgment.

"Someone was calling my name." I watched Michelle for her reaction. It was a gauge to help me decide how I should feel about it.

"Oh. Okay. Um, do you think it was a dream? One of your awake dreams?" She hesitated, then smirked. "Do you think any cute guys saw you in your underwear?"

"I think so. I mean, no. I think maybe it could have been my dream. I don't know. It might just be nerves." I tried to convince myself I was still half-asleep when it happened. That I'd imagined it.

"Hmmm. You were probably still asleep. *Unless....*" She opened her eyes wide. "Someone's trying to reach you. From *beyond.*" And she looked all around, like she was trying to detect a possible spirit hovering above the trash cans and shop signs.

I rolled my eyes, but to be fair, I guess I did sound a bit ridiculous.

Lynch's was right around the corner and I welcomed the distraction. The crowd seemed smaller this time and the band twanged away on their instruments for sound check. My shy boy hid, shielded again behind his amp, and pressed pedals with his foot to find his perfect sound.

A new feeling, maybe it was bravery, washed over me as I made a firm decision to approach him. I needed a good line, different from the standard stuff. Every girl started with, "Oh, you're such a good guitar player, hee hee." I had to do better than that, for once in my life. I hoped I was even capable.

The roadie at the soundboard arranged levers and switches to control volume, sound, or whatever. He had an entire recording studio set up by the looks of it. I could start with him maybe.

I navigated between the tables, wondering where my confidence was coming from. It was brand new for me and felt like Red Bull shooting through my veins. His head lifted as I approached and I kept my eyes on the equipment with false interest.

"Are you recording the gig tonight?" I tried to sound like I knew what I was talking about.

"Yeah, the lads want a demo so they can book more gigs." He took a double-take and said, "You a Yank?"

I nodded. "From Boston." I wasn't sure what to say next. My plan ended and now I was winging it. This was the part where I always froze and made a mess.

"Whatcha doin' in Ireland?" He stopped fiddling with the levers and put his elbow on the stool next to him, looking at me with raised eyebrows.

"Um, taking a couple courses at NUIG. Uh, tracing my family roots." I was already boring myself. His eyes were glazing over. "Personal enrichment...?" I reached for straws, dying a slow death. Someone kill me. End the suffering. He looked back at his soundboard and began fiddling with levers again. "So, I, uh, I hear there's great hiking and cool ruins around here...." My voice trailed off. "I guess...."

"Hiking? Ya mean *hillwalking*. In Connemara." He turned to me again and looked over at the guitar players. "Rory over there, he's the one ya need to talk to. His dad's a hillwalker, covered the Twelve Bens of Connemara buncha times. He's dragged Rory through those hills more times than I can count." He played with some switches on his soundboard again.

"Him?" I pointed to the showman.

"Christ, no. Not Finn. Rory, behind the amp."

A wicked smile grew on my face. He gave me information on my shy boy. And it was good stuff. Relevant. And his name. I loved it!

Rory.

"Oh. Okay. Twelve Bens? Conna…Conna-what?" The complete shut-down process had already taken over and couldn't be stopped, turning me into a stuttering idiot.

"Connemara!" He laughed to himself, shaking his head and focused back on his mixer.

I flew back through the tightly packed tables to Michelle. She was rehearsing her pick-up line for Finn and was confident it should start with, "You're such a good guitar player, hee hee," and she was absolutely fine with that.

Lights flashed for last call and the band started breaking down their gear. Girls surrounded Finn like ducks to bread, leaving no chance for Michelle, so I dragged her with me over to the sheltering amp.

Rory unplugged his guitar and started wrapping cables off to the side. He looked up as we approached. I tried to ignore his deep blue eyes to avoid becoming completely tongue-tied, but everywhere I looked at him was equally distracting.

"Hi. I'm Maeve. This is Michelle." I gestured toward Michelle, trying not to stare at his muscular arms hiding under his loose-fitting T-shirt. There was no way I would get through this without making a complete fool of myself.

Rory looked at me without expression and continued fumbling with his gear. I searched for the rock I would usually hide under, like when Michael O'Brien would come to Gram's house, but got slapped back by something new inside me. I took a silent deep breath, determined to leave Michael O'Brien far behind me.

"We're looking for a place to go hillwalking and that guy over there…." I jerked my thumb over my shoulder to point toward the switchboard roadie, and hit Rory's pint of beer, knocking it off the amp and onto his lap in a big slosh of black stout across his shirt.

He leaped up. "Jazus!" He jumped back, inspecting his gear for any beer damage. Seeing it was safe, he grabbed his rag and started batting at the wet foam on his shirt.

He glared at me like he was about to swear. I nearly crapped myself.

"Oh my God! I'm so sorry!" Horror washed over me as I lost all sense of my plan and reached for him, trying to help clean him up. "I'm so embarrassed. Sorry...." I rambled as I stumbled over some of his gear, trying to reach him better.

"Wow, Maeve." Michelle stepped back, looking around, not knowing what to do. "Clutz much?" She smirked, checking to see if Finn saw.

I shot a look of death at her. Like, *Thanks Michelle. Way to help out.*

Rory took my arm to steady me and blinded me with a huge, unexpected smile. He chuckled while shaking his shirt away from his stomach, revealing more abs than my nerves could handle.

"It's okay. No need for further damage." He held his hand up to stop me on my path of destruction. "That how *all* you Yanks say hello?" His gentle gaze put me in a trance.

"That guy over there," I said as I pointed more cautiously this time, "said you might know some good places to go hiking. Sorry. I was just gonna ask you about that. Jeez, how embarrassing." I splatted my hand onto my forehead.

Rory's face awakened like he had heard a magical word.

"Hiking?" He smiled. "Who? Eugene?" He shot a scowl at Eugene, like he'd get him back somehow. "He's right. M' father's a hillwalker. Has been all 'is life. Connemara's the place for it." The topic brought Rory to life as he stood taller and his eyes brightened. His rolling accent was enough to make me lose consciousness, smooth and sweet and totally distracting. "So, you're a Yank."

My turn to respond. Right. God. I restrained my hand from smacking myself in the head again.

"It's that obvious?" I smirked. "I'm trying to blend in, you know. Pubs, scones, hillwalking—not hiking." I smiled at him, envying his long, thick lashes, unfair to any woman.

"Right. Well, ya *did* say hiking earlier. I caught that slip. Sorry. But, sure, you're doin' okay. No worries." He chuckled. "Have ya much climbing experience?"

No.

"A little," I lied.

"Well, yeh'll like the hills of Ireland. No trees at'all. Views the whole way up. Exhaustin' still, though." Rory held up his empty pint glass and gave it a shake at the barman who returned a knowing nod.

Flicking his guitar pick between his fingers, Rory described the hills, his eyes dreamy and faraway. I gazed up at him as the rest of the pub blurred out. His full lips and boyish grin melted me, helping me feel comfortable and unafraid, like I could trust him or like he wouldn't think I was a joke.

The lights flashed one final time and Rory reached for his jacket. As he picked it up, beer dripped off, proving there had been more casualties than merely his shirt. Embarrassment flooded me again and in defense, I swiped the jacket from him and said, "I got this! Really. My fault."

His eyes widened in surprise. "Oh, a jacket thief too?"

"No. What? Right. No, I'll get it cleaned for you. I promise. I'll bring it back next gig." I left him little choice, moving the jacket to safety behind my back, out of his reach.

He squinted his eyes, acting like I had planned it all. "Fine. Here. This day week."

"Great. Okay. Um…wait, when?" I had no idea what he had just said.

"This day week. Like, same day but next week, ya know." He laughed at my ignorance with a playful jab.

"Oh! Got it. 'Kay. See you." Could he see me flailing?

I took Michelle's arm and moved toward the door while keeping one eye on Rory. She was still sulking at her missed chance to speak with Finn.

"At least he noticed us though," she said. "He saw us with Rory, so that's good." She cheered herself up with a little smile. No wonder she'd been snooty when I spilled the beer.

Rory held my gaze until I turned away. The heat from his eyes warmed me as I left with Michelle, but I was careful to not look back.

Chapter Five

Second Sight

Michelle and I stretched the weekend a little further than it was meant to go and ended up in County Clare, a couple of hours south of Galway—and my awake dream made an encore appearance while we were sitting in a dimly lit, well-aged pub in Doolin. When the mist and the wind faded and my heartbeat returned to normal, Michelle was staring at me, baring clenched teeth.

I glimpsed at her with a sheepish grin and said, "Yeah, so, that's what I've been telling you about. My awake dream...." I lingered on the sentence, waiting for her reaction.

She smiled and reached across the table to give me a huge, warm hug.

"That was freaky," she said. "I would have been really worried if you hadn't warned me about that." She looked at me as if I had barely avoided being hit by a runaway train. "Literally, it looked like you were having a silent seizure or something, like you were awake in a dream world, but you were scared at the end. Really scared. To be honest...." She hesitated. "That was way beyond weird. Sorry."

She smiled right into my face, searching my eyes and said, "Sooooo, what did you seeeeee?"

Traditional Irish music played in the background as the smell of burning turf from the fireplace filled the open spaces. Everything mixed with the essence of seafood chowder and brown bread served at the bar as I began piecing together the new details of my awake dream.

"I could feel the wind coming." I leaned in closer to Michelle. "There was no time to warn you. I froze; I couldn't stop it." My hands shook as the scenes flashed in my mind. "The wind and mist filled the pub. I couldn't see a thing."

Michelle stared, absorbing every word.

"But then there was the stone wall, right up close, with moss and worn carvings, like bizarre faces."

In the dream, I stepped away from the disturbing carvings and as I backed up I had a better view of the size of the wall. It went as high as I could see and as wide as the salty mist would allow.

"It was a castle," I stated. Michelle's eyes widened.

How could I not have known this before? It was so obvious now.

Square at its foundation, stark and gloomy, it rose at least four stories high. It had a pointed roof at the top with a high arched window at the highest level and narrow vertical slits for windows lower down. A large black brooding door, matching the arched window at the top of the castle, marked the entry. Four large stone slab stairs were lined with aged black water marks from the regular visit of high tide, leading up to the threshold.

A powerful force seemed to surround the castle, like it was protected by someone or something, causing my defenses to be on high alert.

"It was like someone was inside. Waiting for me."

Michelle's eyebrows shot up. "What do you mean?"

"I could feel them. I've always felt it. And I heard my name again." The voice lingered in my ears, haunting me. A shiver ran through my bones. "It's been tracking me my whole life. Getting closer. It's here." I looked all around me and moved my hands in slow waves over the table for emphasis.

"Here?" Michelle pressed her finger into the top of our table and sat up straight as her face went white.

Laughter burst out of me at her confusion. "No, not here!" I pushed at her arm on the table. "But here...." I looked around us and out the door. "Here in Ireland."

"Oh, phew!" Her shoulders relaxed. "You scared me. I don't want to get stuck in one of your head trips, or meet the freak who's stalking you in them. No offense." Michelle sat back in her chair with safe satisfaction. Then her eyes focused on me as she reached for my hands. "But really, Maeve, you need to find that castle. That's all there is to it."

***

"Come on. Let's explore a little." I waved for Michelle to keep up. I was ready to find my castle. Now.

"Nah. I'm gonna chill at the B&B. I'm not taking any chances 'exploring' with you and your freaky dreams." She hip-checked me. "I mean, they're cool and all, but really, a little distance is better for me."

My heart sank, seeing the boundary Michelle put up. Though I couldn't blame her, really. Her close proximity to my castle vision must have made it a little too real for her and she was out.

Michelle went without me toward the B&B. I dragged my heels, admiring the quaint shops of Doolin, all painted yellow, orange, or purple to counter the gray skies. I was drawn to a bright pink sweater shop by its luminous green door and thatched roof. I peered through the window at the hand-knit Aran sweaters, but the reflection in the glass of a meandering road stole my attention.

Behind me was a lone country road, traveling up through the green hills. My body turned itself and was crossing the street before I even made the conscious decision to do so. Tempted by the winding path to nowhere, I started up at a steady pace. The smell of burning coal thickened the air and blended with the pungent aroma of silage and fermenting hay from the farms, but as I made my way up, the sweet smell of wet air returned and cleared my senses.

Soon I was high enough to look back on the village and see the countless farms that were hidden behind the shops of the main street. Men with caps worked the land and tended to their cows in a slow-motion dance. I climbed up on a small boulder for a better view, hoping for a glimpse of the coast, and noticed, hidden near the side of the road, a wishing well of some sort.

Moving closer, I hunkered down for a better look. It was a holy well. A small plaque described it as ancient, used for sacred Druid rituals. As I leaned in to see the detail in the limestone, I came face to face with a mythical creature carved into the rock, faded and weathered, with knowing eyes that looked straight into my soul.

I jumped back in surprise and stumbled onto the road, blinking away the ghostly image. As I stepped back, the screech of tires on pavement tore through my body as a car ground to a halt, inches from hitting me.

My heart leaped out of my body a second time, leaving me like dust to blow away in the next wind. Pulling it back into me through a huge gasp, I wrapped my arms around myself to hold the loose bits together.

I gaped at the car in shock. My natural instinct was to apologize, to thank the driver for not killing me. My face said it all before I could.

The driver opened the door and climbed out of the car—much to my horror. My first reaction was to run away mortified, but thankfully, some small form of normality still existed in me, ready to stand up.

My awkward embarrassment was met by a friendly, smiling face— a smirkish grin actually.

It was Paul McGratt.

My heart skipped several beats in my chest, leaving me flustered on top of traumatized.

"My apologies, Miss O'Malley, sure, I nearly ran ya over." He was just as flustered as me and seemed out of breath. "Are yeh okay?" He reached for my arm as if I needed help across the road like an old granny.

I stepped back, raising one hand up and nodding my head to show him I was fine, and stumbled right over the embankment I had come from. My balance left me as I saw each freeze-frame play out, painfully slow, as I headed toward the gravelly mud, face first. Right as I envisioned my humiliating splat, Mr. McGratt grabbed my arm and steadied me, hauling me back to a solid upright.

"Gotcha, mind yer'self. Ya can't go and break something right after surviving almost being hit by a car!" He kept hold of my arm, making sure I was solid. "You okay? I think yer a bit shaken." His supportive touch warmed me to my core.

"No, I'm fine." How embarrassing. "Just a little surprised to see you, I guess. What are you doing here?" I brushed off imaginary dirt as the blunt question left my mouth without going through my normal multiple levels of filtering.

"What am *I* doing here? Sure, I was gonna ask you the very same thing." He laughed. "I mean, yer out here alone, fallin' into the road and then fallin' off the road...." He tilted his head, holding back a chuckle as he waited for an answer.

I felt my spirit returning, probably because I started breathing again, or maybe in response to his teasing. "I'm exploring." My hands on my hips added sass and false confidence for effect. "Field research, ancient artifacts, Celtic stuff, you know," I teased, and looked right back at him.

"Oh, I see. And where's your gear? Rucksack? Field instruments. Anything?" He raised his eyebrows, calling my bluff.

"Fine." I crossed my arms. "No, but really, I *am* exploring a little bit. My friend Michelle is down the road, in town." I nodded my head in the direction of the village.

"Ah, gotcha. That makes sense. So you're not wanderin' aimlessly or hopelessly lost? That's good news." He looked back at his car. "Do ye need a lift? Back into town?"

I looked at his car and noticed the passenger watching me. It was a girl. She was pretty.

"No, thanks. I'll be fine. Really."

Butterflies turned to bats and began to upset my stomach as I thought too much about my situation—talking to my professor, who almost hit me with his car, on a random road, far out in a random village. Weird.

"Okay, well, you're all right then? Feeling better?" He looked at me with a furrowed brow. "Sure, it looked like ya'd seen a ghost when ya stumbled out onto the road."

A flash of the ancient carved eyes ran through my mind, and I bit my lip.

"No, really. I'm okay. I'm gonna head back in a sec, after I make it to the top of this road." I pointed to the rise, which wasn't far. My curiosity demanded I see what was over the hill.

"Okay, well...." He rubbed the back of his neck and took a step back, looking at the ground. "Hey, I'm really sorry I nearly hit ya." He dragged his shoe across the pavement then his eyes met mine. "Once you make it to the top of the road there, great view. There's a little surprise." He smiled at me. "Yeh're an adventurous one, Miss O'Malley," he said with squinted eyes, almost like he was trying to figure me out. "See ya at university. And sure, I hope you won't hold this against me."

I watched his car wind down the road toward the village and began to release the tight embrace around my stomach as he moved out of sight. My butterflies felt their new freedom and traveled throughout my entire body, making me feel like I could fly.

My head fell back as I shook my hands, freeing the butterflies out through my fingertips. I grabbed my pack and threw it over my shoulder, shaking my head in self-judgment, but unable to hide my guilty smile. The mystery of the view over the rise moved me forward.

Chapter Six

Mojo Rising

"I can't believe you're worried he's in a band, Gram. That doesn't make him bad! He's super-nice. And his name is Rory!" I was certain his Irish name would win her over.

I didn't mean to worry Gram but I couldn't help but tell her about him. I hadn't been to Mayo yet to find the O'Malleys. I wasn't ready. I was still researching and basically trying to find my feet. So Rory was the main topic of conversation on my mind. I actually thought she'd be excited that I was smitten with an Irishman. Smitten at all, for that matter.

"Just take care of yerself, Maeve. Don't get distracted. Yeh're on this journey for you, no one else."

I felt another *Dear Abby* moment coming. Gram always had a clipping from the *Dear Abby* column, one that fit each current life moment perfectly. It was creepy. I had to change the subject, fast.

"My classes are cool...." But I was cut off as Gram spoke at the same time.

"Have ya had any of yer strange dreams, Maeve?" Gram's stiff voice had a chill to it.

"What? Um, actually, yeah, a couple." My voice went high at the end. "They're not too bad though. Nothing to worry about." I managed to keep my voice steady but it was laced with false confidence. I couldn't get the balance right and I was sure she could hear it.

I didn't want Gram to know how real my awake dreams had become in Ireland. She'd try to make me come home so fast. Like she was waiting for an excuse to yank me back home, which really sucked because I could actually use her help to figure out what was going on with my visions. But she had tried her best to stop me from coming, so there was no way I was going to chance it by telling her how scary things were becoming now.

Silence.

"Gram?"

"Yes, I'm here." Her voice was a million miles away.

"Everything okay?"

"Well, I'm glad yer all right." She filled the silence with meaningless words, though I heard more between them.

I tilted my head and lifted one brow.

"How's Joey?" I blurted out, leaving no chance of it going back to *Dear Abby* columns or awake dreams. "Tell him I love him."

The phone rustled like it was passing through a pile of laundry and I could hear her telling him my words. The phone was awkward for my grandfather. He had zero ability to hold a conversation on one. I pictured Gram sitting on the couch on her side of the living room, with him in his big chair on the opposite side.

"Tell 'er I gave up me pipe," he shouted, pride in his deep, seasoned voice. His words surprised me. Joey's pipe was part of who he was. His sweater and his chair always smelled of his tobacco.

"Tell him I'm so proud of him!" I shouted back, realizing my raised voice was unnecessary. "Tell him I'm happy here and I miss him."

I strained to hear his replies as Gram and I carried on our conversation from Ireland to America, from Galway to Boston, from me to Gram, from Gram to Joey, from her couch over to his big chair, and back again.

***

"My grandparents say we need to try the Irish bacon while we're here!" I shouted at Michelle as we pushed our way toward the arch at the back of the pub.

Lynch's was crowded again—standing room only. Mojo had

already started playing and the deep tones of the bass guitar vibrated through my body as we squeezed our way in. I had my ammo ready—Rory's clean jacket in my cinch sack.

Michelle was hyper-focused on meeting Finn and didn't take her eyes off him, optimistic about finally making a connection. He was busy putting on his usual show, singing to the girls in the crowd, and from the look on her face it was clear Michelle was sure he sang to her a couple of times too. It only baited her further.

Rory was off to the side shadowed by his amp. My heart squeezed in my chest, sending jitters through my veins. As he knelt and arranged his foot pedals, I admired his worn jeans and the perfect way they hung on him. He glanced up, almost knowingly, and caught me watching him. I prayed I didn't have a stupid love gaze on my face.

He smiled as he gestured the neck of his guitar toward me. My butterflies took full flight and I was sure they were going to find their way right out of my mouth as I sent a quick fan of my fingers to say hello back.

Michelle and I got lost in conversation within the swirling atmosphere of thumping music and packed bodies. I was surprised to see a freshly poured pint of Guinness pass in front of my face and hover there, held from behind me. The creamy foam top slid down the side of the glass of stout as I followed the arm of whoever was offering it to me.

My expectant smile fell from my face as I recognized Fergal, an awkward man who gave Michelle and me a lift home from our trip to Doolin. He was probably around thirty, lacking in basic hygiene, and his clothes were dated, but that wasn't even the bad part.

Meeting Fergal was something I wanted to forget. After picking us up from the side of the road near our B&B, Fergal had been creepy from the start. His eyes appeared to cross a little, making him seem either drunk or deranged. He said he had been watching us in the pub earlier and liked how we "stood out."

I know hitchhiking is a definite no in the States, but we missed our bus by a mile and were told hitching was the main form of transportation for backpackers in Ireland. So I guess we took the "When in Rome" attitude. Dumb.

If Fergal had been our age—and well, less stalkerish—it might have been okay, but that was not the case. I'd known we needed to end the ride fast and cursed myself for being so naïve.

And when he'd reached over for a squeeze of my knee, it was time to get out.

I'd had to pretend I was going to throw up to get him to stop and unlock the doors, and I could still hear his voice yelling at us as we fled to the safety of a nearby shop. "Runnin' away…coward…O'Malley…no place for a woman…." I could swear I heard O'Malley in his rant. Weirdo.

We'd vowed to take the bus from that moment forward, and wrote the encounter off as a cautionary tale.

But now, Fergal was here! In our pub! In Galway! Handing me a pint! In front of Rory!

"What are you doing here?" I took the pint away from my face and placed it on the table next to me.

"In my car, ya mentioned this pub and a great band and, sure, I had ta come find ya." He stood too close with bad breath and a sleazy smile, pressuring me to smile back, which was *not* happening. His body pressed against mine as if the crowd pushed him in. Repulsed, I set a firm stance, ready to shove him away with my shoulder.

"Yeh're feeling better, I see," he said without care. "That was really no way to treat a man who mighta been doing ya a favor now, was it?"

He pressed his weight further into my side and I squirmed as he inspected me. I prayed Rory wasn't seeing this. Michelle grabbed my elbow.

Fergal leaned in closer. "Why are you *here*?" He tipped his head and rubbed his chin.

Why was *I* here? What the hell was he talking about? I was the one who should be asking that question. Warnings went off in my head like the blaring of my school's fire drills. Something sinister about him darkened his space.

Careful not to agitate him, I said, "I'm meeting a guy here tonight, someone I'm dating. I wouldn't want to give him the wrong idea." I began moving away from him.

"Ah sure, that doesn't bother me. I'm not the type to shy away from a good fight." His smile exposed his rotting teeth and sent my panic to a new level.

"Sorry, Fergal. I'm not looking for any fights. Please, leave me alone. Okay? Please." I turned away from him. Michelle's eyes stared blankly at me in frozen helplessness.

"Yer type never shied away from a fight before. Sure, it's in yer blood." His curled lips and the slow drawl of his words sent me flying. Did he know me?

I grabbed Michelle, now pale as a ghost, and pushed her through the crowd away from him.

"Ya can't just come back like that!" he shouted after us. "It ain't right!"

I kept pushing Michelle toward the far wall. I looked back—Fergal was moving away through the crowd toward the door. He was leaving.

Michelle's huge eyes and pale complexion mirrored mine.

"What the hell was that?" she spewed. "He's crazy. Like for real."

We agreed to stay put so we wouldn't run into him on the streets. We'd keep an eye out for him for the rest of the night, to be sure he didn't come back. And now, his coercive gift pint sat there on the table, growing old, taunting me.

***

The band took a break in the middle of their session to refresh their pints and cool down. I kept a conversation going with Michelle so I wouldn't appear as desperate for Rory's attention as I felt.

We went through our run-in with Fergal a thousand times, each time with a worse ending than the one before. We'd gotten off lucky and knew it. A chill shuddered through my body at the thought—and then I felt someone approach me from behind again. I closed my eyes, accepting that Fergal really hadn't given up that easily, and turned to him in disgust. But my grimace flipped to a bright, hopeful smile.

It was Rory.

"How's yer pint?" he gestured with a knowing grin to the stale beer left earlier by Fergal.

My heart jumped as I looked at him with bright eyes, speechless. My concerns about Fergal washed away as my thoughts filled back up with Rory.

"I know," I finally sputtered. "What a waste. So sad, just sitting there like that." I smirked. "An Irish Coffee would have worked much better."

I blushed from my whiskey reference or maybe from his close proximity. He was so cute, standing there with his tousled black hair and deep blue eyes. I could stare into them all night.

Rory chuckled and asked, "Did yeh have a chance ta walk the hills yet?" He shook his hand through his hair as if recovering from his performance and my eyes followed the woven string bracelets on his wrist.

"We went to Doolin," Michelle cut in. "Awesome traditional music in the pubs."

"Oh, yeah?" His attention turned to her, and my eyes narrowed. I could hit her. "Which pub? O'Connor's? Sure, they have great trad sessions."

"Yes! How'd you know that?" Her eyes were wide with surprise.

Rory tapped the side of his forehead and squinted at her. "I know things." He half-smiled. "And, sure, there's only a few pubs in Doolin. O'Connor's is the one." He jabbed at her with his elbow.

I saw red.

"So the hills…." Rory brought his attention back to me and my jealousy evaporated.

I found my voice again. "Yeah, I saw an ancient sacred spring." He nodded, showing some recognition. "At the top of the hill, there was this amazing round tower, like a castle ruin."

"I know that place," Rory interjected. "Been there a million times. M' family, we drive out there for walks in the Burren. Did ya go into it?" His song-like voice sounded like he was reciting poetry.

"No. I didn't know you *could* go in. Are you allowed to do that?"

"Probably not. But ya should'na let that stop ya. Yeh'll need to see it up close. Explore a bit. It's fantastic. I'll have to take ya there again some time." He tapped my arm with his palm to seal the deal.

My stomach flipped. I prayed I'd heard him correctly.

Rory returned a wave to Finn and headed back to the band. A moment later, he was playing again.

I turned to Michelle and my earlier jealousy returned. "What the heck was that?" She'd nearly stolen my chance.

Michelle pulled at the neck of her shirt and looked pale. "I need to get out of here." Her hands shook and a small twitch jolted her chin. Her breathing sounded more like gasps.

"What? Okay, come on." I took her arm and wove through the chaos of the crowd, hiding my disappointment in leaving Rory and fighting the resentment that tied in with it.

After considerable effort, we extracted ourselves from the tightly packed pub and fell out onto the street.

"What the heck was that? Are you okay?" The color began to return to her face.

"I don't know. A panic attack? Let's just walk." I followed her as we moved along the sidewalk. "I think I got claustrophobic or something. Or the Fergal thing. That freaked me out." Michelle took a few deep inhales, letting each breath flow out with control as I looked around to be sure we weren't being followed. "I just needed to get out of there."

She led me into a late-night food dive.

"Sorry, Maeve. I didn't mean to ruin anything for you with Rory." Her eyes glistened with sincerity.

"That's okay. You didn't." I felt stupid now. "I'm just a bit tense. Especially after Fergal."

"I know. That was crazy. And Rory watched Fergal like a hawk!" Her eyes were wide.

"Wait! Are you serious?" I gasped.

"Oh yeah." Her Cheshire grin proved she was loving this. "Once Fergal handed you that pint, Rory didn't take his eyes off you, or him. He acted like he was busy playing his guitar, with his head turned to the side, but he kept his eye on you. Watching what you would do." Michelle smirked. "Like he was pissed at Fergal or something."

We sat at a table after ordering our french fries—well, *chips*. As I placed my bag on the seat, I remembered—Rory's jacket! It was still in my bag, held hostage, or more like collateral. I needed to get it back to him.

Full of chat and curry chips, we stepped back onto the dark streets an hour later, talking about Finn and how to get Michelle a chance at him. People were milling about, heading home from the pubs or relocating to the nightclubs.

We started up Shop Street toward Bohermore and planned to find a cab in Eyre Square for Michelle. Once she was set in a taxi, I would easily walk the short distance to my flat.

As we passed our beloved Lynch's Pub, I heard my name. "Maeve, hey, Maeve, wait up." I knew that smooth lilt and dreamy accent. It was Rory. I turned in disbelief and there he was, coming toward us.

"Where'd ya guys go? Tired of the band so soon?" he joked as he caught up to us. "I'm takin' the gear back to the shed. You girls want a lift home?"

He gestured toward the small, beat-up van in front of the pub. The other guys were still loading in drum parts, clanging and clashing the cymbals. Though Bohermore was just up the road, I looked at Michelle with hopeful eyes and she shot back an expression of, *Hell yeah!*

We squeezed into the passenger's seat together, giggling like two schoolgirls. Before starting the van, Rory pulled off his sweatshirt and adjusted his loose, worn T-shirt around his waist, but only after I caught a quick glimpse of his bare hip. My butterflies took flight again.

He grabbed the wheel and reached for the stick shift in the middle of the console, right where I was squished in. He worked the shift down past my thigh repeatedly, trying to get it in reverse, apologizing every time. I sent a gentle jab to Michelle's rib.

Then my attention pulled past Rory out the side window of the van, toward the red door of Lynch's Pub. In a flash, I saw Fergal waiting there, leaning against the wall, watching the van pull away. He bared his teeth and spat on the sidewalk. I cringed and jerked my head away.

A blanket of relief covered me in the safety of the van. Rory had saved us from another encounter with Fergal, maybe one where I was walking home alone.

"Which way?" Rory asked, tugging on the gear shift.

"I'm out in Tirellan Heights," Michelle said, while I delayed disclosing the close proximity of my flat for as long as possible. "It's a bit of a hike, so thanks for the ride. Maeve's flat is on Bohermore, right back that way." She pointed up Shop Street toward Bohermore.

I wanted to kill her, again.

"I'll make a loop. Tirellan Heights first, then back this way to return the van. Does that suit ye?"

He leaned forward, eyeing both of us. I could feel Michelle's knee pressing into mine as if she was saying, *Oh my God!*

Gram's face filled my head, reminding me of what *Dear Abby* would say. I squeezed my eyes shut and gave it a little shake to get rid of the image.

"Tell us about Mojo. You guys are great." I wanted to know more but mostly for Michelle's sake.

Cymbals clanged together in the back of the van as Rory struggled more with the gears.

"Ach, we're just a bunch of gurriers who like ta play music together. Keeps us out of trouble I s'pose. The lads, well, they're great craic. Two of 'em have families and day jobs. Finn and me, we're the slackers."

Michelle and I looked at him with blank stares.

"What's craic?" I asked, lost already, pronouncing the word like Rory had—*crack*.

"Ah." Rory thought about it. "Craic is, I dunno, good times, I guess." He scratched his head. "Never really thought about it before. It's like, a greeting too—like, how's it going, how's the craic."

"Hmm," I nodded my head, saving the word for future use.

Michelle didn't hold back and asked, "What's Finn like? He seems pretty happy up there. He's such a good guitar player." She dragged out the last sentence with a deep, yearning voice. Her inner groupie was showing.

"Oh, Finn. He's a funny one. His girlfriend's none too keen on his playin' gigs, ya know. He's more about makin' a good run for his money."

Rory's matter-of-fact tone made it clear that Finn was a player, even if we couldn't understand all of the idioms. He must have known full well that Michelle's inquiry had purpose.

Her face hung with disappointment. I peeked over at her and nudged her with my elbow. I shook my head slowly with my lips pursed to the side as if to say, *You're too good for him anyway.*

At Michelle's, Rory hopped out of the van and took her hand as she climbed out, wishing her a good night. She looked back at me before closing the door and mouthed, *Holy crap!* Then her eyebrows rose a quarter inch and her expression changed to, *Are you sure you want to go alone with him?* I nodded with a sly grin while shredding in my mind every *Dear Abby* column ever written.

As Rory hopped back in, my stomach tightened. This was my first moment alone with him. I hoped I wouldn't blow it.

"Want t' check out the beach?" he asked out of nowhere. "It's on the way back, if we go the Salthill road. I want to show ya something." He glanced over to see if his bait had hooked me.

"Yeah, sure." My heart nearly jumped out of my chest. "Hey, I have your jacket by the way." I pulled it out of my bag in slow motion, exaggerating the kindness of my gesture. "See. All nice and clean." I patted it like a puppy.

Rory reached over for the coat and held up the sleeve. "Missed a spot."

"What?" I examined it quickly, certain something in my bag messed it up.

"Just kiddin'. It's perfect. Thanks." He laughed at my reaction.

"Hmmff…sure thing." My lips pursed to the side and then, out the window, I saw the beach of Galway Bay.

Through the darkness, I could make out the light of a distant town far across the bay. Rory parked, grabbed his jacket, and brought me along the promenade. The beach was deserted and the fresh salty air blew at my face and curled my hair. Our hands bumped together and the electric energy shot through me like a jolt.

My hand pulled back close to my body like it was jumping to escape. Hopefully he hadn't noticed, because I actually liked the unexpected touch of him. I wasn't sure why I had flinched like that.

"Here." He turned us down a jetty-like structure, kind of a boat ramp. It led to a two-story framework with platforms and rusty railings for standing and viewing the scenery. "This is Blackrock. People walk the length of the prom to this point, kick the wall for good luck, and then turn back." He paused with raised eyebrows. "It's a tradition for Galwegians."

He smiled at the simplicity of it, then pointed to the high platforms. "Ya can climb up there and jump into the sea at high tide. Sometimes ya have to time it right so ya don't land on any jellyfish." I assumed he'd landed on a jellyfish or two at some point. "Ahh, good craic."

He started up the steps and reached back for me. The thick darkness left me feeling lost but I took his hand, trusting him. My fingers flinched in his palm again as a jolt of pain stabbed at my chest at the same time and I stumbled.

"You okay?" Rory looked back at me.

I let go of the rail for a second, to rub my chest. It felt like a hot coal had landed there.

"Yeah, good craic." I faked a smile while looking down, expecting to see scorch. "Just a bit dark. I got this." I continued climbing with him as the burning sensation festered on my chest. This time, it kept growing in urgency, nagging me.

At the first platform, we looked over the edge and then at each other and decided to go higher. I ignored the rising pain on my skin as he took my hand again and swept me up to the top of the structure.

Leaning against the railing, we gazed across the bay at the lights of the distant town.

"That's County Clare over there. That's where ya saw yer round tower in Doolin, and the holy well." Rory spoke into the night air.

I focused on his accent and the heat that radiated from his body to keep my mind off the burn. But my senses were heightened around him, he triggered them all, making the pain even harder to ignore. It was mellowing to a steady pulsating hot spot now, at least, and I hoped it would stay under control while I was with him. He was the only thing I wanted my attention on.

I shivered from the ache and the chill in the night air, crossing my arms around myself. Rory pulled off his jacket and wrapped it over my shoulders.

"Sure, don't spill anythin' on it." His eyes squinted from his teasing half-smile. He rubbed the tops of my arms, trying to warm me up. I looked up at him, half holding my breath.

His smile went away and his eyes focused on me.

"What is it about you?" His gaze held my eyes locked. "You've got a freedom about ya. But some kind of knowledge, like an old soul. I'm not sure...." He examined me. "Ya make me nervous, though. Not sure why."

He looked away across the water.

"Wait. Is that bad? Like, weird or something?" My eyebrows rose. I didn't know how I was making him nervous. I had been quite sure, actually, that it was the other way around.

"Nah, you don't mean ta. I just feel, I don't know, like I might do something wrong, guilty like. I'm sorry." His shoulders slumped.

A cold breeze picked up, carrying a piercing briskness from the water. It went right through me, stealing my core heat.

"Are you kidding?" I punched him in the arm to snap him out of it. "*You* have nothing to worry about." I couldn't stop my eyebrows from scrunching together as I pondered what he could be talking about. My head tipped as I studied him.

"I'm leaving soon," he spoke into the night. His breath formed white swirls of frost in the air.

"What?" Time froze, along with my own breath. I had no idea where the cold air was coming from all of a sudden.

"There's nothing for me here, really. I'm making plans for England. Bigger music scene there." He avoided looking at me and somehow ignored the bone-chilling air.

My heart sank like a stone.

"When?" It was all I could say without exposing too much of my inner crash.

"Not sure yet. Soon, I think."

We stood in silence staring into the blackness of night. I fought to keep my disappointment from drooping my face. A shudder ran through me as the relentless chill in the air persisted.

He looked at his phone. "Come on. I gotta get this van back to Eugene straight away. I'll take ya home." He took my hand again and led me back down the high structure.

My forced smile faded as I trailed behind him. The throbbing on my chest felt lighter now, allowing my shoulders to relax. A bit too late though, now that the moment was over.

The roads sparkled with evening street lights and front door lanterns while I watched the shops and rows of houses blur by as we drove toward the city center. Outside my window, two nuns stood at the gate of a church. Their dark skirts and jackets made them nearly invisible against the dark stonework of the building. Light tufts of hair stuck out from the front of their habits, highlighting their faces.

One of them hooked onto my stare and held my gaze as we drove by. I was first to break eye contact, looking down at my fidgeting hands in my lap. Guilt washed over me, like I wasn't good enough, pure enough, or like I was a lawless rebel. I couldn't help feeling judged.

"Seriously!" Rory let out a laugh that shook the van. "Shake it off, girl! Don't let the nuns get to you like that." He stopped short at a traffic light and I jerked in my seat.

"How do they do that?" I accepted their superpower without question.

"They do it on purpose, ya know. They know full well the power they hold." He flinched as the light turned green. "And they abuse it too." He pushed at my knee in jest before accelerating again. "Sure, they've done it to me m' whole life."

I snuck a peek back through my side mirror and then reeled my head around in a snap for a better look. Both nuns were looking directly my way. At me, somehow.

"Go! Go! Go!" I shook my finger forward, commanding him to peal out.

"What?" Rory slowed on the gas.

"The nuns! They're still watching us!" I playfully reached for his knee to push it down on the gas pedal for emphasis. "Seriously! Go!"

Rory floored it and we flew over the bridge and along the docks toward Bohermore, filling the van with my squeals and his raucous laughter. My heart was racing as we pulled up to my blue door. Rory watched me with bright eyes, nodding his head.

"See. Told ya. I knew there was something about you. The nuns seem to know it too." He chuckled and watched me walk to my blue door and open it.

He pulled away and uncertainty filled me with sour doubt, as usual: not knowing if I'd see him again, if he liked me, if he thought I was strange. But the insecurity was buffered this time and diluted with a strong dose of wanting more.

Chapter Seven

Clash of the Chieftains

I am sleeping.

I am dreaming.

Dreaming of my awake dream.

The wind drives me from the quiet of my subconscious into lucid awareness within my dream. The gusts slap me in the face, demanding my full attention as I struggle to see my surroundings.

There's great commotion around me and my vision focuses on the scene of men rushing, dutifully carrying out orders and preparing for defense.

We're on the open wooden deck of a ship, far out at sea. I look around at the rough, weathered men scurrying about, attending to their duties. With an unfamiliar sense of purpose and responsibility, I feel prepared to defend those around me, to protect their lives and their mission.

I yield to the unwavering leadership of a powerful woman. All on deck stop to acknowledge her as she emerges from below. She stands tall with hair jet-black, wild and flowing. Her militant clothing and black leather tunic wrap around her strong, lean body, creating an intimidating vision.

Her voice fills every space as she calls out orders. Covered by white ruffles from the sleeve of her blouse, her hand never leaves the grip of her sword. Her commanding tone shoots fear through my heart, but I stare, motionless, as she stands tall, pushing her blade into the air with every word.

A nagging pang of panic hits the pit of my stomach, over and over, until I pay attention to it. My hand leaves my mouth and moves to my stomach to calm it.

Her heavy boots strike the wooden deck as she moves toward me, loose pant cuffs swaying around the worn leather. Her feminine curves are undeniable even hidden beneath her uniform. I bow instinctively as she approaches and without control over my own body, I sink to the wooden planks, hands splayed out in front of me, gazing at her weathered boots.

She is captain.

"Rise!" she commands me as if inconvenienced. The clomping of my own heavy boots as I stand shocks me and draws my attention to my strange clothes, similar to hers but without a weapon. There's sharp focus in her eyes, with the look of a lion ready to pounce, but I recognize something else in her, something she is hiding—a vulnerability.

"They intend to board us!" she shouts for all to hear. "Prepare t' defend our ship, our clan, and our honor!" Her face turns close to mine as she states, "Stay near me. I need yeh to keep me strong." Then she yells again, "They intend ta challenge me power and me fleet, but we won't let them stop us! This is *our* sea! *Our* home!"

I'm on a battleship of some type. The vessel is massive, at least fifteen oars on either side, filled with hundreds of men rowing intensely to the steady beat of a traditional bodhrán or carrying out orders, preparing for defense. Resistance saturates the salty air.

On a raised deck above the skirmish, I stand with the captain and hear unsettling warning calls from the crow's nest. The smell of brine and tar mixed with sweat and rising alarm causes sickening dread to surge through my body. I stand with her, feeling like I belong here.

From behind, a tall man approaches us and takes my captain by her waist, pulling her close into him. Strong and sea-worn, tanned with a lined face and tough hands, he is deeply handsome with a youthful spark in his expression. His ornate metal wrist cuffs cover his muscular forearms like armor and the clawing lion-beasts masterfully carved into them seem ready for a fight.

He holds her tight against him and says, "Fear not, me queen. You are strong. Continue yer quest, no matter the cost." He looks out across the ship and into the oncoming assault and calls out over the chaos, "We will fight! For Ireland! For freedom!" He pulls her body closer to his as if it were his final lifeline and kisses her with a passion I'd never known existed.

As he releases her, he says, "I will protect yeh with all I have. I'll never leave yeh. You are me heart, Grania. Always will be." He lifts her hand, rubs her ring with his thumb and kisses her fingers. He whispers to her slowly, *"Gra, ma croi,"* then hurries toward the commotion and blends in with the blur of rushing devotees.

She follows his form with her eyes until he is out of view, time frozen, then looks down at her ring as if to feel him there again. The ring is ornate, regal-looking, and now seems to be her direct connection to him.

Hurrying footsteps grow louder. Shrill voices shout from every direction. I cover my ears to shelter from the piercing smash of metal, like cymbals crashing all around me. The distress of rising alarm surrounds us. I can see it in her eyes—battle is inevitable. She can't seem to predict how the next minutes will play out but she is ready to defend her ship and her crew with all she has.

I stay at her side as the ship is boarded by the enemy captain and his henchmen. Their crewmen hold steady behind them, on their own deck, with wild, hungry looks in their eyes, frothing for the command to attack. Our crew stands valiantly, blocking their pursuit with a wall of weapons and shields.

A man in a bronze helmet with a protruding spike on top and cheek plates down the sides steps forward, making accusations of stolen land, illegal hunting, pirating—a price to be paid. He threatens to overtake the ship, pointing at my captain as he speaks.

"I will not yield to yer tribe and watch ya control land and sea. No woman will grow mightier than I. You are no chieftain." He sneers and spits on the deck. "You will bow t' me." He motions with his hefty sword to a few of his men, instructing them to go to my captain, to capture her. "Hand her over and we will spare yer filthy lives."

As the invaders attempt to move toward her position, our wall of defense tightens, preparing for full-scale attack. One of her devoted followers bravely bursts out from the barricade to confront them, to defend his captain. His queen.

"No!" My captain lurches forward in alarm and flies down from the platform to stop him and surrender herself, to accept whatever is to happen to her instead. "Stop!"

But her words remain unheard, or unheeded. The one in charge orders his men to seize her loyal supporter. Our crew is frozen by the unexpected situation, knowing any false move could end his life.

He is swarmed by the enemy, with a dagger to his throat before he can make a strike. My captain's crew, ready to pounce with the collective force of an army, is stifled by her scream to halt.

She rushes forward, pushing through her crew to come between them—her courageous lover and the attackers. She's going to offer herself instead but they already know their course and it involves blood and battle.

"Wait! Stop! 'Tis me yeh want!" The power of her voice cuts through the churning sounds of fury and assault. The sea grows angry as swells heave from the bounding main, tossing the vessel with insatiable aggression. The vicious commander draws strength from the rising seas.

Orders are given and my dream falters. I hear no words but understand the sinister intent by the combative gesturing. The captain is tearing toward them with every ounce of her being.

My ears ring with a high-pitched whirring sound and my vision focuses on the scene in front of me, all images from my peripheral vision blurring and fading. My heart thrums in my neck and my arms and legs are electrified with unspent energy. I know this scene is not going to end well.

Taunting the captain, they hold her lover by the arms, pulling in opposite directions to present him to their malicious chieftain. Her crew rises up in an instant, swords drawn, screams snarled, no longer heeding her orders to hold. The pivotal moment plays out in a painful, merciless slow motion.

My feet are stuck to the tarred deck planks and despite the adrenaline that surges through my limbs, they refuse to obey my command to run to her. Her roars turn to cries as she clamors to reach him, and then to screams as she sees the one in charge draw his sword. Her desperate struggle gives him the power and courage he needs for his next move.

Her crew is in mid-air pounce, about to connect their swords to enemy hearts. As she screams, I can finally hear her words: *"No! Hugh! Ma croi!"* but her words are cut short as the heavy blade lifts to full height and drops with a powerful blow against his neck. The weight and force of the sword's blade brings it straight into his body, crushing bone, crushing dreams, and he falls, lifeless.

I can't see any more through the explosion of chaos—shouting, fighting, clashing swords, death cries. The enemy crew is pouring onto our deck in waves, intimidating and armed, some wielding two swords. The gray sky darkens to ominous black swirls and I am caught in the tempest. Every man on the ship erupts in a fury of battle.

Then I find her, slumped to the ground at the body of her beloved. I am paralyzed with fear. The force of the wind compounds the sounds into a horrible fusion of metal, screams, clashing, and bloodshed. The ship rocks as the high seas lap up the sides of the vessel, searching hungrily for victims to pull into the abyss.

I gasp as I am drawn from the depths of my dream state by the stinging salt spray in my eyes and on my face as reality tugs on me, waking me from my nightmare.

I take one final look at the horrific scene and see her again. Through my fading vision, there is another woman there now by her side, consoling the captain as she wails over her beloved's body. My heart stops. I recognize the woman without question.

She is my mother.

My breath sucks in sharply as I gaze upon my mother's face for the first time since she died. She looks healthy, strong, nothing of what I remembered of her in her final months. I feel a great flood coming and know it will sweep me away.

The captain stands up, staring at the battle. With a twisted, lost look of fury and devastating loss in her eyes, she raises her sword and surges toward her vengeance.

***

I forced my eyes open, caught between images of my nightmare and the light of morning. It was the only way to escape the dream.

Holy crap! Sweat streamed down my face, rolling into my ears. I wiped at my cheeks to dry them and felt tears. Thick, heavy tears. It wasn't sweat or sea spray. I was weeping, grieving.

The flood had hit me and the sadness was unbearable. Was this what I had been sheltering myself from for all these years? Avoiding? The pain of losing my mother felt like sickening poison coursing through my veins, causing my muscles to constrict and joints to ache.

God! Make it stop! I writhed in my bed, tormented by visions of the captain slumped over her lover, crying out. My face contorted in grief. I curled into a fetal position, rocking and weeping. The pain in my chest continued to grow. Tightening. Sharp jabs. Jolting, out-of-rhythm heartbeats.

The pain of a broken heart.

I sank in my bed, imploding like a deflating hot air balloon as I entered a dark, lonely place of despair. For my captain. For her lost love, Hugh. And then for my mother.

I'd found her. But she was still just as lost to me as ever.

***

The morning was like a thick fog I could hardly move through. My nightmare left me beaten and exhausted. The sounds and smells of the horrific scene lingered in my senses, flashing back every second. I dragged myself to campus, each step burdened under the ever-increasing weight of my backpack. My destination was the only thing that kept me moving.

Straight to the library, I collapsed at a computer station. Without even removing my coat, I started searching. Famous Irish women, powerful Irish women, female Irish leaders and captains. My results list offered names like Queen Maeve of Connacht, Maud Gonne, Betsy Gray, and Granuaile. But nothing sounded like the name Hugh had called her in my dream. I clicked on Queen Maeve of Connacht, certain there would be a connection.

Queen Maeve: warrior queen, political activist. In Irish Gaelic the name means 'she who intoxicates'. Historical queen or sovereignty goddess? Ruled for over sixty years, two thousand years ago....

Each site I read confused me more. I wasn't finding specific connections with this *Queen Maeve*. Nothing jumped out at me or felt familiar. My head fell on my arms across the keyboard in defeat.

Spent, I dragged myself to Smokey Joe's to find Michelle. She was huddled at a far table, still tucked into her jacket with the collar raised as high around her cheeks as it could go. She held her coffee close to her face and stared into it blankly.

"Hey, you okay?" I asked. "You're not gonna believe this nightmare I had…." I dropped into the chair next to her with a thud.

"Maeve, not now." She continued to stare into her cup.

"No, seriously. This is crazy. I have to tell you," I pressed on.

"Not now, Maeve." Her firm tone took me by surprise. "It's not always about you, you know. And your dreams. Whatever. Other people have stuff going on too." She glanced at me from the corner of her eye.

I shifted side to side, not knowing what to do with myself. Had I really been that self-absorbed?

Probably.

"I didn't mean to ignore you," I said after a long moment. "I'm a jerk. I'm just a little crazy right now." My voice had a shake to it. My throat constricted as I forced it to swallow everything I wanted to blurt out about my nightmare, but it was clear something was wrong with Michelle. And on top of it all, now my feelings were hurt and the sting wouldn't go away.

"What's going on?" I prodded as I dropped into a chair.

She kept her gaze down and said, "I called home last night. No one was happy to hear from me. I don't even know if anyone misses me." Her bottom lip trembled and she tried to hide it, biting her lips.

"I'm sorry," I said, struggling to find more words.

"They didn't want me to come here. Said it wasn't 'proper'. Now it's like they're punishing me for it." Michelle's face moved from sagging hurt to tense anger—lips pursed until they turned white. "They're all about keeping up appearances. Fakes. I'm sick of it. I'm done."

She scraped at the skin around her thumbnail, what was left of it anyway. There were scrapes trailing up her arm as well, mostly hidden under her coat sleeve.

"That sucks, Michelle. It has nothing to do with you. It's them." I reached across and held her wrists as her head fell into her arms on the table. There were more scratches. My natural instinct was to pull away in fear but I fought it.

Her occasional attitude of entitlement had annoyed me so much sometimes—her endless opportunity and secure future. I was jealous. But now I saw a new side. Her broken one.

She peeked up from her arms, muffled by her coat sleeves. "Things have been crap for you, Maeve, but you're still whole. You're not a mess like me. I don't know. How do you do that?" She tilted her head toward the ceiling and let out a sigh. "The way you talk about your grandparents and even your mom. They mean everything to you. I wish I could feel something like that. Anything, really."

I picked lint off my pants as I listened to her, shocked that she would ever want anything I had.

She went on. "Aren't you even pissed off? You know, about your mom?"

The words sent instant venom through my veins and I went blind for a second. The ringing in my ears fueled my rage. No one had ever spoken so bluntly about my mother's death and it sent me over the edge. I regretted every word before they left my mouth but it was beyond my control to stop them.

"Pissed off? Oh my God, Michelle! You have no idea. Clueless! I'm pissed off every damn second of every day. Are you kidding me?" My blood boiled. "I was robbed. She was stolen from me. Jesus!" My voice cracked and tears swelled in my eyes. I stood up to get away. "What did I do to deserve that? Why couldn't I stop it?" My voice reached shrill and the sound of it scared me.

She stared in shock.

Other students throughout Smokey Joe's stared too.

I sat down to hide, calming myself through my breathing, still shaking. "Pissed off? Yeah, I'm fuckin' pissed off," I murmured and glanced at her, my expression tight.

She leaned in and hugged me. "I know you are, Maeve. I don't know why I said that. I'm sorry."

The only thing that kept me sitting at that table with her was the fact that no one else had ever been brave enough to ask me that question. Or any question about my mother. In her haste, Michelle had actually made me acknowledge it for the first time ever.

I drew in a long, deep breath. I thought about how to respond to her. Things felt different now between us. More real.

"Okay, first of all, that sucked." I jabbed her arm. "Second of all, I'm sure of it now. We were brought together for a reason. Like karma. Right?" It sounded silly, but true nonetheless. I reached for her hands for a squeeze and gently rubbed the scratches on her wrists with my thumbs.

"I hope so, Maeve," she said, lifting her coffee cup with a new flicker of light in her eyes. "Come on. Let's get out of here. We gotta get to class." She pulled on my arm, already out of her chair.

We sat in the back of our philosophy class and my subdued mood made me antsy. Michelle had stirred something in me and I couldn't place it.

Our instructor droned on, lecturing non-stop again, as if he was talking to himself in an empty room.

"...A higher, more focused level of t'inking occurs when the mind sustains a single point of concentration known as meditation," the professor blathered on. "In meditation, one can enter a different state of consciousness and one can control the mind to bring about this state and discover a new mode of consciousness which...."

My arm shot up under its own control.

The professor blinked. He stumbled over his words, confused by the concept of an interruption during his lecture. "Um, yes, question?"

"Yeah, hi, um, I have a question about that." I used my mature, sophisticated voice for increased effect. Michelle's surprised smirk burned into the side of my face. Ignoring her with all my might, I continued, "Can meditation happen by itself, even if the person isn't trying? Like, take over?"

Maybe I could learn something about my awake dreams from this guy. That would be a bonus.

He rubbed his chin, flipped his long hair to the side, and answered, "Well, no, not really."

I deflated.

He paused, eyes turned toward the ceiling, struggling to hang on to his place in his memorized "lecture of the day." "Ah, people need to practice and train their minds for meditation. They remain in control during the process."

He observed me, eyebrows raised, encouraging me to accept his answer so he could move on with his monologue.

As if missing his cue, I continued, "Well, is there a name for it if that kind of thing happens, like another state of consciousness, without even trying?"

He pulled his chin in as his eyebrows scrunched together. My cheeks burned with embarrassment. I'd stumped my teacher. He probably thought I was nuts or just a pain in the neck, damn Yank. There went my grade, from a hopeful A to a measly C, if I was lucky.

To clarify, I added, "Sometimes I have strange dreams while I'm awake." My peripheral vision caught signs of life appearing. Some heads picked up, one turned to me. "Not like daydreams, but more like dreams I can't stop and can't control, while I'm awake. It's weird. And it's always the same dream, ever since I was little."

A guy from the front row turned with his elbow on the back of his chair and said, "Sounds like hallucinations ta me." His sarcastic tone made other students laugh. I half-smiled and a weak, nervous chuckle snuck out.

The professor stood and moved to the front of his desk, ignoring the joker, and I could see him make a shift, practically physically, away from his planned lecture and into uncharted territory. His new position in the classroom captured everyone's attention, all eyes on him.

He took a slow, deep breath and began.

"Hypnagogia is a state between wakefulness and sleep. During hypnagogia a person could experience dream-like situations without the power to come out of them, almost like paralysis." He paused, looking around the room and nervously running his hand through his white hair as he continued, "The line between what is real and what is dream is very blurred."

My jaw dropped.

Michelle and I looked at each other, eyes wide, mouths agape, both thinking the same thought: Maybe my awake dreams were a real thing, a scientific thing. Hypnagogia.

But something wasn't right. My awake dreams didn't happen between wakefulness and sleep, like what professor was saying. They happened during full-blown wakefulness, nowhere near sleep. Either way, it didn't matter. I had amazing new information.

I bit my thumbnail in concentration. The professor carried on lecturing about human thought and consciousness and I got lost once again to the steady drone of his voice.

After class, Michelle and I bee-lined back toward Smokey Joe's. I had my Celtic History class next with Paul McGratt. My insides tightened. I couldn't wait to see him again after the Doolin run-in. Fiona and Tish would be so jealous if I told them about our chance meeting. I decided I'd better not.

In synchronized stride, Michelle and I flew down the corridor, in hot pursuit of coffee, but a guy from the class we'd just left shuffled to catch up to us.

"Hey, ye girls are in me philosophy class, yeah?" he panted, stating the obvious, then turned to me. "I thought yer question about daydreams was interestin'. Well, not daydreams, but dreams during the day, yeah?" He stumbled on his words, looked down at his feet to regroup and went on. "I know someone who has the same thing."

I stopped in my tracks, nearly causing him to crash into me. "Wanna grab a coffee?"

***

Declan.

Holding his thick stack of books, papers flying out of his backpack, he struggled to sit in his seat.

"What's all this?" Michelle picked at the mess sticking out of his pack, teasing him. He hadn't taken his backpack off yet, or his wax jacket either. Maybe he never did.

"Hey, leave it. That's me work." He swung his backpack out of her reach like she was a pest. Then he took a closer look at her and a grin tugged at the corner of his mouth, like he was charmed despite himself. His eyes lit up as a smile spread across his face. "Sure, I'm a poet. I write every thought."

"Cool." She tried to swipe one of the papers again, hoping to sneak a read of one of his innermost thoughts.

"Ah, not so fast." One swift movement of his shoulders and his pack was out of her reach again. He kicked one of his Doc Martens at the leg of her chair to force her away. "So, about them dreams...." He looked back to me.

We sat at our favorite spot, coffees steaming, waking our senses as the three of us moved in precision through our caffeine-worshiping ritual, like kindred spirits—smelling, allowing the steam to warm our faces, moving in for the first sip. All sacred.

"Me little sister has dreams in the day," Declan started. "She's pretty much tormented by 'em." He searched our faces for reaction. "Sometimes I'm there with her and I can't shake her out of it. Scares the livin' Jazus outta me."

I nodded, clinging to his every word. "I call them awake dreams."

Declan nodded back. "Yeah."

Michelle broke in and blurted, "I saw Maeve have one of her awake dreams and it was freaky!" She stared at me, wide-eyed, and then at Declan. "It was like she left me completely and entered a new world."

"Exactly!" Declan agreed. "I know instantly when me sister's gone. She gets a look in 'er eyes and 'er face loses all expression. I hate it." He started cracking his knuckles. "I'm pretty used to it now, but I'll never be okay wit' it."

His accent was cute. He put emphasis in unusual parts of his sentences, on different syllables, which made it fun to listen to him.

Michelle smothered him with more details about my awake dream and they didn't come up for air for the longest time, talking about what it felt like to be the observer. Scary. I'd never really thought about that.

"I had one last night. Well, actually, it was a real dream, nightmare really, but it was *directly* related to my awake dream." I sounded lost already, but was dying to talk about it.

"Huh?" Michelle frowned.

"In my nightmare, there was wind, sea spray, fury, fear, and sorrow, everything that happens in my awake dream. Only more detail."

Declan said, "Me sister and I 'ave been researching the condition. It's called atonia." He drew his eyebrows together, waiting to be sure we were interested.

Michelle and I leaned in without blinking, so he went on.

"Like prof said about hypnagogia, it's a form of sleep paralysis while yeh're awake, but with atonia ya have intense sensations of noises, sights, smells, even levitation."

He paused, giving us a minute to absorb what he said, gauging whether to continue or not. I threw a hopeful glance at Michelle but she was way gone, blissfully trapped in her captivated love gaze.

Looking back at Declan, I said, "Yeah…?"

"It's pretty weird, but me sister and I are trying to make connections with what happens during her atonia and maybe something that's happened in the past." Declan looked into his coffee cup and smiled. "We're actually havin' some fun with it right now, looking into past life regression and that kinda stuff. It gets interesting. Maybe some connections to the Great Famine."

Michelle and I sat up tall in our chairs and put our hands out on the table, at full attention. Michelle reached over and nudged his hand in her enthusiasm.

"Past life regression?" She blinked like an anime character, hoping for more.

"They say unresolved problems from past lives can come back and create sufferin' in a person or their family. It's like memories that seem real and as vivid as the actual events, sometimes to the point where the person doesn't know what's true memory or something that's false." His fist went up to his mouth as he cleared his throat. "That's what it's like for me sister. She goes into her trance, as I call it, and comes out with stories and places she believes are real though she's never actually been."

I was lost in his words and the racing of my own mind. I knew it was crazy talk but it sounded so right. It was exactly what I was looking for. A possible explanation.

I glanced at the clock and jumped out of my chair with a jolt, making Declan and Michelle jump too.

"Sorry," I spewed with a chuckle and fumbled with my things. "I'm late for my next class. I'd love to keep talking about this…." But I also wanted the opportunity to ask about the captain in my Celtic History class. If I had the nerve.

I flashed Michelle a knowing smile and turned to race to Paul McGratt's class. "See you later," I yelled over my shoulder.

Chapter Eight

Connemara

Celtic History was a bust. Paul wasn't in class and had recruited a substitute, so I didn't even get to talk to him about the captain like I'd planned. Maybe it was for the best, though—I always seemed to trip over myself when he was near.

Exhausted, I met up with Michelle and Declan and we spent the rest of the afternoon and early evening in the college bar processing every detail of hypnagogia, awake dreams, and atonia. Between coffees, snacking, and chatting, time got away from us.

Michelle and Declan headed home in the same direction together and I carved my own path through the city center. I passed along the cathedral, magically lit by the glow of street lights, and moved toward Shop Street. I hoped I might bump into Rory. He said he'd be in town but the roads were dark and quiet, not a soul around.

I followed my familiar route, approaching Lynch's Castle, a landmark in Galway City that harbored secrets of the darker moments of the Lynch family. It was surrounded by shops and pubs but still held its Old World mystique.

The castle fascinated me, probably because of the eerie stories told about it. The Lynch family, many of the patriarchs mayors of Galway City, built the castle in the sixteenth century. Legend says one of the mayors found his own son guilty of murder. No one in the city would carry out the hanging and poor James Lynch had to hang his own son. They say it's been haunted ever since.

Every time I walked past the castle I thought about the awful predicament James Lynch found himself in, but always became distracted by the medieval details on the castle walls and the ancient stonework. The gargoyles drew me in most and I stopped to look up at my favorite one, a creepy animal creature holding a human baby. Like any gargoyle, it made me uncomfortable and spooked. In the evening shadows it took on an awakened ghostly silhouette. Then I got that unsettling feeling—the one you get when you know you're not alone.

The spine-tingling sense of being watched made my body stiffen. I could have sworn I'd heard footsteps fading in the evening air and now I was sure of it. I looked left and along the front wall of the castle, my body already starting to move in the direction of home. I couldn't see anyone but before I was allowed the luxury to feel a comforting sense of relief, I heard it.

And it was close.

As if the city faded away and the castle stood in its original, lone setting, I heard whispers from an ancient time. My head filled with their lost sounds, a confusing mesh of questions, demands, directions. Wisps of my hair lifted, then began flying around my face, blocking my vision as the familiar wind grew and whirled around me. I bolted along the expanse of the castle wall, running from the wind, groping for the corner so I could turn it and escape.

The voices grew louder and more menacing, accelerating my pace with every syllable. They were on me as I struggled to keep my body out of their reach. I swatted at my hair to bat it down out of my way and caught a quick glimpse of the castle's end. One last step. I let out a grunt of final effort and wrapped my fingers around the edge and pulled. I turned the corner with incredible speed and panted in the immediate relief from the wind. The voices lingered in my ears for a moment, swirling in my head, then faded.

I looked back, pushing my tousled hair out of my face to be sure I wasn't being followed, while moving in the opposite direction to get away from there. I returned my gaze forward, determined to escape completely, and was snapped to attention as I smashed, face to face, into someone who grabbed my arm and yanked me off my path. A quick, high-pitched scream escaped my lips.

"Whoa, whoa, me pretty. Why such a hurry?" Fergal had a vice-grip hold on my arm, preventing me from freeing myself even as I tried to wriggle it loose. "I knew yeh'd come running back to me eventually." He slurred like he'd been drinking and was unsteady on his feet, probably after a few pints at Lynch's Pub.

My body shuddered with shock. The urge to look behind me, toward my invisible stalker, was overpowering but facing what was right in front of me was equally terrifying. I yanked my shoulders back, trying to pull away, and shouted, "Get away from me. Let go!"

His grip tightened and the alarm of losing control fueled me to continue struggling, twisting and pulling to release myself from his hold. His sleeve inched up in my resistance, exposing a hack-job tattoo on his wrist, something tribal that somehow raised more alarm in my core. He restrained me without a hint of effort and my only defense was to scream. He pulled me closer, lodging my scream deep in my throat, and brought his face close to mine, exposing a dark, evil intent in his eyes—a purpose.

"Now that's no way to treat me, missy. Aren't ya happy t' see—"

Fergal's words were cut short by a hard shove against the castle wall that left him keeled over with both arms twisted up behind his back, full nelson-style. My free arms wrapped me in a hold of safety as my legs moved me backward, away from the danger. Tears blurred my vision as I took one last look toward Fergal before running.

Pinned against the wall, face held to the stone, Fergal wriggled under Rory's strong hold. I froze and blinked my tears away for a better look only to be captured in Rory's intense gaze. His worried eyes searched mine for clues of my condition and then he turned back to Fergal and his look went more savage, honing in on his target.

"I'll ask ya kindly to keep yer fookin' hands off her." Rory moved in close to Fergal's head and spoke with authority. "And don't let me see you around here again or you'll regret it. Stay the hell away for your own good." Rory gave him one more shove into the wall and then moved his attention to me. Fergal stumbled along the sidewalk, looking back at Rory with an evil eye while rubbing his sore shoulder.

"Ya defector," Fergal shouted at him.

Rory stopped in his tracks and his face transformed again with rage.

"Sure, I know who ya are," Fergal went on. "Yer scum." Fergal spat at the ground as if onto Rory. "Deserting your people. For her!" He threw a condemning look of disgust my way, as insecurity rushed through me.

"Yer on dangerous ground, man. I'd be more careful if I were you." Rory's deep voice held threat in every syllable. His arm moved around my shoulders as he led me away.

A shaky breath struggled to escape my body as terror seeped out of me. My next inhale filled me with relief as a sense of safety returned.

Rory whisked me up Shop Street toward Bohermore without even a glance back at Fergal.

"I'm sorry," Rory started. "That bastard best never show his face here again. Are ya okay?" He leaned in close, scanning me from head to toe.

"I don't know." My body shuddered from residual shock and from Rory's close proximity.

"I should've been there sooner. It's my fault. I didn't know. I'm sorry." Rory rambled as if he were responsible, and his face carried a burden I couldn't interpret.

"Rory. What?" My pace slowed as I questioned his words. "If you didn't show up when you did…." I stopped and stepped in front of him to force him to face me. "I don't know what would have happened." I couldn't allow my mind to even go there. "Thank you."

"He should have never had the chance to put his hands on you." Rory's face fell as guilt spread over it.

"Wait. I'm lost. Do you know him?" Rory avoided my eyes and looked at the ground, scuffing his foot in search of loose pebbles. "Well, do you?"

He inhaled through his nose as he raised his eyes to mine. "I'm not sure. Maybe. I just don't know."

He searched my eyes for answers and I searched his right back with equal intensity.

**

Fumbling with my things, I raced to get ready for a walk in the hills with Rory. It had been a few days since the Fergal encounter and the voices at Lynch's Castle. After Rory took me home that night, he promised to take me to Connemara.

He had his parents' car for the day and picked me up early. We drove far out of town, leaving behind all pangs of anxiety and confusion.

"Check it out. It's the Twelve Bens." He pointed at the majestic hills that filled the panoramic view.

"Wait. We're going to climb one of those?" My enthusiasm drained out of me as I took in the enormous size of the "hills".

My apprehension turned out to be correct. The hike was exhausting and merciless, a steep climb at an advanced pace. I did my best to hide my fatigue so Rory wouldn't think I was a wimp, but I was dying.

At the top, Rory sat next to me to take it all in. The expanse of green hills and gray sky filled me with wonder. He pointed out the stripes in the land, far off in the distance, and explained the turf cutting fields.

"They're strips of sod," he said, "where they cut out the ancient turf to make the briquettes for fuel. For the fireplace. Burning history." He looked serious for a moment and continued, "They leave those scars in the land."

I watched his elation move quickly to a solemn place and it surprised me how fast his mood could go from high to low.

"I've used those briquettes in my fireplace," I confessed. "I had no idea where they came from. Never again!"

Rory was in a bad place now. Dark.

"You okay?" I prodded his ribs playfully.

"Yeah, fine," he muttered. His blank stare traveled into the distance.

"What is it?" I pressed, knowing something was wrong.

"Leave it." His curt reply stung. "Come on." He pointed to the dark clouds rolling in. "Rain's comin'."

Gravity helped my descent, making it much more pleasurable than the uphill battle. I hip-checked Rory, causing him to stumble, and pushed him further to make the most of his imbalance.

He stepped off our path in an exaggerated fall and I caught a look of mischief in his eye, one of retaliation.

I turned and ran, letting out a quick yelp of pretend fright, and tore across the green toward a boulder for shelter.

"Not a chance!" he shouted, sending more urgency for escape through my muscles as he gained on me with little effort.

A small, laughing scream escaped from my throat as he caught me and pinned me against the far side of the boulder. He pressed into me, preventing my escape, and brought his face close to mine, still breathing heavily from the run.

His gaze put me in a helpless trance as he spoke. "I'm sorry. I've caught you." His smoldering eyes pierced my soul. "I want to kiss you." He leaned in, waiting, listening for a reply.

I stared back, breathless. I wanted him to kiss me.

With his face close to mine, he hesitated as if to prolong the moment, and then his lips found mine. They were warm and full and he smelled fresh of the outdoors. His rough stubble rubbed against my chin. My entire being lit up from deep inside as I felt a new part of me come to life. It filled me with warmth and hope.

Then, out of nowhere, ice coursed through my heart, jolting me as if being woken from a sweet dream. My eyes popped open and I pulled back a little. Had he felt it too?

Rory looked at me, eyes soft, like he hadn't noticed.

"I didn't think I'd ever get a chance to do that," he whispered, still breathless.

Drops of rain began spattering around us and on our faces. Instead of shielding from it, we both lifted our faces up to it. He took my hand and whisked me out from my spell and back down the hill.

"What really brought you to Ireland?" Rory nudged me to redirect me toward the car, which was hidden by a small hill.

"What do you mean?"

"I don't know." He shrugged. "It just seems like there's somethin' more. More to it all."

What could he be picking up on? That was just weird.

We walked the flat road a short way to the car and Rory unloaded his pack from his back. He stepped close to me and reached for a lock of my hair. He played with it, rubbing with his fingers and trailed it all the way down to the ends. I stood, frozen, as he gathered it and gently tickled the shallow at the base of my throat with it, his finger touching the delicate space.

My breathing stopped as his finger traced a line down my chest bone and then stopped short. He pressed directly into my spot that burns when danger is near, and looked me straight in the eyes.

"You're an interesting girl, Maeve. I think I like you." And he winked with his familiar arrogance and fumbled his pockets for the keys.

As my breath sucked in, my hand instinctively went straight to my chest to feel where he had touched me. In an instant, it pulled back in shock. My fingers sailed right into my mouth for soothing. The intense fiery heat coming from the exact spot burned me. But my chest felt fine.

"Time to hit Keane's." Rory threw his pack in the trunk and slammed it shut.

His muted words redirected my attention and I got into the passenger's seat on autopilot. My red fingertips throbbed in my lap.

**

Keane's Pub nestled itself into the side of a hill in Maam Cross, majestic mountains as its backdrop. With no other buildings or homes for miles, the pub looked like a lonely manor from the eighteenth century covered in smothering ivy. A traditional Guinness sign hung proudly over the entryway, beckoning us to come in.

I was pulled to the warmth and glow of the hearth fire and the comfortable, upholstered seating around it. The smell of burning turf and coal filled the welcoming space. We sat at the fireplace, peeled off our layers and nestled in. I rubbed my fingers, which showed no sign of their earlier injury, and assumed my sanity was in question again. In my heart, though, I stored the information, knowing it must have meant something.

Another group of hillwalkers sat at a table by the far wall, relaxing after their climb. Rory ordered a pint and a glass of fizzy orange.

A few random climbers approached Rory at the bar.

"Howya, Mac?" One of them smacked Rory on the back. "Ya in the hills without yer dad. That's a first." They looked over at me, knowingly.

I pulled myself out of my cozy chair, inconvenienced by the need to visit the bathroom.

In the ladies' room, I gazed at my reflection as if seeing someone new for the first time. I looked radiant. My hair was windblown and my face was exhilarated and fresh. My eyes were bright and pretty, with a new sparkle. I was happy and it reflected back at me from the mirror.

Elated, I headed back toward our seats and glanced over at the other group of hillwalkers sitting at the far wall, whom I noticed when we first walked in. A blur of rucksacks, hiking boots, fleeces and animated faces—one of them looking directly at me with a smile of recognition. Caught off guard, I took a double-take.

It was Paul McGratt.

His hair was a mess and his cheeks were flushed from the wind and fresh mountain air. His usually clean-shaven face had weekend mountaineer scruff that was further complemented by his red plaid hiking shirt and well-worn khaki pants.

He flashed a vibrant smile at me, showing me he'd had as good a day as I had. My cheeks burned, blowing my attempt at any form of composure.

He stood up, against the pleading of my inner wimp, and walked over to say hello. I stopped at the corner of the bar, an equal distance between our parties, and watched him approach.

He held my eyes with his, leaned in and with a low voice said, "Are you followin' me?"

He raised an eyebrow. His sly comment and playful demeanor were unexpected. I could hardly speak and felt my cheeks reach a new, humiliating level of hue.

I wasn't sure why he was able to get such a reaction from me but I felt his presence fill every space in my body. *It's no big deal. It's no big deal. It's no big deal,* I repeated in my mind, trying to calm myself. I took a deep breath.

"Actually, I was going to ask you the same question," I said, equally as coy and my heartbeat quickened. "This is getting a little awkward, you know." I snuck a bit of flirtation into my voice because, well, he started it! Then I added, "At least there's no threat of death this time."

"Okay, okay, easy." He held his hand up, to soften my blow. "First yeh're on a lonely road in Doolin while I'm out doing research, jumpin' in front of me car, mind you. Then you're in the middle of *nowhere* in Connemara while I'm takin' a walk. Very suspicious, t' say the least." He waited for an explanation.

"All very coincidental, I assure you." I shot a pompous look at him, with a slow blink, to confuse him about whether I was telling the truth or not.

"Hmm." He considered his options. "You're a bit of an adventurous one, for sure, Maeve O'Malley. What are ya lookin' fer anyway?" He tilted his head to one side, trying to figure me out.

I was stuck on the part where he said my name. The sound sent heat through my body.

"I'm not sure yet," was all I could come up with, eyes narrowing. "But I think I'm getting warmer."

A pleasant smile spread across his face as he nodded. "That's good," he said. "Keep searching." His gaze burned into mine. "You're sure to find it."

A pair of judging eyes held a firm bead on me from behind Paul. My smile faded when I caught a girl staring at me with a fierce expression. Paul saw my reaction, turned, and leaned back toward his table to introduce me to the girl who was glaring at us…okay, at me, just me.

It was the same girl who had been in the car with him in Doolin. She was pretty, in a fancy way, with blonde hair and makeup. She was overdressed for the occasion in what looked like horseback-riding clothes: proper black jacket over a white blouse and beige leggings, with high black boots.

"Patricia, this is Maeve O'Malley, a student from my Celtic History class. She's visiting from Boston."

I smiled at her. "Nice to meet you."

Her stiff posture didn't relax after the introductions and she watched the rest of our conversation closely. I felt the pressure to end our chat even though I was enjoying it.

I rushed to tell Paul about the roughly cut turf fields I had seen. His eyes were warm and welcoming and his bright smile encouraged me to continue but I looked toward Rory and realized it was time to get back to him.

"There's a place you should see," Paul added. "Dun Aengus. It's a ruin on the Aran Islands. It's ancient, full of mystery. I can see you liking it there. Add it to yer list of adventures," he said with a grin. He nodded as a formal gesture of farewell and said, "See ya at university."

***

Rory's face darkened as I told him who Paul was. "What's he doing out here? Shouldn't he be in a library studying?"

The judgment in his tone was laced with a negativity I hadn't noticed before. Rory never finished college and now something that sounded like regret was seeping out of him. Paul McGratt and everything he stood for probably only made him feel worse.

"Not sure." The temptation to look over at Paul again was excruciating.

Rory was sulking.

Back in Galway, he would turn to his guitar and spend entire days playing it. That was pretty much how each day went for him. I wasn't sure but he seemed almost stuck, avoiding what he should really be doing with his life.

"Have you been to Dun Aengus?" I changed the topic to bring him back to me.

He handed me my fizzy orange, poured from a Fanta bottle, and I smiled at the pleasure from such a simple gesture.

"Dun Aengus? Yeah. It's out on the Aran Islands. Why?" He shot a quick glance at Paul and then back to me.

"Wanna go?"

Chapter Nine
Dun Aengus

"What the hell! Where've you been?" Michelle's tone made no attempt at hiding her pissed-offness. I had been out of touch for a few days and now realized she had felt blown off.

"Crap! I'm so sorry! I got caught up in the whole Rory thing. So much has happened!"

My grandmother's words echoed as I spoke, like a sharp slap in the face. Gram was always so right. She knew "this Rory person" was going to distract me. And he did. Big time. I'd lost complete focus on my true mission. How did he do that to me?

Michelle forgot her annoyance in a blink and dove into her Declan story. "Wait 'til I tell you." She baited me for my full attention as we chose our table in Griffin's Bakery. "Declan and I are totally a thing!" She beamed and did a mini happy-dance in her seat. "He's so awesome! And seriously, you need to hear more about his sister's dreams. It's just like what happens to you."

She bounced in her seat, licking off a smear of cream on her lip and then changed the subject in the same breath.

"Soooo, tell me about Roooory," she insisted. "Tell me everything." Her wicked smile closed her eyes to narrow slits.

I wasn't sure what to say. It was all still so new. And now, I was confused about his innate ability to distract me from why I was even here.

"He's taking me to the Aran Islands to see Dun Aengus."

Her head tipped, confused.

"It's an ancient ruin, like an Iron Age fort."

Her eyes glazed over.

"Maybe I'll figure something out about my visions. You know. I need to keep looking, any chance I get."

'Yeah, I 'spose." She nodded, distracted by coffee house clatter.

"It seems like a good start anyway. Paul McGratt suggested it when we were in Connemara. And he seems to know what he's talking about."

Michelle's eyes widened at full attention as her mouth dropped open.

"Wait. Stop." Her hand shot up, judgment oozing. "Are you kidding me? Paul McGratt? *Again?*" Her duck lips and raised eyebrows proved her certainty that a second "chance meeting" was more than a coincidence. "That's too bizarre. Aren't you the least bit blown away by that?"

I shrugged and looked away, fighting the strange tingly feeling of guilty pleasure.

"You can't tell me that's not weird." She began making hand gestures with pointing fingers that became more pronounced as she taunted me with the chant, "Ooh ahh, Paul McGratt, *Ooh ahh*, Paul McGratt!"

I grabbed her hands and slammed them onto the table before anyone might hear. Two girls at another table looked over, freaking me out even more.

"I know!" I struggled to suppress the huge incriminating smile spreading across my face, whispering now to be sure the other girls couldn't hear. "It *is* bizarre. I can't believe I bumped into him twice now, in the most random, obscure locations. Crazy."

I thought about it for another minute, trying not to give it too much credence, but enjoyed the fleeting fantasy. My head shook, waving away the romance-novel daydreams that were forming in my mind.

"Anyway, he's out of my league, taken, and not interested," I assured Michelle more than necessary, hoping to convince myself as well.

"Thou dost protest too much, Maeve." Michelle batted her lashes at me and looked away, chin up with cocky arrogance.

***

The choppy crossing to the Aran Islands took a couple hours, and soon Rory and I were disembarking on the bustling docks of the main island, Inishmore. Friendly faces greeted us and bike rentals covered the docks, making our selection of transportation simple.

We pedaled out of the quaint village into the postcard-worthy landscape. Space quickly opened up and we left a sea of whitewashed, thatch-roofed cottages behind us, along with my pestering seasickness.

We cycled along mazes of stone walls, labyrinths from generations of farmers who'd moved stones to uncover rich soil. The entire expanse of island was networked in a grid of the rocky walls.

Once we made some distance away from the docks, the freedom of the open road pulled us along. My mind raced ahead of me, hoping to find clues to my visions but fearing the same. I didn't want to get hurt again, burned or hunted, but I was adamant about learning something, anything, to help stop it.

Maybe I would recognize some of the fort from my dream. I considered telling Rory about my side mission so he could help me if something went wrong, but my nagging gut told me it was too soon for him.

We came to a point where we could finally see the coast of the far side of the island. Our eyes followed the shoreline and off in the distance we saw the great ruin of Dun Aengus.

The medieval fort, ancient and proud, was a massive semi-circular monument positioned on the very edge of high vertical cliffs overlooking the Atlantic. Two thousand years ago, it was the stronghold that defended Galway Bay.

"Follow me," Rory said. "To the coast." He maneuvered his bike off-road and ditched it. I did the same, looking around to be sure it was okay to leave them. We were the only souls anywhere to be found.

He hopped over a wall, gesturing for me to hurry up. As we approached what should have been beach, we stopped short and discovered the edge of the world—high, steep cliffs. A raw chill shot through me from the unprotected danger.

Moving with meticulous caution toward the cliff's edge, we got down on our hands and knees and crawled. Once we reached the sharp ledge, we lay down and inched our bodies to the very end of the earth and looked downward.

The drop was a straight shot and the dizzying height made my head swim and my stomach lurch. It must have been thirty stories of breathtaking but lethal beauty as far as the eye could see.

Out of nowhere, Rory grabbed my shoulder and moved it further over the edge, shouting, "Look out! Whoa!"

My heart shot into my throat in panic as I caught my breath. His laughter filled the air and we rolled our bodies away from the edge, seeking safety.

Once out of harm's way, I turned on him and punched his arm as hard as I could, hurting my fingers.

"Jerk!"

"Sorry. I couldn't help myself," he apologized and pushed out his bottom lip, rubbing his sore arm.

My gut sent me a signal of warning about him, one I ignored with all my might as he pulled me close.

"I'm sorry. Dumb joke. I don't want to hurt you." He hesitated. "But I always feel like I will." He watched me closely. "Why is that?"

"Oh, so you go and try to push me over the cliff? Couldn't help yourself?" My sarcastic tone helped lighten the moment, buying me time to figure out what he was saying.

We weren't good for each other. I could feel it. Rory needed me, but he was pushing me away at the same time. I wondered if his plans for England had something to do with it.

His face softened, opening up to me. "Sorry. I don't mean to…sorry."

"You apologize when nothing's wrong. Is that an Irish thing?" His apologies went beyond the cliff hijinks.

He reached for my face and pushed wisps of hair away from my eyes.

"I know. I'm sorr—ach—I don't want to hurt you. I can picture your face in pain and I never want to actually see that. It haunts me."

He kept his fingers on my cheek.

I could have predicted the next moment before it happened.

I twisted, wincing in pain, grabbing at my chest. Damn it. The burn brought tears to my eyes.

"What is it? Are you okay?" Rory took my arm, trying to help me upright.

I rubbed at my chest and tried to extinguish the molten fester.

"Yeah, weird spasm or something." I caught my breath and stood.

As if my inner hesitation wasn't enough. I was falling for him, but that sense of warning was growing louder. And now the pain again.

Still, it felt so good to be with him. I couldn't think of a single reason why it could be wrong.

***

I climbed back on my bike as my focus shifted toward Dun Aengus. Bigger than life and as ancient as the time of Christ, it was imposing and impressive, covering the rocky landscape with pride.

As we got closer, I dropped my bike to follow my curiosity and explore. The beauty of the ruins filled me with energy and I looked to Rory, hoping he felt the same.

He looked bored.

"Hey, are you okay?"

Rory's slouched posture and blank stare snapped back to attention in response to my voice. "What? I'm fine." His curt, defensive tone stopped me from prodding. For a second.

"You seem a little uninterested. Like you're not into this anymore."

"Seriously? Why does everyone always assume the worst of me?" His flippant tone sent his response into the open air, not just directly at me, as he threw his hands up and turned with a grimace.

Shocked by his strange accusation, I walked past him toward the outer wall of the ruin. I touched the stones, feeling their history. It was like I'd stepped into a time machine. Rory walked along the side of the fort and looked up its high walls, likely imagining it in full-scale operation. He moved toward the front, to the point that took the direct hits from the Atlantic.

In the exact moment when Rory stepped out of view—

The wind came.

It was slow and seething at first, slithering across the grass and snaking into my hair. By the time I'd managed to unfreeze and turn to run, it built into a gale, shrieking and howling and blasting me back against the wall. The back of my head smashed off the stone of the fort and I crumpled to my knees. I stayed hunkered down, praying for it to end, knowing it was only beginning.

I called out for Rory while holding the back of my sore head. My voice was gone, lost in the chaos, and I tasted the evil bile of dread rising from my belly. Lifting my gaze, the green fields and stone walls came into view—fading in and out of focus.

Then I saw her.

My captain. From my nightmare.

She loomed ahead of me, sword drawn back and dappled with light. Her eyes blazed and her delicate features twisted into a snarl. An avenging angel sent to destroy me.

She raced toward me from within the fort, sword held high, teeth bared on her savage, grief-stricken face. Panic coursed through my veins, freezing me to my spot. In her rage, her long black hair and layered shawl flew around her, giving her the appearance of a goddess, one of destruction and death. She charged toward me with clear intent to kill.

I froze in place as she came at me, her expression contorted. I braced myself for the heinous blow of her sword but felt only wind. She moved through me like a shiver and continued beyond to the outer point of the fort, her violent intent still clear.

Gasping for breath, relieved to be unharmed, I watched in awe as the captain from my nightmare made herself known in my awake dream.

It was her.

It had always been her.

I stared at the swirl she left in her wake, piecing together the fragments from my dreams, grappling to make sense of what I was seeing.

Then Rory called out—desperate cries for help. His shouts were diffused by the wind but clear enough to know she must've gone directly for him. Fists pounding, I ran as fast as I'd ever moved, around to the front of the fort, situated directly on the cliff's edge.

Rory struggled at the ledge, battling the wind. His arms swung and flailed in every direction as his shirt flapped wildly around him. His resistance was no match for the incredible force of the gale. He stumbled back, again and again, as if being pushed. His steps brought him closer to the cliff's edge as the gusts pounded him, beating him from every direction.

Screams of horror blasted out of me. "Look out, Rory! Stop! You're right at the edge!"

The icy chill of my screams filled every part of me but I couldn't hear them for the power of the winds.

It was her.

Her aggressive form, tall and hurtling, was a blackened haze in the surge and her rage blasted through my heart, filling me with the vengeance she carried.

She was going to kill him.

Rory crouched low to the ground to reduce the force of the blasts and as he knelt, one of his feet slipped over the cliff's edge. His entire leg went down the rock face, sending shards of stone scattering down the steep drop. Waves thrashed hungrily far below as if anticipating their feast.

Eyes still closed, Rory clambered for something to grasp but the sharp rock ledge left him no purchase. He was slipping inch by inch over the cliff.

I fought to get to him, pushing through the whirling haze. With fists clenched by my sides I screamed as loud as I could, "Leave him alone! Stop! Leave him!"

And then she saw me. She stood over him but looked directly at me, tilting her head with an expression of utter confusion. Power drained from her as she withered and the wind lost its strength and slowed. Her arm fell from the weight of her sword and her shoulders sank as if she had been let down, or worse—betrayed.

Still filled with terror, I begged her to stop, tears streaming down my cheeks. I fell to my knees and crawled toward Rory, praying I wasn't too late. I felt around the ground ahead of me, blindly searching for his hand. And then it all stopped—the wind, the vision of her—and all went calm.

I reached toward Rory, his head hanging and feet still struggling for a hold, sending more fragments of stone trickling down the cliff's face. I grabbed onto his shoulders with a steel, white-knuckled grip and pulled him up and far away from the ledge, falling back with a thump.

"Jazus Christ!" Rory yelled. "What the fook was that? I nearly went over the cliff!" Rory crawled on his hands and knees, gasping for his breath. He spoke quickly and with force, his accent thick and almost indecipherable.

My body quaked uncontrollably. My awake dream had nearly caused a horrific accident. It was real. Too real.

"That wind came out o' nowhere and the force was incredible," Rory went on. "Updraft from the cliffs. Flippin' dangerous! Jazus! Let's stay far away from there from now on."

He thought it was a force of nature.

He had no idea.

As soon as I was sure Rory was safe, the tears came again in torrents. I cried everything out of me in waves.

"Maeve! I'm here! I'm okay. Don't cry. Please. Stop." Rory held me in his arms on the ground, stroking my head. "I can't take it. Don't cry." He was at a loss with my condition. "You have a bump on the back of yer head." He gently felt it and sounded worried. "What happened? Yeh all right? Dizzy?" He looked into each of my eyes, attempting to check for a concussion.

I rubbed the bump, from when I'd hit the wall, and winced. Maybe I was disoriented. What really happened? I couldn't be sure. It was my awake dream, I knew, but this one was different. It actually knocked me down.

And *she* was in it.

She was in my awake dream. And went after Rory. I was absolutely sure of that.

I knew what I had to say and plunged ahead before I could collect my thoughts. "I'm sorry. I should have told you sooner," I started. "This kinda happens, a lot I guess. I have this awake dream. It's like a dream, but I'm awake." I spoke fast, pushing it all out. "I don't know. It's weird." Then I realized how crazy it must have sounded. I stood there, head down, eyes on the ground, waiting for his response.

Rory paused. "What do ya mean, awake dream?" I didn't look at him but I could hear the skepticism in his voice. "What're yeh talking about?"

I glanced up at him and shrugged, hoping for his understanding. What if he thought I was nuts?

"It's happened to me since I was a little girl. It seems to be getting more intense now." I watched Rory closely and continued. "I think they're a warning of some kind, or a message. And now there's a woman." I hesitated because it looked like I might be losing him.

"A woman?" he said with cynicism in his lifted eyebrows. I could tell from his judgmental tone we weren't on the same page, at all. He wasn't ready for any of this.

But I was in too deep. I needed to wrap it up, fast. "Yeah, she's a powerful woman, a leader, and she has a sword and…." Oh, right, I was definitely losing him. "Never mind, it's dumb. It's only a dream." I reached back to rub the bump on my head again. "Nothing to worry about."

Rory checked my head and helped me stand. "Okay," he said. "No big deal. Let's see how ya do on the bike and try to get yeh back to town. We'll grab a cup of tea at the docks. Sound good?" He watched me like I was a child, checking my ability to ride my bike.

"Yeah. Sounds great," I murmured.

Chapter Ten

She Captain

"It sounds like yeh're having a loov'ly time," Gram said.

I had finished telling her about my adventures with Rory—the hillwalking in Connemara and the trip to Dun Aengus. I tactfully left out the details of my awake dream at Dun Aengus, basically the part where Rory was almost killed.

"Is everything *else* okay, Maeve?" I could hear slow reluctance in her voice but pointed directness in her question, like she had a hidden agenda.

"Yeah, Gram," I said. "Everything's great. Why?"

"Yer awake dreams, Maeve. I want to know if they're bothering yeh." Worry leaked from her shaking voice.

"Gram, you don't need to be concerned about my awake dreams. They don't bother me. Not a problem. Really," I lied, trying not to put it on too thick because, to be honest, they were scaring the crap out of me.

"Be truthful with me, Maeve. What are ya seein'?"

Her direct inquisition took me by surprise. She was fishing but there was no way I was giving up any bait. She'd derail my journey and have me on the next flight home so fast. Avoidance became my chosen tactic for the remainder of the conversation.

"My awake dreams are the last thing on my mind, Gram." I fought to control the tears that were creeping up my throat. "I'm too busy enjoying everything. Traveling, my classes…." I hoped to redirect her growing concern. "I'll be planning my trip to Claremorris soon." Stealth.

Gram changed her anxious tone to a smoother one filled with nostalgia. Having successfully dodged the dream inquiry, I felt my shoulders relax from their tight position up around my ears.

"How's Joey? Is he there?" I asked, knowing full well he was sitting comfortably in his chair across the room.

"Oh yes, Maeve, he's in his chair cursin' at the remote. It's not doing its job again and I'm sure he'll throw it through the telly this time."

I could hear Gram's smile as she described my grandfather's temper to a T. "He asks for ya every day," she added and the lump rose again in my throat, this time bigger than before.

"Tell him I love him." My voice strained. "Tell him I saw an ancient ruined fort and everyone here is drinking Guinness."

Gram relayed my message and then repeated it, louder, for him to hear. He began to respond and hesitated through a long, congested cough, and began again.

"Tell 'er I loov 'er," he said. I pictured his big face with his black-framed glasses, his sparkling blue eyes and warm smile. "Tell 'er to trust herself. Be brave. Be smart," and then his unexpected words of caution became lost in his coughing and I left them there, for fear of their ability to weaken me.

***

At our favorite table at Smokey Joe's with Declan and his friend Harry, Michelle and I sat back wasting time. Harry was a permanent student at NUIG—every campus had one—and he seemed to be a classic fixture in the coffee shop.

I sat next to Harry—and his familiar smell of filterless home-rolled cigarettes that left his teeth tarred and yellow—and looked over enviously at Michelle and Declan. They were in the middle of a "hot coffee drinking contest" to see who would get the first sip down without suffering third degree burns.

Since Dun Acngus, my time with Rory hadn't been great. He seemed content hanging around and doing not much of anything. The last time I saw him, I'd wanted to explore the Bohermore cemetery together for more awake-dream clues, but he'd scoffed and said I needed to stop obsessing about my "dream stuff." He'd ended up taking me to the guitar shop instead—dragging his heels the whole way and refusing to stop and listen to the fun street musicians—and his moodiness dragged the whole day down. When it was time for him to head off to his gig, I was not disappointed.

Declan and Michelle on the other hand lifted me up. Declan was happy, funny, and more connected to spiritual ideas than most guys, so I loved being around him. He always wanted to hear about my awake dreams and would painstakingly compare them to his sister's. His protective nature spiked any time I mentioned the lethal danger in my visions, but his sense of intrigue hoped hers would develop into a mysterious treasure hunt the way he felt mine had.

Michelle looked across the table at me and said, "You've got to hear this, Maeve. Declan and I have been talking about his sister's dream and it's crazy. We're trying to figure it out, but listen...." She looked at Declan to give him an opening to speak.

Declan turned to me and said, "Well, me sister's dream, it's the same one mostly. She's trapped in a small cottage, scared, wonderin' if she should run, and when she looks out the window she sees ragged, filthy people wandering around and scavengin'. Then she sees a woman, healthy and well-dressed, who's watchin' her and waving for her to come out. Me sister's too scared t' move."

I rested my chin in my hands, leaning in to hear every word.

Declan went on. "Each dream is similar but some have differences, like flowers in the field around the aimless people or large mounds behind 'em or even massive ships in the background." His voice dropped lower as he said, "We think it might be related to the potato famine of the 1840s. The ships that took thousands away, the mass grave sites that created large sacred mounds on the landscape. And the woman, she's American. You can tell from the health and sophisticated clothin'. Like New York City style." His eyes were wide and hopeful with his dream interpretation.

"Maybe we had family members who were lost, maybe still are. Searchin' for peace. It's like it's their ghosts or something." He looked at me, eyes round and blinking.

I stared at Declan, adrift on his story. Seeing how my own dream could be pieced together in the same fashion.

"Whoa," I murmured. It was all I could say.

"I know!" Michelle interjected. "Isn't that nuts?"

"That's incredible," I said to Declan. "Freaky. I need to think about that more."

Declan took Michelle's hand as he said, "We've been talking about it all morning and it seems to make sense. I don't know, it's something anyway."

I was in agreement but a little weirded out too. It opened a lot of ideas that scared me. The more the dream was explained, the more real it became.

Declan redirected the conversation and asked, "So have ya planned your next moves for finding your castle?"

He and Michelle leaned in together, like an old married couple, to hear my response. The details of my Dun Aengus story had them completely spellbound and it only fueled their interest in finding more meaning in my dreams.

"Soon, actually," I replied, knowing I couldn't put off my visit to my grandfather's town of Claremorris much longer.

"Lookin' fer castles?" Harry pushed his thick glasses up, causing his eyes to distort and magnify. His tar-stained fingers matched the blackish-brown color of his frames.

"Yeah," I replied. "In County Mayo. I'm gonna look for some O'Malleys and do a bit of castle hunting. Think I'll find anything?" I eyed him, hoping for some of his wisdom or clever comebacks.

"More green hills and sheep." Harry's boredom resonated in his lazy tone as he pulled his black attaché case closer to his legs as if by instinct.

A student passed our table and slapped Harry on the back as he walked by. "Howya, Haych."

"Howya." Harry nodded.

He stacked coins by his coffee cup, largest to smallest, and then added, "But maybe ych'll find some craic. Plenty'a historical seagoing fleets and castles at the coastline. You know." He pushed some of his long, unruly hair out of his face as he reached for some photos in his case and continued. "Mayo's known for its famous seafaring clan and chieftains. There's one in particular I'm sure ya'd find interesting, a—"

"Harry!" An enormous leather portfolio slammed onto the table. "Where've ya been, man? The exhibit's nearly done. We need ya." The blur of a fellow art student gripped Harry's shoulders, pressing on him for emphasis.

"Jeez, Dez. Sure, I'm on it." Harry pulled back with little interest.

Dez pulled up a chair and waved some other students over to the table, probably for reinforcements.

Harry pushed his photos back into his case, pursing his lips to the side, and secured the collection, once again, protectively to his chest. The contents called out to me and with a wink, I assured them I'd be back for more.

***

Paul McGratt held class like always, as if our chance encounters had never happened. I was crushed. Not even a nod or a glance. Nothing.

Shame rose in me, burning my cheeks, as I took a hard landing right on the number one school rule: Thou shalt not fantasize about thy teacher.

Okay, true. But this was different. Right? I felt a strange connection to him. His passion about Celtic history, for one thing. I loved that. But it was more. He seemed grounded and solid about where he stood. He knew what he was doing with his life.

So I pushed etiquette aside and followed him around the room with my eyes, ignoring the distance he placed between us. Probably protecting his professional integrity. Keeping accusations at bay. Unfair grading. Et cetera.

He moved around the room, disguised as a college professor but with fresh air still lingering on his cheeks and in his hair. His red plaid shirt and khakis were still in his soul.

Who was Patricia? Probably his girlfriend, maybe his wife, though he didn't wear a ring and looked way too young to be married. Then, out of nowhere, I heard my name and was jolted back from my distraction.

"Maeve?" It was Paul's voice. "Did yeh have a chance to visit that area yet?"

His eyes were fixed on me, catching me in the middle of my Paul McGratt daydream.

Seeing the lost look in my eyes he continued, "The Burren, the limestone hills in County Clare. Have ya seen them?"

He knew full well I had seen them. That was where he almost ran me down with his car! He must have started his lecture on that region. Heat rose up my neck, threatening to reach my face in an instant when—

"Ach, sure she's been there. Told me all about it," Fiona interrupted, regaling our past conversation about my trip to Doolin. "Had a right ol' good time, I heard."

Paul's eyes shifted over to me and his eyebrows raised a millimeter, inquiring exactly how much information I'd shared with Fiona, if I'd gossiped about seeing him outside of school. His expression was subtle enough that I was sure only I noticed.

"She nearly got kidnapped," Fiona went on. "Amateur." She burst out laughing and then all eyes were on me to elaborate.

Paul exhaled slowly and gave me a small smile, knowing now his name never came up in my chat with Fiona. I returned a soft smile.

"Right, yes," I said, dragging my eyes away from Paul and turning to Fiona. "I've been there." I glared at Fiona in jest, thanking her for the awkward setup, and for bringing up the awful Fergal car ride.

"Anyway, it was amazing and I made it home fine, thank you very much. There was an ancient ruin, a round tower." I wanted Paul to know I saw the "surprise" he told me would be at the top of the hill. "It might have been a lookout or something."

Paul nodded so I continued, "And right off the road there was a holy well. A natural spring, like a wishing well, with a cool stone structure around it, really old. The plaque said medieval sacred rituals took place there." I took a breath and Paul seemed pleased.

"Great. Has anyone else seen that holy well? I believe it was likely Pinnacle Well." He looked across the rest of the students, and many of them nodded. "Did you see anything else, Maeve?"

Okay, so this was how we were going to have this conversation.

He was pressing me to find out what spooked me at the well,

causing me to fall into the road.

A smile on my insides lit me up. "There was a Celticky-looking face carved into the center stone of the well. It looked like a ghost. Most of the detail was worn off but it had hollow, staring eyes."

"Right," he said. "The Burren has many ancient sites going back to medieval times. The carvings date back to the Druids."

I sat listening to his voice, enjoying his fascination with the subject rather than listening to the actual information itself. I was lost again in my Paul McGratt daydream.

Then, I froze.

The wind was coming.

Instant panic. *Oh my God! Not here, not now, pleeeeeease!* My teeth clenched together as I begged for it to go away.

Then it was upon me.

I reached for the metal legs of my chair and held on for dear life, not knowing how my body would react to the assault. My hair lifted up and begin to whip around my face as I was blinded by the biting gusts and the salty spray that pelted my eyes. I scrunched them tight for protection from the thrashing blasts, praying it would stop and return me safely to my classroom.

I opened one eye in a reluctant attempt to look around. I could see now through the squall, and although the wind still pounded against me, I could take a full breath—as if it barely touched me.

Vivid colors and shapes surrounded my vision. Greens and blues. Grays. Rolling hills and coastal inlets. The brackish air smacked my senses to full awareness and then, there it was, standing proudly.

The castle.

The same castle I had seen in my awake dream when I was in Doolin with Michelle. Square at its foundation, rising up four stories with a point at the top.

Beyond the castle, a ship was anchored in the shallows. The strong vessel was black wood with a huge mast up the middle and row after row of long oars reaching down toward the eager waves. It was familiar to me, just like the castle.

A sense of calm washed over me as I began to feel my mother's presence fill the space in my mind. She was here, urging me on, encouraging me to move forward toward the castle.

As I approached the fortress, a shiver from my soul sent panic through every nerve as the rage of the captain coursed through me. She was near.

Like a camera flash, I saw her governing the castle and a fleet of ships. This was her home and her lead vessel. It was the same ship from my nightmare, I was sure now, where her beloved had been brutally slain. I moved closer to the castle, unable to resist my curiosity and the temptation of seeing my mother again. My senses sharpened in preparation for fight or flight as I pushed toward the familiar scene.

The large arched wooden door came into full view, black and brooding, with heavy iron fixtures. Watermarks from high tide curled around the stone slab steps, where the sea had made its claim on the castle and watched over it from below.

I paused at the door, afraid to get too close, and was struck by the smell of iron in the air. It mixed with earth and brine and I coughed to clear my lungs. My cough transformed into a choke as the blood drained out of my head in response to the pounding and straining that came from the other side of the door. It bulged as if being pushed out from the inside. Against great resistance, it finally cracked its seal, and air rushed through the opening as if it had been airtight for a thousand years.

My breathing stopped as I peered into the chasm through the slight gap, ignoring my mind's primal command to run. Then with the force of an army, the door burst open, bowling me over with a powerful blast.

It was her.

I saw her in the surge of energy that exploded out of the castle. Her hair flew wildly in the wind and her sword was drawn, same as when she appeared at Dun Aengus. In an instant, I knew I would be dead. She came hurtling toward me. The glint from her sword filled my vision. I knew I would be....

But I wasn't dead.

I clutched at my chest and winced in pain as I struggled to draw a full breath. My skin burned with an intensity that was escalating, like molten iron on my flesh.

It was more than the wind trying to hurt me. It was the captain. She wanted to kill me and anyone I was with. She had gone after Rory on the cliffs and she wouldn't stop until she got me. I didn't understand why she was intent on tracking me, but I was sure of her determination.

I needed to cry out from the fiery pain and from the fear of being hunted in a place I couldn't hide, but just as I found my voice to scream, the searing pain jolted me back to my classroom in silence.

The rigidity in my arms melted and my locked hands unclenched from the metal legs of my chair. I strained to regain control of my rapid breathing and slowly glanced around the room, without moving my head.

The students were still looking at the map Paul was showing, but he was staring directly at me—wide-eyed, brows pulled together, a frown tugging at the corners of his lips. The students followed his direct line of vision and turned to me too. I dropped my gaze onto my desk, hoping to vaporize, and peeked up again after a moment. Fortunately, they had lost interest and were focused back on the map as Paul stared off into space, like he was in deep thought. After an exaggerated blink, he looked back to me, like he was checking on my condition. I kept my grimaced face tilted downward. Flushed, I shook my head to let him know he didn't have to react or do anything and I fake-smiled to let him know I was okay.

Shit. How embarrassing. He must have thought I had a problem or something. I felt ridiculous.

***

My shame was debilitating and wouldn't allow me the chance to run through the details of my awake dream. I needed to get out of the classroom, fast—out of Paul's sight, possibly forever, to somewhere I could think.

The clock crawled for the final eight minutes of class. As soon as Paul began acknowledging the end of the lesson, I shot up from my seat and headed straight out the door, keeping my gaze down the entire way.

Finally! The freedom of getting out of there. My body quaked with a chill of emotional release as I darted for a private place to think and decompress.

I grabbed a coffee at Smokey Joe's and, head down, snuck off to the far corner where no one would notice me. I sat facing out the window, looking across the Corrib River, wallowing in my humiliation. Michelle had watched me during one of my episodes and described it as "freakin' weird." Great. Now Paul had that same experience with me.

I inhaled deeply through my nose and exhaled forever, feeling my body melt into the chair, accepting my inevitable "fool" status. I brought my coffee up to my mouth and breathed in the smell as I prepared for my first sip. Lost in the scramble of my mind, I tested the temperature on my upper lip, by instinct, to protect my beaten self from any further trauma.

Instead of my lip, the burn came from my chest. Right on the same spot as always. "Ach." I heard my own sound as I reached for the area. My shirt seemed to stick to it. Sound hissed from my mouth as I inhaled at the same time as I pulled on my shirt. I tucked my chin down and tried to see the burn.

Someone touched my shoulder. I flinched as if being shocked, and whoever it was came around, lowering themselves down to my shameful level.

"Are you okay?" Paul's worried eyes searched mine. "I wanted to check on ya." He lingered in my gaze.

I could hardly find my words and looked at him crouched in front of me. I was silent, awkward. His hand still rested on my shoulder and that was the only thing I could focus on.

I looked down at my coffee and shook my head. "Yeah, I'm okay. Sorry about that." I was beyond embarrassed. "I hope I didn't cause too much distraction." I was an idiot.

"Not at all," he said quickly. "I only, ah, are you sure yeh're okay?" His words got stuck, like he didn't know what to think or say either, but he wanted more, like an explanation. How mortifying.

"I'm okay," I started, and my chest actually *was* feeling better. "What happened in class, that's kinda happened before. Not a big deal. Um, did I do anything weird?" I needed to know how much I'd disgraced myself.

"No, well, not really." He hesitated. "Ya just sat there, but I could tell you were gone, in a way." He chose his words with care. He could have easily gone with *crazy* or *possessed*. "Yer eyes looked scared. You were hangin' on to yer chair for dear life." He watched me, probably in hopes of getting more information, but all I offered him was a blank stare. "Well, as long as yeh're okay...." He pressed on his bent knee and began to stand.

He couldn't leave—not now, not after I was exposed like this. He was about to go, to not pressure me, so I raced to think of something to make him stay.

"I saw a castle. And an ancient ship." I held my breath.

Curiosity widened his eyes as he nodded. "Can...can I join you for a coffee?"

Relief washed over my face, leaving an easy smile. He placed his bag and jacket on the chair across from me and went to the counter for his order.

My eyes followed him in disbelief as I scrambled to figure out the next minutes. What would I say to him? He seemed willing to listen and understand but would he shut off once I told him more?

He sat down across from me and my heart constricted. No turning back now. Without enough prep time, I winged it and started telling him about atonia and the information I learned from my philosophy teacher and from Declan, too.

"It's called dream paralysis," Paul said.

I nodded, grateful he understood and knew what I was talking about.

"It's been happening since I was a little girl," I went on, "but it's more graphic now, since I've come to Ireland."

Paul listened about the phenomena of atonia but was far more interested in hearing the details from my awake dreams.

He leaned forward on the table between us and gently prodded, "So, ya saw a castle? And a ship?" His eyes were wide with interest. "What else did ya see?"

My shoulders slackened and I allowed myself to slide down an inch in my chair. This was the most relaxed I'd felt all day, sitting across from Paul McGratt and telling him of my awake dreams, something I never thought I'd do.

"Well, there's always a lot of wind and mist, filled with fury and sorrow. Devastating, really. But now, there's this castle. And a woman...."

He listened without blinking, but when I told him about *her*, it was like time stood still. I described her clothing and her sword, her ship and the castle, and he absorbed every detail, barely blinking.

"It's a sixteenth-century description," he interjected, rubbing his chin. "Have ya been doing research on this stuff? Looking for extra credit, no doubt." His tone turned to jest. "You definitely get points for creativity," he teased.

I flashed him the evil eye, grabbed my coffee in exaggerated offense and took a long sip.

"You must think I'm crazy," I said from inside my cup.

"Not as crazy as yeh might think." He looked at me, mind made up, and said, "You should try to follow the clues in yer dreams. Ya need to find that castle. It would be a fantastic adventure."

My jaw dropped. I pulled it back up before he would notice.

"Yeah, I've actually been trying. Not as easy as you might think in Ireland. There seem to be castles everywhere." I smirked and dropped my gaze. "Maybe Mayo, where my grandparents are from." I looked up again with certainty.

I'd been stalling my trip to Mayo—avoidance maybe, probably from pure fear, or just hoping I'd get more information first. One of the two. Or both.

"Mayo?" His face lit up like he had heard an old friend's name. "I know a castle up the coast in Mayo. It's similar to the one you described. Called Rockfleet. You should have a look."

"Seriously?" Rockfleet. "That's my first *real* lead."

"It's near Westport. It'll take ya couple hours ta get there, just out the Headford Road." He gestured with his head to show the general direction or to emphasize the simplicity of it.

My hand went up to my mouth and my fingers pressed on my lower lip. It *would* be a perfect adventure near where my grandparents were born. And maybe I'd find more clues to my awake dream—figure out why it was haunting me, and get rid of it for good. I committed to the journey as I settled into his bright eyes and trusted them.

"Okay," I said with finality, nodding my head.

Paul's push was just what I needed. He had no idea how much this conversation meant to me—his genuine interest and lack of judgment.

He flashed a heart-stopping smile, stood up, and started to gather his things.

"I've gotta run," he said, checking the time. He looked at me, head tipped. "Take it easy for the rest of the day now. No heavy lifting." He took a long draw from his coffee cup and added, "But really, that stuff is truly fascinatin'. Worth exploring."

He threw his empty cup at the trash barrel. It tipped off the rim and fell in.

"Hey, and thanks for sharing with the class about yer trip to Doolin." He flashed a toothy grin. "Sorry ta put you on the spot like that. And, actually, ya taught me a great new term: 'Celticky-looking.' That'll surely come in handy to me in the future." He chuckled, grabbed his jacket and bag, and was gone.

I leaned forward in my seat to glance in the direction he left, straining to suppress my guilty smile, hoping for one more look at him. My attention was stolen, though, drawn away to the table across the coffee shop where Michelle sat. She was staring at me in shock, wide-eyed, with a look of, *What the hell was that all about?*

Chapter Eleven

Pirate Queen

Harry sauntered into Smokey Joe's from his cigarette break, disheveled as usual, rummaging through his attaché—an artsy thing that looked more like a worn out briefcase than a fancy portfolio case. He grumbled about his lost lip balm and tossed the contents on the table while searching the depths of the tote. Michelle and Declan rolled their eyes at the same time, which gave the effect of sitcom canned laughter.

Harry's binders and notebooks sprawled across the table. The big black binder caught my eye. There were pictures peeking out—photographs.

"Hey, what's this?" I reached for one of the photos. I could see a stony landscape and green hills on the prints, trying to sneak out for a glimpse of daylight.

Harry snapped the binder back, close to his chest. He straightened his spine and stated, "Part of me portfolio. Four years of field research and photography in this baby." He rubbed it like it was his prized possession. "I'll be presentin' it to the arts department portfolio appraisal committee, mind yeh."

He blinked and tried to hide his insecurity with a loud, convincing voice. He was a true artist and I knew enough about artists to know they never thought their work was good enough and self-doubt haunted them like the plague.

"Harry, can I see some of your photos? Those ones sneaking out look really cool. I had no idea you were so good."

"Yeah, well, I have loads of photos from the area," Harry explained, keeping his voice light. "I like the medieval stuff, and historical sites. They have their own stories t' tell. I entice them out, through m' lens."

He pushed the loose photos back into the binder to neaten it up and opened the front cover with care. A picture of a manor covered in ivy filled the first page.

"'Tis a ruin in Menlo," Harry said. "Burned down in 1910 after generations of the same family had been living in it for over 400 years. 'Tis out the way, up the road." He pushed the binder closer to me so I could see better and then turned the page. "This one's a dolmen out in Clare. Ancient. Maybe an altar of some sort or timekeeper. No one's sure."

He riffled through a few loose black and white shots and passed a photo I recognized.

"Hey, that's the round tower in Doolin! I've been there!" I blurted out. I grabbed the photograph for a better look. The light was perfect and the glistening sea behind the castle created a perfect background.

"Well done, Harry. That's an awesome photograph," I told him. Harry beamed, and the smile lit up his face. "I love these castles and the ruins," I continued. "They're so mysterious, full of secrets. I can practically see the ghosts all around them."

I flipped through a few more photos. "Hey," I interjected. "Have you ever been to Rockfleet Castle, in Mayo?" I thought about Paul's recommendation.

Harry started turning the pages of his portfolio binder as if he were looking for something and then paused and said, "Yeah, actually, two summers ago. A friend of mine lives near there. I took some shots. I have one here as one of my portfolio pieces." He continued turning pages quickly, looking for a specific photo.

He opened the binder fully and rotated it toward me, continuing, "The sun was going down, cast the most brilliant light on the wall, golden glimmer shot back off the water in the backgr...."

Harry's voice went into a muted monotone as my mind spun out of control. I focused in on the photograph. I recognized it. My heart began pounding and I froze, staring at the image. My eyes misted with tears. It was the castle from my awake dream. Every detail. Every stone. Even the water marks on the steps.

My hands shook. Sweat beaded on my brow and my breathing accelerating. That was my castle. I had touched the walls in my vision. I had felt the cold, damp stone and seen the carvings up close.

I knew exactly where I needed to go now; nothing could derail me. I had to go to Rockfleet.

With a loud smack, my hands splatted on the table, practically launching me over it. I stared into Harry's face.

"How do I get there?"

***

Rory and I walked up Shop Street, past the pubs and cafes and stopped in a bakery for sausage rolls. We snacked on the warm, flaky pastries as we headed up the road, listening to buskers and moving toward Rory's favorite guitar shop.

Rory held my hand and asked, "What're ya going to do when ya get there?" His melancholy tone sounded bored.

I turned to him with a quick twist of my head, tilted in disbelief. Did he truly have no idea about the nature of my trip? About me?

He went on. "I mean, once you see the castle, will ya come back home then?" His eyebrows shot up, hopeful for a quick return.

"I'm not sure. I need to see what happens when I get there. What it feels like, you know. I don't really know what to expect."

"Well, probably just be another castle on the landscape, ya know. Long way to go, an' all."

Was he discouraging me from going or was he only sulking?

"Don't ya think you're taking it all a bit too far?" he continued. He held my hand with both of his and pulled it toward his chest, as if to suggest staying with him would be better.

My temper flared at his words. He was trying to derail me.

"What do you mean, 'too far'?" I snapped. Even saying the words made me more pissed off. "How can this be me 'taking it too far'?"

"Don't overreact." His righteous tone was condescending. "I'm only saying yeh might be wasting yer time. It's not worth the effort really." He continued leading me toward his guitar shop as if his comments meant nothing.

My blood boiled now.

"Wait." I stopped in my tracks, forcing him to stop too. "What are you talking about? I thought you liked this idea—that it was a cool thing for me to do. Now you think it's a waste of time?" My voice cracked. "What's wrong with you? Even if you think my dreams are silly and the castle is nothing, what about my grandparents? I'm going there for them, too." I stared at him, thinking of my grandparents at home missing me.

"I guess," he said. "Yeh're already here, though. In Ireland. It won't be any different in Mayo." He shrugged his shoulders as he said this, as if to emphasize how futile my mission was.

"Whoa, whoa, whoa." I held my hands up, stopping him. "You're turning on me." The thought hit me like a punch to the gut, knocking my wind out. The scene from Lynch's Castle where Fergal grabbed me flooded my mind. "A defector?" The accusation had been nagging me since the moment I heard it.

Rory's face reddened from the sound of the word and his hands balled into tight fists.

"What did Fergal mean by that? What does he know about you?" I demanded.

I stared at Rory, waiting for something to explain his detached attitude. Through clenched teeth he stated, one word at a time, "Do. Not. Speak. Of. Him. Again."

I stared at him, taken aback. "What's going on? I'm lost. Please, tell me." I held his gaze, forcing him to respond.

"Too many people want too much from me." Rory held a blank expression on his face. "Now you're the same. I'm never good enough." He glanced away, looking betrayed.

"Okay, now I'm completely lost." I shook my head and put my hands up.

"My family. I'm supposed to be this big leader. My father's son. Son of the MacMahon Clan leader. Chieftain. I don't want it." Rory looked at the ground, frowning.

"Chieftain?" I asked. "What's that?"

He pulled up his T-shirt, exposing his ribs, and I saw a Celtic tribal tattoo with the most incredible detail and mastery. '*Ruaraidh*' it read.

My finger reached out for it. "What is that?"

"It says 'Rory' in old Irish, means 'Red King.'" He dropped his shirt before I could explore it further. "It's dumb. I'm tired of letting everyone down all the time. Now you."

I shook my head and took a step back. I could see it all now, what Rory was doing. This was like a setup. He'd set himself up. To fail. Sorry all the time, before anything even happened.

He went on. "That shithead Fergal could see right through me. Just like everyone else." He examined me, waiting for me to confirm his accusation. "I need time to think. I don't want to get too deep in something that I know I'm gonna screw up." He looked to the ground. "I'm gonna go to England. Get away. I've been askin' yer forgiveness from the first day I met ya…and I'm gonna ask fer it again now."

Wait. He was breaking up with me? I stared at him. My head was spinning. I reached for my chest, ready for the pain, the hurt, but it didn't come.

The word "defector" played over and over in my mind. I thought about its meaning, its definition. A defector was someone who gave up allegiance to their group, abandoning them, for allegiance to another. And somehow, Fergal knew this about Rory. Fergal seemed to know a lot.

Rory turned back toward the direction of the shop he wanted to visit and said, "Come on. Let's get out of here," as he motioned his head for me to follow him. His sluggish pace and rolled-in shoulders slowed me down, bringing me to his somber level.

I couldn't help but notice a darkness about him now. Something I hadn't seen before. My heart felt a sickening tightness, similar to the discomfort it felt when I was caught in an awake dream.

"No, I'm gonna head home now. You go." The ache in my chest proved there was nothing more to be done.

As I walked away from him, I understood better what he had been saying. He was pushing me away, and he thought it was for the best. And to tell the truth I wasn't as infatuated with him as I used to be either, standing around watching him play the guitars he dreamed about buying one day. I felt like I was playing a supporting role in his life rather than the lead in my own and it made me sick. Like I was only there for him and his music and anything I wanted to do was secondary and less important.

My eyes opened wider than ever before. I'd spent years feeling like a victim, feeling cheated. And now I started to recognize how it felt to want to fight for something.

It felt good.

I wanted to go on my trip, stop running, face my awake dreams head on, and fight to the finish. I wanted to spend my last moments before leaving for Mayo with Michelle, not with Rory. I wanted to call my grandparents. I wanted to talk quietly with my mother. My throat constricted as I thought about her.

It was time for me to go back to Bohermore.

***

I overstuffed my pack with everything I thought I would need and did my best to leave my Rory baggage behind, though it relentlessly begged to come along for the trip. I wished Michelle could come with me, bringing her lighthearted sense of fun, but her overload of courses had her stressed to the limit.

I left Bohermore with a skip in my step and headed toward Eyre Square to catch the bus to County Mayo. A couple hours later, I found myself standing at the base of the large clock tower that marked the town center of Westport.

Molloy's caught my eye, an inviting pub with a black and gold sign and bright red accents around the windows and door. Inside, it had a medieval stone archway that reminded me of the one in Lynch's, and I took a seat at the bar.

The barman set my coffee on the polished black oak counter and asked, "Where ya headed? Yer from the States, yeah?"

He was an older gentleman, the owner maybe, and looked like he'd worked there most of his life. He plopped a dollop of fresh whipped cream in my coffee and pushed it in front of me.

"Thank you. I love the cream like that." I put my hands around the mug and placed my face over it, taking a deep inhale. "I'm from Boston. My grandparents grew up around here."

He rubbed his chin and leaned against the side bar. "So yeh're going to try to find yer family roots, yeah? Where were they from, tell me."

"My grandfather was from Claremorris, and my grandmother was from Turlough."

"Right, right, I've been through Claremorris many a time, many a time. Farms. Small. Not too far from here now. What's the family name?"

"O'Malley," I replied, eyes bright and hopeful.

He threw back his head with a big laugh and smacked his rag on the edge of the bar. "Right. Well no wonder yeh've come to Mayo. The O'Malleys *are* Mayo. Yeh've got quite a family lineage, young lassie."

"Really?"

He pulled back, as if shocked by my ignorance.

"I'm gonna start looking around here in Westport first. There's a castle, called Rockfleet."

The barman burst out with another raucous laugh and said, "Of course, sure ya are. Couldn't miss that. But first, you'll be going to Westport House, right?" He seemed to know what he was talking about and assumed I did too.

My naiveté was showing again as I asked, "Is that the best thing to do? Start at Westport House?"

"Of course. You'll learn everything ya need to know before yeh see the castle. Set the stage, so to speak. O'Malley...Fantastic. Don't get a swelled head now, thinking yeh're royalty or somethin'." He rolled his eyes at me.

He swirled his damp rag around my setting and moved down the length of the bar, polishing and shining, chuckling to himself.

***

Bright yellow paint and decorative flower boxes helped me choose my B&B. Colleen and her two daughters ran the place with the spare bedroom in their home. They treated me like family with endless cups of tea, biscuits, and a cozy spot by the warm fire.

Breakfast was an "Irish fry." Colleen's daughters, Imogen and Aoife, fought for who would sit next to me and poor Imogen, who lost, pouted. "Eeeee-fa! That's not fair!" Imogen whined at her sister.

"Those are rashers and them's the puddin's," Colleen explained in her thick brogue as she pointed to the bacon and circular cuts of black and white sausages on my plate.

Imogen, maybe nine, chimed in. "The dark one's the blood pudding. It's the best one." And she threw an all-knowing look at her older sister as if to challenge Aoife's preference for the lighter one. All I knew was I preferred the name "black pudding" to "blood pudding" but would be brave and try it anyway.

After making arrangements to stay a second night, I threw a few essentials into my small cinch sack, poked and tickled the girls, and started out.

Colleen pointed me in the direction of Westport House and said, "Sure, 'tis but a wee bit up the road, couple of kilometers out the way. No trouble t'all."

Imogen and Aoife followed me to the end of the driveway and waved excitedly from the hedgerow until I was out of sight. A breeze carried the smell of brine and hinted at the nearby coast as I left the bustle of the town behind me. Low stone walls filled my view and the distant sound of farm machinery broke up the quiet.

Just as I began to wonder if I had made a wrong turn on the single, straight road, I saw a small white sign with a painted arrow pointing ahead. *Westport House, .5 km.*

***

Like a scene out of *Pride and Prejudice*, Westport House looked like an old manor where a great lord would have lived. The three-story estate, built of gray stone blocks, was supported by massive pillars at the front and had impressive first-level windows that went floor to ceiling and were accented with climbing ivy.

Rickety scaffolding on one corner messed it up a bit, but the fancy gardens and topiary made up for it. Peeking out from around the corner, a large bronze statue of a woman stood tall, certain not to be ignored. I'd be sure to find out who she was.

I stumbled along the loose stone driveway that had visitor parking at the side. One small car was parked in the otherwise-vacant lot near the *Visitors Welcome* sign. I made my way to the side door marked

Admissions and entered into a waiting area with a glass display counter, pamphlets, and brochures. It was a museum of some kind.

A woman shuffled to the desk, alerted by the jingle from the door. She was young but dressed like a much older woman—hair tied up in a bun, simple cardigan buttoned to the top, and oversized long skirt— a caretaker of sorts for the museum, the curator or maybe docent. She looked me up and down with a half-shut critical eye while welcoming me in the same breath. She introduced herself as Moira.

Since this was apparently a slow season for tourism, Moira offered to be my personal guide. She launched into her well-rehearsed spiel: "This estate holds much history of Mayo and her sixteenth-century Pirate Queen, Gráinne Ní Mháille, also known as Granuaile. She was legendary to the people of Mayo and to all of Ireland. The 'She Captain' ruled the trade routes of the sea with her fleet and was chieftain of the most powerful clan of the west. Fairy tales and legends were told of Gráinne's conquests and victories, as well as her defeats."

She pointed toward a map like a robot while explaining some of the history of the area, but all I heard was her first words, "Pirate Queen, Gráinne Ní Mháille." This manor was a museum to a pirate queen. My heart accelerated to the point where I could hear it thumping in my ears.

Moira moved toward the entrance of the museum wing, hovering too close to my personal space, and I stopped, needing to enter alone.

"Thank you, Moira," I said. "I can take it from here. I'd like to walk through the exhibit on my own if that's okay." A feeling of hysteria was rising in my chest as I imagined what might be beyond the door. Was this pirate queen connected to my visions? I thought of the bronze statue out front. The "She Captain."

Moira stopped short, affronted by my request, but my mind had already raced so far ahead of me I didn't have the ability to be more polite about it.

I grabbed a pamphlet describing the displays as Moira forced a pleasant smile, opened the door for me, and added a final rehearsed phrase. "Be sure not to miss the dungeons. They're a pinnacle of the tour." She shuffled back to her counter in hopes of a new guest who might need her help.

I ducked out through the door into the wide hall, allowing it to close firmly behind my back, creating a solid barrier between Moira and me. My mind raced with thoughts of finding clues to my dreams. Maybe I would recognize something. My breath sucked in as a jolt of fear struck me. What if I *did* recognize something?

Peering down the corridor, my eyes brimmed with historically ornate detailing: crown moldings, antique white paint, and weathered brass fixtures. Plaques and pictures, panels with photos of artifacts and family trees, displayed on every wall. Each available space was filled with information. Aged tapestries bordered the exhibits, depicting historical events and bringing a regal feel to the displays.

My footsteps broke the deafening silence of the long corridor as I started at the beginning.

Gráinne Ní Mháille, born 1530, died 1603, Chieftain of the Mháille clan…inherited large shipping and trading business from her father…accused of piracy trade…ruled the Irish seas, commanding duties for safe passage…wealth, power, loyalty…arranged marriage, two sons and a daughter…built castles along the west coast for residence and defense…second marriage, a son….

I continued moving from panel to panel, absorbing as much information as possible about her. A feeling of certainty rose in me, that there was a connection here. A link.

Met with Queen Elizabeth I in 1593 for political negotiations, to free son from English captivity and remove Sir Bingham from his tyrannical governorship in her region…known as "the meeting between the Sea Queen and the Virgin Queen," Gráinne Ní Mháille refused to bow to the Queen of England, as she considered her a peer….

I clung to every detail. A powerful force drew me to Gráinne Ní Mháille, like I already knew her, and my heart raced in my chest.

I walked further down the hall, shaking at the knees, absorbing the drawings and renditions of Gráinne and her fleet. Many pictures portrayed her as a staggering beauty with long red hair; others displayed a strong, masculine woman. Her likenesses were dependent upon the artist or historian who depicted her at the time and I was sure they all had it wrong. A clear image hung distinctly in my mind and I searched for its equal on the walls. A large part of me hoped I was wrong, that Gráinne wasn't real after all, that I had imagined it all along.

My eyes were brimming with paintings and sketches of Gráinne's meeting with Queen Elizabeth I, of her many castles and strongholds—and then, there it was, her "galley," as the plaque called it. Her massive ship: fifteen oars on either side, black as tar, single mast with elevated deck and cabin.

It was real.

I reached up and tapped on the glass frame of the galley sketch, recognizing it and connecting it to my memory. I knew the ship. I had been *on* it. My finger moved along the raised deck and down onto the lower deck, tracing the events that unfolded there. I was on that very ship with her, and my mother, and Hugh.

Gráinne Ní Mháille was my captain.

My heart rate skyrocketed and my head throbbed, overwhelmed with pressure. My breaths came short and quick. A panic attack.

I raced to the end of the corridor, suppressing the urge to puke with my fist at my mouth, passing more exhibits and writings in a blur. I collapsed onto a bench and put my head between my knees.

Digging through my bag between my feet, I searched for my water. I gulped thirstily in hopes of restoring balance to my spinning head. I held my face in my hands, rocking, trying to understand the storm of information thrown at me.

She was real.

Pirate Queen, Gráinne Ní Mháille…from my dreams.

She was real.

***

I looked back down the elaborate exhibit hall after rubbing my eyes for longer than necessary. I half-hoped to see an empty corridor, proving the past ten minutes to be unreal. But a sea of maps, paintings, drawings, and plaques filled my sight, proving the reality of my situation. Everything in view was there to commemorate Gráinne Ní Mháille, Ireland's Pirate Queen and famous clan chieftain.

What did she want from me?

Against every ounce of my will, my eyes were pulled to an old, wooden door with the ominous word *Dungeons* painted across it. I stared in an unspoken stand-off, my eyes going in and out of focus, as

I hoped for it to lose my interest.

I was afraid to go down there. The thought alone chilled my core. Moira had said it was the "pinnacle of the tour," but I knew I wouldn't share the same sentiment.

Fear pounded in my heart, urging me to continue my mission. I had to see the dungeons, no matter my inner resistance. I sat for another moment, building up my courage. After one final sip from my water bottle, I put it back in my bag and stood.

My mind swam with every image of Gráinne Ní Mháille, her fleet, and her castles. All of it was familiar to me, every detail. I held on to this for bravery and forced my body to move toward the door to the dungeons.

I approached with caution and hesitated when I saw a small written summary beside the door. It read: *The stairway and spaces below are the only remaining original parts of Gráinne Ní Mháille's home here, which she resided in for many of her middle years. The manor was built several hundred years later around the foundation to preserve it.*

The Westport House was built on the actual site of one of Gráinne's towerhouses...and I was about to go down into her dungeons. The thought sent shivers through my body.

I took a deep breath and deflated slowly, then heaved the heavy wooden door open. Its hinges, large and rusted, let out a groan of resistance as I pulled. Assaulted by the stale, earthy smell that wafted up from the darkness below, I cringed, looking at the uneven stone stairs that curved down into the gloomy abyss.

Dim lighting ran along the side of the stairs and a modern railing led the way down. Forgetting to breathe, I started my descent on the rough stone slabs, feeling the temperature drop with each step.

The stairs curved to the right and opened into a long, narrow passage. I squinted to see in the poor lighting and cautiously moved toward the end of the dungeon space where I could make out a flickering glow.

As I passed small nooks or cells along the sides, I worried about what might be lingering in their dark corners, fearing something sinister would jump out and grab me at any moment. I kept my arms tucked tightly against my body and my eyes fixed on the light ahead.

At the end of the dungeon was a large holding cell. The rounded rear wall was made of fist-sized river stones, pressed closely together to create a barrier to the earth. The floor was the same, only with smaller smooth stones. There were nubs of rusted iron along the side wall and near the opening, maybe the remains of shackles and bars.

A symbol of some sort was etched into one of the back wall stones. I reached for it, tracing it with my fingers. It was worn and faded from time, but its main features were still visible, roughly carved, maybe with the edge of a shackle by a prisoner. My eyebrows drew in as I moved closer for a better look. I stepped back as my body stiffened, my hand covering my mouth. The tribal Celtic symbol was familiar to me. But how?

A shudder ran through me as I rubbed my nose to repel the musty, grave-like air. Then, an unexpected draft of fresh briny sea washed across my face, as if a window had been left open. Hyper-focused on my fear of what I might find in the dungeon, I didn't notice that the fresh breeze was the wind.

And then it came.

The forceful blast plastered me against the wall, blowing my hair in a frenzy. I couldn't see through the swirling wind and thick mist, even right in front of my face. My muscles liquefied, leaving me defenseless. Lost down in the dungeons, trapped and vulnerable, I prayed to become invisible.

I closed my eyes as tight as they would go, wishing it all away, pleading for it to stop, and then felt a break in the gusts like the eye of a storm. Sneaking one eye open and then the other, I peered into a twisting funnel of glowing light. My gaze zoomed to sharp focus—directly on her.

She held a sword in each hand, swinging them with precision in every direction, fully engaged in an unseen battle. Her face was a curled grimace, teeth bared, wild eyes burning. Blood covered her swords and hands, leaving splatters on her face and clothing. A large streak of dried blood was smeared across her cheek like war paint. Exhausted but still radiating an insatiable hunger in her eyes, she fought furiously…and then she saw me.

My blood ran cold, draining from my head straight into my feet as she turned her attention on me. Terror writhed in my gut.

This must be it, I realized.

This was my destiny. But why?

She was coming toward me now, straining with the effort of shouting, calling out with all her might, but I could only hear the fury of the wind. Her swords hung from her hands, by her sides now, pointing behind her as she moved forward.

Though locked in her gaze like hypnotized prey, I held my head high in defiance. She stopped out of reach, her face strained with the efforts of her screams, struggling to make herself heard. I stared into her twisted face. My captain. Gráinne Ní Mháille, the Pirate Queen.

She was my awake dream. My tracker. I was certain now.

She had been hunting me since I was a child and now she had led me to my death, right here on her turf. And I had walked right into it.

I continued to hold her intense gaze, searching for any possible answer. Thoughts of home filled my mind. My mother. My grandmother. Joey. Thoughts of my grandfather blanketed me, offering protection. I felt safe with him in my mind. I strengthened my spine and refused to back down to Gráinne Ní Mháille's intimidation.

We held direct eye contact. Her rage and ferocity, mixed with the blood of her victims, dripped off her. It was a deadlock.

Her spirit passed from her eyes into mine, her life force moving into me, nearly blowing my mind. My entire body felt suspended in the air as I held her writhing, aching soul. Emotion flooded me like never before. I ached, bent over in pain, crying out from crushing grief. The overload jolted me from my dream state back to awareness.

And she was gone.

The wind stopped and I collapsed onto my knees in relief, groping at my chest, searching for a heartbeat. I was sure it was gone, stopped completely. My face fell into my hands and floods of tears poured over my palms while my pulse snuck back to its steady rhythm. I wasn't hurt, but the fact that Gráinne Ní Mháille had lured me here, had revealed herself to me, filled me with dread.

Prepping my wits for my full flight upstairs, I wiped my eyes and stood up on wobbly knees. I forced my way along the passage toward the curved stone stairs. And then I heard it. Right behind me. The sound of metal hitting the stone floor: a loud rattling clang as if a long metal object had been dropped. Something like a...sword.

I lost my mind to pure terror and flew up the stairs. Bursting through the wooden door with all my force, my body shot out from the dungeon with incredible speed. Without even looking up, I ran straight into a gentleman who, at the same time, was opening the heavy door and I found myself buried in his chest as he caught me. It was the safest place I could have been at that moment, and I let the terror gush from my body in massive quakes.

Embarrassed, I slowly opened my eyes and started to release myself from the stranger's safe hold. I shyly looked up toward his face, attempting to make space between us with my arms, and started to apologize and thank him for catching me. I lifted my gaze higher to meet his as I struggled to find my words and to my complete and total shock, I looked straight into the face of Paul McGratt.

My mind spiraled into full overload, all peripheral vision blurred out, and I stumbled toward the bench and crashed onto it with a huge thump, dropping my head between my knees, once again.

::*

"What are you doing here?" The words spewed unguarded from my mouth.

Paul sat next to me on the bench and put his hand on my shoulder. "Yeh're shaking," he said, eyebrows lifted in the middle. "Are ya okay? What happened down there?" His tone was low and cautious, hiding the ring of alarm in the decibels. "You burst through that door like yeh'd seen a ghost."

He bent forward, turning toward me, trying to get a better look at my face. Heat rose in my cheeks and I silently cursed its consistent terrible timing.

I dug into my sack for my water, ignoring Paul's questions, and took a deep drink to finish it off. Paul looked around nervously, probably searching for a place I could refill. I took that second to evaluate my condition and decided that my mind was officially blown, but other than that, I was actually okay.

I turned my body toward him, shoulders slumped, energy drained.

"Exactly what are you *doing* here?" I repeated. His uncanny timing and unexpected appearance had me almost as frazzled as my earlier run-in with the Pirate Queen ghost in the dungeon.

He rubbed the back of his neck and looked at the floor, contemplating his response. He picked at a string on his cuff, looked at me from the corner of his eye and said, "I, um…oh boy." He paused. "This is awkward," he said with an apologetic half smile. "This is going t' sound bad, but I, ah, I followed ya here." His eyebrows lifted as his lips retracted, like he was preparing to get slammed.

"What?" My chin pulled back as my lip curled.

Shock seeped out of me and confusion replaced it with something that made my blood boil. I wanted straight answers, not more questions.

He wriggled under the pressure of my stare and continued. "A friend of mine at NUIG told me you were coming. And a' course, I knew why. Sure, I told ya to come."

"Harry," I stated the obvious.

"Yeah, Harry. We play a bit a' rugby together, since secondary school," he rambled. "Anyway, he told me you were coming here."

Okay. So Paul and Harry were friends.

"Why?" I pushed, making no attempt to hide my annoyance.

He rubbed his hand through his hair like he was preparing for a leap of faith. "T'be honest, Maeve, it's yer dreams. The visions. I gotta admit, I'm fascinated by 'em." He drew in a long breath, considering his next words.

"Seriously? You don't think I'm crazy? Because right now, I'm not really sure anymore." I looked toward the dungeon door to double-check that it was real.

"Well, if I think you're crazy, then I'd be condemning m'self to the same fate."

My eyebrows drew together. "Huh?"

"Ya see, I've had visions like yours m'self, Maeve. Before I even met ya." He paused, looking into his lap. "And you were in them." He turned to me as he said the last part.

The weight of his words dragged me down to frightening depths, stole my breath. My annoyance left me in a heartbeat.

"I recognized you when I first met ya, straight away," he continued.

"Wait. Are you messing with me? You're actually freakin' me out right now." I waited for the punchline to drop. Nothing. "Why didn't you say anything sooner?"

"I had to be more sure. I don't go around telling students I've been dreamin' of 'em. Come on now. I know I'm new at this, but I got that one figured out, at least." He looked down the hall at the displays of the Pirate Queen. "It's startin' to make sense to me now."

I pulled my head back. "Well, not to me!"

He stopped rubbing his knees and asked, "Should I go? I shouldn't have come. Are yeh mad?"

My previous anger had melted away, leaving a strange warmth in my chest. His boyish vulnerability made him incredibly desirable, distracting.

I strained to keep within the boundaries of student/teacher etiquette with my thoughts, hoping he couldn't read my face. As I thought about his dreams, the crimson flush in my cheeks started to cool and was replaced with wide eyed interest.

He looked back at me with hope in his eyes and asked, "Can I stay? For a little while?" His tousled hair and slumped posture left me little choice.

The sound of a door opening down the hall startled us and we turned in its direction. A voice made its way down the corridor: "Closing time. Ten minutes. Please finish up and make your way out to the lobby. Thank you."

I looked back at Paul, who was still waiting for my permission to stay.

"I can't believe you were able to find me." My smile assured him he could stay. "You have no idea what just happened to me down there…." My eyes went wide as a grin spread across my face, proving it was unbelievable.

Then I added, "Has anyone ever told you your timing's impeccable?"

***

Paul and I moved through the corridor toward the exit of Westport House, passing through the displays depicting Gráinne Ní Mháille's life and her impact on Gaelic Ireland. I soaked in as much information as possible and the endless details pieced themselves together like a puzzle, leaving me with a story of Gráinne's life that was bigger than I could ever have imagined.

Paul watched as I craned my neck for a better look at a portrait or to see lines in the sketches of her fleet. He stood off to the side with his jacket folded over his arm and followed my voyage through her history until I was spent.

"So, what do ya think? Is it what you expected?" he asked, walking beside me to the door that led back into the lobby.

None of the day was what I had expected. My visit to Mayo was proving to be incredible and I hadn't even made it to Rockfleet Castle yet.

"I think I'm losing it, is what I think," I joked. "But seriously, I don't know what to think. I'm done. I'm a puddle." I used my last drop of energy to crack a smile.

"Let's get ya back to town. Time for a rest. Come on." He gestured toward the door and pushed through it.

Moira stood idly behind the counter by the maps, picking her teeth with a pamphlet. She snapped back to attention when she saw Paul and quickly tidied any wrinkles in her skirt before pushing an imaginary tuft of hair behind her ear. She shot a flirtatious smile at him.

Her eyes jumped from him to me and back to him. She looked at us with a raised eyebrow, as if she was surprised to see us together...or maybe she was still questioning my mental stability, and at that point, I couldn't blame her.

"Did yeh have a chance to see the dungeons?" she asked dutifully.

I noticed a basket on the edge of the counter with small stuffed dolls for sale, pirate girls with plastic swords, and smiled to myself, knowing *she* was far more fierce than that.

"Yes, thank you, Moira. The dungeons were definitely the pinnacle of the tour." I shot a shaky smile back at Paul as we left, to remind him I had quite a story to tell.

The fresh air of outdoors washed over me, making me feel more like myself.

"Hop in," Paul said as he led me to his car and opened the passenger door. "I'll take you back to town."

Grateful for the ride, I didn't allow myself time to second guess if it was appropriate or not, though my gut sent a signal of harsh judgment. I sat in his car and watched him walk around to the other side and my heart rate accelerated again. His car smelled of him and I liked it, though it made me nervous, like it was illegal or taboo or something.

"So what'd yeh think of the museum? Gráinne's amazing. Right?" He looked at me, his eyes aglow.

How much did he know about her, and the history behind her fleet, her castles, her piracy?

"Um, well, I never heard of her before." I hesitated. "But now, I feel like I know so much—"

"What? Ya haven't heard of her before?" He made it sound like everyone in the world knew who she was. He put on his turn signal and exited the parking lot.

I shot him a glare and said in a defensive tone, "No, I've never heard of Gráinne Ní Mháille. I did research though, to find her. Everything I could think of…."

I tried to pronounce her name correctly, but was pretty sure I made a mess of it. The garbled sounds brought me back to my research results and Moira's speech. *Granuaile.* That was her. A different version of her name, but still her. I'd missed it in my research completely, but it was there the entire time.

"I've dreamed of her," I said, more seriously now, gazing out the windshield at her vision in my mind. "She was the woman from the dream I had in your classroom. I had no idea who she was. Well, until now. But after visiting that place, I feel like I know everything about her. I feel like I know her."

Paul slowed the car and looked at me again. "Well, yeh *should* know her," he said flatly, looking at me to be sure I wasn't pulling his leg. "You *do* know her name, right?" He looked at me again, total disbelief on his face, and I frowned.

"Yes," I said sharply. "I know her name. What are you getting at?"

He picked up on my frustration and spoke more directly. "Sorry, I'm just a little surprised ya didn't already know about 'er." He quickly recovered the conversation and my guard lowered again.

"Gráinne Ní Mháille, Ireland's Pirate Queen. Gráinne is her Celtic name." He said her name slowly so I could get a grasp on the pronunciation, *Grawn-ya Nee Mawl-ya*. "Maybe yeh'll recognize her Anglican name...." He trailed off.

I watched him, one eyebrow peaked. He had my full attention, but didn't go on.

"Well, what is it?" I begged, shaking my head. "I have no idea what her Anglican name is. Should I?"

Paul opened his mouth to speak, then closed it, shook his own head in disbelief, and pulled over to the side of the road. He turned his body to face me fully.

"Gráinne Ní Mháille is the Gaelic name for Grace O'Malley."

My face fell blank. The name resonated through my skull, repeating, echoing, again and again.

Grace O'Malley.

Grace O'Malley.

A burst of adrenaline shot through my veins. I clutched the door handle until my knuckles turned white.

I yanked the passenger door open, flew out and tumbled into the grass, onto my knees.

Grace O'Malley!

My thoughts tangled into themselves as I raced to understand.

"My grandfather was an O'Malley from Mayo." My voice was forced smooth, with only the slightest hint of shakiness. "Gráinne Ní Mháille is my family, my ancestor?" I'd phrased it as a question, but I knew it was true. I could feel it. I stared into the air as the notion settled into my being, recalibrating who I was.

I gasped for air as Paul came to stand next to me.

"My full name is Maeve Grace O'Malley," I whispered up to him.

He nodded and put his hand on my shoulder. "Are ya okay?" he asked. "Yeh look a little pale—"

Out of nowhere, my vision doubled and I heaved into the grass with violent jerks of my body, relieved I had an empty stomach. Otherwise, the shame would have ended me.

Paul was gone. At first I thought he ran away to escape my dry heaving, but then I realized he was digging through his backseat and reappeared with a bottle of water. He put his jacket over my shoulders as I continued to stare at the horizon.

Everything fell into place. A sense of calm and knowing settled over me as I reawakened with the truth of who I was.

I looked up at Paul, clear-eyed and content, and said, "I think I'm okay now," and smiled at him, my words meaning so much more than they sounded.

A new strength was growing in me, like the sun itself. It was fueling me to face the Pirate Queen. To find out why she had been hunting me for so long. And to end it.

Chapter Twelve

Rockfleet

"What about *your* dreams? Have you ever seen Grace O'Malley in them?" I studied Paul as he parked in front of my B&B.

"It's always unclear who the attacker is. You're usually the only one I can see." He cleared his throat with his fist near his mouth and looked away. "Come on. Let's get you inside."

I dragged my weary bones toward my room, still hearing the resonance of his deep voice as he spoke with Colleen, asking her to call him when I woke.

A moment later, his car pulled away. Colleen's doting voice passed through my door as she offered me a cup of tea and a scone. She called it four o'clock teatime. I gratefully accepted the warm gesture and before I could reach the bottom of my cup, I was asleep.

My reluctant eyes blinked open and saw early evening shadows cast across the room. It was already six o'clock. The laziness of my nap lingered in my muscles as I dragged myself into the warm shower.

I pulled on my favorite jeans, rubbing the small tear in the knee with new awareness. My white sweater hugged me cozily and I felt more like myself again. Tipping my head upside down, I shook my fingers through my wet hair and tossed it back. I was refreshed and unexpectedly energized.

In the back of my mind I heard the chime of the doorbell and then the sound of Paul's mellow, deep-toned voice as he greeted Colleen. I swatted at my butterflies as they reminded me that Paul was my teacher. I really wished they would stop doing that. I didn't need any reminding. It was already as big a burden on my soul as having a pirate queen after me.

Paul had freshened up too, looking handsome and well-put-together in khakis with a blue oxford and a thick, three-button pullover sweater. He saw me approaching and stepped forward, searching my face for clues of my condition.

"Ya look like yeh're feeling better," he said with a smile. "Hungry?"

I nodded. Starved.

"Would yeh be interested in walking?" Paul asked.

"Let me grab my jacket." I ran to my room, giddy, to find the extra layer.

Pulling my arms through the sleeves of my coat, I heard giggling by the front door. Imogen and Aoife were crouched by the sitting room, spying on me with wide eyes and impish grins. Colleen took the edge of her skirt and swooshed at the girls, saying, "Be off with ya and yer mischievous shenanigans, ye divels."

***

"The restaurant's on the other side of the river. I think you'll like the bridge. It's very old," Paul said as he put his hands in his pockets, keeping a formal distance from me, making small talk.

I couldn't stop thinking about the earlier part of the day, though, and cut to the chase. "So, Grace O'Malley, *Pirate Queen*." I put extra emphasis on the "Pirate Queen" part for effect and added, "I'm a little freaked out by this whole thing, actually."

"Yeah, I know," he agreed. "We have a lot to talk about."

I wondered if he was referring only to the Grace O'Malley stuff.

"Including keeping you safe from here on." He looked straight at me, as if to be sure I didn't have any crazy ideas. "I'll tell you whatever ya want to know about her, but really, I want to hear about what happened in the dungeon. You burst through that door like you were running for yer life."

"I'm a little embarrassed. I don't want you to think I'm nuts or anything…." I could hear nervous jitters in my voice, left over from the museum.

"Far too late for that," Paul jabbed. "Seriously, though, I need to know what happened down there, if I'm going ta be any help at'all."

I took a double-take at him.

Then, after a long, deep inhale, I let out a slow, deliberate exhale and told him every detail, from the exhibits to the confrontation in the dungeon.

"Did she attack yeh?" Paul's eyes were wide.

I rubbed my hands together to dry them.

"No. It was only when she locked her eyes with mine that I knew she wasn't going to hurt me. But the feelings that shot through me—it was an overload of rage and grief, love and vengeance. It was everything. And then nothing."

Paul slowed our pace as we approached the ancient footbridge. I looked at him with huge round eyes.

"It's cool, isn't it?" he said, smiling at my reaction.

"Amazing."

My hand was drawn to the ghostly, tribal carvings at the start of the bridge. Old Celtic lettering, faded from time and rain, was still visible in the stone. I traced some of the art with my finger.

"It's hundreds of years old," Paul said, leading me onto it.

I stood at one side and looked over into the shallow river.

"So then what?" Paul asked out of the blue.

"Well, then I heard something—it sounded like a sword being dropped on the stone floor. It was so loud and clangy, and so real. I literally flew up the stairs!"

Paul's eyes sharpened as he added, "Yeah. You looked like you'd seen a ghost." He leaned for a look into the water. "I wish I'd arrived sooner, to be down there with you. You shouldn't do that kind of thing alone anymore." He nudged me to follow as he started to walk toward the other side.

"I can handle it alone." Annoyance rose in me. I'd been doing this alone for years. Although not very well.

"I'm sure ya can. But it's just not safe." He kept walking.

I followed, watching him through squinted eyes, wondering if he knew something I didn't.

My hand ran along the raised edge of the bridge as we crossed. My fingers sank into carvings at the far end and I stopped for a closer look.

"What's this?" The markings looked different from the ones I saw at the beginning of the bridge.

Paul turned back.

"Looks tribal. The carving is deeper and more angular than the rest. Almost like it was done at a later time, by a different craftsman." He traced his fingers in the ancient etching.

I stepped back with a gasp.

"What?" Paul froze.

"It's just like the carving I saw in the dungeon. Hacked into the rear wall of the cell. What *is* that?"

"You saw this same thing down there?"

I scratched the back of my neck, looking around me, remembering the familiar, eerie symbol.

Paul examined the marking again. "Yeah, it's a tribal symbol. A warning maybe. One clan trying to show power over another."

"I've seen it before. I mean, before the dungeon. I'm not sure where. But I think it's bad." I moved off the bridge, distancing myself from the disturbing carving. "Stupid ancient graffiti."

"Exactly."

***

Just across the river, the restaurant invited us in. The façade was painted ivory with deep mahogany accents. The hand-painted sign read *An Port Mohr*.

The hostess put us at a private table for two overlooking the river and footbridge. A hummingbird took over for my butterflies and now beat its wings in my stomach.

"Have I seen you in here before? You look very familiar." The hostess batted her eyelashes at Paul without shame.

Jealousy poured out of me and I had to mop it up before anyone noticed. What was wrong with me?

"What're yeh in the mood for?" Paul asked me, oblivious to the hostess' flirting. "Seafood?"

"Something comforting and warm. And Irish." I blushed at my unintended play on words and prayed he hadn't noticed. Ah, jeez.

What was *wrong* with me today? My inner voice was killing me.

The Irish stew was served to us with a basket of thickly cut homemade brown bread. I inhaled the comfort of it and allowed it to replenish my hollowed-out bones.

"I wondered when we first met if ya might be a descendant of Grace O'Malley. Obviously yer name, but more than that. It was my dreams." He hesitated. "I thought I was seeing a ghost."

"Are your dreams like mine?"

He thought about it. "Sort of. Well, yeah, actually, a lot like yours I guess. Though I'm not awake when they happen. That's a major difference. Well, except for that time in m' classroom."

"What time?"

"You know. That time when you had the vision, of the castle and the ship. Yeah, well, funny thing. I had a strange vision at the same time. Didn't really think anything of it in the moment, but after you described your vision to me, I started putting it together. The visions were related somehow, I think."

Blush flooded my cheeks as the humiliation of having an awake dream in Paul's class returned to me, full force. "Wait. I remember you were staring off into the distance, in the middle of lecturing. Right as I was coming out of my dream."

"Yeah, well, it was the same as my recurring dream. Only that time, I wasn't sleeping." He smirked at me. "You're always in 'em, though. The dreams. Someone or something's after you. I'm always stuck, trying to help but never able. It's quite a burden, actually, you needin' ta be saved all the time." He laughed into his glass of water.

"I do not need to be saved! Thank you very much."

"Oh yeah ya do! Every time!" And he huffed into his bowl, shaking his head at the absurdity. "I always knew there was something about ya though. Something different." He looked down at his stew and searched with his spoon for the perfect bite. "Ever since my keys got stuck in yer hair." He chuckled at the memory and I instinctively reached for my hair to smooth it.

I let my mind wander while he looked at his dish and became lost again in my Paul McGratt daydream. The fact that he was my teacher faded from the forefront of my thoughts and I saw him as a man, lost in his own search—but for what?

"How is everything?" The waitress rudely interrupted my daydream. She paid attention only to Paul.

"Great. We're all set, I think," he said, looking at me to see if I needed anything.

"Wait. Are you from Galway?" She stared at Paul. "NUIG! Right?" She pointed at him like they were old college roomies.

Paul fidgeted and shot a quick look my way. "Yeah. How do I know you?" He remained steady.

"We were in class together a couple years ago! What was it…archaeology or something. I was so undecided then. But you were so into it!" She giggled, batting more lashes. "Are you still there?"

Paul played with his fork, avoiding too much eye contact. "Actually, yes. Lifer, you could say."

"Oh my God. I'll have to tell my sister. She's a sophomore there now." More giggles.

Paul kept his eyes on me and she finally took the hint and left us.

The silence was deafening.

"Was bound to happen, I guess. We're not that far from home." He rubbed the back of his neck. "You okay?"

"Huh?" I blinked and took my first breath since she came to the table. "Yeah. That was weird."

"Don't worry about it. We're fine." He swallowed and looked out the window.

"Okay, so your dreams…Castles…Grace…." I was stuck, trying to change the subject from inappropriate behavior to inexplicable visions. "Help me."

He laughed.

I refolded my napkin on my lap. "Okay, so how do you know so much about her?"

He lifted his bright blue eyes, which actually appeared deeper now, to meet mine and said, "Me mother. She always told stories of Grace O'Malley when I was a kid. The legends had fantastic detail and my imagination ran with it. I loved her tales of the Pirate Queen, and I guess the fascination grew with me."

His voice was warm and gentle when he spoke of his mother. It made me think of my own mother.

"Wow." I scraped the bottom of my bowl in hopes of finding one last bite as a pestering question gnawed at me. "I wonder why my family never told me stories about Grace. You would think they would have talked about her, especially after my mom died." I had told him about my mom, earlier in the car, and he had become very quiet and pensive.

Paul refolded his napkin and returned it to his lap. "Maybe you never asked the right questions."

My wind blew out of me like I was punched in the gut.

"What do you mean?"

"I don't know. Sometimes, if a person isn't ready for the truth, they just don't ask the right questions."

"Oh, so it's my fault they didn't tell me?" I pulled back, eyebrows lifted.

"I'm not saying that. It's just an interesting human trait." He refolded his napkin again.

As I sat fuming, insulted to the core, like I had missed the entire "Grace O'Malley thing" completely, our coffees were brought to the table.

Our waitress pulled out her phone and moved closer to Paul. "Can I take a pic? For my sister, Fiona, in case she bumps into you at university." She cozied down next to him, leaving him little choice.

I choked on my coffee. "Hot!" Cough. "Sorry." Cough.

Did she say Fiona? Jesus. There have to be at least a thousand Fionas at NUIG. Right? My heart pounded into my eyes, making them bulge. If anyone found out I was out to dinner with Paul McGratt, it would be a disaster. I regretted taking such a risk. The university would probably kick me out. Then Gram would probably make me come home. Nausea twisted in my stomach as my inner battle raged on.

"Yeah, sure." Paul didn't flinch. He angled himself away from me, so I'd be out of the shot.

"Thanks!" She giggled and bounced her chest near his face. I could have killed her.

"Can I have the check when you get a second? Thanks."

Her smile faded slightly but she finally left to get the bill.

I looked into my coffee cup. Anywhere but at him.

"Sorry. Awkward." He looked into his cup as his eyebrows scrunched and became heavy. He rubbed the back of his neck again.

"It's okay. Whatever. I'll kill her if she interrupts us again though. Just watch." I grinned at my ability to lighten the mood, but on the inside was a scowl, noticing myself becoming territorial. It was weird. "I want to hear why I was never told about Grace O'Malley. And it's not because I didn't ask!" I threw a sugar packet at him.

His hands shot up in surrender. "Okay, no need to get violent. Although, that's the right tone to set. Some of the stories of Grace were brutal," he said with a more serious voice. "Grace was legendary in battle, bringin' men to their knees, and she didn't hesitate to take their castles by force, any amount of force, if they had scorned her."

I couldn't swallow right, tipping my chin under.

"It was different then," he said with a shrug, as if it couldn't be helped. "'Twas a lawless time. No country, no government. Everyone had ta fight for what was theirs, and Grace was no different. The only difference, actually, was her being a woman. Back then, only men were chieftains, leading armies. Grace broke the rules and kicked butt doin' it." He smiled to make me feel better.

"Well, she definitely seems to want to kick mine," I mumbled into my coffee. "But why? What did *I* ever do? Or my mom? Now I don't even know if Grace wants to hurt me or if she actually needs something from me." The thought got stuck in my brain and stayed there, opening my eyes.

Paul stared off into the distance, mulling over the same thought.

As our waitress approached with the check, Paul had a card ready and handed it directly to her. She took the hint and kept moving.

"Wait, I want to…."

"Ah, no. My treat. I've crashed your party. It's the least I can do to keep my welcome."

Take that, Dear Abby! I'm sure you'd have something to say about this. Though I knew, deep down, Gram wouldn't want me to be indebted to him either. She was probably home clipping the advice column at that very same moment, getting it ready to add to the growing pile on my pillow.

I'd already lost my inner battle anyway. Paul was my teacher and that made all of this questionable and borderline inappropriate. But it was bigger than that. Somehow he was a part of all of this and I had to risk it.

The chilly evening mist washed over us as we walked back toward my B&B.

"So, what're yer plans for tomorrow?" he asked, looking across the road as if distracted by a sign or something.

Tingles danced in my belly, hoping in my deepest fantasy he would still be here.

"Rockfleet. It's hers, you know." I figured he probably already knew that. "I saw it on the panels at the museum. Actually, Harry showed me the first picture I saw of it."

"I know. I've seen Harry's photo, too. It's brilliant," Paul mused. Not the direction I hoped he'd go, and I felt a pang of disappointment stir in my gut.

He turned his head to me, looking over sideways, and said, "I can take ya there if you want."

"Really?" My high pitch revealed my enthusiasm and his shoulders relaxed when he heard it. "That would be great! Really?"

"Yeah." He chuckled.

I turned to him with my eyebrows scrunched, perplexed at how he was so available and he added, "I'm, ah, stayin' at the B&B down the road."

He gave a crooked smile as his master plan of following me around on my dream quest unraveled and revealed itself.

***

The fluffy duvet on my bed made it extra-cozy and my body screamed for a long sleep, but as the day settled into me, my eyes grew wider and my heart beat faster.

Michelle picked up on the first ring with a groggy voice, surfacing from sleep. "Are you okay? It's late. What's going on?"

"I didn't mean to wake you but I had to talk to you. You're not going to believe what's been happening." My excitement shot through the phone line.

"And you couldn't wait until morning?" She smacked her lips.

"Oh my God, you're right. I'm sorry. What a—"

"Just kidding, Maeve. What's going on?" The phone rustled as she pulled herself up onto her pillows.

After pouring every detail of Grace O'Malley over her in fast forward, her only response was, "Oh. My. God." Pause. "I can't believe Paul's there."

We burst out laughing at her one-track mind.

"I had a feeling that might happen," she added.

"What? How?"

"Harry. I swear Paul has a crush on you." If she could poke me through the phone, she would have. "I can't believe he actually went there."

"He does not have a crush on me." I rolled my eyes, for my own benefit. "He's just into this sort of thing. It's what he does, Celtic history and stuff." My pitch went higher as the words came out too fast.

"What-everrrr." I could hear her roll her eyes back at me as she continued her relentless teasing.

My next call had to be Gram. Boston was five hours behind, so no worry of waking her.

The conversation started the same way it did with Michelle: "You are not going to believe what's been happening…." but I needed to censor the majority of it for Gram.

"Gram! I'm in Mayo and my awake dreams…They're real. They have meaning!" I didn't stop talking long enough to take a breath. "Grace O'Malley. What do you know about her? I've learned so much about her at a museum, and her dungeons…." Panting now, I stopped long enough to give Gram a chance to respond.

Silence.

"Gram?"

Silence.

"Gram? Are you still there?"

"I'm here." Her stiff voice sounded frozen.

"I found Grace O'Malley. She's the source of my awake dreams. Gram? I might be able to find a way to stop all of this." I begged for her to respond in the way I wanted her to.

Gram hesitated again as I hung, waiting.

"Yeh've found more than I ever expected ya would, dear. More than I thought possible." Caution laced her voice. "How did yeh find her?" The unnatural calm in her voice straightened my spine.

"How did I find her?" The words came out harsher than I meant. Gram was hiding something. Holding it, just out of reach. "What do you know about this, Gram?" My voice fell flat and accusing. I wanted *her* to start explaining to *me*, not the other way around.

"You should head home now, dear," Gram said without affect. "Back to Galway and call me when ya get there. You're excited and tired. I think it's time for you t' come back home to us now. To Boston." Her tone held a note of finality.

My eyes narrowed.

"What? This is what I've come here for, Gram. I need to know more. This is about who I am. I'm finally starting to figure things out." My anger seeped out of each word. I was tired of being sheltered, of being left in the dark. I took a deep breath. Anger was only going to make things worse with Gram. "What are you worried about?"

She paused and stuttered, searching for the right thing to say or measuring how much to tell me. At last she said, "I'm worried ya won't come home to us." Her voice cracked as she took a shaky breath through the phone.

"I'll come home to you, Gram. I promise. I just need more time." I drew in a deep breath and asked, "Who is Grace O'Malley?"

Gram considered her words before speaking. "Grace O'Malley was your sixteenth great-grandmother. On your grandfather's side. You are of her lineage." Gram's voice began to tremble. "Yer mother had dreams of Grace too."

The world stopped around me. All I heard was my breathing and my heart pounding in my ears.

My great-grandmother, separated from me by sixteen generations? My mother had dreams about Grace O'Malley too?

Now I was really scared.

"What happened in Mom's dreams?" I asked Gram with the best

calm voice I could fake.

"Yer mother had dreams about Grace in the night, while she slept. Ever since she was a little girl. She would wake, frightened and confused." Gram cleared her throat. "As she grew, she dreamt of ships and castles, and the Pirate Queen." Gram's voice cracked and she paused.

When she spoke again, her tone rose to a high pitch I had never heard before. It sounded like panic. "Before yer mother died, she said Grace tried to reach her, to have yer mother join her. Yer mother's weakened heart was givin' out and Grace helped her feel safe, at peace. Yer mother wanted to go with her. She wasn't afraid. She felt she knew her, all her life."

Gram paused but I was speechless.

"When yer awake dreams returned, after yer mother's death, I was afraid Grace was coming for you too. And not only in the night while you slept, like yer mother. She made bold contact with ya while you were awake." Gram's voice cracked while tissue rustled against her nose.

"Gram, don't cry, please. I'm not going away. I don't think Grace is trying to take me. I think she needs something. Mom will protect me."

I believed every word I said. Everything came clear to me now. And the best part was, I now knew I wasn't going crazy.

But my throat tightened anyway—because Gram had known all this, known the source of my awake dreams from the start, and hadn't said a word.

"Why didn't you tell me? Why didn't you?" I choked out.

"It's a ghost story, Maeve. Don't you see? How could it be explained? It makes no sense. Not even to me. I'm supposed to hold this family together, not have us called 'crazy people with visions.' We got a fresh start." Gram spoke frankly, her steady voice armored and stoic.

"What?" She lost me for a second. "But you let me come to Ireland? Without knowing?"

"I wanted you to find the truth. An explanation behind the O'Malley's troubles. Not more visions, ghosts, and pirates!" Her sudden shrill tone took me aback.

"Well, I'm sorry. It *is* real. Grace O'Malley is real and we can't ignore her anymore." My eye twitched. "Does Joey know?"

"Bits. He doesn't know the full story. Doesn't want to." Gram had a sob in her voice. "I hoped too somewhere in my heart it wasn't true. That yer going to Ireland would make it all stop. But it hasn't. I'm worried about ya, Maeve. I want yeh to come home now. Come home to us, please."

Gram's words terrified me. Not the part about Grace coming for me, but the part about going home. I didn't want to go home, not now. I needed more time. I needed to calm Gram and convince her that I'd be okay and safe.

"I'll head back to Galway," I assured her. "I'll focus on my studies at NUIG and call more often." I paused a beat, pulling my plan together. "But I want to stay in Ireland, to finish my classes." I avoided telling her about my visit to Rockfleet in the morning—I still had to see what was there.

***

I cracked my window, allowing the fresh morning air to wash across my face as Paul navigated the narrow road to Rockfleet.

"My grandmother didn't want me to come here. She wanted me to go straight back to Galway. Back to Boston, really." I looked down at my wringing hands. "And I hate to admit…I wonder if she was right."

"She didn't want ya to come? Why?" His fingers tightened around the wheel.

"She told me everything on the phone last night, about Grace. She's known all along. Grace was my sixteenth great-grandmother, on my grandfather's side. How could she not tell me that before?" My blood boiled all over again.

"She wasn't ready. Or you weren't ready." His tone was matter of fact.

"What? No. I've been asking her about all of this forever." I stared at him with daggers.

"I know. But trust me, it wasn't the right time. You needed to figure this stuff out on your own. You would never have believed it otherwise."

"No. I...." Mmm. "I hate when you do that! Whose side are you on?"

"Yours."

Staring out at the rolling green hills, I replayed her words until they were worn out.

Paul glanced at me, noticing my fidgeting hands.

"Can't blame 'er for being concerned about you coming out here." He jabbed at me with his elbow. "But no worries. That's what I'm here for." He sent me a lopsided grin. "But seriously, we can go back any time. Whenever you want. We *do* need to use caution."

Tension filled my spine, causing me to sit up straight. We were approaching Rockfleet. I felt it. It would come into view any second and I held my breath, waiting for it.

Familiar grassy fields, moorland, and hills surrounded us. The view began to open up as we approached an inlet of the sea, and the fresh, briny smell in the air awoke my senses. One final bend and there it was, standing tall and proud. Rockfleet Castle.

Four stories high and dark as night, it held a rectangular corner turret rising above the parapet. I couldn't shake the foreboding sense that it was waiting for me.

Struck by the intensity of the sight, I threw my head back in disbelief. I closed my eyes to clear the image, shook my head a little and opened them again, only to see the exact same vision. The castle of my awake dreams, right in front of me.

"I know this place." My palms sweat and my heart pounded its way nearly right out of my chest. "Stop the car. Please. Stop. I need to get out." I couldn't breathe. Was this another panic attack?

I reached for my door before the car had stopped and flung it open. Paul jammed on the brakes and the vehicle came to an abrupt halt, leaving black marks in the gravel behind it. I stumbled out onto the rocky side of the road and fell against the bordering stone wall, staring.

I definitely had never been to this place before, but I knew it well. I knew the water. I knew the castle walls. The briny smells mixed with damp earth. I knew the hills and the view.

As Paul came around from the car, I pointed toward the castle and the sea and rambled, "The water becomes really shallow when the tide goes out, so boats can't move in or out, and then it becomes really deep at high tide, right up to the corner foundation of the castle, and boats can move quickly and easily then. That's what made this location perfect for Grace."

Paul stared at me with raised eyebrows as I continued.

"Unexpected visitors wouldn't know how to navigate the waters at low tide and wouldn't be able to sneak attack." I looked at him with one eye squinted. "How do I know that?"

More images and ideas came to me as I looked around. "The sun sets on the ocean and the sunrise can be seen from a window on the far side, barely more than a narrow slit. A bedroom with a massive fireplace is behind that large arched window at the top." I pointed to it.

Paul cleared his throat, eyebrows still high on his forehead. "Well, let's have a look. See if yeh're right." He eyed the castle, as if trying to confirm the details I had shared.

I bent over with my hands on my knees and dropped my head down. Paul reached for my shoulder to steady me and asked, "Are yeh gonna be okay? I can take you away from here. Right now." His assertive tone convinced me he had already made up his mind.

"No, I'll be okay, really. I want a closer look. I just need a sec." I mustered the strength to look up at him, half grinned. "But I'm afraid."

He nodded at my apprehension, understanding my fear. "You got this." He stood back, giving me room to make my choice and my breath came a little easier.

"This is definitely the castle from my dreams. I'm sure of it. I've been aware of this place my entire life." The words sounded ridiculous in the open air and I instantly regretted saying them.

"I was hopin' so," he said.

"I just didn't expect to be so afraid." My eyes misted as I stood frozen to my spot.

Paul leaned in close. "I'm going to help you." He searched deeply into my eyes. "I'll keep ya safe. I promise."

I held his gaze, allowing the tension to melt out of me. My

breathing slowed and became deeper. I wanted him to stay like that with me forever.

"I know I shouldn't say this...." He stopped, struggling for words. "But it's been eatin' me alive. You need ta know."

"What?" My lips pursed together.

"There's more to my dream than what I've told you. There's another part you need to know." He looked out across the ocean.

"Tell me."

He turned back to me. "In my dreams, the ones you're in, you know, where I'm savin' ya...every time." He smirked. "You see, each time I save you, well, I end up gettin' killed. Time and time again." He pressed his lips in a tight smile and nodded his head in acceptance. "Yeah. So, that's my dream."

My heart dropped.

"But sure, does that stop me?" He let out a stifled laugh.

So that was it. In his dreams, he died saving me.

There was no way I'd let him come, then. He needed to stay away. Far away. He should have told me sooner.

My teeth clenched, and my head started to ache as I considered going alone. If he was killed in his dream saving me, then what would happen to me if he's not there? Was he supposed to come and protect me, die for me, so I could live and finish whatever was happening? Was that his fate?

Screw fate. This was my choice, and no way was I going to let him die for me.

"Well then, you're not coming." I put my foot down, decision made.

His gaze sharpened. "Like hell I'm not. I've been waitin' my whole life for this." He pushed his shoulders up and out, looking broad and strong, but I still saw the worry hiding in his eyes. "I only needed ya to know about my dreams, in case there's real danger. Ya need to be careful."

"Wait. I thought you can't die in a dream?" The number one dream rule jumped to my mind.

His shoulders released some of their tension. "Right, true enough. Funny that's all you're thinkin' about right now, but sure, you're right.

I never *actually* die. I'm about to die, every time; arrow flying directly toward me heart, sword hurdling straight at me, fire, bludgeoning of...."

"I get it!" I grabbed his arm to stop him. "That's terrible!"

"Yeah, weird really."

"No. Tragic." I saw the conflict play out clearly in my head.

"How so?"

I glanced toward the castle and said, "We're on this journey, drawn together somehow, and though you're driven to save me, you're doomed to die for me." My words sank my heart like a stone. "Or, you would be if we believed your dreams are fated to happen. Which they aren't," I added, determined to believe it.

Paul's eyebrows shot up at the idea, but he only said, "Sounds about right." He reached for my arm and turned toward the castle. "Shall we?"

Chapter Thirteen
Her Chambers

Crossing the rocky way leading to the castle, I became smaller and smaller as the stronghold grew bigger and bigger. It stood steadfast in its foundation. Looking up at its steep, dark gray walls made me dizzy as I found ancient swirl-like carvings, hidden randomly in the stone. A blanket of sadness surrounded the structure and the dull gray skies set the somber backdrop to its mood—solemn and lonely, isolated in its lost inlet of the sea.

I moved closer and reached up to put my hands on the cold stones, like in my dreams. I looked to Paul before touching and he gave an encouraging nod.

My hands pressed onto the bone-chilling wall and I closed my eyes and waited. Flashes of awake dreams went through my mind, bringing me back to my mother's arms, the cemetery, my grandmother's kitchen, and Bohermore in the blink of an eye. And then thoughts of the dungeon at Westport House: the swords, blood, and terror.

I filled my lungs and exhaled slowly. Everything was okay. Paul stood back watching, eyes wide, waiting for some form of wild event to unfold. I pushed out my lower lip in a fake-disappointed sulk.

The large, brooding black door stole my attention and I nodded my head toward it to get Paul to come along.

The dark wooden door arched at the top with a heavy metal ring for a knob—no lock, no bolt. It stood strong like a loyal castle guard. My heart beat faster as I stood in its shadow.

Paul grasped the rusty, weathered ring and heaved to haul the door open. It groaned in resistance as it reluctantly gave way to its uninvited guests. Air hissed through the first crack, releasing the pressure, making it easier to move.

As Paul pulled the stubborn door further, I stepped up to peer in through the crack, wondering what my first impression would be. I leaned forward, eyes adjusting to the darkness—and, like a sucker punch, was struck back by the agitated force of the wind.

The burst blasted through the open door with an energy that knocked me backward. Paul stood a couple of feet away, unaffected by the violent gust, and watched as I stumbled. He leaned back in for a look through the door, confused. The wind surrounded me quickly and I lost sight of him.

Pushing into the squall, I squinted against the force. Tears tore from my eyes and trailed back into my hair. Arms outstretched, I pressed forward toward the open door until the gusts began to move around me, as if avoiding a protective force field. I had a clear view now and tracked sudden movement from deep within the castle, following it with precision as my heart pounded out of control. It took form as it filled the doorway. Tall, with shoulders back and chin up, the figure moved with confidence and power. I recognized her immediately.

It was Grace O'Malley. Pirate Queen.

In a wide stance, she held her sword with two hands high above her head, ready to confront an aggressive intruder. Her dark cloak flapped around her body and the heavy chain and pendant around her neck emanated royalty. With her hair flying wildly about her, she searched, as if through centuries, for her assailant.

Tears poured from my eyes now as I gazed upon her intimidating posture and unworldly beauty. I froze to the core and stared, mouth hanging.

Then she saw me.

Like a missile detecting its target, her attention homed in on me. Her curled, bent expression of aggression filled me with terror as she lurched out of the castle, lunging toward me, sword drawn.

My mind and body instinctively shifted to defensive mode. My arms shot up to protect my body from the imminent blow as she came hurtling toward me. Swirls of smoke streamed behind her as she barreled forward, assuring me she'd plow right through and leave nothing but a pile of dust and broken pieces in her wake.

She was on me in an instant. Defending her castle, she raised her sword against me as I held my breath, never breaking eye contact. Looking into the soul of her victim, she tightened her grip and then suddenly weakened.

Her eyes widened.

She knew me.

The vengeance gnarled across her face faded as recognition took its place. Her sword dropped to the ground with a familiar clang.

My balance shifted as she locked her arms around me in a powerful hold. Her desperation was clear as she held on to me for dear life, like a mother who had found her long-lost child. Her mind opened up to me: her turmoil and her power, her love and her hate.

"*Ta muir ar cheann, Méabh,*" she said to me in an ancient Irish cadence as she filled my brain with her strong voice, authoritative, but carrying a smooth tone of compassion and nurturing.

I could be lost forever to Grace O'Malley. I looked back toward the castle for reassurance of my existence in time and place. There, watching from the doorway, stood another woman. Her long, dark hair swept across her cloak in the wind as she gazed upon me with tear-filled eyes. I hadn't seen her alive in over six years. Unconditional love poured from her directly into my heart, and I knew immediately.

She was my mother.

She was the woman with Grace on the ship, consoling her after Hugh was slain. Here now with Grace, again by her side, she knew we were all together again. Home at last.

Searing pain, like the glowing red tip of a hot iron sword melting into my chest, forced me to recoil and drop to my knees. I frantically grabbed at my chest to extinguish the blaze, tugging at my shirt for a cooling effect. When I looked up again, they were gone.

Grace was gone. My mother, gone. The wind, gone.

Paul ran toward me in alarm but my focus shot down to the pain on my chest, still burning like fire. I sprang up and ran to the water's edge with Paul right behind me. Splashing cooling handfuls on myself, the relief was miraculous, loosening the vice grip from my tense muscles. As I pulled the neck of my shirt down for a better look, my gaze jolted back up and I gaped at Paul in horror as he reached me.

I was burned. My chest blazed red and blistered. Paul and I stared, mouths open, at the ancient Celtic art forms seared into my skin.

"It was her necklace," I blurted out. "There was a big charm. It burned me." I sputtered in my confusion as Paul gaped with a baffled look on his face. He didn't seem to know what to believe. He said he'd watched me peer into the doorway, fall backward with a terrified expression, and then crumple to the ground.

I babbled on while splashing water on my burnt skin and explained, "I saw her. The wind came and I saw her. She saw me, too, and she recognized me." My words felt awkward. It all sounded so crazy but I couldn't stop myself. "It was when she held me, that was when her necklace burned my chest." I strained to get a better look at it.

I knew I sounded irrational but surely Paul couldn't deny the evidence. The burn was plain to see.

"And my mother was there, in the doorway. It was like we were all meant to be together." I continued to splash water on myself while looking off into the distance, trying to recall the details. The intense pain clenched my teeth but I kept talking through them. "Grace spoke to me. She said my name."

Paul froze at my words. "You saw your mother?" His eyes searched mine.

"Yes. At a distance." I looked down.

"Did *she* speak?"

"No. Only Grace."

He nodded his head and rubbed his chin. He looked at me again with a cautious, sideways glance.

His concern formed a huge lump in my throat.

"I'm okay."

"Yeah? It's a lot to take in."

"Yeah. I'm okay. The fact that Grace spoke my name, though. That blew my mind." He was lost in how to interpret my feelings about seeing my mother. And honestly, so was I.

"Did she say anything else?" he asked, allowing me to move on.

I pinched the skin between my eyebrows, trying to remember. Her words were in Gaelic and I'd never heard them before but I did my best to repeat what she said. "It sounded like, 'Thaw mw-air ar k-yan.' Something like that." I didn't do it justice. Her voice turned the words into song, and I only made them sound choppy. But Paul's wide eyes revealed he recognized what I'd said anyway.

"*Ta muir ar cheann?*" he asked. His smooth-toned accent made the words sound lyrical again.

"Yes! Exactly!" I blurted out. "What does it mean?"

Deep in thought, Paul said, "It's an old expression. One used by the clans, when discussing tribes. It means something like, 'We are together,' basically, 'We are one.'" He looked at me cautiously.

It all began to make sense. We were connected. By blood, by clan. The O'Malley lineage made us one.

But there was more. She wanted something. Needed something from me. I knew it. I just didn't know what.

The nagging pain of my burn distracted me as I continued dripping cool water on it, clumsily.

"Let me help you," Paul said as he tried to get a better look at my burn.

He cupped water into his hands and gently trickled it on the wound. The water cascaded down between my breasts, drenching my shirt. It calmed the burn and stopped the pain. His close proximity and attention distracted me as I watched his handsome face, focused on its task, and imagined him holding me.

"Is that any better?" he asked hopefully.

"Actually, yes," I said, still lost in my thoughts. "It's much better." Surprise blinked my eyes. "The pain is gone." The burn was still completely visible and angry-looking but the discomfort had faded.

"Maeve, yeh're soaked," he said, noticing my shivering. He started removing his bulky layers. "Take off yer jacket," he instructed me. "At least that's still dry." He was quickly down to his T-shirt and pulled it over his head with one arm and passed it to me.

"Here, wear this. It'll be big but should fit under yer jacket. Take off yer wet blouse. Go on, put this on before yeh freeze." He continued handing his shirt over to me, giving it a little shake, encouraging me to take it.

I stood riveted, captivated by his shirtless form, muscular and lean. Sudden urges raced through my body and mind. I stared at him, trying to control the craving that left me defenseless while attempting to appear natural and unaffected.

"What?" he asked defensively, wondering why I was unresponsive to his offer. Or more likely wondering why I had become a mute. "Don't worry. I'll turn around," he said, clueless, as he pulled his heavy sweater back over his head.

A chuckle escaped my lips at his innocent ignorance as I grabbed the T-shirt from him.

"Gimme that!" I jokingly yanked it from him. "No peeking." I giggled, nerves shot to the wind as I turned my back to change clothes. I secretly reveled in the fact that I had my cute, silky, light blue bra on—just in case he had seen it while he helped me with my burn. Now I was sure I had gone completely mad.

The smell of his shirt took me to another world as it passed over my head. It smelled of him, woodsy and clean, like heaven. I drew in a long, slow inhale as I emerged from inside it and said, "Okay, you can turn around now."

As he turned back toward me, I put one hand on my waist and stuck out my hip, striking a flirty pose, and said, "How do I look?"

With a wide smile, he began wrapping his outer jacket around my shoulders. "Perfect," he answered.

"Now tell me everything. Every detail," Paul said as he scouted for a spot we could sit comfortably. The sun snuck through the overcast clouds, bringing new life to the view, helping keep the chill away. Any residual fear from "the event at the door" had passed and the brightening skies lifted my mood toward elation as I pondered everything that happened.

We settled on a long flat rock near the water's edge.

"That was the worst one yet. By far," I said. "I mean, we've found her, right? I should be scared to death right now, but somehow, I only feel happy. Everything feels good."

I pulled my knees up to my chest and gave myself a squeeze. Her message clung to me: "We are one." So maybe, just maybe, there was a solution here.

"Are *you* good?" I asked him. "I mean, that was beyond weird, I know, but are you okay?"

"Absolutely," he said without hesitation. "I'm good. A bit shaken. But good. Okay, my mind's blown and all. I mean, you've a burn on your chest. Jazus." He rubbed his brow. "What about her sword? Tell me about it. What was it like?"

"It looked heavy, with shiny silver on the blade part and black on the handle, some carvings and curves...."

I struggled with my description but Paul masterfully turned my scattered words into a visual replica in my mind.

"Was there a line down the center of the blade? Was the blade flat or diamond shaped? At the quillion, the crossguard, the part that stops her hand from moving down onto the blade, what were the details there?"

His interrogation made me dizzy. I had no idea there could be so many details on a sword.

My brow scrunched as I thought about Paul's questions and was able to visualize the details of the weapon, piece by piece. "The blade was flat, sharp on both sides, with a line going down the middle—"

"The blood gutter," Paul added.

"Gross!" I gaped at him with exaggerated repulsion.

"What? That's what it's called, for obvious reasons."

"Okay, well, the crossguard was blackened silver with scrolls that swirled down on each side, like Celtic circles. The grip part was wrapped in black leather and the top, rounded part of the handle—"

"The pommel."

"The pommel, it was the same as the crossguard but reversed— the scrolls were swirling upward. There were finer engravings, Celtic knots and more eternity circles. It was a work of art really," I panted.

He nodded in satisfaction and told me stories about the Pirate Queen while I lifted my face to the sun. He spoke of her historical meeting with Queen Elizabeth I to secure the land that was rightfully hers. He promised to show me a copy of an ancient map, drawn by one of the queen's men, that labeled the area of Mayo as Grany O'Maille's territory. Hers was the only female name on any map at that time—and for all time, to date.

The tide began creeping in. It rose gradually, making its unyielding, twice-daily visit to the base of the castle. Nudged by its persistent encouragement, we moved to a drier, more secure site closer to the door of Rockfleet.

My stomach gurgled and I looked down. I was starving and savagely could think of nothing else. Every ounce of my energy had been sucked dry and I looked to Paul with a hand on my growling stomach and wide puppy eyes. He nodded with a grin and hopped up, holding his finger in the air. "One sec. I got this," he said, heading to the car.

He walked away and I secretly admired him from afar. His casual gait was confident and relaxed. His pants hung on him perfectly as he patted his back pockets, as if to look for his keys. I smiled, blushed, and redirected my fool-hearted gaze toward the door of the castle.

I blinked, certain I saw movement. A quick twitch and then a swoop. Straight for me, a black bird careened and then, at the last minute, sailed up and over me. As it spread its wings, preparing for its ascent, it exposed its regal red shoulders. A red-winged black bird. It rose straight up, then curved, gliding down toward me again and cascaded past me and soared off into the distance.

I stared, mouth open.

My next move was clear. I had to go inside. Now that I knew who the Pirate Queen was to me, and that my mother was with her, I needed more. To find out what Grace wanted. What she needed.

Paul returned with his pack and like a knight in shining armor, pulled out a wax bag that held two wrapped sandwiches. He continued his chivalrous act and produced two Fanta bottles, cracked the tops, and balanced them adeptly on the rock where we sat. He spread out his pack like a makeshift tablecloth and handed me my sandwich. It might as well have been steamed lobster with melted butter by candlelight.

I ate hungrily, replenishing my starving body and soul. Paul watched with amusement as I chowed, crumbs flying, manners shot to the wind. He laughed when I attempted speech through my full mouth, wiping at it with the back of my hand, trying to say, "Ohmi…so good, th-you."

Picking at whatever crumbs were left and coaxing the last drips of Fanta from the bottles, we enjoyed the view of the sea and the hills. With legs stretched out, leaning back on my arms, out of nowhere I looked at Paul and asked, "Who's Patricia?"

I'd been wondering about this ever since the time we bumped into each other in Doolin. I'd seen Paul with her twice now, and I needed to know who she was before another moment passed. My heart thumped heavily in my chest. What if she was his girlfriend—or worse, his fiancée?

Paul fidgeted as he folded the wax paper from his sandwich, smoothing out any creases. Then he looked squarely at me and said, "She's my girlfriend."

My heart plummeted like a stone and a sickness rose in my belly. I didn't try to hide my disappointment.

"Well, she *was* my girlfriend." He tried to recover. "It's a long story really. I'm trying to put space between us now, to gently move away from 'er. It's complicated."

How could I have got it so wrong? When did I lose touch with reality?

Holding back my urge to cry, I loosened the vice grip of my now-crossed arms, but continued to glare at him.

He continued, "Our families are close. They've done everything to ensure we'd be together ever since we were kids." His tone lowered, sounding sullen. "I was never comfortable with it but was pressured by my parents. I did my best to make it work. For them, for her." His eyes squeezed shut, grimacing in pain from the position he was placed in.

I didn't know what to say.

"Anyway," he continued, "I've been talking with her about putting space between us. She's not happy about it and she's gettin' the family involved. It's a right mess." He raised his eyes in frustration.

He struggled now, looking like he didn't know if he should say more or less or just run away.

I still had to wonder, should I believe him? Was this okay? Could I trust him? The questions ran through my mind, *Dear Abby* columns dancing about, but I felt his honesty and believed in it. His explanation was more than he needed to give.

I nodded at him and looked out to sea.

"What about the guy? From the pub in Connemara?" His voice surprised me. He wanted to know about Rory.

I had no idea how to answer his question. Rory and I had grown apart and he clearly pushed me away right before I left. And he made me feel bad about myself. I knew that. He was lost and made no effort at finding his way. But Paul made me feel alive. Amazing. So, no matter what happened, either way, I knew I wouldn't go back to Rory.

"Um, I don't know. It's confusing. But I think it's over." I felt the sting of my last conversation with Rory.

We smiled gently at each other and started to pack up our picnic in comfortable silence.

Paul walked to the car and my attention turned toward the castle and in that instant, I made up my mind. I wasn't going to be afraid anymore. I was going to walk into that castle to face the force that had been chasing me since I was a small girl, and I was going to trust Paul and allow him into my world.

I smiled to myself and walked toward the brooding black door.

With my newfound courage, I marched alone toward the menacing entryway to Rockfleet Castle. Without reservation, I placed my hands on the heavy metal ring and pulled. The door didn't budge at first, so I put my full body into it and heaved. It fought me, groaning against my persistence, but finally yielded to my efforts.

I poked my head in and a cool, stale breeze brushed my face. The damp, grave-like air surrounded me as I held my breath and stepped further into the ancient ruin. Dark and tight, its windows were narrow cuts in the wall, letting in little light.

The entry space was bare and must have been the level for housekeeping and dealing with outside affairs. The upper floors were probably where the actual living took place. As I walked around the tight space, I peeked out each slim window to see the restricted view Grace would have seen.

Something moved behind me and my heart stopped short, causing me to suck in a quick gulp of air. I froze and pushed my way through the fright to turn around. Paul's silhouette filled the space as my eyes adjusted to the low light and the tension left me as quickly as it came.

"Crap! You scared me to death!" My voice echoed through the castle, creating an incredible sense of life and energy within its walls.

As I stepped back from him, ready to show him around, he looked at me through squinted eyes and said, "No, you scared *me* to death. I didn't know where ya were! I was walking to the car and then, poof, you were gone. Ya can't do that t' me."

His angry tone made me chuckle, which pissed him off more.

"Aww, you worried," I teased.

"Ya bet yer arse, I worried. Did ya see that burn on yer chest?"

"Come on. Let's go up!" I turned with a spin, knowing he would follow.

***

A rickety ladder took us up to the second floor. Unable to help himself, Paul explained its unstable installation as another form of defense. The ladder could be drawn up to prevent intruders from gaining access to the higher levels of the castle. I was tempted to pull it up.

We explored the second and third stories, and the sounds of our feet on the wooden floors echoed throughout the castle. I spied secret hidden passages in the walls and looked into fireplaces with large stone arches. A spiral stairway tempted us to the top floor above.

Without a solid sense of balance, I made my way up the awkward counter-clockwise staircase as Paul laughed at my clumsiness.

Only *after* enjoying his stolen entertainment, he explained, "The staircases in these tower houses spiral in the 'wrong' direction, as yeh can see." He chuckled again at my effort to stay upright. "They do this to put attackers at a disadvan'age. Swords need ta be wielded with the left hand, making accuracy near impossible."

Paul hopped two stairs in a flash as if he were about to pounce on me. I fended him off with my free left hand, trying to push at him, and lost my balance, proving his theory. I fell right into him, as he knew I would, and pushed against his chest for balance.

Even in the playful moment, I was lost in the intimacy of the touch. I'd never actually touched him before, full-on like that, and my mind swam in the excitement of it. He felt good. Strong. Steady.

I pulled my hand back like I'd done something wrong.

He was still laughing from the setup of his attack.

"Hey! Looting marauder! Out of my castle!" I kicked at him, trying to keep him down, and scrambled up the next few steps.

With perfect stealth, he climbed the steps in pursuit, sending a rush of playful panic through me.

A quick scream flew out of me as I rushed toward the top. "Get back! I'm warning you!" The words came out as laughs, slowing me down even more.

He clipped my ankle as I made it onto the top floor and I squealed with excitement as I reached safety. I filled the doorway and put my arms out to block him from entering. He came up behind me but then we both fell silent, looking into Grace's private chamber.

I took a deep breath and moved into her sacred space, Paul close behind.

Gráinne Ní Mháille's top floor chamber was massive, open, and airy. The space was bright with windows that were large and freeing. She had an enormous medieval fireplace and I ran my finger along the back, certain I might collect some soot. At the top of the hearth, the keystone was a carved coat of arms depicting crossed swords, a boar, and a proud galley with the name *Mháille* carved below.

The space felt barren now, but I imagined it furnished and warm, with Grace's battle gear displayed proudly on one side, swords mounted on the walls, a huge four-post bed, booty from her expeditions piled high in every corner, and her personals tucked away like treasure on the far side.

Lost in time travel, I stared out at the amazing view from the chamber and felt like I was on top of the world. It must have been here where she stood to dream, to plan and plot, and to remember her stolen love, torn from her, leaving nothing.

I felt her devastation in my own heart. The Pirate Queen had connected with me in a way I never thought possible. Her presence filled my mind as I stood at her portal to the sea. She was all around me and within me.

A cool breeze washed across my face as I looked down at my hands. I hardly recognized them. They were strong and worn, rugged even. I brought them to my face to convince myself I was still me as the breeze picked up.

It was the wind. It was coming.

Paul approached me from behind. I jerked around to see him and as I gazed at him standing in the middle of the room, a sense of urgency took me over. It was like he was the most beautiful man I had ever seen and I was starving for him. Desire took over and passion flooded me.

I sprang at him and wrapped my arms around his neck. He stumbled back but regained his balance, holding me at arm's length. I pushed against his resistance, trying to embrace him again, struggling to be close to him.

"*Grá mo chroí*," Grace's voice repeated in my head again and again. Paul reached for my wrists behind his neck and with controlled strength brought them together in front of him, forcing space between us.

I fought against him as he bent forward, looking into my eyes.

"Maeve, are yeh all right?"

The words echoed in my head from miles away.

"Maeve, it's me. Are yeh okay?" His voice sounded closer this time and more clear. Confusion staggered me. *What happened?*

From under my eyelashes, I peered up at him as embarrassment washed over me like seasickness.

Shame rose to all new levels. "Oh my God," I said, cheeks flushed. "I'm so sorry. That was weird." My hands flew up to my face, hiding the blaze. Had I been trying to *kiss* him? "I think it was my dream again." Every ounce of me wanted to melt to the floor and drip through the cracks into oblivion.

Paul chuckled. "That one didn't seem so bad." He tilted his head to be sure I was okay. "But, seriously, what *was* that? What happened?"

"I have no idea. It was like Grace took over. Like she was *in* me." It sounded ridiculous as it came out. "It felt like I was starved for you, I needed you."

Paul's eyes darted back and forth between my eyes as if trying not to miss anything.

"I kept hearing the words 'graw ma cree' over and over…and then I had to ravish you." I put my hand over my eyes. "Sorry about that." My lips pursed to the side as I waited, wondering what he was thinking.

He rubbed his chin and said, "'*Grá mo chroí*' is Irish. It means 'love of my heart.'" He grinned and raised his eyebrows at me. "Sure, you've just expressed to me yer undying love."

***

Paul led me out of the castle, walking behind me with his hands on my shoulders—warding off ghosts maybe, or making sure I didn't stray. Once I stepped out onto the stone steps, he turned and closed the black door behind us with an extra push to tighten the seal.

The freedom of the fresh salty air and bits of sun that shined through the mist sent shudders of relief through my body. The burn on my chest pulsated now, distracting me.

I pulled the neck of my T-shirt open and pushed my chin to my chest to try to see it. Paul reached for the neck of my shirt, hesitated for my permission, and gently pulled it down. He bared his teeth and hissed when he saw the burn.

"It's okay. It doesn't hurt. Just feels…weird." I shivered, turning to the black door to be sure it was still closed.

My hair fell across my chest, blocking his view. He reached for it and moved it back to my shoulder. But he didn't drop it. He rubbed it between his fingers. looking at it, and then he looked at me, at my mouth, and into my eyes.

His chest heaved as he took a sharp inhale. He was going to say something. I gazed back into his eyes, waiting, hoping.

He dropped his eyes and my hair and took a swift step back.

"Let me take a pic so you can see it better. Yeah?" He fumbled for his phone in his pocket and angled it discreetly at my exposed chest. His hand was shaking.

When he handed the phone to me, I zoomed in to maximize the features of the wound as he stood against me, leaning in to see. Celtic art forms danced where I'd expected to see charred flesh. I recognized the Celtic designs and could see part of a mythical creature. It was like a fire-breathing lion beast. One I knew well.

And then I realized….

I had seen those patterns before. I'd seen the medieval lion creature. These were the designs from the ring on Grace's hand, when I saw her on her ship in my nightmare. The ring her love kissed before he was brutally murdered.

But I knew these shapes from more than that. I'd seen them my entire life, right in front of my face. They were the exact designs on the bulky charm hanging from my grandmother's necklace. The charm she had been wearing at her heart forever. They were a perfect match.

Grace's ring and my burn were the same pattern my grandmother had worn around her neck for as long as I could remember. Gram's charm was a ring. It was the ring of the Pirate Queen, Gráinne Ní Mháille—given to her by her beloved.

My grandmother was the keeper of Gráinne's ring!

My head swirled as my surroundings spun around me. Colors blurred. This was the discovery I had come so far to find, but there it was, always within my reach.

My grandmother's words came back to me as I remembered what she had always told me about the ring: "The O'Malleys have had this relic for generations and pass it down for safekeeping, to protect it from being lost forever. 'Tis the heart of the O'Malley Clan."

I never truly understood what any of her words meant—until now. It was the ring given to Grace by her true love. The only remaining piece of what they'd had and what they'd lost. Like a time capsule, holding their eternal love.

I was still staring into the phone when Paul finally spoke.

"It's fading."

I looked at the photo again and didn't see any difference.

"No," he said. "Yer burn. It's fadin' away. I can't make out the designs anymore." He strained for a better look at the mark on my chest.

But I barely heard him. I grabbed onto his hands, excited, and held them to my chest as I told him everything I'd just realized about the ring.

Chapter Fourteen

Archenemies

"Through all my studies, all my courses, never have I experienced history like that before." Paul shook his head, bewildered, keeping his eyes on the road.

We were convinced that what happened at the castle had no rational explanation. What we experienced was inexplicable. It was supernatural.

"Try teaching that to your class," I teased. "No one would ever believe you. You'd probably get fired." I watched the road signs for Galway—fifty kilometers to go. We'd be back to town by dusk.

"Yeah, I've been worryin' about that, actually." He glanced over at me for a second, long enough to see me dart my eyes over to him. His gaze jumped back to the road before we had time to read each other.

I wanted to ask more but wasn't sure if I should. This was awkward territory. He had a lot to lose. His reputation. His career. I stared out at the green fields.

He was silent, driving faster than usual with a strong grip on the wheel. His focus on the road was sharp.

"Are you okay?" I broke the silence.

His foot lightened off the gas, releasing the tension in the car.

"Yeah, I'm okay." He bit his thumbnail. "I just didn't expect any of this to happen. I didn't believe it could."

"Me neither. It's not exactly normal."

"No, I mean this." He waved his finger between us. He slowed the car and watched me from the corner of his eyes. "I want to keep doing...this...with you."

My breathing stopped. Did he mean the ghost-hunting? Or could he have meant "us?" I refused to shame myself again in the same day and went with the safe assumption.

"Yeah, we do make a good ghost-hunting team. The 'visionary' and the 'historian.'" I smiled at him, and some of the tension melted from his shoulders.

A familiar nagging prickled in the back of my mind: Rory. Guilt smothered me at spending all this time with Paul. But still, I felt good. Happy.

Flying down the narrow hedge-rowed streets, I cleared Rory from my mind and allowed my thoughts to return to Paul. What if he *did* mean "us?" I thought about the almost-kiss in the castle and wanted to smack my hand over my face again.

"What about Gráinne's love life?" I smirked from my awkward timing and pretended to have an itch on my lip to hide it.

He looked at me with a laugh, welcoming the change of subject. "Right. Well. Aside from two arranged marriages, she did actually have quite a scandalous love affair."

"Tell me! Every detail." I rubbed my hands together.

"Well, she found 'im washed up on shore while scavenging a shipwreck, searching for booty." He grinned and I couldn't help but chuckle. "He was barely alive, probably'd been left for dead, but she liked him. Took him to her castle and basically brought 'im back to life."

"So they fell in love?"

"One of those epic, big-movie loves. Movin' mountains." He turned to me and then back to the road. "Soulmates."

"So, what happened?"

Paul hesitated for a second, then said, "Disaster. He was an Irishman from Wexford, called Hugh DeLacy."

I cocked my head. Hugh. The Pirate Queen's true love.

"Once he recovered, he swore to honor her, never leave her side. He knew she was a queen to her people and the land, a true chieftain. He loved her."

"And?" I pushed, though I already knew how this story ended. I braced myself.

He took a deep breath and said, "Hugh was murdered by the rival MacMahon Clan. Made an example of, ta show the competin' clan's power. Story goes, it was done right in front of Grace."

My hand went to my mouth as I relived the memory. The shouting, the sea, the Pirate Queen's cries.

Paul took it as a cue to continue his story. "But they'd messed with the wrong woman." His tone deepened. "Grace took her army and ravaged the castle of the MacMahons, decimated it, took it over. It was brutal and gory, bloody and thorough."

He began picking up speed again.

"Few men had ever seen a woman in battle before and hesitated to attack her. She used that to her advantage, establishing her reputation as one to be feared. But still, she wasn't satisfied. She became consumed by it and...What?"

I stared at him in disbelief, clinging to his every word, not moving a muscle.

Paul slowed the car and glanced at me. "What?"

"I know this story, Paul. Every detail. I was there when he, when Hugh, was struck down, murdered. She raced to him, to stop them. It was horrible. And the blood...everywhere...the screams...."

He narrowed his eyes.

"In my nightmare," I clarified. "I was there and saw the attack. It was on her galley."

Though his eyes were still on the road, his full attention remained on me. His perfect stillness and subtle leaning begged for more detail.

"What happened?"

"Pirates of some sort came aboard. At first, it seemed like they were there to negotiate, but then Hugh stepped up in Grace's defense. They murdered him. Brutally."

The horror I had witnessed pulled my face down and my eyes started to fill.

"They were trying to intimidate her and her crew." My voice squeezed. "No one had a chance to stop them, it was so unexpected. And he died. Right in front of her." I choked on the last words, recalling her desperation and her haunting screams. "It broke her. Completely."

I forced myself to swallow, trying to relieve the tightness in my throat.

"I know. I think I've actually seen him in me own dream. You know, the one you're in. But only recently."

"Wait. How recently?" I stared at him, hard.

"All the time, Maeve. More so now. The last one, he was there. I know it was him…now that I'm sure it's Gráinne Ní Mháille tryin' ta kill me."

I nodded, realizing I'd made the same assumption about Grace and his dream.

"So, right as she's about to kill me, he shows up and stands with me. Throws her off completely. She drops her sword and tries to reach him. And he's trying ta get ta her too, but it's like there's a force field between them. It's torture to see it. They're desperate ta be together." He rubbed the back of his neck.

I stared at him, mouth open, for the longest time.

"So that's it." The sureness in my voice convinced even me. "There's no way she can rest now. Like an unsettled soul, out for vengeance but also seeking her love. It makes sense, right?" It was like a revelation, pulled together by Paul's dream. "Her bond with Hugh— it was…is…eternal."

Tears fell from my eyes and the grief crept in, same as when I had the nightmare. Then an odd certainty settled over me and I lifted my chin. "That has to be what she wants," I told Paul. "That's why we're here."

He raised an eyebrow, but I didn't see him. I saw the Pirate Queen's lover, stretched out and presented to her enemies. I saw the blood, and the sword, and the horror on my ancestor's face. I saw them reaching for each other, desperate to be together but doomed to separation.

"We have to help her reunite with Hugh."

The spoken words became our unspoken pact.

***

At the first roundabout leading toward the city center, Paul asked,

"What are ya going to do now? You okay to be alone?" He leaned forward to get a better look at my face. "Ya might be a bit traumatized, ya know. A little PTSD maybe." He shot a teasing glance, causing my butterflies to re-awaken.

"Yeah, probably. But, no, I'm fine. Thanks though." I really just wanted some alone time to think.

We drove down Bohermore past the cemetery and the calming comfort of home blanketed me. But as the car glided toward the space close to my door, I bounced from an unexpected jerk as Paul hit the brakes. A man stepped recklessly off the curb into the street directly in front of Paul's moving car. My heart stopped.

It was Rory.

He leaned forward to see into the car, a scowl covering his face. He glared straight into my eyes through the windshield. The fire in his gaze made my heart jump into my throat.

I hopped out of the car with too much phony exuberance. I grabbed his arm and pulled him back onto the curb as Paul moved his car further into the spot.

Rory was rigid, his defenses high, as he scoffed, "Where've ya been? Who the hell is that?"

Insecurity oozed from every syllable. I felt bad for him and regretted not planning ahead to avoid this. We were basically broken up, but maybe he'd misinterpreted things? Either way, his expression made me uneasy.

"Oh my gosh," I said, keeping it light to prevent the situation from becoming any more awkward—and to keep him from paying any more attention to Paul than he already was. "It was incredible. I have so much to tell you."

He started pacing and hadn't really looked at me yet. He kept watching Paul, calculating his every move. Paul seemed unsure what to do, hesitating with his door slightly opened, and I nearly died when he started to get out of the car. I wished he would just drive away, avoid this whole thing.

Paul stepped away from his car toward us. "Is everything all right, Maeve? Do ya want me t' stay?"

Oh God. Worst words ever. Bad timing. Didn't he know that was going to start something?

Rory puffed out his chest and moved into Paul's personal space. "Who is this guy?" He looked down his nose at him, sounding like he was talking about a dirty dog. Paul stood his ground, with no intention of avoiding Rory's advance.

All I could do at the moment, besides run, was introduce them. "Rory, this is Paul McGratt. Paul, this is Rory MacMahon," I said as politely as possible.

Paul looked Rory in the eye. "Aren't ya a musician in town? I think I've seen some of yer gigs. Mojo, right?" He tried to defuse the situation like a pro, but Rory wasn't having it.

Rory ignored the question. He turned to me as if Paul were invisible and said, "I thought you went to Mayo on yer own? I didn't realize yeh had a travel companion." His voice was thick with judgment.

"I did go alone. Paul and I bumped into each other in Mayo and he gave me a ride home." My voice rose defensively and I left out all the middle details. Rory kept glaring anyway. I wasn't sure what else to do but extract myself.

I cleared my throat. "So, I'm gonna go now. I really need to rest...." I left the words hanging, waiting for them to take the hint and leave. I watched my foot twitching back and forth, moving pebbles.

When I looked up, I caught Paul glaring at Rory with a level of hostility I'd never seen from him before. Maybe they had a past I didn't know about, but by the look of it, Paul definitely did not like Rory. And actually, it was pretty clear Rory didn't like Paul either. His wide stance and squared shoulders sent clear signals of aggression.

I grabbed my bag and whispered to myself through my inhale, "Oh my God."

I looked up. "Thanks for the ride." I gave a weak wave to Paul, acting as casual as possible, though my mind was going crazy. I nudged my chin at him, signaling him to get going.

He nodded and turned toward his car. "Welcome. Have a lovely evening." His curt, formal tone worried me. He glanced at Rory with another nod. "Rory." And he left. I watched him from the corner of my eye as he drove off, leaving behind a hollow emptiness in my chest.

I turned to Rory, irritated now that Paul was gone, but feeling bad for him at the same time. "Sorry about that. I guess it was a bit awkward."

I paused, but he gave no answer.

"Thanks for coming to see me." I forced a toothy smile. I kept my face plain and my body stiff. I didn't want him to come up.

I picked up my bag and started to head toward my blue door.

Rory stayed in the same spot. His shoulders fell as his arms flopped down and his palms turned out toward me.

"That's it?" His tone sounded harsher than I expected. "Yeh're just gonna go inside? What? Are yeh *with* that guy now?" His eyes were round and forehead creased as he pointed his thumb limply toward where Paul had parked his car only moments before.

I frowned at him for going there, but didn't respond.

Rory's face fell. A transformation washed over him as he grew agitated, leaning side to side and balling his fists.

I dropped my head, staring at the ground to avoid his pressure as my heart rate increased. My pulse pounded in my flushed ears.

"Let's go upstairs and talk about this," he growled.

No way I wanted him up in my flat, but his rising angst was scaring me. I wanted to get him to calm down, and maybe talking about it upstairs would be the quickest way. His glare and aggressive posture made it feel like he was giving me no choice, even though I wished he would leave.

Struggling with what to say next, I looked up from my feet to speak to him. Whatever words had been forming on my lips were quickly lost when I saw his angry expression. Bile rose up in my throat—taunting me for my inability to deal with this situation.

Planning my quick exit route, which involved Mr. Flaherty's paint shop for starters, I saw movement behind Rory.

It was Paul.

He was coming back. With a forceful gait.

His car, lights still flashing, was double-parked a few spaces down Bohermore, and I heard the faint sound of the chime coming from the open door. He walked toward us, eyes set on Rory like a missile on its target.

"Everything okay?" He was louder than necessary.

The force of his voice shocked me. It wasn't a question. More of an interjection, directed at Rory.

"You all set?" he pressed.

I looked around, sure this must be drawing attention.

Rory jerked around to face Paul.

"What in hell are yeh doing back 'ere?" Rory crossed his arms, clearly pissed off. "Who the fook do you think yeh are!"

Paul stood with shoulders squared, feet planted, as if preparing for an attack. He was taller and his confidence overshadowed Rory. Fidgeting now, Rory struggled with what to do next.

"She's ready to call it a night. Do yeh have a problem wit' that?" Paul edged closer to Rory.

"No. But I do have a fookin' problem with you. Not mindin' yer business." Rory shifted his weight from one foot to the other. Preparing.

"Rory, please," I butted in. "He's trying to help."

I regretted the words the instant they left my lips.

"Oh, you need his help now? What the hell is this?" Veins bulged from his neck.

"No, I'm just tired. I'm going to bed now. Please."

Paul slowed things down with a mellower tone, clear and steady. "You ought to be going now. I won't be leavin' this spot 'til yer gone." He stared Rory down. "It's been a long day. For everyone."

Paul remained composed, putting his hands in his pockets, but he didn't budge from his stance and held his eyes fixed on Rory's.

My heart throbbed in my chest. Rory might react emotionally and lash out; it appeared to be his only option at this point. I opened my mouth again, this time with more caution.

"Guys, please. Go home. Everything's okay."

I grabbed my things, again, and walked straight to my door without looking back. I wasn't sure what my plan would be if they stayed there, squaring off against each other. I pushed my door open and turned for a last look, like turning to see a car crash.

Rory sniffed, unimpressed, ignoring Paul to save his pride. "Yup.

I'll see yeh later."

He said that as much for Paul's benefit as mine, I was sure.

Rory glared at Paul and didn't begin walking until Paul started off too, back toward his car. Each of them set a similar pace away from my door.

As Paul left, he nodded good-bye to me with his mouth pressed to the side, as if to say, *Sorry that had to happen.*

I closed my door without giving either of them preferred acknowledgment, wanting to be sure they kept going on their separate paths.

I ran up the stairs to my flat, skipping every other step, and flew into my bedroom to peek out the window. Paul's car pulled out, moving into the light traffic of Bohermore. Down the sidewalk, Rory was walking, dragging his heels in a relaxed strut, moving toward the city center.

***

I hung at my window until Rory was out of sight. As I perched on the sill, my head rested on my arms as I gazed down Bohermore. A hollow sadness emptied my insides as I said goodbye to Rory in my heart. Every cell in my body was breathing Paul, and pain, like a vile sickness, twisted in me as our separation settled in and became real. I stared down the road, attempting to make him materialize. Maybe his car would appear if I tried hard enough. Maybe he would come walking up the road toward my flat.

A figure moved along the sidewalk, dark and blurry at first, and my heart quickened. I picked up my head for a clearer view. As it got closer, I recognized the bounce in the step and a smile spread across my face like the crack of dawn.

It was Michelle.

Grease from the scrumptious kebabs had already stained the brown bag. The wraps from my favorite shop were her chosen elixir to get me talking. With Paul and Rory long gone, in body anyway, her plan worked perfectly and together we caught up on the past few days. I inhaled my food as she went on about Declan.

She crammed her last bite into her mouth and spoke through it, firing crumbs everywhere. "He actually likes to read and stuff." She shoved a bit off her lip, back into her mouth. "Oh, and I saw some of his poetry too. It's really good."

My mind wandered as she gave me details, talking about how she didn't know what she was going to do after the school year ended and it was time to go home.

"So what *are* you going to do?" I asked when she was done.

"About what?" She tipped her head, flipping her hair out of her eyes. I noticed for the first time it wasn't perfectly straightened anymore. It had delicate waves throughout and even some…frizz?

"Well, your relationship, and having to go back home."

She looked up through her wisps and said, "I want to be with Declan."

My eyebrows shot up. Her family would never allow it. She stood on delicate ground.

"So, how? Will you have to move here or something, or will Declan follow you back to Boston? How does it work?"

I bit my lip. I was rushing their relationship without knowing why, but I felt like I needed an explanation. I was desperate to know how this sort of thing would play out.

"I've actually been thinking about that too. It's a no-brainer." She shrugged her shoulders. "I'm gonna stay here."

I leaned forward. "Are you serious?"

"Totally. Why not, Maeve? I'm happy here. Let's see—happy Galway, sad Boston, happy Galway, sad Boston." She used her hands like a balance scale.

I gathered up our trash and took it to the counter.

"I can't believe you would just *do* that." I stared out my kitchen window. "What will your family think?"

"Oh, they'd cut me off. Even more, I mean. Out of the family. A disgrace. That sort of thing." She picked her teeth. "But I have a little nest egg, like a cushion, tucked away for when I turn twenty-five. So that adds a little safety to the equation." Her foot shifted and hit my chair. The yellow stitching on the sole caught my eye. Her pine green Hunter rain boots had been replaced by black Doc Martens. "I like it here, Maeve. I really do."

I stared at her in disbelief. And then I looked again at her shoes, and her hair, and her smile—carefree, happy, *honest*.

Michelle had found her true self.

"Now you. Tell me everything! Did you find your castle? What about the Pirate Queen? And *Paul?* Tell me about Paul." She inched to the edge of her seat.

I grinned and blushed, and told her everything.

***

I woke to the persistent brightness of morning reflecting off every surface in my room. As empty consciousness turned to complex awareness, heartsickness took over my innocent bliss.

My mind cranked up to a marathon pace of thoughts from the previous day. What would have happened when Paul dropped me off if Rory hadn't been there? Would he have left or would he have made a plan for when we would see each other again? Or would he have come up? Now I'd never know.

And what about NUIG? I had class with Paul in two days. We'd go back to a charade of not really knowing each other, not having been through the most intense experience ever together. A sterile teacher-student relationship. What if that was how it would be? Maybe it really was only field research for him and I just so happened to be a really informative student.

I accepted that none of this would surprise me. What could I really expect anyway? He had a life carved out here and I was certainly not a part of his master plan. My thoughts went into dark places and I was beginning to sicken myself with doubt.

I dragged myself to the bathroom to splash water on my face, brush my teeth, and bring life back to my spent soul. That was when I got a really good look at the burn on my chest. Incredibly, it was much better. It didn't hurt at all and the redness and markings were almost all gone. A part of me wished for more of the wound to remain, to remind me that it was all real.

I leaned on the sink while I looked at my reflection in the mirror and gazed into my own eyes. At first, I thought I was looking into the eyes of a stranger, and then I saw myself clearly. I looked content. Comfortable in my own skin. I could see deeper into my own soul now, more than ever before, and I liked it.

The doorbell rang and I jumped a mile, knocking my wet toothbrush onto the floor.

Crap. I bet it was Rory. I wasn't ready to face him yet. I was too exhausted, in every way, and I didn't want to hurt him. He had been trying to make things better with us, probably. And it turned into a mess.

And *I* was a mess. Of course I still had Paul's T-shirt on and my hair was wild from sleep. I moved down the stairs, heart pounding, praying it would be Mr. Flaherty from the paint shop below.

I hurried down the open air corridor, running my fingers through my untamed hair and apprehensively pulled the door open. My heart stopped as I looked into Paul's face.

He was here!

Happiness lit me up from the inside, clearing my head of any darkness. But what did he want? His expression was so serious.

"Hi." I sounded more surprised than I wanted to and suddenly became self-conscious about my pajamas and messed-up hair. "Sorry," I said as I tried to straighten out the T-shirt. "I just woke up…ish."

He stood there, speechless, looking at me. He leaned forward slightly, like he wanted to come in. I raised my eyebrows at him to encourage him to speak and maybe tell me why he was there.

"Hi," he finally said. "Good morning. Or almost afternoon." He gave a weak half-smile. "I, uh, wanted to check on yeh, be sure you were okay." He sounded uncertain. "When I dropped ya off, things got a little intense with Rory."

"Oh. Yeah," I mumbled. "I'm good." I wasn't sure what to say either. "Thanks for helping me with that."

He regained his confidence as he stepped closer and held on to the door near my hand. "I really wanted to see you again." He watched me, with unshielded eyes. "We didn't have a chance to say goodbye properly yesterday and I, uh…." He stumbled on his words. "I couldn't stop thinking about ya."

He looked intently at me, waiting for a response. My heart jumped out of my chest. I hadn't stopped thinking about him either.

I pulled the door farther open and asked, "Do you want to come in for coffee?"

My own bold gesture took me by surprise as I prayed he would come in. Before I could finish the last syllable, he was entering the corridor and closing the blue door behind himself.

I had him in my space, my home. I couldn't believe it. I started to walk down the corridor, looking back at him, encouraging him to follow.

"This is my alleyway, basically." I filled the initial silence with mundane explanations and gestured around the narrow space that led to my door. "My flat is there." I pointed down the length of the passageway and continued to move toward it.

As I spoke, I felt his arm reach around my waist. He stopped me and turned me toward him, drawing me closer. I instinctively reached for his upper arms as if to hold him back but it turned into more of an invitation for him to pull me near.

He held me, looking down into my eyes and spoke with his glorious Irish cadence. "Maeve," he said in an enticing drawl. The words came from deep in his throat. "I dreamt of holding you all night." His embrace grew stronger with each word. "I worried yeh'd slip away from me."

He closed his eyes and dropped his head down near mine, brushing his face across my cheek without actually touching me, sending chills through my entire body.

"I thought I was losing my mind." He stroked the side of my cheek and pushed back my hair, causing my head to tilt and my face to lift toward his. He leaned down. I could hardly breathe.

I looked him in the eyes as he spoke, inviting him to come even closer to me. I felt his breath on my lips as he whispered, "This isn't right, I know it. I can't stop it though. I want to kiss you."

And in an almost silent whisper, he added, "Please...." and lingered there, waiting for me.

His words sent heated currents through my entire body. His "please" drove me over the edge and I responded to his touch and his words without hesitation. I tilted my face to bring my mouth closer to his, to invite him to kiss me.

And he did.

His hand moved around the back of my neck in an instant and his fingers ran up into my hair. Pressing me against the wall, he kissed my mouth and my face. He was powerful but still sweet and gentle, which made me want him more. I ran my fingers up through his hair to hold him to me with no intention of ever letting go.

His hands glided up my back and he lifted me. My weightlessness sent me soaring as tingles ran through me and time stood still. It felt so natural, so effortless, as we moved together. Lost in each other's kiss. I begged for the moment to last forever. He lowered me down onto the tops of his feet and his hands moved down my back and held my waist. Then he paused, his breathing jagged.

He tilted his head back as if to remove himself from temptation and I could see the effort of restraint etched on his face.

He took my face in his hands again and kissed me softly. Once. Twice. And then kissed the tip of my nose.

I took his hands and started walking backward, leading him toward my door with a mischievous smirk on my face.

"Coffee?" I offered.

Chapter Fifteen
Bohermore Cemetery

"*Are you crazy?*" Michelle shrieked with her eyes bugging out of her head. She was dying for more details about my surprise visit from Paul.

I jerked across the table and grabbed her hands. "Shhhh, not so loud!" I reminded her where we were, in the middle of Smokey Joe's. "It's not like that. Shut uuup! I'm already freaking out enough as it is." I begged her to tone it down but could barely keep a handle on myself. I bounced in my seat.

"Oh. Wow. This is huge," she went on, looking around suspiciously to be sure no one was listening in. Her indiscreet surveillance had the complete opposite effect, I was sure, and was bound to generate curiosity in anyone sitting within a mile.

"What are you going to do?" Michelle asked in a more serious, hushed tone. She bit around the nail of her index finger, considering my new "situation" with Paul. "But he's your teacher...." Her voice raised with the last syllable, along with her eyebrows, as she stared at me.

"I don't know what I'm going to do. I certainly won't take any more of his classes, I can tell you that." I gave a half-smile.

I couldn't stop myself there though, as much as I tried. My mouth kept moving and the words poured out. "He's all I can think about, Michelle. I want to be with him all the time." I stared at her, helpless. I was getting into something complex but I couldn't stop it. It was too late.

Michelle stared back as if I were speaking another language. She blinked at me, her jaw hanging in amazement.

"Holy crap," she murmured.

***

I snuck a smile to Paul as I entered his classroom and then kept my eyes down, finding my way to my desk through rote memory. Intimidating stares bored into my back, probably Fiona and Tish, and I made every effort to ignore them and appear normal.

As I sat down with exaggerated casual affect, I glanced over at them to say hi. They were watching me, as I surmised, and their expressions of suspicion shot fear into my heart. I prayed I was being paranoid. There was more than one Fiona at this school and Michelle had already put the fear of God into me, making me feel like the center of a scandal. Now I was sure I was wearing a plaque of shame for all to see.

Remaining falsely aloof, I said, "Hey. Are you guys making any progress on your papers?" They continued to look at me in silence. "I'm suffering major writer's block." I figured this might distract them from whatever they were scheming. My paranoia continued to grow.

Fiona finally spoke. "Yeah, I guess. A bit of a pain in the arse, I'd say. Too long really." She continued to watch me.

I forced myself to think positively and figured they were merely intrigued by my new look. I had finally transitioned to some practical Irish wear, more conducive to the weather and steel gray skies. I had black leather boots now, like hiking boots, and wore a dark, common wax jacket, made of a slick fabric for repelling mist and rain. I looked more like a local. Maybe they noticed.

Paul moved to the front of the room and placed his hand on the desk, moving some papers with his fingers. I looked everywhere but directly at him, which challenged every natural urge in my body. His fresh white oxford with the top button undone made his face beam, colored by fresh air and adventure.

"So, let's begin. We'll start with, em, let me see…." He shuffled through his papers. "We, ah, left off with the Iron Age, no?" He stumbled on his words, distracted. I flushed beet red from the idea of running my fingers through his hair.

If I looked directly at him my eyes would betray me and expose my wandering thoughts. Instead, I listened to the gentle cadence of his voice and fought my sharp pangs of jealousy any time he answered the question of another female student.

The minutes crawled by as I planned my swift, seamless exit from Paul's classroom. As the big hand crept toward the twelve, I gathered my things and bent down to fill my backpack.

Paul summarized some points, ending class and giving reminders on deadlines. I was ready to hop up and leave at the stroke of twelve when Fiona leaned in toward me. My bones become disjointed as a wave of panic melted my inner structure. With terror shooting out of my pupils, I looked at her.

She leaned in with precision and whispered, "Ya got an extra tampon in there by chance?"

Within an inch of incontinence, relief swept over me like a silk blanket. I had no idea how she was able to make me so tense and realized I had brought the panic on myself. I really had nothing to worry about.

"Actually, yes, I think so." I dug in the side pockets of my pack, still shaky and sweating from my near brush with exposure, and fumbled longer than necessary to find one. Finally, I found the damn thing and discreetly handed it to her, turning twenty shades of crimson.

"T'anks so much," she said as she wrapped her fingers around mine, holding onto my hand instead of the tampon. "Mum's the word, Yank. For him." She glanced at Paul, then took the tampon and made a beeline out of the classroom toward the loo.

My blood pressure sank to new lows. What the hell did that mean? A nervous quake moved through me as my inner voice tried to convince me everything was okay.

At that point, my stealth escape at the top of the hour had been thwarted and I inconveniently found myself the last to leave the classroom. The last, except for Paul McGratt.

Paul cut down the aisle of desks and walked toward me. His eyes were gentle but intense and I felt my joints become unhinged again.

He was Paul in this moment, not my teacher. I could see it in his gaze.

A new blush rose in my cheeks, blending with the previous shades, and I could only imagine how it must have looked to him—which of course, made it worse.

He stood with my desk between us as I swung my pack over my shoulder. "I want to take ya to Claremorris," he said, watching me for a response. "To help ya find your grandfather's home. Sure, we can't stop now."

I labored to piece my brain back together before I could respond.

"Yeah. I'd love that," My heart jumped right into my throat. I looked toward the door to be sure no one was watching. "You're sure?" I tipped my head and looked at him from the corner of my eye.

"Very. How about this weekend?" he asked as he put his hands in his pockets and leaned back onto his heels.

"Really?" I blurted, almost too eagerly. "Yeah. Definitely. Thank you."

"Great. It's a plan then," he confirmed as we started toward the classroom door. "I'll figure out the details and we can talk about it when I see you again. Which I was also wondering about." He turned to me with a boyish grin.

At the door, I joked, "Well, unfortunately, I'm super busy with a research paper I have to do for my Celtic History class." He rolled his eyes at me. "No, but seriously, I found some cool information on tribal markings. Trying to trace the ones from the dungeon and the bridge. I have to show you some of the stuff I found out. Like, enemy tribes and centuries-old conflict." We turned down the hallway toward Smokey Joe's, as if on auto-pilot.

I put on a plain face and casual air for the public, looking down at the floor as we walked. Although we kept a proper distance from each other, the electricity between us still buzzed me, sending a vibrant glow radiating from my cheeks without shame.

"Hey, you don't think Fiona could be the sister of that waitress from Westport, do you? She said the weirdest thing to me…."

As I glanced down the hall, my eyes were pulled toward the ominous figure of a woman standing squarely in the middle of the aisle. My face fell, turning sheet white in an instant. It was Patricia,

Paul's ex-girlfriend or not-girlfriend or…girlfriend.

She glared directly at us as if nothing else existed in the world. My words froze in my throat and I kept my gaze forward, trying not to flinch, while watching Paul from my peripheral vision. I continued moving down the hall in an awkward, robotic motion, with Paul next to me, as we fatefully walked toward her.

I moved to create more distance, physically and emotionally, between myself and Paul. I continued walking when we reached her, turning slightly to say a quick hello, acknowledging my recognition of her from our earlier introduction at Keane's Pub in Connemara. She kept her face fixed on Paul but her eyes followed me with an antagonistic stare as I passed. No reply. And then her eyes darted back to Paul.

My ears piqued as I heard her first and only word to him as he stopped to greet her.

"Really?" Her unimpressed judgment made it sting.

There was a pause and all I heard was the sound of my steps and the throbbing in my ears.

"It's not…." and his words got lost in the distance between us, which grew exponentially as their meaning sunk in.

***

Michelle's head shot up as I barreled into Smokey Joe's like a wreck.

"Come on. We gotta get out of here." The words flew out of me. "Please. Don't say anything. Let's get out of here, then I'll tell you everything. Come on." I was already speed-walking toward the exit as Michelle swept her things across the table into her backpack and caught up to me in a flash.

"What's going on?" she panted.

"Just keep walking," I begged. "Oh my God. Crap. Oh my God." Panic was rising in my voice.

"Oh no." Michelle's powers of perception kicked in. "Everyone knows? Do all the other students know? Holy crap. That was fast. What happened?"

My mind felt scrambled and blurred. Michelle's questions brought focus to the mess. "No, they don't know. Well, maybe one or two. I'm not sure. I don't think so anyway."

Michelle's eyebrows scrunched together and she slowed our urgent pace. "What then?"

"Patricia." I said her name out loud and then smacked my hand over my mouth while looking around to be sure she hadn't materialized somewhere next to me. "She's here. She saw us together."

"Crap! Let's get out of here!" Michelle grabbed my arm, practically lifting me out of my shoes as we ran off campus to hide in the shelter of the bustling city.

We found ourselves in Griffin's Bakery at our favorite table near the back. My shaking hands made it nearly impossible to drink my coffee.

"Well...." Michelle mused, "it's not like he hasn't been straight with her, about breaking up and all. She knows he's moving on. Right? At least he's been honest with her."

"I guess." I stared into the abyss of my cup.

"No, really. He told you he's moving himself away from her. So, basically, you're okay." She shot me a reassuring grin like everything was going to be fine. Then it faltered. "Well, maybe a little wrong. He *is* your college professor." But behind the uncertain smile her eyes were sparkling, because Michelle was a die-hard romantic and there wasn't anything more romantic to her than a forbidden relationship.

"That's not all."

"What do you mean?" The sparkle in her eye turned flat.

"I heard some of what he said to her. Like, it's not...what you think, or it's not...anything. Something like that." My stomach twisted. "And she was just so angry." I stared back into my coffee for guidance. Its reply was a swirling, steaming cloud of cream and confusion.

Patricia scared me. Her history with Paul sent chills through me. She had the power to end the ride I was on and all my newfound happiness would be over in the blink of an eye. And not knowing what Paul's first words to her were was killing me. Could he have written us off so easily?

Either way, the one thing I was certain of was my feelings for Paul. I couldn't just turn them off. There was no turning back. He filled my thoughts in every breath and the idea of being without him scared me. I could hardly stand to think about it. My throat tightened and a deep emptiness tore open inside me. I fought back tears to keep it all away. To keep it from happening.

Michelle grabbed a cab in Eyre Square and made me promise to meet her at McSwiggan's at eight. "I don't want you to be alone too long, Maeve. It wouldn't be good for you. Have a quick rest and I'll see you later."

Back at Bohermore, I dragged my battered body up the stairs into my flat. The kitchen called to me to have a cup of tea or a sit by the fire but I fell face-first onto my bed instead. The luxury of emotional control was long gone and tears poured out of me.

Eventually, I succumbed to the months of build-up. I cried for missing my grandparents. I cried for my mother. I cried for Rory. I cried for Gráinne Ní Mháille. I cried for losing Paul. It all poured out of me like never before in my life.

And then, I slept.

***

My nap went hours longer than intended and I woke up groggy and unsettled, having to race to McSwiggan's to make it there in time. Michelle was waiting for me in a dark oak alcove with a thick wooden table and cushioned benches. The pub was full of college students and the band was warming up with sound check.

"Hey. Sorry I'm late," I said as I peeled off my wax jacket and hunkered in. The line of shiny taps at the bar pulled my eyes along the rows and rows of pint glasses. My eyebrow shot up, considering the options.

"No prob. I just got here. Why didn't you answer me? I texted and called, like, fifty times. Snagged this table right up though. Score!" Michelle spread her arms out territorially.

I pulled out my phone to check. It was dead, again. "Damn it. This thing only lasts for like a minute." I shook it, hoping to generate more battery life. "It's crap anyway." I shoved it back in my bag. "So, where's Declan tonight?"

"Out with the guys. Slightly wounded that I made other plans, but he'll get over it. Girl time." She sang the last part and winked at me.

"So, any word from Paul?"

Ugh. Why'd she have to ask that?

"No. I don't really want to talk about it." I slumped on my bench, broken. "It's like, I thought I was finding answers, it was all coming together, and then the rug was pulled out. Everything fell apart."

"No, it hasn't. You can still do more. Even without Paul. He doesn't have anything to do with this. Find out more about her ring, or whatever that thing was that burned you."

Her words sounded right. But they weren't. Paul *did* have something to do with my visions. He had them too. I just couldn't tell her that part; it seemed too private, but he was totally connected to what was happening to me. And now he was being ripped away.

"I don't know what to do next. Go to Claremorris, I guess." The wind had been stolen from my sail and the journey had lost its luster.

Michelle tilted her head. "I know this is gonna sound weird, but have you ever tried to *make* an awake dream happen? Like start one yourself? Maybe you'd have more control that way."

"Hell no! No way! Are you sick?" I slammed my hand on the table.

"Just wondering." She raised both hands in innocence.

I sat up and looked into the growing crowd, watching the movement like a flickering fire. Make an awake dream happen? Was she crazy? But now I couldn't help but think about it.

"What should we order? I'm in the mood to try something new," I said. A strange sense of rebellion rose to the surface and made me feel fearless.

Michelle's eyebrows shot up. She drew in a breath but as she was about to speak, we were pushed deeper into our nook by people trying to find room to sit. We fought back, holding our space until we saw who it was. Declan and Harry were making themselves comfortable at our table, laughing at their own boisterousness in crashing our girls' night out.

Harry looked different tonight—more outgoing without his photo portfolio attaché, which otherwise seemed permanently connected to his body. My smile brightened to see him outside the walls of Smokey Joe's.

Declan reached around Michelle's neck and gave her a sweet kiss.

Harry leaned in to me in a similar way, saying, "I've got one for you too if you'd like," and he puckered up. I shoved him playfully as the band started up, filling the pub with lively music and energy.

The boys had ordered pints of Guinness before they found us and now set their glasses on the table. Harry said, "Okay, coin challenge. Let's see if you can float a penny on the head of me pint."

I wondered if it was even possible. Michelle and I searched for a penny, one that wasn't covered in dysentery, in hopes of beating the challenge.

The band picked up tempo with a beat I recognized and as I strained to guess the song before the singer began the lyrics, I was jolted back by a pint of Guinness. The sixteen-ounce glass of black Irish stout, with its creamy foam top dripping down the side, was being passed in front of my face. My mind jumped to the instant when creepy Fergal passed me a similar pint in Lynch's Pub and my skin prickled.

Terror rose in me as my eyes locked onto the glass. With enormous effort, I followed the arm and was met by Rory's smiling face. He laughed at me, knowing full well he had re-enacted a most heinous moment for me and his clever trick made me chuckle. I punched him and glared up, one eye squinted. "That was low."

"You know," Rory began, "that guy showed up at Lynch's Pub again, after the night I told him to get lost—rather forcefully I might add." He raised his eyebrows at me, knowing I would squirm. "Kept coming to the gigs looking for you, half drunk. Said he was one of me henchmen, workin' at keepin' you away from me." Rory shook his head, knowing it didn't make any sense. "Had ta give him a little reminder to fek off. Told him ya went back to the States." And he let out a laugh of sympathy for the guy, shaking his head.

"Well? Are ya gonna take it?" Rory wiggled the pint in front of me. His smile was so charming I couldn't refuse it. I took the glass and placed it on the table in front of me.

"Thank you," I said. "Wow." I was surprised to feel happy to see him, even after all the time I'd spent with Paul. Something about Rory still attracted me and I couldn't be freed from his pull. My head and heart throbbed with the implications.

"It's a rite of passage," he said.

"What?" I blinked my eyes to clear them.

"Yer first pint of Guinness. It's your true initiation into Ireland. I want ta be the one to give it to ya." He smiled an unfairly beautiful smile and I felt my insides melt.

"Oh. Wow. I didn't know that. That that was a thing." I stumbled over my words and felt dumb.

"Well, it is. Go ahead. Try it."

I looked at Rory out of the corner of my eye. "You're a troublemaker and I won't crumble under peer pressure." I smirked at him as I reached for the glass. "But, today, I will make an exception."

I brought the cold, heavy glass toward my mouth. Time stood still as everyone at the table stopped talking and stared at me. No one wanted to miss the moment of Maeve having her first pint of Guinness.

I brought the glass to my mouth and took a sip but made no progress because the froth was so thick. I had to tilt the glass further than expected and the creamy top sloshed all over my upper lip. As I swallowed a large gulp, I returned the glass to the table, landing it with a loud thud and looked to everyone for their approval. They laughed out loud as I took my time reaching for a napkin to wipe the large foamy mustache off my upper lip.

"I'm impressed," Rory stated, nodding his head and pursing his lips. "Yeh're like a pro. And on yer first time." He gestured toward his own lip to let me know I missed a little foam on mine.

I licked at my upper lip and got it, this time a little more self-conscious as I thought about the kisses Rory and I shared. A revealing blush heated my cheeks, annoying me.

Rory took my arm and leaned in close. "Hey, I'm sorry about the other night. And everything else. I didn't mean for it ta go down like that." His voice was low so only I could hear. "Ya mad at me?" He bent his head and gave me sad puppy eyes.

The pull from the depths of his eyes was strong and I looked down at my glass for safety.

"It's okay. I'm sorry too." I took the risk to look him in the eye again. Ah, jeez, shouldn't have done that. His pupils were wide, inviting me in.

"Hey, I thought you were headed to England." My redirection was genius.

"Ach, sure, England can wait. I got some new business to tend to here." He took a sip from his pint. "I'm happy to see yeh." He playfully pushed his knuckles into my shoulder. "Glad ya made it back safe from your adventure trip, unscathed." He tipped in closer to me. "I know I was a jerk. Pushin' ya away and all. I shouldn't have tried ta end it with ya like that. I was stupid."

I sucked in air and straightened.

"Will ya gimme another chance? I'd like ta see you again." His lashes fanned me as he waited for a reply.

I hesitated a second before answering, testing my emotions. Rory was sweet. He was apologizing. And there was no denying I was still attracted to him...but I wanted Paul. Nothing could change that. Not even Rory's pouting lip and big, hopeful eyes.

Paul was gone, though. It could never work. She had come back for him.

And Rory was right here.

But he wasn't good for me.

"I can't, Rory." I shook my head and took a small step back. "I need time to figure stuff out. I'm sorry."

His mouth pursed with resolve like he'd expected that answer.

"Maeve! Maeve! Look, look, look, look, look!" It was Harry, vying for my attention. "The penny!"

Everyone was staring at his pint as a copper penny tilted in the foam and sank to the bottom of his glass.

"Ohhhhh! Yeh missed it!" he whined.

But everyone's half-shut eyes and twisted lips proved I hadn't missed a thing. The penny had sunk instantly.

I turned my attention back to Rory as he said, "Okay. Well, no harm in tryin'. Might try again too, so...." He wiggled his eyebrows at me with a grin, then gestured toward Eugene, who was hanging with the band. "Well, I should probably go. They might be needin' me."

He held me hostage in his warm gaze. I swear he did that on

purpose.

"Enjoy the rest of your pint. It means something. Don't let it go stale now." He kissed my cheek and disappeared into the crowd.

I continued to stare into the sea of people, trying to follow his form, and finally turned back to my friends. They stared at me in a freeze-frame of open mouths and shocked eyes.

"What?" I said defensively. Then I grabbed my pint and took a long, deep drink from it, landing it back down on the table with a loud clunk. I wiped my foam mustache with the back of my hand and asked, "Who's up for a nightclub tonight?"

***

The sun shined on my face, waking me from a dead sleep. I wondered if the thumping in my head was from the paint shop below, remnants of the nightclub beats, or a reminder of my first acquaintance with Guinness. It was well worth it though. Kept me distracted from the reality that didn't spare a moment before crushing me now.

Thoughts of Paul with Patricia sent sharp pains through my chest. I wouldn't see him in class for another day and figured he'd probably ignore me anyway. I considered for a brief moment going to NUIG to hang around and see if I would bump into him. The shudder that reverberated through my body was enough convincing that it was a bad idea.

Coffee, though. *That* was a good idea.

I dragged myself down Bohermore, shielding myself from the bright sunshine as I followed the aroma of dark roast right into the city center.

What was I going to do now? I didn't want to do any of my Pirate Queen search without Paul. That sounded so dumb but I couldn't help it. Not only because he could "save me" in my visions, but also because he believed in it with me. Fully. He was a part of my journey and belonged there.

I sat on a bench in Eyre Square, watching the water splash in the fountain around the majestic sails.

I was ready to go home. It was over. I failed.

My throat constricted at the thought, but I couldn't do this. Who was I kidding? I was the girl from Boston who couldn't leave her own backyard. Lost in dreams, but no reality. I wasn't as powerful as I'd been beginning to believe. I was the same girl as when I started.

I had something though. The ring. Gram had the ring. I guess that counted a little. But I knew there was more to be done, more to discover. I just couldn't do it. I was tired. And scared.

The thought of my visions haunting me again back home made me sick. I sat up at the thought. And what would Mom think? She'd raised me to be strong, to confront danger, not to run like a rabbit just because her would-be boyfriend couldn't confront it with her.

My head turned on instinct like I was being watched. A figure, a man, passed behind the fountain as soon as I looked and I waited to see it come out the other side. It never did.

My neck hairs bristled, sending chills up the back of my head.

Damn it.

I jumped up and ran toward the fountain. I went around the side where I saw him and circled the pool. He was gone. I scanned the pedestrians for anyone odd and saw a strange, hunched man heading up toward Bohermore.

I grabbed my bag from the bench and followed.

Courage coursed through my veins as I felt myself standing taller again. My heart accelerated and my resolve hardened. Screw it. I was going to do this. With or without Paul, I was going to finish it.

I picked up my pace to a near-run.

Then I lost sight of the disheveled man altogether, like he disappeared into thin air, and my pace slowed as I scanned the area. He'd been following me, watching me. My mind was turning again, considering my next moves.

With the sun in my eyes, I squinted to clear my vision and saw a red car driving down Bohermore. The double flip of my heart proved that I hoped, foolishly, it might be Paul.

I strained to get a clear view of the car, sunspots blurring my sight. It was a long shot but my breath stopped anyway. I watched as it got closer, as if it held my future in its hands.

It slowed and swerved into a space on the side of the road, almost hitting the curb. I froze. Paul jumped out and walked directly toward me with determination.

My bag fell from my hand and hit the ground in a splat. I stood solid without a flinch.

He was coming toward me. His eyes pierced into mine, holding me to my spot. His handsome features were crunched up like he was ready for a fight and his pace moved him like a freight train. I braced myself for impact.

He threw his arms around me, picked me up and turned with me to absorb the force. His face softened and with no concern for being seen, he kissed me. He lowered me down and kissed me again.

"Hi," I said as I caught my breath and looked into his anxious eyes, wondering if my feet were even touching the ground.

"Hi," he whispered. "I found yeh." He smiled and kissed me again sweetly.

"Yeah, you did." I beamed, so happy to see him.

"I've been looking for ya since last night," he said. "I needed to see you, to tell ya what happened. Where did you go?"

His lost eyes looked wounded, like I'd abandoned him. I immediately felt awful about avoiding everything, but I had feared the worst and escape seemed the best route at the time.

"I'm sorry. I freaked out a little, I guess. I went out with Michelle. I didn't know what else to do." I looked helplessly at him, remembering how lost I had felt.

"Oh, well that's good. Michelle's good." He paused. "I wasn't sure what you were thinkin' and I...." He stumbled on his words. "I worried that maybe yeh, I don't know. I'm just glad I found you." He looked at the ground and then back at me. "Will ya walk with me? To talk?"

His eyes searched mine, as if I might say no. Like maybe I hadn't been freaking out about losing him for the last twenty-four hours. Worry lined his brow. "To the cemetery maybe?" He tipped his head up the road.

I nodded, waiting for my voice to catch up. "Yes."

We walked in silence for the first few minutes, a safer distance from each other now, looking into shops and watching cars pass and then Paul broke it.

"That was God awful." He ran his hand through his hair. "Jeez, I'm surprised I wasn't throwin' pebbles at your window in the middle of the night like a school boy. Sure, crossed my mind more than once, I admit."

"I wasn't sure if I would see you again. You know, out of the classroom." I watched my feet.

"Maeve, I'm in this with you now. I told ya that. Nothin's gonna change it." He bent his head to see my face. To see if I believed him.

I smiled. Tears sprang up out of nowhere and I kept my eyes open without blinking, hoping the moving air would dry them out before one took a fall.

"There are some pretty famous people buried in the cemetery, you know." He checked me again. "I'll show yeh some of the gravesites. I've looked around in there before. It's fascinatin'."

My face relaxed into a gentle smile as he went on but I didn't hear a single word he said. I was simply happy to be with him.

"It dates back to the 1800s, when Victorian graveyards were popular, elaborate, and expensive, which explains all the big Celtic crosses. Around World War I, they got smaller, less 'Celticky-looking,' as you would say." He jabbed me with a teasing elbow.

"Hey! That's what you get for putting me on the spot like that!" I chuckled at the memory of Paul calling on me in his class, asking me to describe the ancient well I saw in Doolin. I was also aware he was avoiding what we really needed to be talking about.

We reached the entrance, marked by a granite slab reading *Reilig An Bhothair Mhoir*, carved in old Gaelic script with the translation printed below: *Bohermore Cemetery*. The sea of Celtic crosses drew me in and the array of squared-off plots and ornate crypts created an intricate maze.

We snaked through the endless paths, reading carvings and personal tributes. I stopped to examine an old, weathered, Celtic carving on one of the oldest stones in the yard. Paul stood with me and reached for my hand, without a word or even a glance, and held it.

His energy entered my body through his warm hand and his firm grip assured me of his feelings. Relief moved through my body like morphine.

"I told 'er about us." He spoke toward the garden of crosses.

I looked up at his face and he turned to me with his lips pursed to the side and his eyelids low. He cared about her.

"It was hard," he said. "She made it difficult at first, accusations of inappropriate conduct, but she couldn't deny the truth. It was time for us ta move on."

His face squinted like he was in pain, as if he were separating himself from something that was once good, something he would always cherish.

"I'm sorry that happened," I said.

"It had to happen. I guess I'm glad it's done now." His weak smile shared a sense of relief. "She asked about you, after seeing us together in the hall." He hesitated.

"About me?" Panic constricted my throat.

"She wanted to know who yeh were to me." He looked into my eyes for reassurance before saying another word. "She wanted ta know if we were together." He hesitated, proceeding with caution. "I wanted to be honest with her. Not mislead her in any way."

I held my breath, waiting a year for each word he said.

"I told her we were." He paused. "After that, she left."

I still couldn't remember how to breathe, especially when he shot me his heartbreaking boyish smile.

"I hope that's okay," he added, dangling, waiting for a reply.

Word formation proved more difficult than necessary.

"Yeah. It's good." I exhaled, releasing the breath I had been holding since the day before, feeling the toxins of doubt leave my body. "I actually thought you told her something very different."

He took a step to the side. "Like what?"

"I don't know. I heard you say something like, it's not…anything, or it's not…what you think. Something like that."

"No." He moved close enough to me that I felt his breath. "What I said was that it's not appropriate for her to be there. Sure, what'd she think would happen?"

My hand covered my eyes. I'd let my insecurity create a scene that left me in broken pieces when actually I had a fighting chance. "Do you think she'll make any trouble about it, you know, the school thing?"

"I don't think she would. I hope not anyway." He squeezed my hand.

We walked out of the cemetery and turned down Bohermore.

"Hey!" A loud, confrontational voice barked at us.

Paul's hand automatically tightened on mine and my eyes darted toward the sound.

A disheveled man, the stranger from the fountain, stood in our way.

"I thought that was you." He slurred, pointing at me with his brown-bagged bottle. "Good ta see ya left Mac alone finally. Let him get back to his right callin'. Sure, he can't ignore his clan fer'ever."

It was Fergal.

I pulled on Paul's arm. He squeezed my hand and spoke to Fergal.

"Hey, man. You've got the wrong person. See ya 'round." And he moved himself between Fergal and me, ushering me away.

"Wait. Who are you?" Fergal turned on Paul. "It ain't right. I can feel it. Yer with her. Sure, it can't be true." He shook his head in disbelief and followed behind us, scratching his face in confusion. "I said, wait! How's this possible?"

Paul turned to him, sheltering me behind his back.

"I don't know who the hell ya are, buddy. But you better stay t' hell away from us. I'm warning ya." The look in his eye was sharp and piercing.

Fergal's hands went up. He hopped back, exaggerating his fear. "Whoa, whoa. Payback's a bitch, I know. I'm sure I'll feel the burn from the two of you." He stopped in his tracks. "I just can't believe it. We didn't see this comin', not in a million years."

His arms still raised, the blotchy tattoo on his wrist exposed itself again. The tribal Celtic design jumped at me and made me gasp. The same symbol that was carved into the cell wall in Gráinne's dungeon. And the bridge. Panic surged through me. He was an enemy.

Paul pulled me close and cut through the traffic to the other side of the road.

"Come on. That guy's nuts. Keep walking, all the way to town. I don't want that lowlife knowing where ya live."

We sped toward town and I kept looking back to be sure he wasn't following us. "Paul, I'm scared. I know him. His name's Fergal and it's like he knows me or something. He keeps showing up, following me, saying the weirdest things. He knows Rory too. Kept calling him a defector."

"Shit."

"What? What's wrong?"

"That explains a lot." He rubbed his chin. "Sounds like clan stuff. Feuds. Ancient politics."

"His tattoo. I know it, from Grace's dungeon and the bridge."

"I saw it too. It's his clan marking." He looked back.

Fergal had stopped and was leaning against a wall, looking up at the sky, mumbling.

"What does this have to do with me?"

"I don't know yet. I want you to keep far away from him, though. If you ever see him again, run."

Chapter Sixteen

Ruined

Flying down the N17, destination: Claremorris, I pulled out the folded paper my grandfather slipped to me when we said our goodbyes and I studied its unique markings. It revealed vague directions on a simple hand-scrawled map. Roads were generally named after whatever they led to, so I was looking for the O'Malley farm on the Drumlin Road, no formal address.

My grandfather had said, "Be brave. Be strong." I dismissed the words at the time but they lingered now in my ears.

My crumpled map depicted a three-way fork in the road leading out from the town center. It was decorated by my grandfather's unsteady hand, with a cross representing a church and a W for a pub he recalled but couldn't remember the name of. It wasn't much to go on, but hopefully would be enough.

"We're almost there," Paul said as he reached over and held my knee. "Ya look worried."

"I'm nervous," I admitted. "It's like I'm opening a treasure box with no idea what could be inside." I worried about what I might find. Maybe danger. Maybe worse.

This was likely my last shot. I didn't have any other leads except this—finding the O'Malleys and learning about the history of the Pirate Queen and her effect on the family. Discovering a way to stop a centuries-old curse.

As if pushing through a dome, we entered what felt like a time warp. Claremorris. The ancient architecture, dated buildings, and nostalgic signs must have been the same ones when my grandfather lived there: Old World and traditional.

Leaving the car in a lot, Paul reached for my hand and held it as we walked. I worried at first about being seen holding hands with him in public, but something about this small town made it seem safe.

"Coffee? Before we get too lost?" Paul gestured toward a large pub on the corner.

It was an old building, probably one of the original structures in the town. The pub had a stone front and its black signage ran the length of the building. *Michael Warde Pub,* it read in gold Celtic lettering. Two large, vintage Guinness signs on either side of the door generated a steady pull into the building that couldn't be resisted.

Padraic, the barman, wiped our counter and placed small square napkins in front of us as we waited for our coffees and cheese sandwiches.

I leaned into Paul and asked, "Paw-rick? I've never heard that name before."

"Irish for Patrick," Paul whispered.

"What brings you into Warde's today?" Padraic asked with a wide smile. "Haven't seen yeh in here before."

Paul replied, "We're visiting. Maeve, here, her grandfather grew up in Claremorris."

Padraic looked at me and said, "Is that right, lassie? Where ya from?" His aged eyes were still bright and inquisitive.

"Boston," I said. "My grandfather left when he was eighteen. He's never been back."

"Ah, yes." Padraic nodded. "That's how it was. So many left to find a better life in the States and then never returned. All got rich there, ya see." He looked off into the distance, likely remembering his own family members who left. "What's the family name?"

"O'Malley." I watched for his reaction.

My family name carried more interest in this part of Ireland than I ever realized it could and now my heightened awareness of that fact noticed his expression come to life.

"Ach, Christ, the place is overrun with O'Malleys," He laughed as he swatted me on the shoulder. "Yer family here, lassie," and he made his way down the bar to tend to other patrons.

I looked at Paul, wide-eyed, and he returned a hopeful smile.

"So what's our next move?" I asked with growing impatience. I pulled out my grandfather's map and smoothed it on the bar. I used my small square napkin to remove any moisture or crumbs from the area and left it, crumpled, beside the map. I shoved the rest of my cheese sandwich in my mouth, ready to press on.

Paul moved his finger across the map, along the main road toward the fork, and said, "So, let's head back out on the main road and look for that split. It's tough t' know distance but we can...."

As Paul strategized, Padraic returned, intrigued by our cryptic map. "So yeh've got some idea of where yeh're headed then?" he asked. "That's sure a rough map to be usin'. Can I have a look-see?" He tilted his head sideways to get a better perspective of the markings.

"Does any of it look familiar to you?" I asked, watching his face for a reaction.

Padraic turned the map to have a better look and burst out laughing. "Yer grandfather drew this map?"

"Yes, from what he could remember anyway."

"Well, he's got a shockin' good memory, sure. Yeh're at the heart of it." He beamed as he pointed to the W in the center of the map. "In Warde's. See the W on the map? See the W on your napkin there? Sure, you're in Warde's Pub, lassie," he teased. "I'd say yer grandfather likely sat in that same spot."

He waved an open palm across my location and the idea struck every cell in my body. A huge smile spread across my face. Paul reached around my shoulder and pulled me close.

Padraic drew his finger along the line on the map that led to the forked road and his finger moved left, following the arrows all the way to the X that marked the spot. He stared at the map and the tip of his finger without looking up.

"What?" I became impatient.

He continued to stare at the page and I could swear his hand began to shake.

"What?" I persisted.

He looked up in slow motion. Pale. Beads of sweat formed on his brow. "I'm sorry, lass. You should na go there. It's not safe. Them O'Malley's was cursed somethin' awful."

I grabbed Paul's hand.

Paul's voice was low and serious as he said, "What do you mean, Padraic? This is her family you're talkin' about."

"I know, lad. I'm sorry." He shuddered. "Please, do not go." He turned to me. "Especially the lass. Don't go. It's not safe for them O'Malley women. Cursed. Surrounded by death."

Paul stood up gathering our things. "Come on, Maeve. Let's go."

Padraic grabbed my wrist on the bar and leaned in near me. His eyes were wide and his voice low like a whisper. "I don't know what you'll find there now. If ya *do* go, please, may God be with ya."

***

"So I guess we keep an eye out for a right turn?" I eyed the map again for reassurance, trying to ignore Padraic's warnings.

I envisioned a traditional white-washed cottage, probably with a modern, cost-effective tin roof instead of a thatched one. But inside, that's where everything would unfold. Warm embraces from family long missed. Tear-filled eyes swelling with joy. Endless questions and cups of tea.

The road led us toward farmland and stone walls. Cows spotted the fields and sheep moved together far off on the hills. The smells in the air changed from those of a bustling town to earthy, farm-like odors of silage, mud, and manure.

My eyes moved across the horizon and I saw it—what looked like a lone mountain in the distance, with a sharp drop off on one side and gradual slope off the other: a drumlin.

"Oh my gosh!" I pulled on Paul's arm as my heart rate accelerated. "Look! It's a drumlin, right?"

"Definitely. That's a drumlin." He looked at it and then back at the map. "The Drumlin Road! It must be around here somewhere."

He picked up the pace at the exact time I did.

We flew along the path, looking for a right turn after every stone wall or land plot we passed. Excitement mounted in every part of my body. We were getting closer to my grandfather's home. My nerves fired sparks within me, reminding me of Padraic's words that internally battled my own hopes and expectations.

Paul noticed the apprehension in my slowing pace.

"Hey, what is it?" he asked. "Are yeh okay?"

"Yeah, I think so. Nervous I guess. I can't believe we're here, so close." I let my air out through pursed lips. "I'm a little overwhelmed. I need to slow down for a sec."

We were close, I knew it. I could feel it in my bones.

I stopped walking.

"Do you think he was right? About the curse?" I looked back toward town. Toward safety.

"Could be old superstition. I mean, that guy spent his entire life in this small village. 'Tis all he knows." He reached his arms around me and hugged me close. "We just need to see for ourselves."

I breathed into his jacket, finding my courage again. I didn't want anything to happen to us, to Paul. I'd dragged him into this.

"I'm putting you in danger. Again." I pulled back from his embrace.

"Oh, not this again. Please, Maeve. Stop. I'm in this now, whether you like it or not." He squeezed me again and took my hand, turning back to the map.

Maybe we were close to ending this thing, for good.

"Come on. It's time to find where X marks the spot." Paul released me, holding my shoulders as if to steady me.

A gathering of spruce trees marked a right hand turn down a lost, lonely lane. Lined with more spruce on either side, it meandered out of sight. Paul and I looked at each other and then checked the map.

Goosebumps covered my forearms and chills raced on my upper arms and thighs. This was definitely the turn, the road that would lead us to the X on my grandfather's map.

There wasn't a soul in sight. No cars, no houses, no one.

We kept walking along the desolate road, wondering if there would be anything to be found at this final stage of our journey. As we were about to question our orienteering skills with our roughly sketched map, a small cottage came into view. It appeared neglected with overgrowth around the perimeter stone wall and rusting farm equipment decomposing in the front garden.

A small Jack Russell Terrier came racing out, barking an alert to its owner. Once it got us in striking distance, it aggressively paced around our feet, herding us until its reinforcements arrived.

The front door of the cottage flew open, hitting off the exterior wall with a bang, and an elderly gentleman stepped out, calling to the dog, trying to stop its incessant barking.

"Jack, be done with it. Jack, ya pain in me arse, ya. I'll have yer guts for garters! What in hell are yeh barking at? In Jazus' name…." and as the final words left his mouth he saw us, standing in the road outside his property. "Sorry," he called to us. "Mind. The bitch thinks she's in charge."

I turned to Paul, shocked. He discreetly murmured, "Common term for a female dog on a farm. No disrespect." My shoulders relaxed again as I reached down to the female "Jack" to let her smell my hand. She kept her distance and continued to herd us with the confidence of a much larger dog.

"Hello," Paul called out to the man who was hobbling over to us. Dressed in a worn, aged suit, he looked out of place for a farm. "Our apologies for bothering yeh. We're looking fer the O'Malley farm. Do ya know of it?"

The old man wiped his hand across his nose and sniffled as if to clear his thoughts. He jimmied his rusty, crooked gate open and stepped into the road with us. His close proximity brought with it a stench that curled my hair. The man was pungent, with filth on his face and hands that was crusty and thick. Cakes of grime had settled in around his ears and in lines on his neck. As he spoke, it was clear he was missing most of his teeth, and the ones he had left were rotten beyond repair.

With squinted eyes, he looked down his nose at us. "Who's looking fer the O'Malleys?" He inspected us up and down as if we might be government agents.

"Actually, I am." My voice sounded mousy at first. "My grandfather grew up here and I'm looking for his home and his family. I'm Maeve O'Malley, and this is my friend Paul."

"Yeh won't find 'em here, lassie. No sir-ee. They're gone. All gone...." He rambled into the open air, scratching up his nose with his thumb. My suspicions about his mental stability were confirmed the more he spoke. "Mad they were. Sure. All gone mad. Won't find them here, sure you won't," he jabbered on.

Paul tensed and his shoulders squared up; he was getting annoyed by the man's disrespectful responses. "We don't understand what you mean. Can yeh tell us if we're on the right road? Is this where the O'Malleys lived?"

"Ah, sure 'tis. This is it. Just down the way." He gestured with his arm further along the road. "You won't find much. Gone they are. Only bones now, bones are all you'll find of them. Mad she was. All them lassies, mad they were." He shook his head in disgust.

A chill ran up my spine and I shuddered from the man's words and his appearance. I had no idea what he was talking about but I didn't like it.

"Well, thank you." I strained to remain cordial. "I think we'll head that way to take a look around." I nodded to Paul to go, to get away from this lone, wild man. Long periods of solitude had apparently taken what was left of his sanity.

"The woman, she gone mad, like the rest of 'em. The man and two sons buried her and left. Done buryin'. Never to return. Bones is all yeh'll find." He scratched into his matted hair and down the back of his neck.

Paul asked, "What do yeh mean, bones? Where will we find bones?"

"Nothin' left of the house. But the cemetery, at the end of the road, that's where they is now. O'Malley boneyard. All that's left. Nothin' to find here. All that's left...." He continued scratching and kicking at Jack, the terrier, who was still pacing around us as if we were her prized cattle.

I grabbed onto Paul's arm and moved away, thanking the man for his time as he continued mumbling and remembering things from his past in waves of lucidity. I considered dementia or Alzheimer's as Paul and I removed ourselves and continued down the road, away from the man and his Jack Russell.

I looked back to be sure we weren't being followed, and the man was carrying on an animated conversation with himself and his dog as they made their way back to his house. Relieved to be moving on from that interaction, I squeezed Paul's arm to release the stress that had built up inside me.

"Okay, that was unfortunate. What was wrong with him?" I asked.

"Yeah. That was bizarre. He's been alone too long. No one checking in on him. Sad, really."

"But do you think there was any truth to what he said? I'm worried now," I muttered.

"I don't know. Let's keep going, see what we find. It's the only way ta know." He seemed grateful to at least have a heads-up in case things weren't as perfect as I had hoped they might be.

We turned a gentle bend in the road and the spruce trees reduced their numbers to open up a better view. There was a lone structure on the right side, a home. Paul glanced sideways at me with anticipation and took my hand as we got closer. His firm grip offered needed security, but then it tightened in response to the open view.

We were approaching a ruin.

The abandoned cottage remained proud, as if it had nothing to hide, even with its collapsed roof and weedy overgrowth. Its thatch roof was rotted and had fallen in with chunks of wet, blackened mash breaking away from all sides. In such a state of disrepair, the elements were saturating the interior of the house, decimating it to rubble. Weeds grew out of the broken windows and the exterior white-washed walls were peeled down to bare cement and stone.

Despair poured over me like I was viewing the corpse of a deceased loved one. The condition of the O'Malley home sent sadness into my soul—mostly for my grandfather, but also for me. The disappointment was crushing.

I looked to Paul and his forlorn expression sent heavy tears rolling down my cheeks. He was equally devastated by the sight.

"I'm so sorry, Maeve. Terrible shock t' see the house like this." He hugged me, allowing me to dry my tears on his jacket.

"It's not what I expected," I murmured, wiping my eyes. "I never expected it to be this bad."

I turned toward the house again and looked at it, this time from a different perspective. "I still want to see it. All of it."

I accepted the fact that no one was there. I wouldn't be meeting any relatives or having any reunion hugs, but I still wanted to explore what they left behind. Any clues of their existence, of who they were, were now my new focus.

"Okay. Let's get a little closer then. Come on." Paul found a spot on the outer stone wall where the overgrowth allowed passage and he climbed up and over, reaching for me to offer assistance.

In the muddy yard, we had to avoid cow patties, proof the local cows had the run of the place. The splatters of manure marked the yard like landmines and I put in considerable effort to avoid them— not without noticing Paul's entertainment.

As we got closer to the cottage, I smelled the damp, moldy scent of rot warning us it wouldn't be safe to go in, but I was determined to at least have a good look through the windows.

We peered in. As if time had frozen inside the cottage, furniture was still in place, plates and bowls sat on shelves in the armoire waiting to serve up the next meal, and piles of rotting linens and pillows spilled out of the broken loft area.

I yearned to go inside and take a plate or a cup for a keepsake but the structure didn't seem stable enough for safe entry. I admired the peeling wallpaper that exposed countless layers of paper beneath, each displaying the fashion trend of its era.

"It's fantastic," I said. "I love it. I can feel the O'Malleys here and all their energy. It's still an amazing visit." I looked at Paul with a satisfied smile.

"I'm glad. I like it too." He returned my smile with equal contentment.

I leaned farther inside the window to be sure not to miss any details and took photos at various angles. As I reviewed some of my shots, in one of the pictures I saw an ornament hanging on the inside wall near the window. I hopped up on the sill again and leaned even farther in, wriggling on my belly to get a better look. There it was, hanging right next to me. A wooden cross. I twisted my body, reaching in at an awkward angle. Paul grabbed on to my legs to be sure I didn't fall in.

"What is it? Can you reach it?" he called in.

"Yes. I...almost...got...it." I strained to speak as I contorted. "Got it!" And I pulled the cross into my chest as I wriggled my body back out of the window.

We examined the cross in my hands. It was hand-carved with a simple rendition of Christ on it, along with a few additional symbols. It was worn but the wood was polished from years of being held and cared for.

"It's a penal cross. This is the type of crucifix Catholics would sneak around with when worship was forbidden, to avoid being caught by the English," Paul explained. "See the short arms of the cross? So people could easily hide it up their sleeve on the way to secret mass."

I admired the beauty of the crucifix.

"I didn't realize there was a time when the Irish had to sneak around like that." I turned the cross over in my hands to observe its every detail. "I want to bring this home to my grandfather," I said. "Maybe he'll recognize it."

"Yeah, that's definitely a cool find," Paul agreed. "It would have been lost forever in the ruin. Looks like it's carved from bog oak." Paul ran his fingers down the length of the cross. I wondered how many people before him had done the same.

Closing my eyes, flashes of my lost family filled my inner vision. Faces, farmers, church-goers—full of chatter and welcomes for all. Now only silence. Where were they?

"Want to search for the cemetery?" I blurted out of nowhere. That was where I would find them.

I had to keep looking. Whatever "curse" Padraic was referring to, I knew deep in my soul he was right. It was the same curse that tracked me in Boston. And my mom. He was talking about the Pirate Queen. Constantly stalking me, hunting me. And it wouldn't stop. She would keep going. If I didn't figure it out, stop it, it would end me.

"Do yeh really think the boneyard exists?" he wondered. "I kinda thought that guy was talking shite, total gibberish."

His right eyebrow lifted as he contemplated the possibility of the existence of the cemetery and I watched his eyes widen as he imagined it.

"It's our last shot. What else is there?" I glanced down at the crucifix and then toward the thicket of spruce at the end of the nearly non-existent lane. Weeds had overgrown any gravel or cart-wheel marks that had once been there, but the deteriorating stone walls on either side led the way.

If the graveyard existed, there might be markers, with names and dates. I wanted to know, for my grandfather. But if Padraic was right, and worse, the old man, then we could be walking straight into danger. Or a trap.

"End of the road," the wild man had said. I considered the double meaning of his words, shaking my shoulders to release the rising tension.

We hopped back over the cottage's stone wall at the same spot where we had entered the yard and found sure footing again on the old road. We walked toward the lonesome glen of spruce.

Overgrowth and broken hedgerows led us toward a low, ancient stone wall, the border into sacred land. We entered the dense shelter of the graveyard. Each spruce dripped in ivy, creating an insulated, shadowy world.

As my senses adjusted, I was struck by the silence, the stillness, the sorrow in the air. We moved a few steps deeper into the cemetery and I froze, staring at the worn, aged gravestones, scattered about like a battle site.

Tipped and tilted in random directions, some stones had Celtic crosses on them while others were limestone slabs, broken, fallen, or leaning haphazardly. The ones on the ground were covered in moss, recognizable only by the impression left in the earth.

My posture slumped. This was all that was left of my grandfather's family.

Paul put a gentle hand on my shoulder. "It's not unusual for a family plot to fall into disrepair. Especially when they don't live nearby anymore."

"I've never seen a cemetery like this, except maybe in a horror movie or something."

Paul edged his way farther in, straining to read the markings on the closest gravestone. I zipped my jacket right up to the neck and hunkered down into it.

We stepped deeper into the graveyard, feeling like the first intruders on the ground for what must have been decades. The spongy earth absorbed our footprints and the air awoke, creating misty swirls around us.

I stood in the center of the cemetery. A muted sunbeam shined through an opening left by a broken spruce branch, and the foggy light illuminated some of the stones at the back. Each gravestone had every form of my family name: O'Malley, O'Mháille, Máille, Malley, Meally.

"I'm surrounded by my family," I whispered to Paul. "I feel like they know I'm here." I swallowed hard, pushing against the rising nag in my stomach.

Off to the side, a mound-like structure poked up higher than the rest. It was covered in earth and ivy.

"What's that?" I pointed, scrunching my nose as I moved toward it. Paul followed with equal curiosity.

Overgrown with vines and moss, it was a burial chamber a crypt of sorts. Rounded at the top and crumbling from the pressures of time, it still held its secrets safe. The back side was almost fully covered with soil and overgrowth but the front stonework was clear. It was a door.

Paul pulled the ivy and weeds from the front of the burial mound, looking for carvings and more details. He exposed the thick stone-slab door sealed against time and eternity, with a capstone at the top—a plaque.

We leaned in, pushing against each other for the best view. I couldn't help but scan for a way to open the tomb. The carvings on the plaque were weathered from the elements, and Paul began to trace the engravings with his finger.

"It's numbers I think, and a few letters. Not much." He continued to concentrate while mumbling his interpretations.

I jittered with anxiety, waiting to hear what he was seeing.

"I think it's a date, 15-something. This thing dates back to the

1500s." His astonishment rang out in his voice.

"That's incredible." I stepped back with my hands folded in front of me. Part of me felt like I'd looked at something that should remain unseen.

"G…R…A." Paul looked up at me, fingers still on the plaque. "That's it. Just G-R-A."

"Grace?" Her name stuck in my throat.

"Or *'Gra.'* Love." He glanced at me in thought.

An urgency lit up my insides, sending adrenaline through my veins, rounding my eyes. Paul took a double-take at my face and tipped his head to one side, eyebrows drawn together.

"What is it?" he asked.

I searched for my voice. My mouth was dry, trying to move, but nothing came out except the vapors of rising fear.

We shouldn't have come here. I knew that now. Every muscle in my body wanted to flee. I wanted to grab Paul and run.

I didn't want to die here. My grandparents wouldn't be able to bear it. I didn't want Paul to die here. It would be my fault.

But I felt it in every space of my body. I knew. This was it.

Then the wind came.

Swirling mist blasted my hair in every direction. I reached for Paul through the turbulence, stepping toward the spot where he last stood, but I was alone in the squall. I was always alone.

My outstretched arms groped for him anyway—and reeled back in surprise when I touched him. I reached again and this time latched on, his hands reaching for mine with matched desperation. He pulled me into his chest, sheltering my face from the wind with his arms clamped around me.

"Maeve!" he yelled against the force of the gusts. "Are yeh all right? I've got ya." His voice was broken and diffused by the thrashing wind but I heard enough to know, somehow, he was with me.

"It's my dream!" I cried back to him. "She's coming!" Her wrath was mounting in the air, in my soul.

The gusts pounded all around us, firing twigs and leaves at our faces. My arm lifted, shielding my eyes as I squinted against the blasts, trying to see Paul.

Could he really be here? In my dream?

Ice went through me. If Paul was here, in my awake dream, he wasn't safe. Had I played right into her hand? The burn on my chest throbbed to life, confirming imminent danger.

Paul continued to shelter me, moving his back toward whichever direction the force came from most. We squatted down, leaning into each other, as the wind pelted us with debris.

Then it stopped.

Everything fell into silence.

I peeked, one eye open, as Paul opened his. We grabbed at each other, checking to make sure neither of us was hurt, pulling bits of leaf and twig from our hair and straightening one another's jackets.

"Holy Jazus! You okay? That was crazy." He helped me to my feet.

"It's not over. That's how it always starts." I looked around, my knuckles at my lips, turning toward any small sound.

Paul stared at me, face frozen, waiting for something to happen. His breath was loud and fast.

Then the unnatural silence was shattered with a blood-curdling shriek. A battle cry of centuries of suffering. I covered my ears for fear of losing my sanity to it.

We turned toward the cry and there she was, Gráinne Ní Mháille, sword drawn, defending what was hers—the crypt—against enemy intruders—us. She held no recognition in her steely gaze, only vengeance and aggression, teeth bared as she barreled toward us.

Paul spun me around, tightening his grip on my hand as he yelled, "Run!"

We flew over weeds and rocks. He moved faster than I could and tugged me along as I faltered and stumbled with every step. The high-pitched cry rose up behind us, stiffening my spine. She was nearly on us.

My foot tangled in the creeping ivy and I went airborne. My hand yanked from Paul's as I fell.

"Paul!" I screamed as I splatted into the vines.

I jerked onto my back to see Gráinne just above me, still screaming a wretched, twisting screech. Blinded by the bright light reflected from her sword through the mist, my arm shot up to shield my eyes. Cowering in a defensive position, I kicked against the ground in an attempt to retreat further.

From behind, Paul grabbed my shoulders and pulled me into his knees.

"This is it! I've seen this before!" He tugged me up to standing as Gráinne's figure shadowed us. She raised her sword high over her head, tears streaming down her face. Paul shoved me with all his force, launching me away, yelling, "Run! Now!" as he reached up to stop her swing of the blade.

I stumbled away, hunched over, looking back over my shoulder.

He reached for her raised arm to stop her from slashing her sword at him. Burned by the metal cuff on her wrist, he recoiled, pulling his hand into his chest as she prepared for a second swing.

Her eyes seared into him with hate, as if accusing him of causing her grief. His resistance and fight fueled her anger further.

She swiped and struck him with a powerful blow from the hilt of her sword, knocking him to the ground. I turned back in horror, realizing his prophecy was coming true. I barreled back toward them with incredible speed as she raised her sword again, ready to drive it through him.

"No!" My shriek was fueled by terror as I threw my body between them. "Stop!"

"Maeve! Get out of here!" Paul pushed, trying to get me out of her range, but my arms flew up to guard him from her and the crucifix sailed out of my sleeve into the ivy.

"Stop!" I stared her in the eyes, ignoring the tears pouring out of both of us.

She tilted her head, looking into my face. Her mouth twitched as her eyebrows drew together. She glared back at Paul and then to me again, her grip tightening on the hilt.

I reached for the crucifix on the ground, keeping one arm raised up against her. As my hand wrapped around it, I yanked it up and held it at her in defense and pleaded, "Gráinne! Please!"

Knocked back by an invisible force, Gráinne stumbled as if the air had been knocked out of her—like she'd seen a ghost. She stared at me and then at both of us, lost.

She reeled back and dropped her sword. It wasn't the crucifix but our faces, particularly Paul's, that shocked her. She took another step forward and recoiled again, then crumpled to her knees.

Behind her, at the mound grave, I spotted a form—someone struggling. It was a man chained to the tomb, pulling frantically at his bindings, trying to get to Gráinne.

Fear shot through me like hot lightning. Who was that?

Gráinne continued staring at us, pleading with her eyes.

"What do you want?!" I cried, pouring a lifetime of anguish into the question. "What are you looking for?"

I stared into her face, searching for the answer I'd been seeking my entire life. One that something deep within me confirmed I already knew.

Gráinne looked back toward the tomb. She reached for the man, who could only be Hugh, as she held the ring on her necklace. My burn hit a new level of agony, like molten lava. She moved toward him but was held back, as if she were chained too. They were kept apart, eternally.

"Come on!" Paul pulled me up and held me tightly, and we ran toward the stone wall. I looked back toward my Pirate Queen; she was still reaching for Hugh, turning to me like she'd been abandoned. Her eyes were wide with shock. She dropped to her knees as her face fell into her hands.

A sharp glint of golden light shot out to me from the ivy near Gráinne's form and I squinted at it. The long metal object, hiding in the vines, begged for my attention and refused to be ignored. My hand covered my mouth as I gasped, realizing what it was.

Paul lifted me over the wall like I was weightless and Gráinne's image started to fade, becoming part of the mist. I watched the distance grow between the cemetery and us and felt I was leaving something behind. Everything.

The brightness of day outside the shroud of the cemetery punched me like being woken in the midst of a vibrant dream.

We were safe. But she was still lost.

The only evidence of the encounter was my pounding heart and shaking limbs…until Paul dropped to his knees, wincing in pain.

"What is it?" I fell to my knees, nearly knocking him over with my awkward attempt at helping him.

He cupped his left hand under his right, cradling it carefully while inspecting his palm.

"I'm burned." He looked around for something to ease the pain. "It was 'er wrist. She had a metal cuff of some kind. It burned me." He sucked air in through his clenched teeth.

His fascination outweighed his discomfort as he examined the wound. We studied his palm, seeing the faint designs in the reddened skin. Celtic art forms filled my eyes and danced in my brain—symbols of the O'Malleys, the same as the burn on my chest. They were a perfect match.

I looked at Paul, eyes gleaming, and met his similarly awed gaze. But his sparkle faded as he stood up and glared at me, fire in his expression.

"What were ya thinking, running back toward her like that?! Yeh could've been killed! We have no idea what she's capable of!" His face reddened with anger. "Jazus, I'd seen all that before, and sure, she killed me in my dream, every time! Ya shouldn't a—"

I reached up and grabbed him behind his neck and pulled him down to me, kissing him mid-sentence. He resisted at first, still angry, but then his tense body slackened.

"I know," I murmured, staring into his deep blue eyes. "I couldn't let that happen."

"Still. It was crazy." He rubbed the back of his sore hand.

"But what you never realized is, you always woke up when she was *about* to kill you. You never actually died." I smirked. "Because I was there, every time, and saved you." I poked him in the arm with the look of the devil in my eye. But it was true.

His lips turned upward in a slight smile and he leaned back. "Okay, right, so you saved me, I reckon." He nearly choked on the words, and I looked to the ground to avoid his intense gaze. He took my hand and squeezed it until I lifted my eyes to his. "Thank you, Maeve."

The corners of my mouth turned up as I hid under my lashes.

With a grin he added, "And, sure, I liked yer move with the crucifix. Very horror movie-ish."

And we burst out laughing at my ridiculous attempt to ward off Gráinne Ní Mháille's ghost with the relic. But not before I gave him a swift punch in the arm and a good shove for his teasing.

Paul led me back toward Claremorris town center, tucked tight under his arm. Our determined pace took us past Jack's farm and out onto the bigger road, clearing our heads and returning us back to civilization.

"I'm sorry," Paul blurted out. "I definitely underestimated yer dreams. I mean, the burn ya got last time was intense, but this time, she was actually attacking us, both of us. Scared me half to death." He looked at me with surprise in his eyes. "How the hell have ya endured these for as long as you have? I'm not sure I'd like to see another one of them."

I sighed, grateful someone finally understood, and rubbed my hand over my face.

"I guess I'm just used to them. But it's different now. I don't feel as afraid anymore."

My own words made it truth. I wasn't being haunted or stalked, like I'd always thought. I was being recruited. She needed my help. Our help.

"She wants something from us." I paused, chewed on my thumbnail, and then added, "Did you see the man? Chained at the tomb."

"I did. It was Hugh. I'm sure of it. I've seen him before, in my dream. And there's more, Maeve. My mother always told me I was connected to Gráinne, but I never guessed she meant this close."

Exhausted and starving for more information, I looked to him for answers, a missing clue of some sort, anything.

"Let's get back to Warde's, see what else Padraic knows," Paul said, whisking me toward town.

***

Padraic cleared our spots at the bar as we painstakingly removed our outer layers, material and emotional, as if returning from battle. We pulled ourselves onto the stools, assessing our aches and bumps through each movement.

"What in the divel happened ya?" Padraic said with a surprised smile. "Ye look wrecked. A shockin' sight." He leaned into us, squinting one eye. "Sure, ya went there, didn't ya?"

He saw it written all over us; shock, dirt, drawn faces. Fully windblown and battered, we looked nothing like our first impression.

Padraic continued wiping the bar through force of habit. "So, tell me, what happened?"

"Not quite what we expected," Paul said calmly as if we were returning from a routine, boring family visit.

"Hmm, whatchamean?" Padraic froze, waiting for details.

"The cottage was a ruin. Nothing left. Roof caved in."

"Ah, 'tis a shame. I'm sorry ta hear that." Padraic took back to rubbing the shiny counter with his rag. "Been abandoned for some time now."

"We found the family cemetery, near the ruin," I interjected. "An old graveyard for the O'Malleys."

"Yeh're talking 'bout the boneyard, sure." Padraic nodded his head, like he knew it well.

"What do you know of it?" Paul put his elbow on the bar and his hand on his chin, looking for details.

"Those O'Malleys was cursed. Poor souls. Illness of the brain, I think. Sorry, lassie." His eyes deepened, filling with sympathy, as he turned his full attention to me.

"Do you know what happened to them?" I asked, feeling a hollow despair rising in me.

"I can't be sure exactly, but there was plenty of chatter 'bout it some twenty, thirty years ago. Eddie and Margaret was their names, I think, farmers. They had two sons and a daughter."

"It was Brigid. Their daughter. She was the one." A voice came from the far end of the bar, a dark alcove.

Padraic turned to the man, his eyes widened. "You remember them, don't ya, Donal?"

"Brigid was in me class, near graduation. Sure, I remember."

The man got up from his stool and lumbered into the light. His large, muscular hand held his pint as he moved closer to us, dwarfing us in his shadow. Paul and I were speechless as he approached.

"She wasn't crazy. Not cursed. Lovely girl. But she had them visions. They sent her to the laundries, thought she went mad. No one could stop 'em." He looked down into the froth of his pint, lost in the memory of a girl he once knew.

Padraic watched Donal with a heavy gaze. There seemed to be more to Donal's story that Padraic knew. Maybe something between Donal and Brigid.

Padraic turned to us and added, "Margaret, the mother, lost her wits after they took Brigid. Poor Maggie was found dead in the cemetery soon after. Rest her soul."

He crossed himself as he spoke of it.

"Eddie and the sons, they buried 'er in the family plot and up an' left. Haven't been seen or heard from since." He lifted his chin at Donal, looking for any additional information.

Donal pursed his lips and nodded.

I turned to Paul as my eyebrows rose. I wasn't the only O'Malley in Ireland who had visions of the Pirate Queen. He gripped my knee under the bar, acknowledging his understanding too.

"There was an old man with a dog at a home near the O'Malley's…." I started to inquire.

"Ol' man Rooney," Padraic stated with confidence. "He's stark ravin' mad, that one." Then he took on a more serious tone and added, "'Twas loss of his wife and then time that stole his mind." He shook his head and pursed his lips, showing his disappointment in the outcome of poor Mr. Rooney.

"I think he needs to be checked on."

"Ach, sure, he's better off on his farm with his beloved dog than he'd be in some old folks' home, rottin' away. There's no two ways about it. And, sure, the church ladies check on him each and every Sunday."

Padraic shook the image from his head.

He pulled another pint for Donal, who had moved back to the end of the bar, content in his solitude. Paul drew me back with a gentle squeeze of my knee and the easy lull of his voice.

"So, yeh're not alone in this. Goes way beyond you and yer mum."

He watched me closely, waiting for my reaction to the news.

I stared back at him without emotion, eyes blank.

Brigid? Sent to the laundries? I wondered where she was now, how old she must be. Fifty maybe. And visions. She had them too. She was like me. And she was the same age when they got bad.

My thoughts swarmed as Paul waited for me to say something and finally, all that came out was, "What are the laundries? What does that mean?"

His face fell and eyelids drooped. He looked down as his mouth set a hard line, processing his response.

I burned with curiosity, waiting for his reply.

"I don't want to tell you this. It's not good." He rubbed the tops of his thighs.

"Just give it to me," I demanded. "What is it?"

"A while back, years ago, girls…girls who were unwed mothers or promiscuous, were sent to live with the nuns. Considered a shame to their families. Sometimes, they would send mentally unstable girls as well," Paul explained.

"Why do they call them 'the laundries'?"

"That was their job, ta do laundry for local businesses, hotels, clergy. They worked hard. No pay. And they couldn't leave. Weren't allowed. Like institutions, prisons in a way."

I sat, mouth agape. "So if a girl got pregnant or was a little boy-crazy, she was sent to prison?"

"I suppose you could say that, yes. Back then." His head tipped down. "Ireland was very rigid, very Catholic, proud. There was no tolerance for breakin' the laws of the church." He hesitated. "Sounds preachy, I know. It was only in recent times the truth about the laundries came out: neglect, abuse, human rights violations basically. They've all been disbanded now, I think."

"And Brigid was sent to one of those places?" I couldn't imagine how that could have happened.

"If she was considered 'mentally ill' at the time, then yes, she would have been sent to one. It was the way. People didn't understand anything about that sort of thing. They might have thought she was possessed."

My hand shot to mouth. "They would have thought I was possessed too." The realization that my fate could have been the same as hers made my bones freeze in fear.

Paul's mouth squeezed to the side as he huffed, knowing it to be true.

"Well, I need to find her," I thought out loud. "To know what happened to her, if she's okay. And tell her she's not crazy."

I stared at Paul, searching for a clue where to begin. His eyes held mine with a steady gaze as he took my hand.

"I'll look into it," he said. "One of my colleagues knows a good bit about the history of the laundries." He tightened his grip on my hand.

I hopped off my stool, took his face in my hands and pulled him down to me. I kissed him. Hope swam behind my closed eyes, swirling with warm color. "Thank you."

Chapter Seventeen

Family Tree

My fingers tightened around the phone and my body went numb as my senses constricted. All I heard was a high-pitched tone that droned off into the distance. Sound soon came back, but this time it was the familiar voice of my grandmother as she spoke calmly. She was explaining and consoling as my senses reawakened and freed themselves from their tight vault. I found my voice at last.

"I'm going to come home right away, Gram."

The words passed my lips without hesitation but their bad taste left a sick feeling in my stomach and a tightness in my throat. My head was spinning with the sudden change of events.

Her words made real two situations in my life. First, I had to leave the most exciting and defining time of my life, and second, I had to arrive home to the most devastating and heartbreaking time of my life.

Joey was dying.

They'd found a spot on his lung. He'd put away his pipes and tins of Sir Walter Raleigh for good that same day. It made sense now why it was getting harder to hear him from across the room these past several weeks.

The reality of the situation took a while to sink in. I refused it at first and believed it would go away if I wished for it to, but as Gram spoke more about his deterioration, the true terror set in.

I had to get home.

***

Michelle groaned in the jewelry store. "I can't believe you have to leave. I don't want you to go." She leaned in over the glass case to get a better view of the rings, but looked back to me, biting her lip. She was heartbroken by the news. She knew how much my grandfather meant to me. But that didn't stop her from begging me to stay.

"What am I going to do when you leave?" she whined.

A heavy emptiness bottomed me out. I wanted Michelle to be in my life forever. Not knowing when I could return made it even worse.

I thought back to Paul's face after I shared the news. He was the first person I told. His crushed eyes couldn't hide behind his supportive response. It was like he was hit by a bus, and everything just crashed. It haunted me.

Michelle and I continued to peruse the array of Claddagh rings in the jeweler's case. We had promised, when we first met, we would get matching rings.

"What are *you* going to do?" I asked as she tapped the glass over a ring she liked.

"I'm going to be a writer." A satisfied smile crossed her face and she watched for my response.

"What?"

"Yup. Declan and me. We're going to write a book about the visions. His sister's, yours. Don't sue me! I promise not to use your real name in it." She poked my ribs and then looked right at me. "What are *you* going to do?" It sounded like a loaded question.

"I'm taking my exams early. It's all arranged." The words nearly got stuck. "I'm not sure when I'll be able to come back. It depends on my grandfather…and then my grandmother. She'll need me."

She tilted her head and asked, "No. I mean, what about Paul?" She slid a ring on her finger and examined it.

"I don't know." My bottom lip quivered.

I replayed the moment again in my head, when I first told Paul, and cringed. He'd hugged me sympathetically but I saw in his eyes he was feeling the crush of equal loss.

Michelle looked down and rubbed her arm. "So, Rory was at NUIG the other day. Weird, right? Was he there to see you?" She handed me a ring to try on.

My eyes darted to her and widened. "What are you talking about? Rory was at NUIG?"

Michelle pulled her chin back. "Oh, I thought you knew."

"Wait! That's a big deal, Michelle. You didn't think to tell me! When?"

I stared at her, waiting for more information. I couldn't imagine any reason for him to be at NUIG.

"Like, last week some time," Michelle's voice shook. "Don't be mad. I just forgot."

"What if he was there to make trouble with Paul? This could be bad." A feeling of dread hatched in my belly. "Do you think he was there to see me?"

"Um, yeah." She avoided eye contact. "I'm pretty sure he saw you. At Smokey Joe's, you and Paul were going through the coffee line. Rory was at the far corner, with his hood pulled up around his head, watching you. And, okay, glaring at Paul."

Her forehead wrinkled with worry, likely realizing what she witnessed was not normal and that she probably should have reported it a lot sooner.

"I was sure he must have gone over to you but I was distracted by Declan and Harry and didn't see what happened after that." She bit her thumbnail.

I closed my eyes and rubbed my temples.

"I'm sure it's fine. Come on," she said. "Let's go to the Spanish Arch to open our ring boxes. The swans will be happy to see us."

***

I had to say a proper goodbye to Rory. He deserved it, and we needed closure. I also needed to know his true feelings and intentions. I was secretly hoping for an explanation about why he'd been at NUIG.

At Lynch's Pub, we chose a quiet table at the back. Rory complained of his sloppy pint, leaving the glass wet on all sides. My coffee smelled burnt and they only had milk, no cream.

Rory's face was sullen and his body slouched in his chair.

"You didn't do anything wrong." I reached for his hand across the table. "You changed everything for me. Made me believe in myself."

"I was bad for you." He looked down at his glass. The collar of his combat jacket was pulled up around his ears and his long lashes hid his eyes, making my heart flutter just like when I'd first met him. He'd been everything I was looking for when we first met: rebel, rule-breaker, slacker.

But things changed for me during my time in Galway. I wasn't lost anymore. That was clear to me now, sitting across from him in the place where I'd first laid eyes on him.

"So what are yeh gonna do when you get back to Boston?" Rory asked as he made brown circles on his coaster with the bottom of his wet pint glass.

"I just need to be with my grandfather. To tell him everything." I looked at Rory, realizing he didn't know the half of it. "I'll be telling him a lot about you, you know."

Rory's eyes brightened and his head picked up.

"I bet he would like me." He grinned. "I bet he'd have a pint with me." He thought about it and then added, "Actually, he'd probably hate me. Yup. He'd hate me. Wouldn't have a choice. Prob'ly kill me."

My eyebrows scrunched together and I tilted my head.

"Sure, he'd know I was bad for ya."

I pulled his hand toward me as I reached across the table to hug him.

"One last kiss?" He held me close to him.

"Rory!" I pushed off him and landed back in my seat.

"Just a kiss, Maeve." He pouted.

His lower lip glistened from his pint and his eyes invited me in.

"So, what are *you* going to do?" I snapped my gaze away from his. "Is England happening?"

Rory laughed noncommittally and said, "Nah. Sure, the lads in Mojo would miss me somethin' awful." He inspected his pint, contemplating his next sip. "I'm gonna see about the clan thing. You know, chieftain. Can't avoid it anymore."

My face brightened. "I can't believe it."

"What, I'm not chieftain material?" He squinted sideways.

"No, not that. I just didn't think you were gonna go for it. You know, face it so soon." Something shifted in me. Like a light turned on deep within my mind. It made me see him differently. And myself. What *was* that?

He wiped his lip after a slug of his pint. "You could say things got a bit real these past couple months. I mean, you…and you know, Fergal."

My eyes jolted onto his at the sound of Fergal's name. "What about Fergal?"

"Turns out he's from an allied clan of the MacMahons. Been allies for hundreds of years. There's a way old feud, for land, power, territory rights basically. He's one of the rebel fighters, holding grudges you might say." He huffed into his glass at the absurdity. "I kinda feel obligated now to keep the Macs on top, keep his clan under our thumb. Wouldn't want the likes of him takin' over."

My hands were wringing under the table. Fergal creeped me out and I wanted him to stay far away from anyone I cared about. Maybe that was why Rory was at NUIG recently.

"Hey, Mac!" the barman called over to Rory. "Ya left these, last gig. Catch."

He hurled a fuchsia sweater and first aid kit. Rory caught them, one-handed.

"Thanks, man."

Okay. A girl's sweater and wound care. I was at a loss.

Picking at my napkin, I said, "Michelle saw you at NUIG recently. I know they have bands in the college bar sometimes." I felt the quake in my voice and prayed Rory couldn't hear it.

He pulled his chin back and looked at me like I had two heads. With a huff he said, "Wasn't at NUIG. Haven't been for months."

He picked up his pint glass and gulped down what was left of it in one chug. He wiped his mouth with the back of his hand, acting cocky, and started to get up.

"I gotta go. I've got a gig later and Eugene needs help settin' up for it," he said. "Thanks fer coming, Maeve. Means a lot." He reached for my hand and started to walk toward the door.

I heard sincerity in his voice but was distracted by his denial about NUIG and his abrupt attempt to exit. I was speechless.

Outside the red door of Lynch's Pub, Rory hugged me. His arms wrapped all the way around and held me close. I heard his breathing through his chest. He took my face in his hands and brought his mouth close to mine. Time stood still as he gazed into my eyes. He kissed my lips softly and then pulled back. His unexpected goodbye kiss was sweet and tingled my fingers and toes.

His hands remained on my face as he continued to stare into my eyes. Something turned in his gentle gaze, something more intense, and his hold on me tightened. He pulled me into him as he kissed me again, this time with a hunger and a passion that surprised me.

"Rory!" I pushed at his chest but he continued to hold me. "Rory, stop. What are you doing?" I wriggled to pull away from him. I shoved him in the ribs and he keeled over in pain.

Holding his side with both hands, he looked up at me, wincing. "I'm sorry, Maeve. I didn't mean ta." He spoke through clenched teeth, his accent stronger than I'd ever heard it. "You've got a hold on me. I cannot break it." Small spots of blood seeped through his shirt as defeat clouded his eyes.

"Rory, you're hurt! What happened? Let me see that." I reached for him.

'It's fine. I'm fine." He pushed my hand away. "Really. Not a bother. I'll tend to it inside." With misty eyes, he reached back for my hand. "Let me know how things go for yeh back in the States. And, Maeve, I'd like ta see you again. Ya know. If ya come back."

Heavy tears rolled down my cheeks as we said goodbye. "Thank you, Rory. For everything."

"You're welcome," he said with his classic arrogance and flashed his brilliant blue-eyed smile. He turned back to me and added, "Hey! An' keep them dreams in check, will ya? Quit makin' trouble for ev'ryone." He winked at me, and walked back into the pub.

***

My final time with Paul was what I dreaded the most. He had swept me off my feet so unexpectedly and became deeply woven in my story. And now I had to leave him. Saying goodbye didn't seem like an option.

The only thing I knew for *sure* was I had to get home to Joey. He'd spent his entire life without answers. I needed to tell him every detail, every connection to Gráinne Ní Mháille and how it all fit together for his family. He deserved this.

***

Paul insisted on driving me to Shannon. It gave us precious time together, right up until the final minute. I couldn't help but think a quick break and a hop on a bus would have been easier though.

The silence in the car made the impending torture more real. I wondered if he had a lump in his throat anywhere near the size of mine.

At the airport, we sat in the car, each waiting for the other to make the first move. Paul reached into his bag and pulled out a brown paper package. Placing it on my lap, he said, "It's nothing fancy, but I want you to have it."

"What is this?" Surprise filled my voice as I inspected the package.

He looked at me with eyebrows raised, waiting for me to open it.

The parcel felt solid and heavy. I tore the brown paper across the front. It was an old, weathered book. Actually, a *really* old book. Irish history or heritage, or something. My eyebrows scrunched together as I turned my gaze to Paul.

"It was my mother's," he said. "She gave it ta me on my eighteenth birthday, so I'd know about my family lineage. There's stuff in there I think you'll be interested in. Really. I want yeh to have it."

"I can't take this!" I started to hand it back. "It looks like a family heirloom."

"Please." He pushed it back. "I want you to have it." His eyes were intense, convincing me to take it.

I looked at the book and flipped through several yellowed pages to show my appreciation. I wondered what part of such an old book would be remotely interesting to me, but it was from Paul, so I loved it.

"Thank you." I hugged the book to my chest.

Paul smiled at me with closed lips and warm eyes and moved to get out of the car. He pulled my bags out as I gathered my things from the front seat and he had my door open before I could.

He helped me out but stood right in my way so I couldn't move.

He trapped me in his gaze, and I tingled from his closeness.

Reaching for my face, he spoke gently. "I love you, Maeve O'Malley. Always have."

My voice was lost and my vision blurred. Totally caught off guard. I'd been so distracted with thoughts of home.

Misinterpreting my silence, he backpedaled. "I'm sorry," he said, "I didn't mean to do that to you. It just came out." His vulnerable eyes pleaded.

His face fell, like he was in pain or grief. I pulled him close and kissed him. My raw feelings for him rose within me like a wild tiger and took the form of words.

"I love you, Paul McGratt," I said with certainty as I smiled into his eyes.

And together, our hearts soared, but at the same time, they broke.

I had to leave him.

Holding hands, we walked into the airport together. He put his hand through my hair one last time and leaned his head down to the side of mine.

He whispered, *"Grá mo chroí,"* and kissed me gently on my mouth. My heart ached as I tore myself away from him.

***

In my narrow window seat, the drone of the engines and garbled message from the pilot about weather, altitude, and travel time filled my ears, but my mind had shifted from my destination—Boston— right back to Galway and Paul. The unexpected, almost violent shift caused a sense of vertigo. My heart sank into a deep abyss as my plane took flight.

As each mile grew between us, my heart broke proportionally. I couldn't bear it. The pain was sharp and vivid, as if a physical wound festered in my chest. Tears streamed down my face, soaking it. Too many to catch. Too many to hide. I let my head fall back and the salty sorrow poured out.

Every moment of my Irish journey came back to me in a flood. I allowed it to flow freely as I relived every emotion.

My swollen eyes finally fell closed, against every effort to keep them open. A flash of yellow light tried to unlatch my lids, but with no luck. Its efforts became relentless and I finally pushed my eyes open to narrow slits, annoyed at the incessant reflection.

The radiant light filled my senses and my eyes burst open as I stared at Gráinne's spectacular sword lying secretively in the ivy of the boneyard. I dropped to my knees to reach for it as it offered itself to me, showing off its every glorious detail.

The Celtic designs and handsome craftsmanship skillfully seduced me and I couldn't resist the temptation to touch it. Avoiding the sharp edges, my hand slid along the fuller blade, toward the crossguard and past the cruciform hilt and, as if by instinct, each finger took its turn to curl around the leather bound grip.

It took both clasped hands and all my strength to raise the weight of the sword up for closer inspection. I turned the weapon back and over, to view it from all angles and moved it through the air in slow, delicate strokes. I was comfortable with the new extension of my body and felt its protection and power course through my veins.

"Chicken or beef?" The offer of food brought me back as the flight attendant instructed me to lower my tray.

I glared at her and she recoiled in surprise. Her wide eyes and scrunched eyebrows slapped my manners back into place and I apologized, my cheeks burning crimson, for my rude behavior and told her I had been lost in a dream.

"No worries, loov. Chicken or beef?"

I couldn't eat. "No thank you," I said. "Just tea please."

The vision of the sword was still clear and I could feel the shadow of its weight in my hands. Gráinne dropped her sword in the cemetery during her attack and I knew it lay there waiting for me, hidden in the vines. I wanted it.

I fidgeted in my seat, considering my next move with this new information. I couldn't be perfectly sure of the sword's existence but it felt so real. Paul would want to know about this. Thoughts of him burst back into my heart and caused a burning ache that made my shoulders roll in and my hands move up to my chest for self-consoling.

I reached for the book Paul gave me. It was the only thing I could touch and hold, to try to feel close to him. I flipped through the aged, worn pages and smelled time and history within them. Handwriting on the inside of the front cover stole my attention and I took a closer look at it.

There were two different inscriptions, one much older looking than the other. The first was difficult to read as the script was faded and fancy, Old World scrawl in blotchy ink. It read something like, *Passed to me by the 1st Earl of Ulster from his father, Lord of Meath. His Lordship*…I couldn't make out the rest and impatiently moved on to the newer script.

The more recent writing was easier to decipher and I glanced through it: *Dearest Paul, The DeLacy family has a long and rich heritage. My father, Walter DeLacy, passed this book down to me, after several generations before him, and I am now passing it to you. Please keep it safe and forward it along to your next*….I froze.

I read it again.

And then again.

I flipped back to the front cover. It displayed a coat of arms with a purple, fire-breathing lion in an attacking position. It was the coat of arms of the DeLacy family.

I jumped to the beginning of the book, which had several pages illustrating a rich family tree titled *Crann Teaghlaigh*. The name Hugh DeLacy popped out at me from several locations on the family tree. I scanned for the time period between the 1500s and 1600s and found Hugh DeLacy, born, died from unnatural causes, with the side bar note: *murdered by the MacMahon Clan*.

My mind spiraled beyond control. Paul's mother was a DeLacy and shared this book with him so he would know his family lineage. He gave it to me so I would know he came from DeLacy descent.

Shivers quaked through my body as the reality of our connection became clear to me. I looked back at the pages of the family tree and stared, absorbing the information they shared. And there, between the pages, a corner of fresh parchment stuck out. I pulled and it slid from the book and landed in my palm. It was a note from Paul.

My Maeve,
I'd nearly forgotten this book existed. My research led me to it, just before you

had to leave. It holds more significance now than ever before.

You had to go before we had time to fully understand all of this.

I don't know what you are thinking now. But I do know our meeting was not by chance.

Hugh DeLacy was my great, many times over, uncle. I am connected to Grainne's story more than I ever knew. And so I'm connected to you, as I've always known. With all my being,

Paul

Our bond was not a mere coincidence. And he knew it.

He was a descendant of Hugh DeLacy, Gráinne's lost love. Paul was connected to Gráinne, just as I was, through time and centuries of sorrow.

Gráinne recognized Paul in Rockfleet Castle when I made a complete fool of myself trying to ravish him. God. And again in the cemetery where he confronted her and was burned. She saw his face once I stopped her, and she knew him as part of Hugh.

My thoughts were spinning in a rapid attempt to generate answers and I looked back into the book.

Hugh DeLacy; Died from unnatural causes, it read. *Murdered by the MacMahon Clan.*

True. He was murdered, ruthlessly. Murdered, it said, by the MacMahon clan. My head tipped in comprehension as I matched the name—and its ancestry—to someone I knew well.

Rory.

Paul never said a word but he understood Rory was a MacMahon. A descendant of the MacMahon Clan, responsible for murdering Hugh. No wonder he despised Rory. It had looked like he actually wanted to kill him that night, by my blue door.

And Rory. He knew too, somehow. He fought it though, pushing away his obligation to his clan. Always apologizing. My head nodded in understanding.

Gráinne also saw Rory as the enemy. She attacked him on the cliffs at Dun Aengus—her vengeance and rage as caustic as five hundred years ago.

Fergal came to mind. Rory said he was "from an allied clan of the

MacMahons." So he held responsibility in this as well.

I held my head to keep it from exploding as I understood the new levels of my situation. I kept coming back to one thing....

I had to get back to Ireland.

I belonged there. I wasn't a lost stranger anymore. I was part of her ancient story. A story whose next chapter was waiting for me.

And my mind kept spiraling back to one other certainty.

I was in love with Paul.

Everything was so clear to me now and he needed to know too. I loved him. I'd told him already, but now it was different. We *needed* to be together. To complete our quest for Gráinne Ní Mháille. To end the curse, to the finish.

We were meant to do this.

Epilogue

Return to Grace

I should have come home sooner. I missed so much of his last days. The pain of regret stung fiercely in my heart. The ache would last a lifetime, I knew. The little time we had together, though, was good. And that was what I would hold onto.

Joey's brow wrinkled as he formed his thoughts and the words came out in wheezes. "The girl, Brigid. She would be my niece." His eyes misted as he thought about his lost family. "I had a sister, Maurine, when I left Ireland. She was sick, like how you described Brigid. Thought she was possessed by demons. She had the visions." He rubbed his temple as he told me about the doctors, priests, and then the nuns who came to take Maurine to the laundries.

"Everything fell apart." He coughed. "Me mum fell apart. There was chaos and fear. Then me mother gave me the ring. Believed it was responsible in some way, powerful. She told me to take it far away and protect it, under a woman's protection, but to *never* speak of it and *never* bring it back to Ireland."

A shudder ran through me, stealing the warmth from my core as I heard the tragic story of Joey's sister. So many generations of O'Malley women had suffered. My heart pinched in my chest, pointing to Mom's fatal heart condition as a symptom of centuries of heartache and despair within the clan.

During Joey's final days, I told vivid stories of my time in Ireland as my grandfather looked out the window, gazing farther than he could see. I spoke of Mayo and her Pirate Queen, Jack the bitch, and Warde's Pub. He wept for his homeland: the hills, the sea, the green. And he wept for his clan, for what might have been.

He wiped his nose with his cloth hanky and cleared his throat with a cleansing huff. With whatever strength he had left, he pulled himself upright. He had a twinkle of hope in his eye that flickered right into mine, lighting my insides with a bright glow.

"Yeh must go back now." It was a command. "Ya understand, don't ya? What you must do?" He nodded his head at me, as if offering approval for my next moves. "Yeh found what you were lookin' fer and that is the best gift you could ever have given me."

Contentment relaxed the muscles in his face and shoulders, though his fingers still firmly gripped the penal cross from the Claremorris home of his youth. Peace covered his face like Irish mist as he died and a bit of my heart died with him.

In its place though, a dream began to grow. A hope. A hope for restoring balance to the O'Malley family.

I resolved to complete my journey for Joey. To return to my Pirate Queen, with my grandfather by my side. To help her find her lost love Hugh, and revive her lost hope for Gaelic Ireland, bringing her back to the memories of her people. For my captain, the chieftain of the O'Malley Clan. I promised to do this.

***

Sitting on the porch overlooking the backyard, I stared out at the garden, missing my grandfather. His voice echoed in my mind whenever I sat idle.

His words, "the key to finding Grace," danced in my mind and I closed my eyes, curious as to why he'd repeated the phrase so many times.

I held his hand as he passed. In his final moments, he looked at me and said, "The garden, St. Brendan...."

Was he going toward the light, seeing paradise? St. Brendan must have been taking him to heaven.

"In the jar. The key. Take it with you."

"The key...." replayed in my thoughts. "The key to finding Grace?" What was he talking about? I pressed the skin between my eyebrows. "The garden. The jar. St. Brendan." The words swirled within me and then all around, moving powerfully in a torrent of sound and then tightening around me to a final point of clarity.

Brendan! The Navigator. The statue of St. Brendan!

My heart raced. I jumped up as my eyes darted around the yard, looking for a key, hoping it would materialize in response to my desperate search. Feeling stupid, I slowed my pace and focused on his words.

"In the jar. The key." My eyes moved down the porch stairs and toward the garden shed. I bit my bottom lip, thinking about the small padlock blocking me from Brendan's secret. I had spent little time in Joey's shed, as it was full of my grandfather's tools and bags of fertilizer. It scared me with its strong smell of earth, intimidating metal forks, saws, and axes, but I thought of the shelf—the shelf where Joey kept his trinkets.

I raced down the steps and tore across the lawn, throwing open the garden shed door. I froze in the space that was my grandfather. It smelled of him and held the essence of his soul, the land. His garden jacket hung on a hook and I instinctively reached for it, hoping to feel him one more time. I lifted the sleeve to my face and smelled it, causing a surge of emotions. As tears choked me and regret began to take hold, my eyes shifted to the light reflecting off glass—the glass jar.

The old-fashioned jar must have held peanut butter or pickles at one point but was now home to small bits: screws, leather ties, washers. I held the jar up, shaking its contents, and impatiently spilled them out onto the floor. I pushed through the varied items, beginning to lose hope and questioning my own gullibility. Within the messy clump, I grasped a loose leather cord, entangled amidst the mess. I pulled and watched it snake its way out from the pile, dragging behind it a small, aged key.

Pulling the key to my chest like a treasure, I rushed out of the shed with a putty knife from the shelf and dashed into the garden. I fell to my knees at the base of St. Brendan's statue and said, "Told you I'd be back."

As I pressed the greenery away from the base of the statue, a rustle and flapping made me jump back. A blur of black circled around me and landed on top of Brendan's shelter. The black bird stood tall, holding its red shoulders high, and tilted its head and bobbed at me. A smile crossed my face as a brightness lit up my heart and I reached for it. The red-winged black bird jumped and flew across the yard, turned back, glided over the garden and out of sight.

I stared after it. Then looked at the small key in my hand.

I jimmied the key into the lock, working it with both hands. A perfect fit. It took some fidgeting and twisting, but the lock finally popped open.

Prying and scraping at the secret door in the cement foundation, I grabbed a rock from the dirt and used it like a hammer on the putty knife. I worked my way around the edges, loosening the seal of decades of paint from the secret door. Using my hands, I pulled it fully ajar and peered in.

There, inside the secret space, was a small leather satchel wrapped with a weathered cord. I pulled it out, sat in the garden, and placed the small parcel in my lap. The leather was stiff, cracking at the corners, and smelled of must and mold. I delicately untied the cord and began unfolding the leather. It unrolled several times and covered my lap with its length.

In the last fold, a heavy object filled my palm. A long, thick piece of iron revealed itself. Almost the shape of a big toothbrush, it was bent at the handle with four solid prongs at the top where bristles would be.

I knew what it was. The pictures I'd seen at NUIG in the history and archaeology cases displayed a variety of them. Always eroded from time or broken from neglect but always displayed in the same setting—a burial site.

It was an ancient tomb key.

***

Gram placed her hands on my shoulders. "I could never have dreamt up this day. You've been brave, Maeve. A true warrior."

Tears swelled in her eyes and her head tilted, as if she was seeing me as someone new.

"You carry all the truths of the O'Malleys. And yer to be the keeper of the ring now, the heart of the O'Malley Clan."

Gram reached around her neck and lifted the chain over her head. Gráinne's ring hung proudly as it swayed and twirled in its freedom. Its weight settled into her palm as the chain coiled around it and she closed her hand, securing it for a silent farewell.

"You were meant ta have this ring, Maeve. Sure, all these years, I've just been mindin' it for ya. Never truly understood its significance, but now...now it's bound to you, strengthening yer connection to Gráinne. It will guide you and protect you."

Gram lifted the necklace from her palm and the ring twirled, showing itself off with pride, enjoying its temporary weightlessness. She placed it over my head and adjusted my hair from beneath, allowing the ring to fall with its full weight onto the middle of my chest. It lay directly on the faded red burn mark left there by Gráinne and nestled into the matching imprint. Its power and energy entered my heart in an instant, widening my eyes and clearing my head, and I knew I would never be the same again.

I was now the keeper of Gráinne Ní Mháille's ring and the lifetimes of truths that it carried.

***

I had Paul's book to return to him.

I had a distant cousin, Brigid, to find.

I had a ring and a key to guard.

My path now was clear.

Paul and I had to find Gráinne's final resting place. We had to return what was hers. We had to show Grace that her love with Hugh lived on powerfully within us and her valiant fight for preserving Gaelic Ireland would not fade from history but would be forever remembered.

We would share all of this with our Pirate Queen.

***

I feel the wind coming.

I turn toward it. Hands outstretched behind me. Chest out. Chin up.

It feels good.

THE END

Thank you for reading! Find book two of the *Pirate Queen* series INISH CLARE available now. And keep reading for an included special excerpt! For more from Jennifer Rose McMahon, check out www.jenniferrosemcmahon.com and join her mailing list.

Please sign up for the City Owl Press newsletter for chances to win special subscriber-only contests and giveaways as well as receiving information on upcoming releases and special excerpts.

www.jenniferrosemcmahon.com

www.facebook.com/jenniferrosemcmahon/

@ BohermoreSeries

All reviews are welcome and appreciated. Please consider leaving one on your favorite social media and book buying sites.

For books in the world of romance and speculative fiction that embody Innovation, Creativity, and Affordability, check out City Owl Press at www.cityowlpress.com.

Inish Clare

Chapter One

Scrambling over shifting stones of the ancient rock wall, laid by hands of countless generations, I cursed the stinging Irish nettles as I vanished into my family cemetery. Every inch of the hallowed space was familiar, from the oldest tombstones with weathered medieval carvings to the "newer" centuries-old gravestones—Celtic crosses that were cracked, tilted, or fallen. The decrepit O'Malley boneyard was in the same state of time-crushed ruin as last winter when I'd almost lost my life there.

Cloaked by heavy spruce boughs laden with hanging ivy, the silent stillness of the graveyard was ethereal, isolated from the outside world. Mist stirred like thick smoke around the foundation of each tipped cross or limestone slab as I moved deeper into the solemn sanctuary. My curiosity drew me in farther as thoughts of my haunting visions swirled in my head.

Tracking my ghostly hunter was my primary focus, because I was growing weary of the torment of forever being stalked. I had new information now that made me stronger, smarter. I intended to end the curse before it ended me and any future I might have.

The raw scar on my chest burned back to life as I crept close enough to read the gravestone epitaphs. My hand jumped to the ancient ring hanging from my necklace and closed around it with a fist as I looked back for Paul.

Thoughts of my grandmother placing the relic around my neck

sent chills through me. It had only been a few months since her passing, back in Boston. She'd died two months after my grandfather. Of a lonely broken heart, I was sure. My return to Ireland after their deaths was an easy choice for me. My family was gone. Ireland was where I felt most at home now. For many reasons—my roots especially. Rebuilding my life here made sense.

I released the heavy ring and it dropped back to its rightful spot, nestling into the scarred burn as a micro-pulsing of molten intensity returned. The rising discomfort, then pain, sharpened my senses, reminding me of the other ancient relic in my jacket. My hand moved to my pocket by instinct and pressed around the outline of the contents to be sure the leather parcel was still there.

"Come on," I whispered like a sneaking child and waved for Paul to catch up. "What are you doing?" My eyebrows scrunched as I watched his paranoid gaze scan the perimeter of lumbering trees that dated to far before my grandparents ever left Ireland. I peeked back over my shoulder in the direction he was perusing, half expecting to see a spook.

"Wait, Maeve. Somethin's different." His brogue thickened and his head tilted as he froze, listening.

"No. It's exactly the same." My classic impatience poked at him. "Just like when we flew out of here last time. Look." I pointed. "That's the ivy that snagged my foot as we ran from her and the...." My eyes moved to the tomb mound and I fell silent. The danger of our last visit brewed in my muscles and turned my bones soft. Fear crept back in, once again, to curtail my plans.

The heat generated from my pounding heart turned me to rubber as I moved from confident explorer to skittish quarry.

"Aren't we safe this time? I have her ring...." My words faded into the mist, losing any promise they may have held.

Facing my ancestor from five hundred years ago, the great pirate queen Gráinne Ní Mháille, shot fear through my soul. The medieval legends of Grace O'Malley told tales of piracy, battle, and revenge.

I'd always believed she was responsible somehow for my mother's death, and for the centuries-old curse that had plagued generations of the O'Malley women. I needed to end it if I was going to have any semblance of a normal life and any hopes of a future for the women of my family. If any were left.

"Shh." Paul's finger went up to freeze time and he moved his palm across the air as if to detect any disturbance. "We're not alone."

My ears flinched, like a deer sensing its hunter.

"What?" My quivering feet carried me to him in a millisecond and I grabbed his arm, turning then to see his view. I watched and listened. "Do you think it's *her?*"

The wind hadn't whipped up yet. The blasts and the terror hadn't come. All the wrath and vengeance of her soul, ready to attack. But nothing happened. How could she be near without the terrifying accompanying wind, violent bursts, and screams?

The screaming.

The blood.

My body shuddered at the memory of my visions.

Every muscle in my body tensed around my bones, turning me to a rigid statue where only my eyes could move.

She would come for the ring.

I was sure of it.

That was why I brought it back.

It was like it connected me to her, somehow, and I would use this to my advantage.

My hand wrapped around the ring on my necklace again, feeling its heat and vibrating anticipation. It was the ring from her true love, Hugh, given to her over five hundred years ago before he was murdered by the rival MacMahon Clan. Visions of the brutal slaying replayed in my mind as I recalled the vivid details of my horrific nightmare that played out the devastating historical event.

I swallowed hard and wondered if I was playing with fire. My impulsive nature always got the best of me and somehow landed me in situations like this—in a cemetery with the ring of the wrathful pirate queen. My second thoughts crashed in on me, making my knees tremble.

My grandmother had protected the ring for years, back home in Boston. It had been passed down and kept safe for generations, but now I'd brought it back. Back to Ireland's legendary chieftain, the pirate queen. She'd been hunting me my entire life, in my strange visions—my awake dreams. All for this. I squeezed the heirloom, feeling its centuries of suffering.

I opened my hand and looked at the ring. The ornate Celtic designs swirled in my eyes and the heavy gemstone protruded among the mythical beasts and spirals, holding secrets of medieval times. This ring could be Grace's direct connection to Hugh. Maybe it held the power to heal her eternal suffering and grief... to settle her tormented soul.

All I knew was that the power of the ring was strong enough to cause my grandfather's mother to send her eldest son away to America to hide the ring and never come back. Thoughts of Joey leaving his Irish home to protect his family filled my heart with sadness.

I missed my grandfather and hoped my final hours with him back in Boston, telling him every detail of my original trip to his homeland, the discovery of Grace, and my hopes to end the curse, were enough to bring peace to his soul. A part of me knew I had come back to Ireland for him. My Irish roots ran deep, especially through my grandfather. Patrick Joseph O'Malley. My Joey.

I figured I could use the power of the ring to stop Grace from hunting and terrorizing me. And future generations of O'Malley women, like all those from the past who suffered the same visions and stalking. Many losing their lives to it in one way or another, including my own mother. I had to end it. Confronting Gráinne Ní Mháille and offering her ring back seemed to be my only option for a resolution.

I looked at Paul's face and traced his stubbled jaw, chiseled with clenched focus, but his warm blue eyes softened with caution and concern. Guilt washed over me as I worried about putting him in harm's way... *again.*

Grace attacked us here last winter, with clear intent to kill, and there was no certainty that she wouldn't try again. But she had recognized him then, right before attempting to strike him with her sword. She looked straight into his soul, like she knew him, and dropped her sword in the ivy. She fell to her knees and buried her face in her hands.

The memory of her grieving form constricted my throat.

A glint of light flashed in my eyes and my head twitched in its direction. Paul's chin jumped toward it at the same time.

His wide eyes turned to mine and I met them with equal hope.

The sword!

It visited my dreams again and again, glinting its vibrant light at me, luring me back to Ireland from its ivy-covered bed.

I squeezed Paul's hand. "Oh my god! It's her sword. Do you think it's the sword?" My nerves bounced me in my shoes. "Come on."

I pulled on him to follow me as my other hand held the ring at my chest. The scarred spot where it burned me months ago was throbbing to a point of warning and hysteria.

Paul's hand tightened on mine.

"Don't move. There's someone here." He stopped short.

Blood drained from my head, leaving me dizzy at the thought that he might be right. Though he was no longer my professor, thank god, I still knew enough to believe his every word.

Crack. Snap.

At the edge of the trees. Motion.

A dark figure lurked in the shadows of the gloom. It moved like fluid away from the far edge and into the maze of gravestones. My feet stepped backward along with Paul's, though I didn't take my eyes off the… person.

His tall frame, masculine in its size and stature, was covered in a dark brown cloak. The oversize hood draped over his bowed head, concealing any features. Only his hands remained exposed in a creepy, prayer-like position. He continued to move toward us, as if he were gliding across the ground.

"Let's get out of here." My whisper caught in my tight throat.

"Come on." Paul turned with me and moved in a determined gait, heading toward the bright light of day radiating just outside the sallow shelter of the graveyard.

Following his steady pull, I turned back to the ghostly figure and let out a yelp as I saw his form moving toward us at a sprinter's pace, hands extended forward, palms facing each other, beating up and down for stealth speed.

My head spun back toward the light of day.

"Run!" I screamed.

I pulled on Paul in a panic and before he had a full view of our attacker, his pace amped up to full sprint as he yelled, "Jazus! What the…."

He raced with me toward the ancient stonewall—the border between our ghostly world and the real one. I fell in sync with his strides as my ears filled with a blood-curdling growl from behind us.

It started out low and grew into a complex sound of a runaway freight train or an evil boar possessed by the devil himself. The terrifying sound shattered my mind as it pushed through my hair and coated my skin, proving he was nearly upon us.

We flew over the wall, slipping on damp moss and knocking loose a top stone that rolled past my feet, tripping me up. Paul gripped my elbow in a steel lock, steadying me as we ran for the car, stumbling on rocks and gravel.

I looked back over my shoulder, expecting to be grabbed any second by terror in human form, but the cloaked stranger was nowhere to be seen.

Paul fumbled for his keys as my eyes darted all around.

"Hurry up!" The shake in my voice worsened with every quake of my body.

The engine revved to life and Paul threw it in reverse and blasted us backward down the lane as I watched the graveyard move farther and farther away from us.

Regret brewed in my stomach as the desire to go back overtook me immediately.

"Wait. We didn't get to…." My words of longing to go back for the sword were cut short as my eyes jumped to the tall figure standing rigid on the stonewall, watching us pull away. His hands interlaced again in a prayer position and his head tipped down, allowing the hood of the cloak to flop over it.

He remained motionless as we drove away.

***

"In here, in here." I pointed to the parking lot near Warde's Pub. My hands rubbed my knees until they were hot. "We can't just go home after that. We need answers," I panted. "Let's find Padraic." I brushed my messy hair away from my face. "He knows a lot about my family… and Brigid."

My defeat at the cemetery turned to determination in a heartbeat.

Paul turned to me with tight lips, then parked the car. "Fine. It's worth a shot."

Our stools in Warde's Pub beckoned us back since our last visit months ago, and Padraic welcomed us as he wiped the counter and set our square napkins in place.

Though it was just a couple miles from the O'Malley graveyard, the safety of the pub made it feel like light years away.

"Ach, sure, was wonderin' when I'd see ye again. Back for more, are ya?" Padraic snapped his towel at me.

I leaned forward to get a look down the length of the bar, hoping Donal might still be at the back of the pub, dwelling in the shadows. Stories of my distant cousin Brigid began with these men in Warde's. Tales of a possessed girl with visions. Not unlike me, really, which made it even more disturbing.

Their tales said she was taken away from the O'Malley farm when she was eighteen and sent to the Magdalene laundries. My eyes closed to clear the haunting thoughts. I could have ended up just like her—committed, institutionalized in an asylum, and forgotten.

I looked at Padraic, still unsure how to feel about him. He had been the bearer of bad news about the laundries last time we were here, but shooting the messenger wasn't going to help. "They was a cursed family, them O'Malleys," he said last winter with little empathy or filter. "The women had all gone stark ravin' mad."

My mouth pressed into a frown remembering his crass words. I shook it off with a twitch of my shoulders. I knew different. I had the same visions as Brigid, of the pirate queen, and knew Gráinne Ní Mháille wouldn't stop tracking the O'Malley women until she got what she wanted. The ring.

If I could just throw the ring at the vision of Grace O'Malley and have it all poof into oblivion, I would. I'd throw it and run. But there was more to it. I was certain. The unfortunate nagging in my gut told me the ring needed to be passed, directly and cautiously, at just the right moment, like a sacred ritual. My lip curled up in disgust and self-loathing, wishing I didn't have to take it all so seriously, but I knew I was right.

Facing her was my plan, and not a pleasant one. She scared the crap out of me and worse, she had the power to end me.

"Yeah, back for more. I guess you could say that." I huffed at his comment. "It all feels very unfinished." I tipped my head at Padraic. "Like the O'Malleys just disappeared from their homeland and no one knows what happened to all of them… particularly Brigid. Where could she *be* now?"

I wrapped my hands around my coffee mug, searching for warmth, wondering where all the local O'Malleys had gone.

"Ach, lassie, 'tis all but legend now, fadin' into the mist of time." Padraic moved down the bar, wiping in a rhythm of decades of similar strokes. "The O'Malleys dispersed. Lost their land through the ancient Brehon Law and moved on. Shame 'tis." His voice faded as he went farther down the bar. "'Twill always be their land, though."

I turned to Paul and raised my eyebrows in question. "What's Brehon Law?"

He nodded, as if in agreement with Padraic, absorbing what he said.

"It's ancient Celtic ruling, from medieval times. Governed the people through laws that were actually quite modern for their time." He looked down the bar toward Padraic. "He must be referring to its property laws, which basically granted ownership of 'property in question' for a fixed amount of time. Generations, really."

"Fixed amount of time?" My eyebrows scrunched, narrowing my eyes.

"Basically giving the original owners time to prove their rights to the land. Once the deadline hit, though, Brehon Law would grant the land to the current holders, if the original landholders couldn't prove their claim, that is."

My eyes widened. "That's a bit harsh. Isn't it?"

"It's actually quite fair. Particularly since the deadlines are generally set for hundreds of years." He flipped his hair away from his face. His windblown look sent tingles into my belly and warmed me.

It was much more than legend though, as Padraic called it, with a flick of his rag. Paul and I knew there was more to it. I had her ring. And in my pocket, the leather satchel held promises beyond imagination—an ancient tomb key.

My grandfather kept the medieval key back in Boston, hidden safe in his garden with St. Brendan the Navigator as its protector. The iconic statue in the backyard held the secret within its stony base, behind a camouflaged mysterious little hatch, for countless years. And now the key was back here in Ireland, right in my pocket.

My smile quivered as my throat tightened. I missed him. Every day. I missed Gram and my mother too. The hollow emptiness of grief carved out my heart each day. Feeling alone and lost, my love for them had nowhere to go. It festered in me, trapped. My journey back here, to Ireland, was the best way for me to stay connected to them in some way.

And Gráinne Ní Mháille, Grace O'Malley, she was my family too. And my hunter. My sixteenth great-grandmother. She'd been terrorizing me my entire life, and even worse, I knew she had something to do with my mother's untimely death. I was sure Mom's "heart condition" had a direct link to Grace's tortured soul and broken heart. It made sense. I reached for my own heart to be sure it held its steady beat.

I ran my hands through my hair, pondering the enormity of the task in front of me. I was determined to break the cycle that plagued the O'Malley women and get my life back and would let nothing stop me.

Paul reached under the bar and took my hand, reminding me of the other reason I'd returned to Ireland. He ran his fingers through mine, sending chills all the way to the ends of my hair. He bent his head to look into my face.

"Maeve, this isn't going to be as easy as we thought," he said with gentle raised eyebrows.

My response to his touch distracted me from his words as I focused only on his mouth. He'd turned my world upside down in every imaginable way. And I just wanted to devour him every minute.

I blinked into his wide pupils and reached for his windblown hair, attempting to control it a bit, then flashed back to the ominous figure in the cemetery.

"Who the hell was that anyway? Or *what* was that?" My hands slapped down on my lap.

My teeth clenched in annoyed distraction.

I wanted to find Grace's sword. I wanted to see if the tomb key was a match to the ancient mound in the cemetery. Its capstone read G R A, 1500-something. Even if it was a match, though, I had no idea what I would do next. It's not like opening a burial crypt like a grave robber was something I could actually do.

My head tipped and I stared into space for a minute.

No. No way.

I pushed on my temples and looked straight into Paul's eyes.

"I want to go back to the cemetery. We have to." My eyes begged his.

He shook his head and rubbed his scruffy chin.

"I don't know. It's dangerous." He pressed his lips together. "I know it's important to you, but I'm not going to put you in harm's way again. We need a better plan." He glanced down the bar. "We need to be prepared for anything, everything."

Paul cracked his knuckles in thought. He looked back into my eyes and hesitated.

My eyebrows shot up.

"We need Brigid," I said.

A chill shuddered through my body.

My lost cousin Brigid was the missing link. She was the only person on this planet who had the same visions as me, the same violent assaults that interrupted our lives and made us freaks. Brigid could have answers.

I nodded my head at Paul as our next moves fell into place through our connected eyes.

"Padraic. Two pints."

Paul bought more conversation time with Padraic as the stout took its own sweet time settling in the glasses before being topped off.

"So, Padraic," Paul continued, "the laundries... which one would they send the girls to from around here?"

Padraic's back stiffened.

The laundries were an unspoken topic, one of disgrace. If they weren't discussed, then maybe they never existed.

The shadow of shame that washed over Padraic's face was a national reaction to the matter.

Paul had done his graduate studies on Irish history and the Magdalene Laundries were a vague part of it, always shrouded in mystery, but enough for him to be able to enlighten me. I remembered his stories of the laundries, all disbanded now— institutions for "fallen women" where young girls were sent if they became unwed mothers or if they showed promiscuity or any signs of mental illness. Ireland's religious laws were rigid and these "physical and mental" conditions were considered unholy. The nuns would come and the girls would never be heard from again.

My pint sloshed in the glass as my shaking hands struggled to remain steady, making it worse, but my visceral response to the idea of the laundries couldn't be controlled. My lips pressed together in loud silence.

"Ya should'na be askin' about the laundries. They're gone now." Padraic eyeballed Paul like a criminal.

Paul adjusted himself on his stool and cleared his throat.

"Understood. But you remember, Padraic, Maeve's cousin was sent to one." He gestured his head toward me. "Brigid. We aim to find 'er."

"Right. Right. I know, lassie." Padraic's head hung and he nodded to me. "God bless 'er soul."

"She's my only family, Padraic. I need to find her. To tell her she's not alone. That she's not crazy."

My heart tore at the thought of Brigid spending all those years thinking she was insane or possessed from the visions. She must be somewhere around fifty by now—tormented her entire life without any explanation. The intense visions started with her at eighteen, same as me. And then she was gone. Taken away.

"I'm sorry. You're a fine pair with good hearts. But it's a dead end fer ya."

Padraic stopped his serving and wiping and looked straight at me, as if it were my final hour.

My heart skipped a beat as his sympathetic gaze shot fear into me, like he knew something.

"How so?" Paul grew impatient.

"She was sent to the House of Tears, I reckon." His eyes avoided ours. "St. Mary's. In Tuam. 'Twas where all them girls from around here was sent."

Paul jolted back as if he'd been punched.

"St. Mary's? The Tuam babies?" Paul gasped.

Padraic nodded.

"I've been studying the excavation. Christ." Paul shook his head and looked down into his pint glass, into oblivion.

"*What?*" My voice pierced the air.

Had they forgotten I was even here?

Padraic moved away from us to attend to other patrons, who seemed all set to me.

"I know where St. Mary's is. They might know about Brigid." Paul's lips turned up in a fake half-smile, but his worried eyes gave him away.

"House of Tears? What is that place?" I asked in a revolting tone, pulling away from him.

It sounded to me like a made-up horror movie script. My imagination spun evil scene after evil scene as sickness soured my mouth.

"The laundries," Paul admitted with flat affect.

Acknowledgments

All of my thanks, love, and gratitude:

To my McMahon Clan. My husband Dara and my children Rory, Harry, Declan, and Maeve. You believed in me from day one and have been my biggest inspiration.

Again, for Dara. My Galway man. For your unconditional love and support, always. My best friend.

To Gramma and Joey. Patrick Joseph and Katherine Mawn O'Malley. For being everything to me during my youth and forever in my heart. Who I am. Now, forever in my book.

To Mom, Cecelia Rose O'Malley. You were the first to read my manuscript, cover to cover, and gave me the confidence to move forward with it. My biggest fan. Always.

To Dad, "Grampa Bobby." For embracing us fully and enjoying the Jameson…and for always emphasizing the importance of proper grammar usage.

Ted. My brother and my scribe who can vouch for all of it. RIP.

To the O'Malley Clan. "A good man yet there never was of the O'Malleys, who was not a mariner; of every weather ye of prophets; a tribe of brotherly affection and of friendship." ~ O'Dugan 1372

To Pat and Margot McMahon, my Irish parents. From the hills of Connemara to freshly baked brown bread, you've always offered unwavering support and reminders of what truly matters.

To my amazing high school beta-readers! The Lovers vs. The Shredders. For your dedication to reading every chapter, marking them up with your red pens, and engaging in the lively discussions that followed. Special thank you's to Aoife Cannon, Anthony Navarro, Penny Kourniotis, Jess DeBenedictis, Libby Hodgman, Inna Kagan, Madeline O'Neil, Anastasia Galperina, Gray Pitt, Jacob I. Komissar and Josef Komissar, and all the others, hidden by names such as Voldemort, Groot, Zero, Blue, The Cat in the Hat, and Maximum Ride. Additional gratitude goes out to Starlord. You know who you are. You were fierce. You made me cry. But you also made me a better writer. Thank you.

To artist Jake Peterson, for creating the fantastic rendition of a 16th century map of Western Ireland depicting Gráinne Ní Mháille's territory.

To all my friends and family who encouraged me to keep moving forward with this project, sending love and well wishes all along the way. Thank you from the bottom of my heart.

To my fabulous freelance editors, Kristen Hamilton and Naomi Hughes.

To City Owl Press. Tina Moss, Executive Editor, for all your support and guidance along the way, and Amanda Roberts, Associate Editor, for your expert fine-tuning and stealth precision.

And last but not least, Maeve…again. My beautiful daughter. Your awake dreams were the spark that pulled this story out of its ten-year hiding place in the attic and glued it together perfectly. Thank goodness the awake dreams are mostly gone from your days but will be forever remembered in these pages.

About the Author

JENNIFER ROSE McMAHON has been creating her Pirate Queen Series since her college days abroad in Ireland. Her passion for Irish legends, ancient cemeteries, and medieval ghost stories has fueled her adventurous storytelling, while her husband's decadent brogue carries her imagination through the centuries. When she's not in her own world writing about castles and curses, she can be found near Boston in the local coffee shop, yoga studio, or at the beach...most often answering to the name 'Mom' by her fab children four.

www.jenniferrosemcmahon.com

About the Publisher

CITY OWL PRESS is a cutting edge indie publishing company, bringing the world of romance and speculative fiction to discerning readers.

www.cityowlpress.com